A GOOD
MARRIAGE

ALSO BY KIMBERLY MCCREIGHT

Reconstructing Amelia

Where They Found Her

A GOOD MARRIAGE

A NOVEL

KIMBERLY MCCREIGHT

HARPER

An Imprint of HarperCollinsPublishers

A GOOD MARRIAGE. Copyright © 2020 by Kimberly McCreight. All rights reserved. Printed in the United States of America. No part of this book may be used or reproduced in any manner whatsoever without written permission except in the case of brief quotations embodied in critical articles and reviews. For information, address HarperCollins Publishers, 195 Broadway, New York, NY 10007.

HarperCollins books may be purchased for educational, business, or sales promotional use. For information, please email the Special Markets Department at SPsales@harpercollins.com.

FIRST EDITION

Designed by Fritz Metsch

Library of Congress Cataloging-in-Publication Data

Names: McCreight, Kimberly, author.
Title: A good marriage : a novel / Kimberly McCreight.
Description: First Edition. | New York, NY : Harper, [2020]
Identifiers: LCCN 2019033129 (print) | LCCN 2019033130 (ebook) |
   ISBN 9780062367686 (hardcover) | ISBN 9780062367709 (ebook)
Subjects: LCSH: Murder—Investigation—Fiction. | Man-woman
   Relationships—Fiction. | GSAFD: Mystery fiction.
Classification: LCC PS3613.C386444 G66 2020 (print) | LCC PS3613.
   C386444 (ebook) | DDC 813/.6—dc23
LC record available at https://lccn.loc.gov/2019033129
LC ebook record available at https://lccn.loc.gov/2019033130

20 21 22 23 24   LSC   10 9 8 7 6 5 4 3 2 1

For Tony,
The beginning of everything good.
And the only ending that matters.

Love never dies of a natural death

—ANAÏS NIN, *The Four-Chambered Heart*

PROLOGUE

I never meant for any of this to happen. That's a stupid thing to say. But it is true. And obviously, I didn't *kill* anyone. Would never, could never. You know that. You know me better than anyone.

Have I made my share of mistakes? Definitely. I've lied, been selfish. I've hurt you. That's what I regret most of all. That I caused you pain. Because I love you more than anything in this world.

You know that, right? That I love you?

I hope so. Because that's all I think about. And solitary gives you lots of time to think.

(Don't worry—I talked my way into "the box." That's what they call solitary. It's too damn loud out there in the general population. All night long, people talk and scream and argue and mumble nonsense. If you don't come in here insane, you'll end up that way. And I'm not insane. I know you know that, too.)

Explanations. Would they make a difference? I can at least start with the why. Because this is so much harder than I thought it would be—marriage, life. All of it.

It's so simple at the beginning. You meet someone gorgeous and smart and funny. Somebody who's better than you—you both know it, at least on some level. You fall in love with them. But you fall even more in love with their idea of you. You feel lucky. Because you *are* lucky.

Then time passes. You both change too much. You stay too much the same. The truth worms its way out, and the horizon grows dark. Eventually all you're left with is somebody who sees you for who you really are. And sooner or later, they hold up a mirror and you're forced to see for yourself.

And who the hell can live with that?

So you do what you can to survive. You start looking for a fresh pair of eyes.

LIZZIE

JULY 6, MONDAY

The sun was sinking lower in the skyscraper forest outside my office window. I imagined myself sitting there at my desk, letting the darkness fully descend. Wondering if tonight it might finally swallow me whole. How I hated that stupid office.

A light in the tall building opposite went on. Soon there would be another—people getting on with their work, their lives. All things considered, it was probably better to accept I was in for another late night. Finally, I reached forward and switched on my light.

In the small circle of brightness cast down onto the floor sat the uneaten lunch Sam had packed for me that morning—the special pepper turkey and Swiss on the right rye bread with carrots because he worried, justifiably, that I was vitamin-deficient. Sam had been packing my lunch every day for the eleven years we'd lived together in New York—eight of them married—even on those mornings he never made it to work himself.

I gave my uneaten lunch a halfhearted kick as I checked the clock on my computer: 7:17 p.m. It wasn't even that late yet, but time always crawled for me at Young & Crane. My shoulders sagged as I tried to focus on the still utterly lackluster response letter to the DOJ that I was revising for another senior associate, one with zero criminal experience. The client was a cell phone battery manufacturer with several board members being investigated for insider trading. It was the typical criminal matter the firm handled: an unexpected wrinkle for a preexisting corporate client.

Young & Crane didn't have a dedicated white-collar criminal practice. Instead, they had Paul Hastings, former chief of the Southern District of New York's Violent and Organized Crime Unit. And now they had me. Paul had predated me at the US attorney's office, but he'd been close with my mentor and boss, Mary Jo Brown, who'd insisted four months ago that Paul give me a job at the firm. Paul was an impressive, well-known attorney with decades of experience, but at Young & Crane he always seemed to me like a recently retired racehorse, desperate for the gates to snap back again.

M&M's. That was what I needed to get through the letter, which, despite my best efforts, remained three paragraphs of unpersuasive dodge-and-weave. There were almost always M&M's in the overflowing Young & Crane snack cabinet—a perk meant to ease the drudgery of the all-nighters. I was about to go in search of them when an email notification popped up on my cell phone, sitting on the far side of my desk—so it didn't distract me. The message, to my personal account, was from Millie, and the subject line read "Call Me Back Please." It was not her first email in the past couple weeks. Millie wasn't usually this insistent, but it also wasn't totally without precedent. It didn't necessarily mean it was an actual emergency. I swiped the message into an "old emails" folder without opening it. I would eventually read it and her other recent ones—I always did eventually—just not tonight.

My eyes were still on my cell when my office phone rang. An outside call to my direct line, I could tell from the single ringtone. Sam, presumably. Not many people had my new direct number.

"This is Lizzie," I answered.

"*You have a collect call from a New York State correctional facility from . . . ,*" a computer-generated male voice intoned, followed by an endless pause.

I held my breath.

"Zach Grayson," an actual human voice said, before the message reverted to the automation. *"Press one if you agree to accept the charges."*

I exhaled, relieved. But Zach . . . I drew a total blank. Wait—Zach Grayson, from Penn Law? I hadn't thought about Zach for at least a couple years, not since I'd read that *New York Times* profile about ZAG, Inc., the wildly successful logistics start-up in Palo Alto he was running. ZAG was creating the equivalent of Prime membership for the endless small companies trying to compete with Amazon. Shipping didn't sound very glamorous, but it was apparently extremely profitable. Zach and I hadn't actually spoken since graduation. The recorded voice repeated the instruction, warned that I was running out of time. I punched 1 to accept the call.

"This is Lizzie."

"Oh, thank God." Zach exhaled shakily.

"Zach, what's going—" The question was an unprofessional slip. "Wait, don't answer that. These calls are all recorded. You know that, right? Even if you're calling me as an attorney, you shouldn't assume this conversation is confidential."

Even well-versed attorneys were sometimes comically stupid when acting in legal matters on their own behalf. With criminal matters, they were completely useless.

"I don't have anything to hide," Zach said, sounding like every lawyer who'd found himself on the wrong side of the law.

"Are you okay?" I asked. "Let's start there."

"Well, I am at Rikers, so . . . ," Zach said quietly. "I've been better."

I could not remotely imagine Zach at Rikers, a jail so sprawling it occupied its own island. It was a ruthless place where Latin Kings, sadistic murderers, and career rapists were held perilously alongside the guy awaiting trial for selling a dime bag of weed. Zach was not a big guy. He'd also always been kind of, well, meek. He'd get ripped apart in Rikers.

"What have you been charged with? And I mean only the facts of the charge, not what happened."

It was *that* important not to disclose anything incriminating, and *that* easy to forget. Once, my office had built an entire prosecution around a single recorded jailhouse conversation.

"Uh, assaulting a police officer." Zach sounded embarrassed. "It was an accident. I was upset. Someone grabbed my arm and I jerked back. My elbow hit an officer in the face and I gave him a bloody nose. I feel bad, but obviously I didn't do it on purpose. I had no idea he was even behind me."

"Was this at, like, a bar or something?" I asked.

"A bar?" Zach sounded confused, and I felt my cheeks flush. It was a weird leap. A bar wasn't where most people's problems started. "Um, no, not a bar. It was at our house in Park Slope."

"Park Slope?" That was my neighborhood, or close to my neighborhood. Technically, we lived in Sunset Park.

"We moved to Brooklyn from Palo Alto four months ago," he said. "I sold my company, stepped away completely. I'm launching a venture here. Entirely new territory." His tone had turned wooden.

Zach had always been that way, though, a bit awkward. A weirdo, my law school roommate Victoria used to call him, and worse, in her less charitable moments. But I'd liked Zach. Sure, he was a little nerdy, but he was dependable, smart, a good listener, and refreshingly direct. He was also as relentlessly driven as me, which I'd found comforting. Zach and I had other things in common, too. When I arrived at Penn Law I was still emerging from my grief-hardened shell, the one I'd been tucked inside since I'd lost both my parents at the end of high school. Zach had lost his father, too, and he knew what it meant to pull yourself up by your working-class bootstraps. At the University of Pennsylvania Law School, not everyone did.

"I live in Park Slope, too," I offered. "On Fourth Avenue and Nineteenth Street. What about you?"

"Montgomery Place, between Eighth Avenue and Prospect Park West."

Of course. The only time I ever went to that wildly expensive part of Center Slope was to browse (and browse only) at the equally over-priced farmer's market at Grand Army Plaza.

"Why were the police at your house?" I asked.

"My wife—" Zach's voice caught. He was silent for a long moment. "Amanda was, um, at the bottom of the stairs when I got home. It was really late. We'd been at this neighborhood party together earlier in the night, but we'd left separately. Amanda got back before me and when I walked in— Jesus. There was blood everywhere, Lizzie. More blood than— I almost threw up, honestly. I could barely check for a pulse. And I'm not proud of that. What kind of man is so scared of the sight of blood that he can't help his own wife?"

His wife was dead? Shit.

"I'm so sorry, Zach," I managed.

"I got myself to call nine-one-one, luckily," he pressed on. "And then I did try CPR. But she was already—she's gone, Lizzie, and I have no idea what happened to her. I told the police that, but they wouldn't listen, even though I was the one who called them, for Christ's sake. I think it was because of this one guy in a suit. He kept eyeballing me from the corner. But it was this other detective who tried to pull me away from Amanda. She was right there on the floor, though, and I couldn't just leave. I mean, we have a son. How the hell am I going to—" His voice cut out again. "I'm sorry, but you're the first friendly voice I've heard. Honestly, I'm having a hard time holding it together."

"That's understandable," I said, and it was.

"Anybody there could have seen how upset I was," he went on. "They should have given me a minute."

"They should have."

The fact that the police hadn't was surely a harbinger of bad things to come. They must have already suspected he was responsible for his wife's death. What better way to keep track of a potential suspect than to lock him away in jail on a lesser charge?

"I really need your help, Lizzie," Zach said. "I need a good—a *great* lawyer."

This was not the first time a former law school classmate had called for help with a criminal issue. It wasn't easy to find top-flight criminal defense lawyers, and few Penn Law School graduates practiced criminal law. But people usually wanted help with small matters—DUIs or petty drug possession charges, occasionally white-collar offenses—and always for a family member or friend. They were never calling for themselves, and certainly not from Rikers.

"I can help with that, for sure. I have connections to some of the best criminal defense lawyers in—"

"Connections? No, no. I want *you*."

Fuck. Hang up. Right now.

"Oh, I am not remotely the right lawyer for you." And, thankfully, that was the absolute truth. "I only started working as a defense attorney a few months ago, and all my criminal experience is in white-collar—"

"Please, Lizzie." Zach's voice was awfully desperate. But he was a multimillionaire, with countless lawyers at his disposal, surely. Why me? Now that I'd thought about it, Zach and I had drifted apart long before graduation. "You and I both know what's happening here—I'm probably going to end up fighting for my life. Don't they always end up blaming the husband? I can't have some slick suit standing next to me. I need someone who gets it—who knows where I came from. Someone who will do what it takes, *whatever* it takes. Lizzie, I need you."

Fine, I felt a flush of pride. Being singularly driven had always been my defining characteristic. I certainly wasn't the smartest student at Stuyvesant High School or undergrad at Cornell or law student at Penn. But no one was more focused. My parents had taught me the virtue of raw determination. My dad especially, it was true. And our diligence had served us similarly: it was the rope we used to pull ourselves up—and also to hang ourselves by.

I still wasn't taking Zach's case.

"I appreciate the compliment, Zach. I do. But you need someone with homicide experience and the right connections at the Brooklyn

DA's office. I don't have either." True, all of it. "But I can get someone amazing for you. They can be down to see you first thing in the morning, before your arraignment."

"Too late," Zach said. "I was already arraigned. They denied bail."

"Oh," I said. "That's, um, surprising on an assault charge."

"Not if they think I killed Amanda," Zach said. "That's got to be where this is headed, right?"

"Sounds plausible," I agreed.

"Obviously, I should have called you before the arraignment. But I was so . . . in shock after everything happened, I guess. They gave me a public defender," he said. "He was a nice enough guy, seemed reasonably competent. Earnest, definitely. But if I'm completely honest, I was kind of checked out during the actual proceeding. Like if I pretended the whole thing wasn't happening, it wouldn't be. That makes me sound like a moron, I know."

And now was the moment I could have pressed for details—when was he arrested exactly? What was the precise sequence of events that night? All the questions Zach's lawyer would ask. Except I wasn't his lawyer, and the last thing I wanted was to be drawn deeper in.

"Checking out is a totally human response," I offered instead. And in my experience, being accused of a crime did do something to even the most rational people. And being falsely accused? That was something else entirely.

"I need to get out of this place, Lizzie." Zach sounded scared. "Like, immediately."

"Don't worry. No matter what the prosecution's strategy, they can't keep you in Rikers on an assault charge, not under these circumstances. We'll get you the right lawyer, and they'll appeal the denial of bail."

"Lizzie," Zach pleaded. "*You* are the right lawyer."

I was not. I was the wrong kind of lawyer, without the right connections. It also wasn't an accident that I'd never worked a homicide case, and I planned to keep it that way. But even taking *that* whole issue aside, my life was already out of control: the last thing I needed was to get mixed up in some old friend's shitshow. And, if nothing else, Zach's situation sounded like exactly that.

"Zach, I'm sorry, but I—"

"Lizzie, please," he whispered, sounding frantic now. "I'll be honest, I am fucking terrified. Could you maybe come down and see me at least? We could talk about it?"

Damn it. I was not representing Zach, no matter what. But his wife was dead, and we were old friends. Maybe I could go see him. It might even be easier for Zach to accept why I couldn't be his lawyer if I told him face-to-face.

"Okay," I said finally.

"Great," Zach said, sounding way too relieved. "Tonight? Visiting hours are until nine p.m."

I checked the clock: 7:24 p.m. I'd have to move fast. I looked again at the draft letter on my computer screen. Then I thought of Sam, waiting at home for me. Now I wouldn't be at the office late like I said I'd be. Maybe that was reason enough to go see Zach at Rikers.

"I'm on my way," I said.

"Thank you, Lizzie," Zach said. "Thank you."

GRAND JURY TESTIMONY

LUCY DELGADO,

called as a witness the 6th of July and was examined
and testified as follows:

EXAMINATION

BY MS. WALLACE:

Q: Ms. Delgado, thank you for being willing to
testify.

A: I was subpoenaed.

Q: And thank you for complying with that subpoena.
Were you at a party at 724 First Street on July 2nd of
this year?

A: Yes.

Q: And how did you come to be at that party?

A: I was invited.

Q: By whom were you invited?

A: Maude Lagueux.

Q: And how do you and Maude Lagueux know each other?

A: Years ago our daughters were in the same
kindergarten class at Brooklyn Country Day.

Q: This party is an annual event, is it not?

A: I don't know.

Q: You don't know?

A: No.

Q: Let's try this another way. Have you been to this party in previous years?

A: Yes.

Q: What happens at this party?

A: Um, socializing, eating, drinking? It's a party.

Q: An adult party?

A: Yes. Kids aren't invited. Anyway most of them are away at sleepaway camp or summer immersion or whatever. That's the point of the party. Sleepaway Soiree, get it?

Q: I do. And does sexual intercourse take place at these parties?

A: What?

Q: Does sexual intercourse take place on the upstairs floor during this party?

A: I have no idea.

Q: You are under oath. You do recall that, correct?

A: Yes.

Q: I'll ask the question again. Does sexual intercourse take place on the upstairs floor during the Sleepaway Soiree at 724 First Street?

A: Sometimes. Not actually *on* the floor. There are beds. It's a regular house.

Q: Have you ever engaged in sexual intercourse during these parties?

A: No.

Q: Have you had sexual relations of any kind during these parties?

A: Yes.

Q: With your husband?

A: No.

Q: With somebody else's husband?

A: Yes.

Q: Did others engage in similar behavior?

A: Sometimes. Not everyone and not all the time. It's not that big of a deal.

Q: Partner-swapping wasn't a big deal to the people at this party?

A: Partner-swapping sounds so, I don't know, purposeful or something. This was only for fun. Like a joke, sort of. A way to blow off some steam.

Q: Did you see Amanda Grayson at the party on July 2nd?

A: Yes. But I didn't know who she was at the time.

Q: How did you learn that you'd seen her?

A: The police showed me a picture of her.

Q: They showed you a picture of Amanda Grayson and asked if you had seen her at the party?

A: Yes.

Q: And where did you see her?

A: In the living room. She bumped into me and spilled wine down my shirt.

Q: When was that?

A: I think around 9:30 or 10:00 p.m. I don't know exactly. But I was only at the party until 11:00. So sometime before then.

Q: Did you see her again after that?

A: No.

Q: How did she seem when you saw her?

A: Upset. She seemed upset.

Q: Upset like crying? Or angry?

A: Scared. She seemed really scared.

Q: Did you speak with Maude Lagueux at the party that night?

A: I was going to talk to her, but when I went over,

it seemed like she and her husband Sebe were arguing about another woman.

Q: Why do you say that?

A: Because I heard Maude say something about "naked pictures of her," and she was *really*, really angry. I mean, I've never seen her like that.

Q: Thank you very much, Ms. Delgado. You may step down.

AMANDA

"What do you think?" the decorator asked, waving her manicured hand around Amanda's office at the Hope First Initiative. There was the brand-new tailored orange couch, the gray wool rug with wide white stripes, and the absurdly expensive end tables, handcrafted by some Williamsburg woodworker.

When Amanda glanced up, the decorator—a tall, determined woman with hawkish features who wore only draped clothing in various shades of gray—was looking at her, waiting for a response. There was a right thing to say at this moment. Amanda had no idea what it was, but when she didn't know exactly *what* to say—which was often—she had found that selecting just a few good words could make up for a lot.

Luckily, Amanda had been collecting good words ever since she and her mom used to snuggle side by side in one of the oversize corduroy beanbags in the children's section of the St. Colomb Falls Library. That ended when Amanda was eleven and her mom got sick and died all within a few weeks—lung cancer, even though she'd never smoked a single cigarette. After that, Amanda wasn't sure she'd ever be able to go back to the library. But then, there she was, only days later, still needing someplace safe to be.

The sour librarian had come out of nowhere with a pile of books for Amanda the second or third time she was there alone. She didn't ask about Amanda's mom. She'd just said with a wrinkled frown:

"There are these." Then she slapped the fat stack down—*Lord of the Flies, Catcher in the Rye, Little Women.* After that, the librarian's special deliveries became a regular thing. In the end, it was from those books that Amanda's best words came. And so they were *her* words; Amanda needed to remind herself of that sometimes. She'd read those books. That part of her was real.

And right now, the decorator was still waiting.

"It's splendid," Amanda ventured finally.

The decorator beamed, admiring her own handiwork. "Oh, Amanda, what a way to put it. I swear, you are my most delightful client."

"Splendid?" Sarah had appeared in Amanda's office door, arms crossed, looking beautiful as always with her smooth olive skin, sharp dark brown bob, and huge blue eyes. "Easy, Jane Austen. It's a couch."

Sarah came in and flopped down on it for emphasis, patting the spot next to her. "Come on, Amanda. Come sit. It's *your* couch, not hers. You should at least test it out."

Amanda smiled and went to sit next to Sarah. Despite her very petite frame, Sarah was an imposing figure. Amanda always felt much stronger next to her.

"Thank you for all your help," Amanda said to the decorator.

"Yes, bye now." Sarah waved dismissively.

The decorator's mouth pinched at Sarah, but when she stepped toward Amanda, she smiled brightly and kissed her on both cheeks. "Amanda, you feel free to call me if you need anything else."

"Buh-bye," Sarah said again.

The decorator snorted before turning on a tall, thin heel and striding for the door.

"Nothing more galling than an asshole like that insisting you *must* spend fourteen thousand on a stupid couch she could never afford herself," Sarah said once she was gone. She was looking down at her phone to finish a text, probably to her husband, Kerry. The two texted nonstop, like teenagers. "And that lockjaw? People who are actually fancy never try that hard. You know that, right?"

Sarah had been raised in a struggling, single-parent home outside Tulsa, but Kerry's family was heir to a button fortune. Like, actual buttons, apparently. It had been dramatically misspent by recent generations, so that Kerry didn't end up inheriting much of anything, but Sarah had spent plenty of time around his very moneyed older relatives.

"Zach hired her. She's apparently very well known," Amanda said, looking around. "I do like the things she picked out."

"Oh, Amanda. Forever the diplomat." Sarah patted Amanda's knee. "You never will say anything negative about anyone, will you?"

"I say negative things," Amanda protested weakly.

"Just very, very quietly," Sarah whispered. Then she shrugged. "Hey, I could probably learn to hold my tongue more. You should have heard me ripping into Kerry this morning." Sarah looked off, considering for a moment. "Though, in my defense, he *is* too old and paunchy for bright-red Air Jordans. He looks ridiculous. And I've seen some of the guys he plays with in that pickup game of his. They are young and in shape and attractive and very *not* ridiculous. Come to think of it, you want to come watch with me? There was this one with these blue eyes and a little bit of a beard . . ."

Amanda laughed. "No, thank you."

Sarah loved to joke openly about attractive men who were not Kerry. She could because her marriage was so rock solid. Sarah and Kerry had three beautiful boys and had been married for ages. They'd met in high school—Kerry the football star, Sarah the cheerleader. They'd even been prom king and queen, something Sarah seemed slightly embarrassed by, but also very proud of.

Sarah sighed. "Anyway, I think Kerry was actually hurt when I wouldn't let up about the shoes. There is a line, even when it's all in good fun. Sometimes I forget where it is."

Sarah was forceful, it was true. She demanded Kerry do this, that, and the other thing—fetch their sons, clean the leaves clogging the storm drain on the corner, help Amanda change that light bulb above their front door. Kerry grumbled sometimes, sure—the leaves, especially, he thought were the city's problem—but it was always with affection. Like he enjoyed their back-and-forth. Amanda found the entire thing baffling and enviable.

"I think Kerry likes you exactly the way you are," Amanda said. "Besides, I'm sure Zach would love for me to be as assertive as you. I'd be able to handle everything here at the foundation so much better."

"Yes, but then Zach would be stuck coming home to *my* harpy ass. Let's face it, neither your husband nor I would survive a single night together."

They both burst out laughing at the thought, leaving Amanda feeling breathless and flushed.

She did love Sarah. Only four months into her time in Park Slope, and Amanda was already so much closer to her than she'd been to any of the women in Palo Alto, who'd ruthlessly guarded their perfection like starving dogs. Sarah was no Carolyn, of course; it was impossible to compete with that kind of history. But Sarah didn't have to compete with Carolyn. There was plenty of room for both friends in Amanda's life.

Sarah was an invaluable help with the foundation, too. A former educator, fellow Brooklyn Country Day mom, and president of its PTA, Sarah knew the ins and outs of the tangled New York City education system. Sarah hadn't worked since before her own children were born, but she'd agreed to take the job at the foundation as assistant director because she wanted to lend a hand. Over Sarah's objections, Amanda had insisted she be paid generously.

It would have been worth any amount of money not to have to deal with the foundation alone. Having grown up disadvantaged herself, Amanda believed deeply in the foundation's mission—providing scholarships that allowed needy middle-school students to attend some of New York City's best private schools. But running the Hope First Initiative was very stressful. And Amanda needed to get it right. After all, it had been Zach's brainchild.

Zach's parents—a pair of Poughkeepsie crack addicts—had abandoned him when he was nine. After that, he'd bounced from foster home to foster home. Zach had told Amanda all about it shortly after they met, how growing up in the shadow of swanky Vassar College he'd always known there was more to life. And he'd wanted it. All of it.

And so, Zach had gone out and grabbed it. At the age of fourteen, he began working an illegal overnight shift stocking supermarket shelves to earn enough for the requisite testing and applications to boarding schools. He was admitted to three, including Deerfield Academy, which he attended on full scholarship. From there, he'd gone on to Dartmouth, then a dual JD/MBA from Penn. Amanda had found it all so very impressive. She still did.

Once he and Amanda were together, Zach had shot up the corporate ladder, too, at start-up after start-up in California—Davis, Sunnydale, Sacramento, Pasadena, Palo Alto. Amanda gave birth to Case in Davis, and he was four when Zach decided that if he wanted to really get somewhere, he'd have to create something himself. It was then that ZAG, Inc. was born. (ZAG as in zigzag and also Zach's initials, plus the A; he didn't have a middle name.) Within five years, ZAG, Inc. was worth hundreds of millions of dollars. But Amanda was not surprised when Zach resigned and stepped away, saying he was ready for something new. He'd always been a big proponent of challenging himself. Whatever the finer details of the new company Zach had started in New York—they never talked about the minutiae of his work— Amanda was sure it would be a big success, too.

"Why must my husband text to ask what we're having for dinner in the middle of the day?" Sarah huffed, punching out another text. "It's not even lunchtime. He should have better things to do."

Amanda's office phone rang. She startled, but made no move to answer it, even when it rang a second time.

"Um, you are aware we don't have a receptionist yet?" Sarah asked. "That phone isn't going to answer itself."

"Oh, right." Reluctantly, Amanda moved to her feet on the third ring and headed for her desk. She picked up the phone. "Amanda Grayson."

There was no response.

"Hello?"

No answer. In an instant, dread all but overwhelmed her.

"Hello?" Amanda asked one more time. Still, there was nothing except that familiar sound in the background. Heavy, horrible breathing. Her gut twisted.

"Who is it?" Sarah asked from the couch.

There was only a series of zeroes on the caller ID. Amanda slammed down the phone.

"Whoa, killer!" Sarah called out. "What did they say?"

"No. Nothing. Sorry, I don't even know why I hung up like that. There was no one there." Amanda smiled, but it was not a good smile. She needed to change the subject. "It's just— Case being so far away, it's putting me on edge. I even had this ridiculously awful dream last night. I was running through the woods, barefoot, sticks cutting my feet. I think I was trying to save Case from something. God knows what." When Amanda looked at Sarah, her eyes were already wide, and Amanda hadn't even mentioned the most disturbing parts—the blood that had been all over her, and she'd been wearing something, a fancy dress, a wedding dress even; and then Norma's Diner, from her hometown, appearing out of nowhere like some haunted house in the middle of the woods. Who dreamed such strange, awful things? Certainly not Sarah. "Obviously, it was just a nightmare. But every time the phone rings, I am worried it's Case's camp."

Amanda knew that Case was safe at camp. She just felt unmoored without him. The only time he'd ever been away this long was when he'd been hospitalized with food poisoning as a toddler, and even then Amanda had slept in the hospital with him.

Sarah's face softened. "Well, *that* I do understand." She came over to lean against the desk beside Amanda. "I always chew off all my fingernails when camp starts. Until I get that first letter, actually. And you're dealing with a new camp. My boys usually go every summer to the same place."

"You worry, too?" Amanda asked.

Sarah's youngest son, Henry, was in Case's class, which was how she and Amanda had met. Sarah was one of those blasé mothers who always had everything so under control no matter what new disaster her sons careened into. And there were a lot of disasters.

"Don't let this tough exterior fool you!" Sarah exclaimed. "It's just easier for me if I don't let myself think about it—out of sight, out of mind. It's like the 'come in and see us' message from Country Day I got about Henry right before the school year ended. You wanna know what I did?"

"What?" Amanda asked, on the edge of her seat. What she wouldn't have done for one ounce of Sarah's bravado.

"I *ignored* it. Did not even respond. Can you imagine?" Sarah shook her head as though she was disgusted with herself, but really she seemed a little pleased. "Honestly? I couldn't deal. I needed a break from everything kid-related. Of course, now we have this emergency PTA meeting tonight. So I guess the joke's on me."

"What emergency meeting?" Amanda asked.

"Come on, I told you. Remember? The contact list has been compromised!" She pressed her flattened palms to her cheeks and widened her eyes for a second, then smirked. "I know that Brooklyn Country Day isn't one of those loosey-goosey progressive schools. We all love rigor and discipline and structure. That's why we send our kids there. But honestly, you'd think the Country Day parents were all in witness protection or the CIA or something. They are *losing* it."

Oh yes, Sarah had told her about that and Amanda had deliberately pushed it straight out of her mind. Zach would lose it, too, if he found out about some hacking situation. He was obsessive about their privacy. If their information got into the wrong hands, he would definitely hold it against the school, which he had picked specifically because of its attention to every last detail. He might even want Case pulled out and *that* could not happen. Despite its demanding academics, Brooklyn Country Day was the only bright spot for Case in an otherwise rough transition.

Amanda had hoped to wait until the end of the school year to move ten-year-old Case east, but in the end that hadn't been possible. At least Case made friends easily. It helped that he fit in many different places socially. On the one hand, Case was an outgoing, athletic baseball fanatic, and on the other he was an introspective artist who could happily sit alone, sketching his favorite animal—jaguars—for hours. But a new school with only a few months left in fifth grade was a lot to ask of any child, even a flexible one.

There had been tears and some nightmares. Once Case had even wet the bed. Having often been plagued by terrifying dreams herself, Amanda had always taken her son's sound sleep as a sign she was doing something right. Now even that was gone. At least Case had perked up once Amanda agreed to sleepaway camp: eight weeks all the way back in California with his best Palo Alto friend, Ashe. But what if her son's sadness returned after camp ended and he came back to Park Slope? Amanda didn't want to think about it. She'd always made whatever compromises necessary for Zach's career, but never at Case's expense. Her most important job was to protect her son, but in balancing Zach and Case, there were no easy answers.

"Oh, now don't *you* get all freaked out, too," Sarah said. "I see that look on your face."

"I'm not freaked out," Amanda lied.

"Anyway, the school is pulling out all the stops to investigate," Sarah said, but she sounded a little like she was trying to convince herself. "Hired some fancy cybersecurity firm. You know Brooklyn Country Day. They take no prisoners."

"I just—I had no idea," Amanda said.

"That's because the administration is being too close-lipped. I keep telling them that," Sarah said. "It makes it look like they're hiding something. So you'll come to the meeting then?"

Amanda had been to one Brooklyn Country Day PTA meeting thus far and had found it extremely intimidating.

"Oh, I don't know if I can—"

"Sure you can. Anyway, I need your moral support. These parents are looking for someone to turn on," Sarah said, as though she wasn't far more likely to cut them all down to size. "Eight p.m. My place. I won't take no for an answer."

Sarah didn't need Amanda there, but she wanted her to be. And that was enough.

"I'll be there," Amanda said to her friend. "Of course I will."

LIZZIE

JULY 6, MONDAY

Rikers looked worse than I remembered, even in the dark.

The larger prison buildings seemed deliberately designed to clash, and the smaller buildings and assorted trailers—administrative offices, maybe, or guard barracks or weapons storage—were unlabeled and sagging. A massive concrete prison barge floated impossibly on the water, housing another few hundred inmates who—I'd read—had recently managed to cut the barge loose and almost escape by slowly floating away.

Barbed-wire fencing loomed everywhere. Tilted and flecked with rust, it ran in straight lines and formed squares and bent in circles, giving you the uneasy sense of being simultaneously locked in and locked out. But what I dreaded most from the last time I'd been at Rikers—years before, to interview a witness—was the acrid smell of sewage and the rats. Unlike ordinary nocturnal skittering vermin, the Rikers rats walked around boldly in daylight, aggressively standing their ground. One more reason to be glad for the dark.

Once inside Bantum, the building where Zach was being housed, it took another fifteen minutes of clearing security before I was finally sitting in a little box that smelled of urine and onions and sour breath, staring at a cloudy plexiglass divider as I waited for him to be brought up.

On the drive out, my friendship with Zach had come back to me in fits and starts. It had been ages, but we had spent quite a lot of time together for the better part of first year—studying, meals, movies. My forgetting the extent of our friendship wasn't necessarily a reflection on Zach either. I had a very selective memory. But I did now remember this so clearly: I'd liked Zach because he'd felt familiar—in good ways, and bad. It had been especially evident the day our beloved contracts professor had spontaneously given us an impassioned "career counseling" lecture in class.

When Zach and I met for dinner later that night at Mahoney's, the pub on Rittenhouse Square, he was already all worked up.

"Can you believe that bullshit with Professor Schmitt?" Zach had said, squirting ketchup on his burger as a rowdy group of Penn football fans tumbled in.

"You mean the bit about soulless corporate law firms?"

Zach nodded, eyes locked on his burger, probably so he didn't have to make eye contact with any of the very large, very drunk football fans closing in around us. "It's too bad. I really liked that guy. But now he can go to hell as far as I'm concerned."

"So you think corporate firms are soulful?" I teased, turning to watch the giant next to me, who was swaying ominously.

"Don't pretend you don't know what I mean. You're the biggest gunner I know." Zach's leg had started to bounce the way it did whenever he got nervous, which was often. "People around here like to pretend that being ambitious makes you a monster. But I refuse to lose, and I'm not ashamed to admit it."

He didn't mean anything by it, but sometimes Zach did sound like the bad part of my dad, the part the customers and employees and neighbors who loved him knew nothing about. To them my dad was all jokes and warm, silly charm. And he was those things. But he was also obsessed with status and achievement for achievement's sake, to the exclusion of things that mattered, like people. Like my mom and me and what we wanted. He wouldn't even let my mom teach me Greek like she wanted and he avoided the few Greek friends she'd made. The real him was always unsatisfied with who we were. What my parents had managed to build for themselves—the restaurant, our "cozy" two-bedroom on tree-lined West Twenty-Sixth Street that was always filled with my mother's homemade *diples*, her amazing stories about Kefalonia, where she'd grown up, and all her endless affection—was pretty amazing. Idyllic, as far as I was concerned. But it had never been enough for my dad, even before we lost it all.

"Are you suggesting that the students at Penn Law aren't competitive enough?" I'd laughed. "Isn't that like saying the problem with a pack of lions is that they're too into vegetables?"

"But they like to *pretend* they aren't competing. It's hypocritical." Zach's eyes flashed up at me pointedly. That was Zach: too much eye contact or not enough. He did not excel at moderation. But then, neither did I. And Zach at least didn't try to hide behind some jovial persona like my dad. Zach was honest about who he was and I respected that. "My mother was a waitress and a house cleaner and my father worked in a steel plant. Blue-collar and not educated, but, man, did they work their asses off. Look at your parents, as hardworking as mine and defrauded into the grave." He pointed a finger at me. "Success is an abstraction only to rich people."

I shrugged. "I'm going the public interest route."

Zach raised an eyebrow. "Public interest? That's noble and everything, but people like you and me don't have those options."

"Speak for yourself," I snapped back. "I'm prepared to do whatever it takes to work at the US attorney's office. And I don't give a shit about money."

I also didn't like being underestimated. I was going to devote my life to protecting people like my parents, hardworking immigrants who'd been convinced by a kindly-seeming regular into borrowing $100,000 against their bustling diner in Chelsea and investing it in a "secret" Hudson Yards project. Really, it was just my dad who'd been convinced. He'd invested without consulting my mother. Then, poof: the money had vanished, and so had the regular. With whiplash speed, the bank foreclosed on the restaurant. Millie, a customer turned family friend and sergeant in the Tenth Precinct, had jumped into action, breathing down the FBI's neck to find the guy. In the end, Millie's pressure wasn't the reason he was found. But found he was—in the worst possible way. It didn't change anything. Everything my parents worked for had already been destroyed. And so had my family. I was sixteen at the time; they'd both be gone before I turned seventeen.

I stumbled through the rest of high school, shattered, living with my mother's sister, who was counting the minutes until she could return to Greece. My world had turned so suddenly hostile and incomprehensibly dark. For months I was dangerously depressed. Throwing myself into my studies had eventually brought me partway back to life.

The compulsive studying also earned me a free ride to Cornell and by senior year there, I'd started thinking about law school and an eventual job as a federal fraud prosecutor. The idea of a future career protecting people who'd been taken advantage of like my parents was a lifeline tossed out to me. Not talking about the rest of what had happened? That had given me the strength to pull myself to shore.

"Hey, no offense." Zach was staring down at his burger as he held up his hands. "You'll make a great prosecutor. I'm just saying, you work ten times harder and are more driven than anyone else in this damn school, even me. Maybe you should reap the rewards."

"Don't worry. I will. They'll just be the rewards I want."

"You know, I believe that." Zach had smiled. "Actually, I have absolutely no doubt."

But no matter how close Zach and I may have been for a time, nothing he said would change my mind about representing him now. I would listen, make him feel heard, and then—as promised—find him that truly excellent lawyer who was not me. And that was all I was going to do.

There was finally a buzz on the other side of the airhole-dotted plexiglass. When the door opposite opened, there, after all this time:

Zach. Or his right eye. Because that was all I saw at first. Swollen closed, it had a deep cut above it. The whole side of his face was a spectacular purple-crimson. It was painful to look at.

"Oh my God, Zach," I breathed. "Are you okay?"

He smiled weakly, nodding as he sat. "I was standing in somebody else's line spot. There are a lot of rules in here. Learning them is a process. It's not as bad as it looks."

Even injured, Zach's face was better-looking than I recalled, the angles more defined, stronger after all these years.

"I'm sorry that happened," I said. "It looks painful."

"Definitely not your fault," he said, eyes darting down in that familiar way of his. "Thank you for coming at all. It's been a long time." He was quiet for a moment. "Luckily, I don't make a living as a model. But ideally, I would like to get out of here so that I can keep the rest of my face."

"A reminder: they're not supposed to record these conversations, but . . ."

"Who knows, right?" Zach said. "I've got nothing to hide, but I hear you. All due care. I was listening, I promise."

His eyes shot up to meet mine as his body started to vibrate slightly—that leg of his doing its thing out of sight. Poor Zach. He was in real trouble in there. He smiled then, sad and eager. I felt a queasy sinking in my gut.

"I'm here to help, Zach, in any way that I can," I began. "But as I said before, I'm not going to be able to represent you myself."

Zach peered at me through his one good eye, made a helpless gesture with his hands. "Okay. I mean, that's not what I want to hear, but you can only do what you can do. I guess."

My chest unclenched a little. I'd been more afraid than I'd realized that Zach would get angry. Not that I'd ever actually seen Zach angry. Did that mean he was incapable of murdering his wife? Of course not. Besides, eleven years was eleven years. I knew nothing about Zach's life now apart from what I'd read in that *New York Times* profile that

I'd discovered during one of my what-happened-to-every-guy-I-knew-before-Sam retaliatory googling sessions.

"Honestly, it's my new job," I said, this very real, very legitimate, and much better excuse having occurred to me on the long ride to Rikers. "I'm a senior associate at Young & Crane. Only partners take on cases. I have to defer to their procedures."

"How did that firm thing happen anyway?" Zach asked. "All you ever wanted was to be a US attorney. No judgment, but I was surprised when I saw that you'd left."

"Saw?" I asked.

Then I remembered: the *Penn Law Annual* class notes. Victoria had an incongruous sorority streak that compelled her to attend every re-union and submit an update to each and every alumni quarterly. I had no doubt she'd been trying to be supportive—a senior associate position at Young & Crane was a prestigious and extremely lucrative job; the complex cases, the sterling reputation, the salary to match. I was even on partner track, albeit a slightly delayed one. But the change in my original plan—to devote my professional life to good work and low pay as a prosecutor at the US attorney's office—had not been voluntary.

"I would have been less surprised to see that you'd left law alto-gether than to see that you'd switched to corporate defense."

I winced, but tried to cover it with a smile. "Life. Things don't al-ways turn out the way you expect."

"What does that mean?" Zach asked. "There's no way you got fired. You're way too good for that."

"It didn't make sense for us to have me stay there."

That was true, though far from the whole truth: that my husband had driven our life into a ditch that my job at Young & Crane was sup-posed to dig us out of.

About a year before, Sam had gotten so drunk at a work lunch that he told his editor at *Men's Health* to fuck off, then fell asleep on the bathroom floor. Facedown, under a urinal. *Men's Health* had already been the last of many stops on a steep slide for a career that had started at the *New York Times*. The jobs had all been lost in one way or another because of Sam's drinking—factual errors, missed deadlines. Belligerence.

Fortunately, when Sam was finally fired from *Men's Health*, he had a contract for a book based on his popular advice column. Unfortunately, we'd long since spent the modest advance, and he was nowhere near finished with the book. These days, Sam wasn't writing much at all. Despite all that, we might have been able to squeak by okay on my paltry government salary were it not for the accident.

The weekend after Sam got fired from *Men's Health*, we took the jitney out to a friend's place in Montauk, trying to get our minds off the whole thing with a good meal and a glass of wine. Apparently, sometime after I went to bed, Sam decided he was "totally fine to drive" and "borrowed" our friend's restored antique convertible to run out and get some more beers. He ended up smashing the car into the Anglers, a historic pub downtown, completely destroying both it and the vehicle. The accident had, remarkably and thankfully, left Sam completely unscathed, but to compensate for the destruction of some priceless family heirlooms we'd been sued personally by the owner of the Anglers for intentional conduct not covered by insurance—in other words, Sam being drunk. The settlement required us to pay $200,000 out of our own pocket over the next two years.

This was a fact I'd intentionally left off my Young & Crane financial disclosure form. The lawsuit was against Sam personally, and hence in a gray area in terms of my own credit history. I did know better, of course. Law firms didn't want associates in debt because it might make them vulnerable to undue influence, and our sizable debt was a joint obligation. Even with my Young & Crane salary, paying it off would not be easy either. But it could be done over time and without claiming bankruptcy, provided we dispensed with "nonessentials" like the IVF the fertility specialist had recommended as our next step. But then, that did simplify things. The last thing Sam and I could handle was a baby.

Was I angry about all of this? Of course. Sometimes I was positively enraged, but never so much that hope didn't win the day. After all, if I stopped believing that everything would work out, if I stopped trusting in Sam's golden-hued worldview, I'd be left only with the reality of the way things were. And that was totally untenable.

"It didn't make 'sense' for you to stay at the US attorney's office?" Zach pressed. "What does that mean?"

There was that directness I'd always liked.

"We've run into some unexpected financial challenges. It's a long, complicated story. Anyway, working at the US attorney's office isn't exactly the best way to earn extra cash."

"Marriage," Zach said, then shook his head ruefully.

"It's obviously not the end of the world," I said. "I'm working at one of the best law firms in the country, not a salt mine."

Zach's one eye looked sad. "Still," he said. "I know how much that job meant to you. I'm sorry."

A burn blazed up my throat. I looked away.

"That's the hardest part about marriage, isn't it?" Zach went on. "Somebody else's problems become your own. It doesn't always feel fair."

"It doesn't," I said. Zach saying the exact right thing was nicer than I wanted it to be.

"So your husband. Richard, is it?"

"Richard?" I felt a guilty pang when I remembered where Zach was getting that name. "No, not Richard. His name is Sam."

"I'm guessing he's not a lawyer . . ."

"A writer."

Zach searched my eyes for a second.

"A writer sounds . . . very, um, creative." Zach smiled. "I'm glad you're happy. I've thought about you over the years, wondered how you were. It's good to see it all worked out."

It didn't. None of it worked out.

I looked down at the table in silence. We needed to get back to the point.

"Where is your son?"

"He's at sleepaway camp in California with his best friend." Zach smiled weakly. "Amanda didn't want him to go, but we moved here in the middle of the school year, and he missed his friends. Amanda was good that way. She always made the choices that were best for Case, even when they were hard on her. I can't tell Case on the phone about what's happened—that would just be so . . . But he needs to know about Amanda."

"What about your mom?"

He looked confused for a moment. "Oh, she passed away."

"I'm sorry. Maybe the parents of Case's friend should tell him, then?" I suggested. "Do you think they'd go get him from the camp?"

"Yeah, maybe," Zach said quietly. "To be honest, I don't really know them. The friend's name is Billy, I think."

"I could call and ask the camp," I offered. "I'm sure they'd know how to reach Billy's family."

"That would be great, thanks," Zach said. "But I don't even know the camp's name. Amanda handled all that." He paused. "That probably makes me sound like an asshole, doesn't it? I bet you aren't rushing home to put a hot meal on the table every night for Richard."

I laughed a little too loud.

"No, but every marriage is different," I said, and my judgments aside—because I was judging it—it didn't make Zach a bad person if he had a traditional marriage, provided that's what his wife also wanted. "Is the information on the camp at your house somewhere?"

"I'm sure it is. There's a small desk in the living room where Amanda kept her papers. All the forms and information for the camp should be in there."

"Does somebody in the neighborhood have a key to the house?" I asked. "That would be much faster than me trying to track down yours in inventory here."

"There should be one under the planter out front," he said. "Amanda kept it there for Case, for emergencies."

"You have a key to your house under a plant in front of your door?" I asked. "In New York City?"

"It does sound stupid now," Zach said. "Honestly, I never thought about it before. Park Slope feels so safe."

"We should make sure the police know about the extra key. It opens up potential suspects," I said. "Is there anybody else I can call for you? Extended family, friends? Somebody from work?"

Somebody, for instance, who Zach had actually seen in the past eleven years? At a minimum, he must have had whole teams of employees who would be clamoring to step up to the plate.

Zach looked down again, shook his head. "The people in my life now, they don't really *know* me." He motioned to his injured face. "I can't have them seeing me like this."

I nodded. "I understand."

But did I? Was there really no one he was close enough to? And what was that little flutter in my chest? Was I flattered that *I* was apparently an exception?

"You and I," he went on, answering the question I hadn't asked, "I always thought we were kind of kindred spirits, you know? I never felt like you judged me."

"I didn't," I said. "I wouldn't."

Zach looked up at me, his one eye glassy. He hadn't just gotten better looking, he'd softened, too.

"Anyway, I know the front door was locked when we left for the party because I locked it. But the alarm was malfunctioning. Amanda had an appointment to get it fixed—one of the last things I did was complain that she hadn't done it yet. Nice, right?" He closed his eyes for a moment as if in pain. "Anyway, Amanda would have locked the door behind her once she got home, too. She was like that: nervous."

"Nervous how?" If there was a reason, maybe it pointed to something, or someone, other than Zach.

He shrugged. "She was from a really small town, and her family was poor, like going-hungry poor. She didn't like to talk about it, but sometimes I think she got overwhelmed by these neighborhoods we lived in, the people. Even the wives who don't work are impressive: fancy educations, community involvement. Amanda was smart, but she didn't even go to college. I think she worried about being found out. It made her jumpy. Maybe I pushed her too hard to be something she wasn't." He looked up at me. He seemed genuinely regretful. "But she was more capable than she realized. I just wanted her to be her best self, you know?"

The way he said "best self" set my teeth on edge. But then Zach had always been big on self-improvement, even for himself. And it was hard to argue with his results.

"Sure, yeah," I said, because Zach seemed to be waiting for me to agree. "That makes sense."

His face darkened then. "I went to do the CPR, you know, but Amanda was ice cold. And the blood, when I stepped in it, was so thick, like glue. And I—" Zach pressed a hand to his mouth. Hadn't he said on the phone that he *had* done CPR? I could have sworn that he had, but maybe he'd misspoken. Or maybe he was ashamed to admit the truth. "The police made something of that when they came, like 'Why didn't I have more blood on me?' 'Had I changed my clothes after I killed her?' 'Did I not even bother to do CPR because I didn't love my wife?' 'Which was it?' It had to be one or the other, according to them. But she was so cold, that was the explanation, and I—people think they know how they'll act. But you don't know until something like that happens to you. It's much worse than you think."

It was. I knew that firsthand. Only last week, I'd woken to find Sam passed out on our living-room floor with a gash to his head. There had been so much blood. On Sam's hands and shirt, smeared under his head on the hardwood floor. I'd rushed over, sure he was dead. But he moaned when I touched him, the alcohol radiating off his body. I could not imagine what it would have felt like if he'd been cold to the touch.

"You're right," I said. "No one does know what they'd do."

Nonetheless, Zach's clean clothes were a problematic fact that the police had already demonstrated could be used to their advantage in multiple ways. Though presumably they hadn't yet located another, bloody set of Zach's clothes—otherwise he'd surely be under arrest for murder.

"I don't know what happened to Amanda, Lizzie. I wasn't home when she died," Zach went on. "But she might be alive if I was a better husband."

Whatever that meant, Zach needed to never say it again. It was tantamount to a confession.

"Um, I wouldn't—"

"I left her at that party, texted her after I was already gone. Because that's what I do: leave. Leave it to Amanda to explain me. Leave it to her to build our life. And she always does." He paused, sucked in some air. "Did. She always did. I probably never once said thank you, either."

"No one is perfect," I offered. "Especially no one who is married."

He gave a grim smile. "We didn't argue. I'll give us that. We were not fighters. Our home life was pleasant. Case is a great kid. Were Amanda and I exceptionally close?" He shook his head. "Honestly, I always looked at marriage as a practical arrangement. And now my wife is dead, so that's going to be the reason I did it, right? Because I'm detached? Unemotional? The asinine part is that I didn't even have to leave that party. I left because I got bored. I went to go take a walk on the—"

My hand shot up like a traffic cop's. "No, no. Don't get into specifics."

"But my story isn't going to change, Lizzie. Because it's not a story. It's the truth."

"It doesn't matt—"

"I was on the Brooklyn Heights Promenade. Walking. By myself. The water, the lights of Manhattan. I used to go walking when we were in Philly all the time, remember?" Did I? I wasn't sure. I was sure Zach was going to make for a frustrating client. He didn't listen.

"Anyway, I already told the police that's where I was. I told them everything they wanted to know about the golf club, too. They were like, 'Is
that yours?' And I was like, 'Yeah, it's—' "

"Zach!" I shouted so loud this time he flinched. "Seriously, stop it.
This isn't helping your situation."

"But it was my house, *of course* it was my golf club," he said defi-
antly. "I didn't kill Amanda; why should I have to lie about anything?"

Ugh, admitting ownership of the alleged murder weapon to the
police was a statement against penal interest. Admissible hearsay. I
made a mental note to tell whatever attorney I eventually secured about
the statements—dealing with them would need to be near the top of
his list. I needed to get out of there before I did any more damage. I
just needed enough information to get Zach a lawyer and to get that
lawyer started on the bail appeal.

"Can we get back to the physical altercation with the officer? The
alleged assault." This, any lawyer would want to know about before
taking Zach's case.

"Obviously, I wasn't the one who started it," Zach said, motioning
to himself, presumably to his slight stature, which, while significantly
more solid than it had once been, still did not make him seem especially likely to pick a fight with a cop.

"The officer did?" I asked.

"I don't know what you consider 'starting it,' but there was this one
police officer who got in my face after the crime scene people got there,
pointing at the golf club: 'You hit your wife with that club, didn't you?
Why? She nagging you? Cheating? Maybe you grabbed one of your
clubs to scare her. You swung it and next thing you know she's down.
You panic.' He wouldn't let up. And then somebody else started in, calling me a liar, saying that I was making up that I was out taking a walk.
That it was a stupid lie. 'You stupid?' he kept saying over and over
again." This seemed exaggerated, but not totally impossible. Rattle the
suspect by screaming at him: it was a thing that was done. "Anyway,

then that plainclothes detective came over to my one side and was like, 'Come on, let's go outside to talk more about this.' And I said, 'I'm not leaving my wife.' Then somebody on my other side grabbed my arm, and I jerked back. Hard, definitely. But it was a reflex." He lifted his elbow and swung, demonstrating. "Anyway, I guess there was another officer behind me, and I ended up hitting him in the face."

"And then they arrested you?"

"There was some back-and-forth first. An EMT looked at the cop's nose, then everybody calmed down and it seemed like they were going to drop it," Zach said. "Then the guy in the suit talked to the plainclothes detective—I didn't hear what he said. But a minute later they arrested me for assaulting an officer."

"But not murder?"

Zach shook his head. "Only the assault. I think even the cop I hit wanted to let me go, and he was the one bleeding. He kept saying, 'The guy's wife is dead.' But I got the feeling the guy in the suit was looking for a reason to arrest me."

Which, of course, would make sense. If you have reasonable cause to hold a murder suspect, you do. Period.

"Did you tell all of this to the lawyer who represented you at the arraignment?" I asked. "The public defender."

Zach frowned uncertainly. "I'm not sure. Like I said, I wasn't very clearheaded at the time."

"It's okay," I said. "I can track down your public defender and ask him. Do you know his name?"

"Um, Adam," he said. "Roth something. He has a new baby and lives on Staten Island. We talked about the ferry."

I could picture a nervous junior public defender—the kind assigned to pick up cases at arraignment—going on and on about his personal life with a half-catatonic Zach.

"I'll find him. If he's already spoken with the DA, he may have a better lay of the land."

"Does that mean you've changed your mind? That you'll take my case?" Zach reached forward and gripped the small edge of the plexiglass frame in front of him.

"I am sorry, Zach," I said, more firmly, but I hoped with kindness. "You really do need someone with extensive state felony experience. Murders, specifically. Someone who knows DNA, crime scene forensics, blood typing, and fingerprints. I know forensic accounting. I also don't know any of the players in the Brooklyn DA's office. A lot of what you need in these cases is back channel."

"What I need is a *fighter*, Lizzie." Zach's eyes were fiery now. "My life is on the line."

"I'm not a partner. I cannot bring in my own clients at Young & Crane. Period."

"I can pay the fees, whatever they are."

"You could probably buy our whole firm if you wanted to," I said. "These decisions aren't about fees."

"Ah." Zach nodded and sat back. "They don't want their name associated with an accused murderer. I get it."

"You know how these firms are. Their morality is arbitrary."

"Hey, I wouldn't want my company associated with any crime, much less a violent one. Beyond reproach, that's the goal."

"Five minutes remaining," a voice over the loudspeaker called. *"Visiting hours will conclude in five minutes. Please proceed to the nearest exit."*

I stood and lifted my pad. "I'll make some calls. I'll find you a fantastic defense lawyer, and I'll get them up to speed. The priority is obviously getting you out on bail." I studied his bruised face and damaged eye. "Anyway, I wouldn't know who to ask at Young & Crane about taking on a case."

Zach pulled his chin back. "Wait, but you *could* ask someone? You haven't already been told no?"

Shit. I looked down and exhaled in a long stream. Why, why, why had I said that? Then again, maybe it wasn't the worst approach—

Young & Crane would certainly say no. Paul had once specifically said something about associates not being able to take on their own cases. After he officially said no, I would officially be off the hook.

"I guess I can ask," I said finally. "But they *will* say no."

"Sure, yeah. Okay," Zach said, but I could tell he wasn't listening.

"Zach, I'm serious," I said. "It won't change anything."

"I understand, I do. And thank you." His stare lingered. He smiled slightly.

"Visiting hours have now ended!" came a louder, more insistent voice on the intercom. *"Please proceed to the exit immediately!"*

"I've got to go," I said. "I should have a lot more information by end of day tomorrow if you call then. Let's say seven p.m.? Here's my cell." I wrote out the number and held it up so Zach could copy it down correctly. "I'll be sure to pick up."

"Thank you, Lizzie," Zach said. He pressed a hand flat against the dirty plexiglass, looked at me imploringly. "Thank you."

I hesitated before pressing my hand up to meet his. It was a weirdly intimate gesture, even though we weren't physically touching.

"Try not to worry," I said, and pulled my hand away.

"Because there's nothing to worry about?" he asked. "Or because it won't help?"

"Both," I said, before heading for the door.

I was breathing hard as I made it up the stairs to our fourth-floor walk-up. I'd googled Amanda on the way home. There was nothing specifically about her death, but there had been stories in the *Post* and the *Daily News* about a murder in Park Slope over the weekend: "Peril in Park Slope" and "Slope Slay" were the headlines, respectively. Both stories featured a nearly identical photo—an ambulance parked outside a brownstone, a half-dozen police cars, police tape. Both had also been very light on detail, with no mention of Zach's or Amanda's names: "Pending notification of the family," the papers demurred. They did not mention a cause of death either, but did indicate that an arrest had been made and that the police did not believe there was any risk to public safety. Sam and I had been at an old friend's house at the Jersey Shore for the July Fourth weekend, so I'd missed the entire thing.

My searching did unearth lots of other pictures of Amanda and Zach elsewhere online—charity events, profiles of Zach. Amanda was beautiful. Hauntingly so. Thin and gazelle-like, with long, thick blond hair. She was the opposite in every way of my dark features and sturdy, capable frame. I couldn't find mention of her age anywhere, but she looked young. Very young.

I was trying to imagine just how young as I stepped inside our apartment, the quiet and that familiar stuffiness greeting me. It was late, almost eleven. But Sam was usually up. Please don't be out, I thought. Please don't be out.

I dumped my bag in the hallway and worked my way out of my high heels, before stopping in the kitchen for a glass of water and something to eat. I grabbed a handful of Twizzlers out of the huge bag I kept tucked, pointlessly, out of sight. As I pulled the Brita from the refrigerator, I saw tomorrow's lunch already packed for me. *Oh, Sam, if only there existed enough turkey sandwiches in the world to make up for everything.*

From the doorway to the dim living room I saw him, dead asleep on the couch. And I was pretty sure asleep and not passed out. He was curled on his side, the Yankees–Red Sox game on, sound muted.

I approached quietly and leaned over him. He didn't smell of alcohol—that's what we were reduced to, me smelling him—and on the coffee table was a bottle of seltzer. I lowered myself onto the edge of the table and watched him sleep. He looked so perfect like that, sandy blond hair tousled over his angled cheekbones. Sam's deep-set, bright blue eyes were lovely, but so troubled these days. Asleep, he was only beautiful.

He was trying, too. So hard. I did love him for that. Sam had stopped drinking cold turkey for two whole months after the car accident. Since I'd joined Young & Crane four months ago, there'd been the occasional beer at a baseball game, or a glass of wine at a friend's dinner party. But he hadn't been drunk again—certainly not passed out, bleeding drunk—not until last week.

Once upon a time, I would have said that blacked out was the same as passed out. Someone asleep, basically, facedown on the carpet. Eight years into being married to Sam, I was now an expert in drunken vernacular. In a blackout, a person—your husband, for instance—stays completely ambulatory, going through all the regular motions, albeit clumsily. He does not seem "passed out" in the least, though he is not "there" either, because the most essential portion of him—the him you love—has effectively vanished. Leaving you speaking to someone who looks like your loved one and sounds like your loved one but is not him in any meaningful way.

Ten stitches and a mild concussion, that was all in the end despite the blood. Such a short time later, and the gash was so neatly hidden by Sam's hair that even our friends in Jersey hadn't noticed. Part of me wished Sam had been left with a ghastly scar right in the middle of his perfect forehead. I would never forget those moments of thinking he was dead. Why should Sam? Zach was right: the worst part of marriage was the way somebody else's problems became your own.

Rehab. That was the obvious solution. But, as Sam was always quick to point out, we didn't have the money for the high-quality private treatment that wouldn't be covered by insurance. The kind both of us had heard was really the only effective kind. Getting sober and staying sober is expensive. But there was one option Sam refused to consider: his parents.

Sam came from an extremely wealthy family, generations of money, going all the way back to the railroads. These days, his father, Baron Chadwick, was a tax partner in a prestigious Boston law firm and his mother, Kitty Chadwick, a society wife. But Sam had not had a happy childhood. No abuse, just unbearable coldness that had frozen into cruelty as Sam continued to disappoint his father with the passionate, creative, sensitive person he turned out to be. Sam's father wanted an athlete, a class president, a lawyer, for a son. He wanted a corporate raider and a locker-room brawler, someone who would cut down enemy and friend alike. Anything to win. Meanwhile, Sam handed over study guides to struggling classmates and had once decided not to interview for an impressive internship his best friend had his heart set on. Sam's dad couldn't really see the point of a son like that. He couldn't see the point of Sam. Sam had been estranged completely from his parents since right before our wedding. It seemed only fair to me that they pay for the damage. But Sam couldn't bear the thought of asking, which was absolutely understandable, and also totally convenient.

"Oh, hey," Sam said sleepily, stirring on the couch. He looked toward the windows, where he was always sure to keep watch for my cab. "Sorry, I missed you coming in."

"It's okay," I said. "I'm fine."

But I was not fine. I was suddenly overwhelmed by this deep, tar-like anger. Stuck to everything. Was it sweet that Sam stood sentry, waiting for me to get home? Sure. Would I rather he express his love by getting himself sober once and for all? Um, yes, definitely.

What I could not explain for the life of me was how I could be that angry and yet want to climb up on the couch next to Sam and curl my body inside his.

"What time is it?" he asked.

"Almost eleven."

"And you just got home?" Sam squinted his blue eyes, bright even in the dim light. "That's late even for the gulag."

"Yeah."

And then I was supposed to tell Sam everything. About Zach and Amanda and the call out of the blue. About my trip to Rikers, and how I'd backed myself into a corner by saying I'd ask Young & Crane. On the way home, I'd been puzzling over my impulse to blurt that out to Zach, but I had no interest in looking under that particular rock.

And so I also decided to say nothing to Sam. To keep it all a secret. After all, what was one more?

"That's like a . . ." Sam reached and spun his fingers through my hair, his voice dropping sleepily as he fumbled to calculate. "A twelve-, no, fifteen-, sixteen-hour workday." He exhaled loudly. "I'm sorry, Lizzie."

I shrugged. "You don't assign the cases."

"But it is my fault you're working there in the first place," he said, and he sounded so sad. The way he always did whenever he apologized, which was often. Still, I believed he meant every word.

"It's okay," I lied. Because nothing good would come from more of Sam's guilt.

I closed my eyes, lost in the warm feel of Sam's strong fingers in my hair, in the memory of how he'd done the same thing on our second date and in our second year and last week. And in the end, wasn't that the key to marriage? Learning to pretend that a few unspoiled things could make up for all the broken ones.

I remembered back to the first weekend Sam and I spent together in New York City. When I'd traveled nearly three hours from Philadelphia, first on the SEPTA train and then New Jersey Transit and then the subway, all just to get to him and that electric pulse he'd sent through my bones the night we met. We'd had sex three times, then slept on Sam's pullout couch, the only piece of furniture that would fit in his postage stamp of an Upper West Side studio, our heads pressed up against the stupidly oversize refrigerator. Before we went to brunch the next morning, we'd stopped at a nearby homeless shelter so Sam could drop off some notebooks and pencils he'd bought for the kids staying there. Maybe it had been planned for my benefit, but he was wrapping up work on a piece about the need for city-subsidized school supplies. And the way his eyes shone was real. Afterward, he said: "It's not much, but it's the best I can do."

What if this, now, was Sam's best?

"Let's go to bed, Sam," I said as he reached forward to pull me on top of him. "People will see. We need those stupid curtains."

"Let's stay here," he murmured as he unbuttoned my blouse, slid the fingers of one hand inside my bra as the other hand lifted up my skirt. "Let's not go anywhere."

"Okay," I whispered.

And then I closed my eyes. Because Sam wanted me. Because, despite myself, I wanted him, too.

KRELL INDUSTRIES

CONFIDENTIAL MEMORANDUM
NOT FOR DISTRIBUTION

June 24

To: Brooklyn Country Day Board of Directors
From: Krell Industries
Subject: Data Breach & Cyber Incident—Introductory Report

This memorandum shall serve to confirm the retention of Krell Industries by Brooklyn Country Day's Board of Directors to evaluate a potential data breach compromising certain personal information of students and their families. All information contained in this memorandum and all future communications are to be considered Privileged and Confidential Attorney Work Product, not intended for distribution.

Krell Industries' investigation shall include, but not be limited to, the following:

- **System Review:** A detailed review of all available data systems to identify internal failures and external intrusions that led to the breach.

- **Witness Interviews:** Interviews with all relevant parties. Interview subjects shall be informed that confidentiality is critical to investigatory success. Confidentiality forms will be executed.

- **Weekly Progress Reports:** Will be distributed to summarize progress on the investigation.

- **Critical Event Reports:** Will be distributed on an as-needed basis to highlight information requiring a more urgent response.

- **Suspect Identification:** Potential subjects for civil and criminal action will be identified.

AMANDA

When Amanda arrived at Sarah's already crowded brownstone, Kerry was standing near the door, pressed up against the wall like he was trying to dissolve into it.

It was a relief to finally see a friendly face. On the quiet twilight walk over, Amanda had gotten two calls to her cell from an unknown number. The sudden shrill sound had made her heart take flight, even though the phone had rung only once each time, not even long enough for Amanda to decide whether to answer. The calls could have been unrelated to the many that had come before—only a few weeks earlier Amanda had fully believed that was a possibility. But once the breathing started, there was no pretending anymore. Somehow, he'd found her. And whatever he wanted, it wasn't something good.

It was hard not to envy all those parents squeezed into Sarah's brownstone for the PTA meeting with their "cybersecurity" problems. Amanda had real security problems, and it was way more terrifying.

At least there in Sarah's brownstone, Amanda felt safe. Sarah's husband Kerry was a huge guy—over six feet, and with the girth of the defensive linebacker he'd once been. Amanda always had such a hard time imagining Kerry, with his soft, saggy brown eyes and quick grin, intentionally knocking anyone over, even on a football field. She could much more easily picture him as Prom King. Though his face was quite a bit rounder than it had once been. Amanda had noticed from some of the older photographs displayed throughout the house.

Sarah hadn't married Kerry for his looks anyway. Kerry had swooped in with his button fortune and his varsity jacket and swept Sarah right off her feet, made her feel safe and taken care of. Of course, in the end, she and Kerry had ended up not nearly as wealthy as Sarah had anticipated—she was quick to point out—but it wasn't like they were suffering. Kerry was a very successful lawyer.

As far as Amanda was concerned, Kerry's attentiveness was far more valuable than money anyway. Zach had always been more than happy for Amanda to fill the gaps left by his demanding career by hiring people—plumbers, carpenters, nannies, tutors, gardeners, painters. But she couldn't very well hire someone to do something like reach Case's baseball card collection on his highest closet shelf. Mentioning it to Sarah last weekend was embarrassing, but within the hour there was Kerry, standing on Amanda's front stoop.

"I was instructed to come, madam," he'd joked. "Something about baseball cards?"

"I'm sorry," Amanda had said. "It's so late on a Sunday night. I swear I didn't ask her to make you come."

And Amanda hadn't, but she was glad Sarah had sent him. Case wanted his cards at camp, and Amanda wanted to get them shipped first thing in the morning. She'd tried using the extra tall stepladder, but the box remained hopelessly out of reach.

"Oh, don't worry. I know my wife," Kerry had said, glancing around the dark house. "Zach's at work at eight thirty on a Sunday? That's hardcore."

"He has a funding meeting in the morning," Amanda had said, which was often the case, though she hadn't known it to be specifically true on that day.

Kerry had retrieved the box from the shelf without even having to go all the way to the top of the stepladder.

"Be sure to tell Case he's a lucky kid," he'd said as he handed it down to Amanda. "If one of our boys ever wrote from camp asking for something like that, Sarah would pretend the letter got lost in the mail.

You want me to take a look at that closet door while I'm here? It's probably just the hinge making it stick."

"No, no," Amanda had said, feeling mortified that Kerry had a mental list of all her undone chores. Did she mention them that often? "I've already called someone."

It was no surprise then, that Kerry was there at Sarah's PTA meeting, even though he'd probably had to leave work early. He was always wherever his wife needed him to be.

Kerry finally noticed Amanda hovering near the door and waved her over. "Can you help?" he whispered through clenched teeth once Amanda had made her way through the crowd. He rubbed a hand over his shaggy brown hair. "Why are all these people in my house?"

"Because your wife is the PTA president?" Amanda replied.

"But it's *summer*," Kerry whined. "There should be a summer reprieve."

"Don't look at me. She made me come, too."

"On my signal," he said. "Let's run for the door."

Amanda appreciated the way Kerry joked with her, like she was just another person, and not even an especially attractive one.

"No way. I'm too scared of your wife," Amanda said with a grin—a real one—as she slid past Kerry toward the living room. "You should be, too."

"Oh, don't worry," he said with an exaggerated sigh. "I am appropriately terrified."

As much as she would have preferred to stay with Kerry near the back of the room, Amanda needed to get where Sarah would see her, so that her presence would be counted. Then maybe she wouldn't need to stay as long. Amanda was feeling rattled from all the calls—more today than yesterday—and being alone in a large group of Brooklyn Country Day parents was stressful in and of itself. Amanda looked around for Maude, but didn't see her. Her gallery was often open late on weeknights. She was probably at work.

Sarah's living room was warm and tasteful. Well lived-in and loved,

Amanda always thought, the walls crowded with candid family photos through the years—red-faced crying babies, first meals, awkward
Halloweens, and finally sullen teenagers. It was so different from the
pristine surfaces of Amanda's gut-renovated brownstone. Her own
home was beautiful, of course, but she longed for floors like Sarah's
that creaked in some spots and bowed in others. Not that noisy floors
in and of themselves were a good thing. The floors of the trailer
Amanda grew up in had made plenty of noise, each heavy, drunken
footstep on the yellowed linoleum like the squeak of a mouse stuck
on a glue trap. Anyway, the point was, the noises of Sarah and Kerry's
house were nothing like that. They were the sounds of a well-loved
family in the brownstone's bones.

Amanda looked around the room at the usual eclectic mix of Park
Slope parents—women in suits next to men in graphic T-shirts; parents who looked old enough to be grandparents next to parents who
looked like they could be students themselves; parents of different
races and cultures; single parents and same-sex couples. It was a di-
verse group in many respects, though they were almost all very wealthy
and, to Amanda, universally intimidating.

In their corner of Palo Alto, the PTA meetings had mostly been
attended by stay-at-home moms, but in Park Slope men and women
seemed to share more equally in parenting, and almost everyone had
not only a job but a *career*. People were intelligent and accomplished in
Palo Alto, too, but in Park Slope everyone was *intellectual*. The neighborhood was filled with journalists and professors and artists. People
who wanted you to be *saying something* when you spoke. Politics, art,
books, travel—you were expected to have opinions that were informed.
As well read as Amanda was, none of her knowledge ran all that deep,
and in Park Slope they picked the bone of each matter clean, held it up
to the light, and inspected the marrow for consistency. This was true of
people, too. If they ever looked inside Amanda they would find nothing.

"Hi everyone," Sarah began once people had finally settled down.
She winked in Amanda's direction and then looked around the room,

allowing the tension to mount. Sarah had a knack for knowing exactly how to keep a handle on the Brooklyn Country Day parents. "So the dreaded contact list," Sarah finally went on. "First of all: Don't panic. We are all going to be okay. I promise." There was an edge to her voice that she wasn't bothering to disguise. "The PTA is working closely with Country Day to resolve the issue."

Hands shot up. "Working to resolve it how?" asked a tall man with dark brown skin and a perfectly tailored herringbone suit that Amanda was pretty sure she'd seen on the extra-expensive floor at Barney's. A *Wall Street Journal* was folded crisply in his hand. "They aren't telling us anything."

"Country Day has hired a firm that specializes in cybersecurity," Sarah explained. "All they do is figure out what happened in these exact kinds of situations and help come up with solutions. But that can take time."

"Time, my ass," a woman next to Amanda muttered angrily. She was frumpy and unkempt, her white skin pasty and veined. Amanda wondered when she'd last brushed her stringy blond hair.

A petite woman with chin-length black hair, light brown skin, and a trim pencil skirt raised her hand across the room. Her high heels barely touched the ground, and she vibrated nervous energy. "I'm sorry, but if Brooklyn Country Day can't keep our information safe, why are we trusting them with our kids?" She looked around the room for support. Several people nodded in agreement. "Other schools in this neighborhood have had big problems with cybersecurity or cyberbullying or whatever *you* want to call it. Serious problems. I, for one, chose Country Day specifically because of its high standards. Do those standards only apply to our kids?"

A knowing hum passed through the crowd.

Sarah's cheeks flushed. "Cyberbullying? This has nothing to do with cyberbullying," she said sharply. "This has to do with all of us—what—tolerating some extra spam and maybe some junk texts for a while? Because that is what this will be."

Amanda glanced around at the faces of the other parents. Some looked noticeably graver than the rest.

"But what if it *is* something more than just a nuisance?" the tiny woman pressed on. "My neighbor works in IT, and she said they could be planning to access all of our clouds."

She said *clouds* as she might have said *vaginas*, like the word itself was slightly prurient.

"I'm gonna second her point," said a laid-back-looking dad in jeans and a faded Ramones T-shirt. His hair was so gray it was almost white, his skin a similar ashen shade. "Maybe this will get worse, maybe it won't. But they should at least be open about what's happening. It's not cool the way this whole thing went down. Brooklyn Country Day should be an open book, let us all in on the process. We're supposed to be a community."

"And what if the person responsible is *part* of our little community?" Sarah asked. "A student, for instance, or a disgruntled former employee? What if that person is here tonight? There are valid practical reasons for the school keeping this *ongoing* investigation confidential. If the people affected want the school to pursue legal action on their behalf, for instance, evidence will have to be protected."

"Wait, does the school have reason to think this is an inside job?" a tall, broad-shouldered woman asked. She had very short blond hair and very large features, an unfortunate combination. Her bulging eyes darted around the room. "That would be awful."

"Sorry, I thought we covered the part about the investigation being confidential and *ongoing*." Sarah's eyelashes fluttered with irritation. "I *can* tell you that Country Day has hired one of the best cybersecurity firms in the country. And that they've launched an investigation. They'll get to the bottom of what's happened. It's all they do. And when they're done, they'll report their findings. But I don't have any more details at the moment."

"It seems like they should at least tell us something in the meantime," the petite woman spoke up again, but more quietly now. She sounded almost shell-shocked. "I mean, what if we have . . . what if there's been additional suspicious activity that could be relevant?"

When Amanda looked around the room, a few other parents were nodding. Like they were victims, too, of this additional suspicious activity. But what was it? Amanda felt sick. Zach would be absolutely apoplectic if he found out about any of this.

"Well, the good news is that the school has given me a number, a hotline of sorts. You can all call it to confidentially report something that has happened to you personally." Sarah hesitated, raised a curious eyebrow as if she was hoping someone might spill something right then. "You could also share information you have about who could be responsible. Provided you *actually* know something."

"I'd like that number," a curly-haired woman next to Sarah said breathlessly. Her eyes were pink at the edges, with circles underneath. She was already digging in her bag for a pen.

Amanda caught eyes with Kerry again as Sarah dutifully read the information out.

"Now?" he mouthed at her, motioning again toward the door.

Amanda shook her head and laughed. She'd have loved nothing more than to race out the door. But where exactly would she run to? That had always been the problem, hadn't it? No destination. Even now, there would only be darkness out there, more and more darkness. She hugged herself to keep from trembling.

This had happened once before. She'd gotten hang-ups just like this when Case was a toddler, and they were living in Sacramento. Back then, Amanda had also known who it was. Then, too, she could feel his ragged breathing against her neck. But then the calls had just stopped suddenly. Until now.

The din in the room rose as parents began to grumble among themselves. Sarah raised her hands and clapped them loudly until the room quieted.

"Hello! I repeat: call the hotline *only* if you have actual information to share," she went on, voice raised. "This firm charges in six-minute increments. So do not call to try to pump *them* for information. Everything in the investigation is confidential. They will tell you nothing, and *we* will all end up footing the bill." Sarah looked about to say something else but seemed to think the better of it. "Now, come on, everyone. It's summer, and most of our kids are gone for camp. Let's not waste our precious free time obsessing about this nonsense!"

LIZZIE

It was only 8:30 a.m. as I headed toward Paul Hasting's office. Absurdly early by Manhattan law firm standards, where typical protocol involved staying into the wee hours, then not arriving at work until closer to 10:00 a.m. Paul was always in early and out late. But then he was not only an ex-prosecutor, he was an ex–Special Forces master sergeant who ran ultramarathons in his free time. He did not fuck around.

I hesitated as soon as I turned the last corner and spotted the desk outside Paul's office. Instead of his usual warm, matronly secretary, there sat bitter, bracing Gloria typing away. I'd forgotten: Paul's secretary was having her gallbladder removed. It was too early and I was already too on edge to deal with Gloria, who'd had it in for me ever since I'd politely declined to have her installed as my own full-time secretary. Gloria had recently been demoted from partner secretary to floater and part-time receptionist when her partner left the firm and no one else wanted to work with her. She'd sat in for me in my first days at Young & Crane, but I couldn't bear her constant complaining— the weather, her sinuses, some old man who didn't offer her a seat on the subway. Maybe it wasn't Gloria's fault that she was so unhappy, but she also wasn't very good at her job. Rumor was the firm would have fired her if she hadn't already threatened to sue for sex discrimination. Knowing Paul, he'd probably asked to have Gloria assigned to him so he could assess the situation himself.

"Is he in?" I asked, nodding my head toward Paul's open door.

"Of course he is." She rolled her overmascaraed eyes. "He came in early to review every single summer associate's pro bono billing. All because *two* summer associates padded a few hours to play a little golf at Chelsea Piers. Harmless, right? Of course, Paul's out for blood. All he's done in there is shout."

It was exactly the kind of thing that would enrage Paul. He was even more maniacal about ethics than he was about hard work. He'd fired associates for far less. Right before I arrived, he'd even pushed out a fellow partner for "behavior unbecoming." Unbecoming what, no one seemed willing to specify. And yet Paul liked to consider himself an outsider in the corporate world, and hence a renegade at Young & Crane. It was a volatile combination.

I headed over to his open door, feeling even more hesitant about mentioning Zach. I could not imagine that being friends with an accused wife-murderer would reflect well on me. And the one time I'd heard Paul talk about associates taking on cases, he'd been pissed at even the suggestion. I certainly did not want him pissed at me.

Paul was seated with his back turned away from the door, hunched over something. In his early sixties, he had a carefully shorn gray buzz cut and that very fit, weathered handsomeness that only increased with age.

I sucked in a breath, reminding myself that this conversation was merely a formality so I could get on to the real business of getting Zach the right lawyer. Finally I knocked firmly on the door.

"Yep," Paul called, without looking up.

I could now see that he was fidgeting with a small wooden puzzle on his lap, black reading glasses on the end of his nose. I came to a stop in front of his huge, perfectly organized desk. On the credenza behind him were framed photos of his four college-age children with his beautiful, silver-haired first wife. At least, I was assuming. I'd heard from Mary Jo that all of Paul's subsequent wives had been much younger, but that he carried an enormous torch for his first.

"A gift from my oldest son," Paul said, eyes fixed on the block. "It's Senegalese. He's living there. Damn thing is impossible. Probably sent it to torture me. He always was kind of an ass." He looked up, eyeing me hopefully over his glasses. "Want to give it a go?"

"Sorry," I said. "I'm not very good at puzzles."

"Hmm," he said with obvious disappointment.

I often felt Paul sizing me up and finding me wanting. Then again, it was the same matter-of-fact disdain with which he seemed to regard most people. No one met Paul's exacting standards, which probably explained why he'd been divorced three times. Holding the puzzle in his other hand, he extracted a stapled set of papers from a neat stack and tossed it onto the corner of the desk in front of me. He returned to the puzzle.

"Your revisions to the DOJ response were an improvement, but our position remains shit."

After Sam had fallen back asleep, I'd finished my changes to the letter and sent it to Paul. It had been 2:00 a.m. It was 8:30 a.m. now, and Paul had already reviewed them. That was the problem with Young & Crane: no matter how hard you worked, there was always somebody working harder. Paul was especially hard to beat.

When I first came to the firm, I'd worked for several different partners. Lately, though, I worked only with Paul. He and I had come to function as a mini white-collar practice within Young & Crane, one where I did most of the work and Paul criticized it and me. While it was stressful working with Paul, it did spare me the precarious juggling of various partners' demands that other associates had to contend with. It would not, however, make it easier for me to make partner myself, if and when the time came. Partnership required numerous allies and a savvy political strategy, neither of which I had any interest in. Nonetheless, the fact that for the past four months I'd performed well enough to be worthy of Paul's continued criticism was apparently nothing short of a miracle. Thomas, my legal assistant, had told me stories about the dozens of associates Paul had taken only days to dispense with.

"Agreed," I said. "The positions aren't strong, but they are the only ones available."

In other words, the client—Young & Crane's client, *our* client—was obviously guilty. Everything we wrote was simply an attempt to disguise this fact. And as my boss Mary Jo used to say, "Pretty bows on a pile of shit just make it harder to flush."

"Yes, I suppose that's—ha!" Paul shouted triumphantly. The puzzle had snapped loudly into place. He set it on the edge of his desk like a punctuation mark, then looked at it for a moment before composing himself. "Shall I assume from the way you are nervously lingering there that the letter to the DOJ was not the sole reason for your visit?"

"It wasn't." I crossed my arms and then uncrossed them: defensiveness was akin to weakness with Paul. "I have a question about firm protocol."

"This firm's protocol?" Paul scoffed. "For Christ's sake, you can hardly fire people here for arguably illegal behavior. This firm's protocol is bullshit, if you ask me." He paused, took an annoyed breath. "But I suppose I can do my best. Shoot."

"It's my understanding that associates can't take on their own cases," I began. "A friend asked if I could help with something, and that's what I told him, but I wanted to confirm."

"You are correct," Paul said. "We need some kind of quality control. We had one yo-yo trying to sue some Upper West Side bodega because his 'uncle' supposedly 'fell.' I may not agree with a lot of the crap they do here, but at least Young & Crane doesn't chase ambulances. What kind of case is it?"

"Criminal."

Paul narrowed his eyes, then leaned back in his chair. "What type of criminal case?"

"A law school friend of mine was arrested," I began, and there was only one place to go next: the crime. Full disclosure seemed best. "Assaulting an officer. It was accidental, he says. His wife was killed, and he was very upset. He didn't intentionally injure the officer."

Paul's eyebrows lifted as he brought the forefingers of his two clasped hands to his lips. "Killed?"

Shit. Was he *intrigued*?

"Murdered, presumably. They haven't charged my friend in connection with the death yet, but it seems likely they will. Anyway, he needs an attorney. Obviously, I don't think I'm the right person, but he—"

"Why?" Paul was looking at me intently.

"Why am I not the right person?"

"Yes. You *are* a defense attorney now, are you not? And you would not be here if you weren't a very good one."

Oh, this was dangerous territory. Paul had forcibly made his peace with the switch from prosecution to defense. He'd be offended if I hadn't made mine.

"Yes, but all my experience is in white-collar."

"You must have rotated through general crimes at the US attorney's office. Everyone does."

That was true. I'd spent three months in the Southern District's General Crimes Unit right out of law school. But the crimes I'd handled had all been nonviolent. I was actually quite proud of how I'd expertly avoided blood-and-gore cases without hindering my upward advancement. I'd even gotten promoted early to the fraud unit, where there was not a drop of blood in sight.

"I handled mostly immigration violations and minor drug charges. Nothing like a murder," I said. "Anyway, I know violent felonies aren't the kinds of cases Young & Crane usually handles, so—"

"Where did this happen?"

"Park Slope," I said.

"Brooklyn, huh?" Paul nodded, still with the narrowed eyes. "I grew up in Prospect-Lefferts. Raised my kids in Brooklyn Heights."

I felt suddenly like a key was slipping through my fingers, about to be lost forever to some crack in the floor. Whatever I'd gone into that office to accomplish was no longer in my control. I was being cross-examined by someone of far superior skill.

"Anyway, my friend would obviously be better served by a defense attorney with homicide experience."

"I presume you told him that?" Paul asked.

"Yes, I did tell him."

"And what did he say?"

"That he doesn't care. He wants me to represent him." I willed my voice steady. "He's not thinking clearly. He wants somebody he can trust."

"Sounds like he's thinking very clearly," Paul said. "And he very clearly wants you."

There was a challenge to the way he said it. *So what are you afraid of?* Fear was another of Paul's forbidden emotions.

"He's scared." My stomach shifted uneasily.

"As he should be," Paul said. "You and I both know that innocent men go to prison all the time. You and I have probably put one or two there." No, I thought. If I believed that, I would have quit a long time ago. How could Paul suggest that so casually? "And so we return to my original question: why not you?"

Because I have never and will never handle a murder case. For reasons I cannot explain. Also, my life is already so fucked up in general. But I can't tell you about any of that either without you thinking less of me.

"I'm an associate, not a partner. You said yourself associates don't take on their own cases."

Paul picked up a pen from his desk and threaded it through his fingers. "*You're* not a partner, no. Not yet." His eyes were alarmingly bright. "But I am. Now, I'm not saying I'll be burning the midnight oil with you, but I'm in for the assist."

I could not for the life of me figure out how this conversation had delivered me here: to representing Zach.

"Oh, okay, great," I said, because Paul seemed to be waiting for gratitude. But my heart was pounding.

"So who's your friend?" Paul asked. "Our client?"

"Zach Grayson," I said. "He's the founder of—"

"I've heard of him," Paul said. "That, um, logistics company. I read something about it in the *Harvard Business Review*."

"ZAG."

"Yeah, that's the one. Making all companies ship like Amazon." He sounded vaguely disgusted. "Why can't people shop in stores anymore?"

Because they work around the clock for people like you.

"Zach cashed out of ZAG anyway," I offered. "He's starting something new in New York."

"Has he been arraigned?"

I nodded. "Yesterday. For the assault on the officer. They're probably waiting for forensics on the murder. No bail."

"No bail? Where's he being held?"

"Rikers."

"Jesus," Paul grumbled. "So first we file a habeas writ. Get him out of that hellhole. Then we poke around at the DA's office and find out what kind of case they have on the murder. Not much of one yet, or they'd have already charged him." Paul paused, his face flushed with excitement. Like an idiot, I'd flung open the barn door, and he'd made his escape. "You think he's guilty?"

"No," I said. "I don't think so."

Exactly that much was true. I didn't *think* so. I *knew* absolutely nothing.

"But even if he's guilty, he'd be entitled to a defense, right?" Paul looked me in the eye. "You've got to believe that. It's the only way this works."

"I know."

And I did. But in that moment, I regretted leaving the US attorney's office more than I ever had. Everyone was entitled to a defense, yes. That didn't mean I needed to be the one to supply it. I'd made my peace with that fact a long time ago.

Paul studied my face a moment longer. "Well then, what are you waiting for?" he asked, seeming pleased. "Get to work on that writ."

I nodded and stood, feeling unsteady as I made my way to the door.

"Oh, and let me know if you have trouble tracking down the ADA that's caught this one," Paul called after me. "I have people I can reach out to at the Brooklyn DA's office."

When I arrived at Brooklyn Criminal Court in search of Zach's public defender, arraignments were in full swing. I'd called the defender's office and left a message but hadn't heard back. I sat in the back for a while, still shell-shocked from the direction my conversation with Paul had taken.

Unlike the stately federal court in Manhattan with its dark mahogany and gold-trimmed ceiling, everything about this court was decidedly practical. The building was tall and modern, the wood inside a honey-colored pine. There were no heavy oil paintings, no weight of history. There were, however, lots and lots of unhappy people.

The arraignment courtroom was packed—nonincarcerated defendants, lawyers, family, and friends filled the gallery, waiting and waiting and waiting. They looked nothing like the smug, affluent defendants in my federal fraud cases, who would always breeze in at the very last minute, too busy to wait for anything. Most everyone in that courtroom looked exhausted and sad and afraid. On the far side of the bar, at a table to the left, sat the arraignments prosecutor. She had short curly blond hair and a sour expression that may have been caused by her unflatteringly snug wrap dress, or maybe just arraignment duty. If the DA's office was anything like the US attorney's office, the junior assistants cycled through arraignments for a short stint before moving on to more prestigious assignments—sex crimes, felonies, homicides.

For an hour I watched the grim, rapid-fire arraignments drone on, hoping an Adam Roth something would announce himself by making an appearance before the court. Instead my eyes glazed over as pleas were offered, charges were reduced. Files were shuffled. I was beginning to think about abandoning the cause when the next case was called.

"Docket number 20-21345, Raime, Harold, murder in the second degree!" the clerk called out.

From the revolving door on the right for incarcerated defendants came an absolutely enormous man with a shiny bald head and thick pink arms covered in vibrant tattoos. He didn't walk. He lumbered. A guy like that could easily take Zach out with the swipe of a hand. The lawyer next to him—young and gangly, with glasses and a thick head of long, curly hair—looked more like a literature professor than a criminal defense attorney. He leaned over toward his intimidating client and smiled gently, then said something that only made the man scowl.

"Adam Rothstein from the Brooklyn defender office, Your Honor."

Of course he was.

A new prosecutor had appeared, taking over on this matter from the arraignment prosecutor, probably because it was a murder case. These days, there were barely three hundred murders a year across all of New York City. A murder indictment was a special thing. The new prosecutor was much shorter than Adam Rothstein, but his suit was sharply pressed and he looked far better rested. Fresh legs: the benefit of having just swooped in to handle this one very serious matter, instead of the sea of petty-crime humanity—many of whom would nonetheless find themselves locked away in Rikers alongside Zach, and scary Mr. Clean.

"How does the defendant plead?" the judge asked in the same bored nasal voice he had used each time before.

"Not guilty," the defendant said.

The judge continued to look down at his pad. "On the issue of bail?"

"My client has three children and a job that expects him back,"

Adam said, his voice fiery, overemotional. *Tone it down*, I wanted to say. "All his family is local. He has no prior arrests apart from minor property crimes, and he doesn't have a car or a passport. He's not going anywhere, Your Honor."

"Your Honor, this is a murder charge," the prosecutor replied, all cool, calm moral superiority. I remembered what it felt like to be him—in charge of a lowly room. It was a heady sensation. God, what an asshole I'd been, confusing the power my position had gifted me with what I had earned.

"The evidence will show that this is a clear case of self-defense," Adam pressed on. "The deceased came to my client's house armed with a hunting knife."

"And he was shot by the defendant coming up the front walk at a distance of more than thirty feet," the prosecutor drawled. He looked the huge defendant up and down. "Are you claiming your client lacked the fortitude to close his front door?"

The judge didn't seem to be listening to either one of them. "Bail is set at two hundred thousand," he said.

And with a pound of his gavel, that was all.

"This is fucking bullshit," the defendant roared at Adam as he was being dragged away. "You suck, you fucking asshole."

I watched Adam's shoulders sink.

It was only eleven thirty when the lunch recess was called. I waited until Adam had gathered his things, then followed him out the door.

"Adam Rothstein," I called after him in the crowded lobby area.

Adam paused, bracing himself, it seemed, for yet another scolding—from a prosecutor, a client's family. Finally he took a deep breath and turned back, forcing a weak smile.

"Yes?"

"I'm a friend of Zach Grayson's," I began, not able to bring myself to say I was his attorney.

Adam tilted his head for a second, as if trying to place the name.

Surely he had dozens of new cases every day. To my astonishment, it took him only a second.

"Of course, yes, Zach," he said. He stepped toward me with a concerned face. "Did you know his wife? Such an awful thing."

"No. I'm a law school classmate of Zach's. I used to be in the Southern District's fraud unit. But I'm with a firm now. Zach asked me to take over the case. I don't have experience in state court or with violent crimes of any kind, but—"

"Great, I'll get you the file," Adam said. "If you were with the Southern District, then you can definitely handle this. Besides, you and I both know it's the resources that matter. I care about my clients like they're family." He hesitated, considered. "Ask my wife. She says it's twisted. But one expensive expert witness is worth a hundred times any amount of dedication, or experience."

"Your clients are lucky to have you."

"If only good intentions were enough," Adam said. "Look at Zach. He should be out on bail."

"You're right about that," I said. "We plan to file a habeas writ. Anything you can tell me about the arraignment would be helpful."

Adam peeked in through the glass window to a small room marked "Attorney Conference." Having confirmed it was empty, he held the door open.

"Why don't we step in here?" He waited until we were inside with the door closed before speaking again. "The judge based his bail decision largely on the brutality of the scene. The DA managed to get some pictures in front of him."

"Well, that's totally prejudicial," I said. Prejudicial, but not especially shocking.

"Yeah, exactly," he huffed. "It was an assaulting-an-officer charge, and there they were showing photos of this bloody crime scene with this beautiful blond woman in the center. But the prosecution argued I'd put the scene at issue because I'd mentioned Zach's emotional distress over his wife being killed. Next thing you know, the judge is looking at the pictures so he could assess whether that was a valid defense." He shook his head in disgust. "Mind you, *none* of this should have been relevant at a bail hearing where the only issue to begin with should have been—"

"Risk of flight," I finished his thought. But I knew the game the prosecutor had been playing. I'd played it myself.

"Exactly, flight," Adam said. "The judge laid eyes on the pictures, and we were done. They'll hold him until they charge him with murder."

I crossed my arms. "But this is Rikers. It's someone's life." As soon as the words were out of my mouth, I wanted to snatch them right back.

Predictably, Adam's face hardened. "It's always somebody's life." And of course he was right. "Listen, I'd file that writ quickly. Once they've charged him with murder, you'll have no shot for bail. And the grand jury will indict. His fingerprints are sure to be on that golf club. It belonged to him. Toss in some creative blood spatter analysis and some petty marital problems, and they've got a slam-dunk."

"Marital problems?" I asked. "Did Zach tell you that?"

"No, but he was married, right?" Adam said wryly. "What marriage doesn't have problems?" He stood, then snapped his fingers. "Oh, and get that outstanding warrant resolved, too. It wasn't dispositive to the bail issue, but it definitely didn't help."

"Warrant?" My neck felt hot.

"Zach said it must have been a mistake," Adam said, his tone equivocal. "And all the prosecution would tell us—all they claimed to be able to tell us—was that the warrant was issued out of Philadelphia and that it was from thirteen years back on an unpaid code violation, not even a misdemeanor. But nothing from back then is computerized, so no one had access to exactly what code was violated. Zach didn't remember it at all, but he had to acknowledge that he did live in Philly at the time. And since the judge had already seen the pictures, that was enough for him."

"And you found Zach's surprise about the warrant credible?"

Adam considered the question for a long moment, which I found reassuring. "Zach seemed genuinely surprised, yes," he said finally. "He even demanded proof. In my experience, liars don't usually go that far. It could be for something as stupid as an unpaid noise complaint, too. He was a student at the time. I looked into discharging it myself, but with something that old, you have to do it in person in Philadelphia, which wasn't in the cards for me personally. But your firm could send someone, right? I'd also find out which DA is driving this case and why. These judges hate getting yanked around for bullshit reasons. That alone might get Zach another shot at bail."

"What do you mean?" I asked.

"Did Zach tell you about the ADA who showed up?"

"He talked about somebody in a suit."

"Yeah, ADA Lewis. He's a junior guy in homicides. The ECAB assistant who initially processed the case made an offhanded comment: 'Lewis wasn't supposed to be on call that night,' or something like that. I almost had the ECAB talked into dropping the whole thing, given Zach's circumstance with his wife. But then he makes a call to ADA Lewis, and we're done talking. Obviously, a murder in Park Slope is a high-profile case, but I got the sense there's something more driving this."

He was right that this was the exact kind of case that the Early Case Assessment Bureau bounced all the time: a prosecution that, upon reflection, seemed to have been initiated because emotions at the scene were running high.

"What do you think is really going on?" I asked.

"Politics," Adam said. "The Brooklyn DA's retiring this year. From what I hear, there's a whole lot of internal jostling for the role of heir apparent. Not ADA Lewis. He's too junior. Somebody else, though, who stands to benefit. A high-profile case like this—"

"Could make somebody's career."

He checked his watch. "I've got to get something to eat before I have to go back. But if there's anything else I can help you with, let me know."

"Thank you," I said. "I really appreciate it."

Adam reached for the door, then paused and turned back.

"For what it's worth, I don't think Zach killed his wife," he said. "And I'm not actually as gullible as I look. Let's face it: most of my clients are guilty as hell."

GRAND JURY TESTIMONY

BEATRICE COHEN,

called as a witness the 6th of July and was examined
and testified as follows:

EXAMINATION

BY MS. WALLACE:

Q: Thank you for coming, Ms. Cohen.

A: You're welcome. But I don't know what I can tell
you. I don't know anything about what happened to that
woman.

Q: Were you at a party at 724 First Street in Park
Slope, Brooklyn, on the evening of July 2nd of this year?

A: Well, yes. But I don't know what happened to Amanda.

Q: If you could try to answer my questions one at a
time as I ask them.

A: Sorry. Okay. I'm nervous.

Q: I understand. But there's no need to be nervous.
We're trying to get to the truth, that's all.

A: Sure, yeah, right.

Q: Were you at a party at 724 First Street in Park
Slope on the evening of July 2nd?

A: Yes.

Q: Did you attend the party with anyone?

A: Yes. My husband, Jonathan. He knows Kerry. That's how we got invited.

Q: Kerry who?

A: Kerry Tanner, Sarah Novak's husband. She's best friends with Maude. We only saw Kerry for a second, though. When we were leaving. We didn't talk to him. We were too busy trying to steal a beach ball.

Q: Steal a beach ball?

A: Not steal . . . I mean . . . it was silly. We took it home. It's like a two-dollar thing. I think they were party favors anyway. And we'd had a lot to drink. It's a fun party, but everybody drinks too much.

Q: Did you engage in any sexual activity at the party that night?

A: What?

Q: Did you engage in any sexual activity at the party at 724 First Street on the night of July 2nd?

A: How is that any of your business?

Q: Can you please answer the question, Ms. Cohen? Would you like me to repeat it?

A: No.

Q: No, you did not engage in sexual activity?

A: No, I do not want you to repeat the question. It's really intrusive. How is what I do in my private life—I don't want to answer that.

Q: This is not a public proceeding.

A: Those jurors are people. They are the public and they're sitting right there.

Q: Ms. Cohen, please answer the question. You're under oath.

A: Yes, I engaged in sexual activity at the party that night. Not that it's any of your business.

Q: Can you describe the nature of this sexual activity?

A: Is that a joke?

Q: Ms. Cohen, this is a homicide investigation. Please answer the question.

A: I gave some guy a blow job in a bedroom upstairs. Are you happy? This is really so mortifying. And it's not—my husband and I don't usually do this type of thing. There's just something about that party, you know?

Q: No. I don't know.

A: It makes you act crazy.

Q: Crazy?

A: I don't mean in a bad way. I mean having fun. The kids are away. And we've all been parents for a long time. Been married for even longer. The Sleepaway Soiree at Maude and Sebe's—it's harmless. And no one talks about it after. It's like it never even happened.

Q: Harmless?

A: You know what I mean.

Q: Did you see Amanda on the night of the party?

A: Only for a second, when we were leaving. She was coming in.

Q: What time was this?

A: Around 9:00 p.m., I think.

Q: Was she alone?

A: She was with a man. But I don't know who he was. I'd never seen him before.

AMANDA

The whole walk to the Gate for girls' night out, Amanda thought she was being followed. The calls were one thing, but she'd never believed there was somebody actually there, in the flesh. And yet from the second she left the house, she swore she could feel someone lurking behind her in the quiet pockets of Park Slope darkness. Not someone: *him*. Yes, the neighborhood was safe, very safe. But a deserted block was a deserted block. Anything could happen, and no one would be there to stop it.

It didn't help matters that Amanda had been on edge from the moment she woke up. It was that same stupid, awful dream about Case— running in the gown again, barefoot and covered in blood, the haunted diner, sirens wailing, warning her about her son. Carolyn even had a cameo at the beginning this time, before the dark and the running and her burning bare feet. Amanda and Carolyn were giggling and whispering, eating pizza cross-legged on her bed. Both of them in pastel tulle dresses now—Amanda's peach, Carolyn's seafoam blue. Why the dresses every time? Was it Amanda's guilt about her ridiculously over-the-top wardrobe? Her sleeping mind did have a way of making everything menacing.

If only this—the dark block, him maybe there, behind her—were a dream. How had he even found her? Yes, Amanda was living closer now to St. Colomb Falls than she had since she left all those years ago.

But New York City was six long hours away by car. It wasn't as if he could have spotted the moving van.

Amanda checked over her shoulder again as she made her way down the rest of Third Street. She didn't actually see anything. But when she tried to take a deep breath, her lungs were stiff and her skin was prickling in that way it always had back then. Right before.

She knew exactly what Carolyn would say: tell Zach. For her part, Sarah would insist it was a husband's job to protect his wife, and vice versa as a matter of fact. But what of the problems you'd brought upon yourself? Was it fair to foist those on your spouse? And Amanda was supposed to reduce Zach's stress, not add to it. He was already under so much pressure. The least she could do was hold up her end of their bargain.

Amanda had been seventeen that night eleven years ago when Zach stepped inside the Bishop Motel. He was nothing like the men who usually stayed the night at the motel—which by then was not only where Amanda worked, but also where she lived. First of all, Zach was half the size of the truckers and loggers, and so much softer. A man who would live his life without ever dirtying his hands. Not exactly masculine either, but there were worse things. Much worse things. And anyway, he had such a nice smile.

But more than anything, it was that way Zach had looked at her when they met that most caught Amanda's attention. Like an explorer who'd just discovered a rare species in his own backyard—exhilarated, nervous. Amanda had been told her whole life that she was beautiful, but up until that precise moment it had always felt like a liability.

Zach was already so accomplished, too. Amanda learned all about that when they ran into each other again, late the next afternoon. Zach was just back from a long hike, looking fit and strong and sure in his muddy hiking boots and even more handsome with a little shadow of a beard. He'd just graduated from law school and business school— both at once!—and was taking some time to himself, hiking in the Adirondacks to celebrate before going west to work in California.

Zach had such direction and focus. He knew exactly where he was headed.

"Wow, California," Amanda had said, feeling a little tug of envy. "All that sunshine. I've never been anywhere outside St. Colomb Falls."

"Come with me then," Zach had said with a shrug. So direct and simple and crazy. "Whatever is out there has got to be better than this. Forget what I think you should do, forget about me—don't you owe it to yourself to find out?"

Like he *knew*. Though he didn't, of course. Not the details of Amanda's miscalculations. Those he would never know. All these years later, Zach had never cared to fill in any of the very obvious holes in Amanda's past. She'd realized this was one of her husband's greatest skills: focusing only on what mattered to him. It was probably the secret to his success.

But back then, at the Bishop Motel, Zach was holding out a sunshiny, golden ticket: California. Away. Far away. Finally, an actual destination. All Amanda had to do was reach out and grab it. And so Amanda had asked herself: What would Carolyn do? The answer was obvious. Carolyn would take a flying leap.

That was how Amanda found herself waiting by Zach's rental car when he checked out that night. He'd acted surprised to see her there. But she was pretty sure he wasn't. Not really.

He'd smiled in this little boy way that made her feel so good inside, and said: "Let's get the hell out of here."

Soon they'd stuffed her three boxes of belongings into his trunk and were hurtling west—top down, wind in their hair. Safe. Alive. Free. Overhead there was only darkness and all those stars. Amanda knew then: she'd do whatever she had to never to return to St. Colomb Falls.

What she hadn't ever counted on—what she'd never even considered—was St. Colomb Falls coming after her.

Amanda picked up her pace until the Gate was finally within view, brightly lit on the corner of Fifth Avenue. The old-fashioned pub was where Sarah and Maude, and occasionally some other moms, met once every other week for drinks. It had a delightful outdoor area, one of the places where the young and child-free of Park Slope congregated— or so Sarah liked to say, her tone steeped equally in envy and disdain.

Once Amanda was safely within arm's reach of the Gate, she paused and looked back over her shoulder one last time. But no one was behind her, at least no one that she could see.

Amanda spotted Maude and Sarah huddled at one of the worn mahogany booths in back. Maude's head was tipped back, and she was laughing hard, feet tucked up on the seat next to her in a feline way. Sarah was leaning in close, saying something with one of her trademark wicked grins. Already, Amanda was glad she'd come. Snuggled back there in that dark corner were her *friends*. Not sister-friends, maybe, not friends like Carolyn. But friendships like that were a lifetime in the making. And after such a short time, Sarah and Maude were already so much more than Amanda ever could have hoped for.

Amanda had met Sarah outside Henry and Case's classroom, and they'd hit it off instantly. Amanda did best with very confident, outgoing women like Sarah who weren't bothered by the way she looked, or how much money she had, or how fit she was. Amanda didn't consider herself an athlete by any stretch, but she could run ten miles without much thought, and even she had to acknowledge that she was rather fast. Over the years, many women had been eager at first to be Amanda's running partner or her coffee date or her friend. But sooner or later those women always began to eye Amanda up and down, jockeying to stand farther away from her so as not to suffer in the comparison. Inevitably, that jealousy would sharpen into something they'd used to poke at Amanda, cutting her down to size.

Had she *really* not gone to college? How interesting. Had she *really* never been anywhere in Europe? Such a shame. Did she *really* have so little say in the things her husband did? How . . . unusual. And how old was she anyway?

Twenty-eight. Amanda was twenty-eight years old; often as much as fifteen years younger than mothers with children Case's age. But sometimes the gulf between them felt even greater. It felt infinite, and impenetrable.

Standing in the doorway to the Gate, Amanda glanced down at her crisp white blouse and the platform Prada sandals the salesman at Barneys had convinced her were so very New York when she went to buy yet more clothes she hoped would be the right ones. But Amanda hadn't clarified that by "New York" she had meant "Park Slope mom," which was a different uniform altogether. Calculated indifference, that was the look. Park Slope moms were beautiful and fashionable and fit, but they were above caring too much about silly things like fashion. They had more important things to worry about, like causes or children or their meaningful careers. In other words, Amanda needed to master the application of the exact right amount of concealer and precise coating of mascara to appear flawlessly barefaced.

Unfortunately, Amanda continued to make her fair share of mistakes in this regard. That was the problem with pretending to be someone—not even someone else, just someone. It was so easy to overshoot the mark.

Amanda smiled hard as she made her way over to Maude and Sarah's booth, pulling her long hair down and rolling up her white sleeves in an effort to appear more casual.

"So sorry I'm late." Amanda motioned to her outfit by way of explanation and then offered her go-to white lie. "I had a donor meeting."

It said so much and so little at the same time.

"Look at the shoes, Maude!" Sarah cried, pointing at Amanda's heels. "I love them!"

Maude pressed up in her seat. "Let me see." She tipped over to look. "Wow, amazing. Someday you do need to take me shopping, Amanda."

This was her friends being kind. They knew exactly where to shop and had the means to do so anytime they pleased. They chose not to because they, too, had more important things to do.

Maude was an art dealer, her husband a well-respected ob-gyn, and they had a teenage daughter, Sophia, the same age as Sarah's middle son, Will, who was a sophomore at Brooklyn Country Day—which was how those two knew each other. But the age of their children was all Maude and Sarah had in common as parents. Sarah liked to joke that Maude wasn't just a helicopter mom, she was a kamikaze pilot. But Maude and her daughter were extremely close, and Amanda saw Maude's hovering for what it was: love.

In addition to having a successful business and being a devoted mother, Maude was also effortlessly sexy in a way Amanda found especially intimidating, with ivory skin with just the right smattering of freckles, intense brown eyes, and a head of long reddish-brown curls. Her husband Sebe was French, though he'd attended medical school in the States. Amanda had met him a couple times when he'd dropped Maude at the Gate. Tall and extremely well built with light brown skin and bright hazel eyes, Sebe was shockingly handsome, especially with his accent. The first time Amanda met him, she'd been unable to stop herself from staring.

"You should see your face," Sarah had said, laughing, once Sebe had gone.

"My face?" Amanda had asked.

"I mean, no judgment, but you're drooling. Don't worry, that was my reaction, too, the first time I saw Sebe." She'd turned to Maude, who'd been focused on her phone. "It's like a joke, how good-looking your husband is, Maude. And talented and charming and he births babies. And now he's doing that tech start-up thing with the online genetics testing, what is it called again? Digital DNA or whatever. Sebe will probably also end up a billionaire. It's almost too much to take."

"First of all, *he* doesn't birth the babies," Maude had corrected good-naturedly. "The *women* give birth. Also, he's only a medical adviser to that company. There's not going to be some huge payout. Anyway, he still won't pick up his socks. Husbands are husbands, no matter what they look like."

"Just make sure you're seated, Amanda, if you ever see Sebe without a shirt on," Sarah had warned, ducking away as Maude swatted at her. "Ow, it's true. We were at the beach when I first saw Sebe shirtless, and I almost got taken out by a rogue wave."

A waiter appeared before Amanda sat down. He was bearded, short, and overconfident. Amanda noticed the two beers already on the table. The people of Brooklyn were big on craft beers. Among her friends in Palo Alto, it had all been cocktails.

"An IPA, please," Amanda said.

The waiter nodded begrudgingly, as though she'd saddled him with some unreasonable obligation, and then disappeared.

"We were just discussing how our rotten children haven't written to us from camp yet," Sarah said. "Have you heard from Case?"

"Case's camp probably makes them write," Amanda said, treading lightly. "It's one of those extremely touchy-feely places, very West Coast."

Many, but by no means all, Park Slope children were gone by now. Most of the others would leave later in the summer for shorter stints at sleepaway camp. Amanda had been dead set on flying to the West Coast with Case, to get him settled. But he'd insisted on going alone. Amanda hadn't flown on an airplane until she met Zach, much less halfway across the country alone at Case's age. But off he went. Her son had already had such a different life than hers. He lived with the expectation that the world was a safe place. And that was a good thing, Amanda reminded herself. A very good thing.

As soon as the first letter arrived, there was no denying Case was happy. He'd written two full pages about how exciting the flight had been and then all about how he was having the very, very best time. His only worry seemed to be that Amanda might be missing him too much, which made her feel dreadfully guilty.

She'd already written several letters back intended to show Case how absolutely great she was doing on her own, even though that was hardly true. Amanda felt so lost without her son, that was the honest truth. But in the letters she'd insisted otherwise, writing all about how they'd have plenty of time together at the end of summer to share stories. At Sarah's suggestion, Amanda had already rented a house in Wellfleet for the last two weeks of August, and it would almost certainly end up being only Amanda and Case. Zach didn't like the beach. Or vacations.

Sarah looked over at Maude and rolled her eyes.

"I told you, Maude. Of course Amanda has already gotten letters. Case is so sweet and perfect and adoring. Honestly, Amanda, it's disgusting," Sarah huffed. "He holds your hand!"

Amanda thought of Sarah's youngest son, Henry. Sarah was right: Henry was neither adoring nor sweet.

"You may have the best-looking husband, Maude," Sarah went on, "but Amanda has the most perfect son. So spill it: exactly how many letters has Case sent you?"

"Oh, I don't know . . . six, maybe . . . ," Amanda said, though she knew exactly how many.

Eleven. She'd gotten eleven letters in the eight days Case had been gone. It was excessive for a child to be writing home that much, but the letters were all filled with such joy and not an ounce of homesickness. It was hard to be too concerned.

"Sophia has written a couple times from Costa Rica," Maude said, her voice suddenly shaky. "That's not the problem."

"Wait—am I the only mother here who didn't get a fucking letter?" Sarah cried.

"It's what Sophia's letters *said* that was the problem. She just—" Maude's voice broke off in a way that was unusual and alarming. "Sophia doesn't sound like herself. She sounds . . . depressed."

"I'm sure she's fine," Sarah said. "Listen, Jackson wrote me horrid letters when he went on that backpacking thing in Glacier National

Park. He kept begging me to come get him. Of course, he did end up sick as a *dog* and in the hospital with that crazy sepsis. But it was a good experience for him anyway."

"Sepsis?" Maude's eyes widened. "Why are you telling me that?"

Sarah clamped a hand over her mouth. "Oh, God, I'm sorry." She reached forward with her other hand to grip Maude's arm. "I didn't mean— Sophia *doesn't have sepsis*, obviously. The place I sent Jackson was essentially a penitentiary. It was his scared-straight summer, remember? They had to, like, catch their own fish, clean it, and then cook it. He probably didn't wash his hands once the whole summer. Anyway, the camp you sent Sophia to is *nothing* like that, Maude. It's run by Country Day, and you *know* how uptight they are. Besides, Sophia is *nothing* like Jackson. I mean, she might finally be acting like a regular pain-in-the-ass teenager instead of your best friend, but I'm *sure* it's nothing to worry about."

Maude took another sip of her beer and smiled, though she did not actually look any more relaxed. "I hope you're right."

"I'm definitely right." Sarah squeezed Maude's arm once more. "Now, can we please change the subject off our children and onto something actually interesting?" Sarah's face brightened mischievously. "Like your Sleepaway Soiree, Maude. Do you need any help?"

"I think we're all set," Maude said distractedly. "The invitations have gone out, and we're using those same caterers from Red Hook. They've done such a good job for so many years now. At this point, they probably don't even need me to show up. To be honest, with everything with Sophia, this party is really feeling like—"

"The perfect distraction?" Sarah said. Then she fanned herself dramatically. "It's worth it to see the caterers alone. With all their tattoos and beards and hipster plaid. I'm telling you, the two brothers who own that place are everything I should have married."

Amanda hadn't been invited to any party. She was sure that she hadn't been. She shifted in her chair even as she willed herself to be still.

"Come on, Sarah." Maude laughed for real. "I adore them because they do a great job. But those two guys are like peacocks, always preening. You'd hate that. You like doting. Like Kerry, who is attentive *and* adorable."

"I'm just saying I wouldn't mind trying deliberately hot on for size."

"Didn't you already do that once?" Maude batted her eyelashes.

Sarah made a face. "Anyway, Amanda, you'll see what I mean about the caterers."

Amanda smiled awkwardly.

"Wait, Maude, you *did* invite Amanda, didn't you?"

"Oh, no." Maude dropped her head into her hands. "I really have been so consumed worrying about Sophia. I used last year's guest list! I'm so sorry, Amanda. Of course you're invited. I'll send you the invite tonight."

"And you really *must* come," Sarah added. "I mean, you really, really *have* to. Nothing compared to what will be my fabulous cooking at Kerry's birthday dinner, of course, or the fab holiday parties we have. But Maude's is a *party* party." She raised her eyebrows suggestively. "A *special* party. So special everyone will happily delay leaving the city for the Fourth this year to attend."

"Do you think?" Maude asked. "I was hoping the holiday might control the numbers."

"No, Maude, no one will miss it. It's *that* special."

"What kind of special party?" Amanda asked, but only because it was obvious Sarah wanted her to.

"We do a whole summer-camp theme. A little over the top, for sure—party favors, games, themed food," Maude said. "We've been throwing these Sleepaway Soirees every year since Sophia started going away to camp, which was, what, seven years ago now? Hard to believe it's been that long. She was so young, eight, that first summer. But she was desperate to be independent . . ." Maude's voice drifted, lost again, it seemed, in worry over her daughter.

"Okay, Maude," Sarah quipped, glancing Amanda's way. "But I'd say, under the *circumstances*, party favors are like the least interesting thing about your party."

"Under what circumstances?" Amanda asked obediently. "I mean, if you don't mind my asking."

"Oh, can I tell her, please?" Sarah asked Maude. "Because you know I am dying to."

"Go ahead," Maude said, rolling her eyes. "But know that whatever Sarah says is purely for shock value, Amanda. It may or may not have any bearing on the truth."

Sarah pulled herself tall, laid her palms flat on the table, and settled her body as if she were about to deliver a great proclamation. Her eyes remained closed.

"Maude's party is . . . wait for it . . . a *sex* party." Sarah's eyes snapped open gleefully.

"Come on!" Maude shouted, but she was laughing. "That's a ridiculous way to describe it!"

"If by ridiculous"—Sarah was laughing, too—"you mean completely and precisely accurate, then sure: it's ridiculous."

"That is *not* accurate," Maude protested, but it was halfhearted.

"I'm sorry. Do people have sex with individuals who are not their spouses every year at your party?" Sarah demanded. "Or do they not?"

Maude made a face. "But that's not the *point* of the party," she said. "That's what you're making it sound like. A sex party is where everyone arrives and puts on a mask and strips naked or something."

"Hmm," Sarah said with a sly smile. "Now that you mention it, maybe that would be even better."

Even Amanda was laughing now. They all were. Flushed and giggling, loud enough that the pudgy waiter looked up from the copy of *My Struggle* that he was reading at the bar and shot a nasty look in their direction.

"Okay, fine," Sarah said, her voice breathy with laughter. "Maybe 'sex party' is a teeny bit much, but I like the way it sounds. Besides, there is more than a grain of truth to it."

Maude looked down. "Okay, the truth is this: Sebe and I open the upstairs of our home during our annual Sleepaway Soiree for consenting adults to make use of as they see fit. Do people on occasion have sex with people who are not their spouses, while their children are hundreds of miles away at camp? Perhaps they do."

"Please, you *know* they do, even if they all deny it afterward. And you have to explain *why* you decided to offer this public service. You need to give context." Sarah motioned to Amanda. "Tell Amanda. She's a safe space, Maude. Trust me."

"I don't *need* to do anything, Sarah," Maude said sharply, and for a moment she seemed actually annoyed. But just as swiftly her face softened. "Sarah likes to talk about my sex life because hers is uptight."

Sarah held up her hands. "Guilty as charged. That is definitely why," Sarah said. "Although technically, *I'm* not the uptight one. Kerry is."

"You don't have to tell me if you don't want to," Amanda said. "Really."

Maude hesitated for a moment. Finally, she exhaled heavily, her shoulders sinking. "No, no, it's fine. You're a close friend. Sebe and I occasionally have sex with other people. We always have," she said. "I could use all sorts of euphemisms, but that's what it is. And that's all that it is. We have our own boundaries and our own rules and it works for us. I don't know that it would work for everyone. In fact, I'm sure it wouldn't. And, no, Sophia doesn't know about it. Not because we think it's wrong or bad, but because it's gross to talk about your sex life with your fifteen-year-old, no matter how close you are." Maude's face had tensed again. "Or at least, I don't think she knows . . . Anyway, I don't want her to. I don't want her thinking an open relationship is all she's entitled to. If that's what *she* wants, then fine. That's a different story. It was a thing *I* had to talk Sebe into, not the other way around. Anyway, that's why this is the last year for the party."

"What?" Sarah gasped.

"It is," Maude said firmly. "We decided a while ago. When Sophia . . . we've decided, for sure."

"Come on, Maude," Sarah pleaded. "I need your parties. Living vicariously through them is all I have."

"You seemed to have made do just fine on your own when necessary," Maude said wryly.

"Touché," Sarah said, turning to Amanda. "For the second time, Maude is referring to the time I 'cheated' on Kerry. She would obviously like me to tell you."

Maude raised an eyebrow, pointedly. "What's fair is fair."

"Oh," Amanda said, and she could feel herself looking too shocked. She couldn't help it. She was just so caught off guard. Stunned, in fact. Sarah had cheated on Kerry?

"Don't worry, Amanda, Kerry knows. We're totally past it," Sarah said. "And by 'cheated,' I mean I made out with Henry's soccer coach once, for like two seconds, a few months ago."

"Oh," Amanda said again, dumbly. Because she was *still* shocked.

"The coach has this Irish accent, and he was always flirting with me, and I don't know . . ." Sarah shrugged. "Anyway, Kerry was fairly reasonable about the whole thing."

"I can't believe you told him," Maude said.

"Kerry and I don't keep secrets. It's not our style. For better *and* for worse," Sarah said. "He was hurt, obviously, but he knows how much I love him. Eventually, he was like, 'I accept your apology; let's move on.' And he did. I'd probably have been throwing it in his face for years. Kerry's always been a bigger person than me."

"He loves you," Amanda said, without really meaning to.

"He does," Sarah said. "The only time I can ever remember Kerry getting truly mad at me was when I tried to break up with him in college. He was so fucking pissed." She smiled mischievously. "It was kind of hot."

"Hot?" Maude laughed. "That is twisted, Sarah."

"I don't know . . . You want a nice guy, but not *too* nice, right?" Sarah said. "It was reassuring to find a lion buried in there."

"He drops everything to do whatever you say," Amanda added.

"They're *supposed* to do what you say, Amanda," Sarah said, exasperated. "They're husbands. That's the whole point."

"Please," Maude said. "Sebe doesn't do a single thing around the house until I've completely lost it on him."

"But Sebe is, you know, Sebe." Sarah fanned herself. "I'd let him ignore me all he wanted. As long as he did it shirtless."

"Oh, shut up." Maude laughed and tossed a balled-up napkin playfully at Sarah.

"Hey, do you think you guys can handle this open-relationship thing because Sebe's an OB? I mean, he *is* already looking at all those other vajayjays."

"Sarah, that's gross!" Maude laughed some more, her cheeks pink.

"I'm serious!" Sarah said. "That's a serious question."

"One which I will ignore, thank you," Maude said, then turned to Amanda. "What about you, Amanda? What is Zach like? I can't believe I haven't met him yet."

"I can," Sarah snorted. "Amanda's other half is a ghost." But right away, she grimaced. "Oh, I'm sorry, Amanda. That was— I shouldn't have said that. What the hell do I know? A good marriage is the one that survives. And none of us will know that until all is said and done."

"Survival?" Maude asked, quietly. "Is that all we're going for?"

"Low expectations." Sarah winked. "They are the key to happily ever after."

For the first time ever, Amanda didn't feel like offering up some well-crafted version of her marriage. After all, her friends had trusted her with the truth about theirs. Amanda could admit at least something. "Zach does work a lot. Sarah is right. Sometimes we barely see each other."

Maude smiled softly. "Absence makes the heart grow fonder," she said reassuringly. "I do hope you'll come to the party, though. And Zach, too, of course. Regardless of what Sarah says, it's a lot of fun even if you never go upstairs."

Amanda smiled. "I'll definitely come. Thank you."

"Have you heard how Maude and Sebe met?" Sarah asked Amanda.

"No," Amanda said, turning to look at Maude.

"This is me trying to redeem myself for debasing their marriage with my unseemly voyeurism," Sarah said. "It is the most romantic story ever."

"How did you meet?" Amanda asked.

"It is a good story," Maude said, looking wistful. "I was getting my master's degree in art history at Columbia, and I was at a party. Out of nowhere I collapsed, knocked my head into a bookcase, and spilled drinks everywhere. It looked, of course, like I was drunk, but I was stone-cold sober."

"And Sebe *rescued* her," Sarah said, making a moony face. "Looking like he does and with that accent, he picked her up and carried her in his strong arms like a bride all the way to Columbia-Presbyterian, where he happened to be an intern. He saved her life."

"Sebe did not save my life," Maude said. "But he did get me to the hospital. And he did carry me to a cab. He also got me seen right away."

"And you were okay?" Amanda asked.

"I'm diabetic, it turns out. Probably had been my whole life, but I'd somehow never realized. It's manageable now."

"And the rest, as they say, is history," Sarah said dreamily.

"Wow," Amanda said, feeling unaccountably sad. "That is romantic."

"Right?" Sarah chimed in. "You should tell that story more, Maude, but leave in the part about Sebe maybe being a start-up billionaire soon. I'd flap it around like a flag if I were you."

"I don't know. Sebe and I have been fighting so much these days." Maude looked off into the distance. "That story barely feels like it belongs to us anymore."

"Fighting?" Sarah asked. "You and Sebe never fight."

"I know. It's all this stuff with Sophia," she said. "Sebe loves her, but he is so free-range. It's that European thing. As far as he's concerned, our daughter might as well be an adult. But she's my baby. I don't care how old she gets; I will always want to make her problems go away. I don't think there's anything wrong with that."

Sarah opened her lips, but her mouth shut immediately when Maude held up a cautionary hand. "Not tonight. Okay, Sarah?"

"Teenagers. That was all I was going to say," Sarah insisted. "They really do ruin everything. What about you and Zach, Amanda? How did you two meet? I have to be honest, you seem very . . . different."

"I was working for the summer as a housekeeper at a hotel in upstate New York," Amanda began. Over the years, she had perfected the story to make it more palatable. *Housekeeper* was better than *maid*, she'd learned. *Hotel* better than *motel*. But most important had been the insertion of the word *summer*. It avoided the raised eyebrows and pursed lips that followed confessing she was a high-school dropout. "Zach stopped in the hotel while he was hiking in the Adirondacks before moving to California."

"California?" Sarah asked. "Did you guys start dating long-distance?"

"Oh, no, when he checked out, I went with him," Amanda said.

"*Right* after you met him?" Sarah asked.

Shoot. She didn't usually include that part. *Why today?*

"I mean, not right that second. But not long after."

"Love at first sight." Maude smiled. "The most romantic kind."

"Hmm." Sarah eyed Amanda doubtfully but seemed to decide to leave it alone. "Well, all I know is that Zach had better be coming to Kerry's birthday dinner. Because I have not spoken more than five words to him, even though he is my boss."

"He's not your boss," Amanda said.

"Sure he is!" Sarah said. "It's his foundation. I work for you, too, obviously. And I'm fine with both, believe me. But Zach needs to make himself available. You are one of my closest friends. He needs to come into the fold."

Amanda forced a bright smile. One of Sarah's closest friends. She wanted to be that. "He'll be there."

That was a lie, of course. Zach wouldn't come. Sarah meant well, but Amanda had made clear his schedule was *very* demanding. Sometimes it felt like Sarah wanted to fix them. But, honestly, there was nothing to repair. Amanda and Zach's marriage was fine. They were both getting things they wanted. Maybe those things weren't what people were supposed to get out of marriage. But she and Zach were surviving, weren't they?

"So how many years have you and Kerry been together then?" Amanda asked, hoping to change the subject.

"Thirty-three, if you count from when we started dating. We were only fifteen when we met. We married twenty-six years ago, back when you were a zygote, Amanda," Sarah said, propping her chin in her hand sullenly. "If ever there was an excuse for letting a soccer coach put his hands on your butt, I'd say that's it."

"There's something special about that history, though," Amanda said. "I have this friend, Carolyn, who I've known since we were little."

"Yes, but time deepens friendship," Sarah said. "Romances, eh, not so much."

"Does Carolyn live upstate where you grew up?" Maude asked. "What's the place called again?"

"St. Colomb Falls. And, no, she's actually here in New York City."

"Really?" Maude asked. "She should come out with us! I'd love to meet her."

"I don't get to see her as much as I'd like," Amanda said. "She's single and lives in Manhattan."

"We *can* talk about things other than husbands and children, you know," Sarah said. "And the subways run perfectly well out to Brooklyn. Cabs, too."

"Of course," Amanda said. Honestly, she wasn't sure herself why she never considered including Carolyn. "I didn't mean—I should definitely invite her. I will."

"Maybe to Maude's *sex* party. That'll make us seem edgy and exciting." Sarah smiled. "Hey, maybe I'll even take my chances at this year's party and ascend the forbidden stairs. If you really are done hosting after this year, Maude, it could be my last chance."

"Please," Maude said. "That isn't you and Kerry."

"That isn't Kerry," Sarah said, then winked again. "But maybe, just this once, it *will* be me."

LIZZIE

I stopped off at home on the way from the Brooklyn Criminal Court-house to Zach's house. Strictly speaking, our apartment wasn't exactly on the way to Zach's, but Adam's what-marriage-doesn't-have-its-problems comment had left me thinking about my own. Maybe I could forgive Sam for getting fired, and even for the accident, but he couldn't backslide again. Not that I really had forgiven him, for anything. I knew that, and so did Sam. I had just buried my resentment and my rage. I was good at burying things.

Sam cracking his head open needed to be rock bottom, though. He had to go to rehab now. Or else. An actual ultimatum—me or the drinking . . . I climbed our three flights sure I was ready to finally give Sam one. And then, at our apartment door, my phone rang. It was a number I didn't recognize. Just like that, saved by the bell.

"This is Lizzie."

"This is ADA Steve Granz," a man said. "I got a note from Paul Hastings. He asked me to call you. But I've got no fucking clue why. Typical Paul."

Brooklyn DA's office, I was assuming. Such was Paul's power. He wouldn't burn the midnight oil with me, but he was helpful in other ways.

"Thanks so much for calling," I said. "We've got a defendant charged with assaulting an officer in Brooklyn. We were hoping for some back-ground."

It was my job now to pump Steve for information about Zach's case: charges, evidence, the assigned DA, what deal they might be willing to make. Not because *we* were interested in a deal, but because that would give us a clue as to how tight the DA's case was. The stronger their case, the less willing they would be to deal. Mind you, a strong prosecution case didn't necessarily have anything to do with the truth. As a prosecutor, you never knowingly pursued something you didn't believe in. But your job was to build cases to win. That meant the truth was sometimes a parallel, nondependent variable.

"Gotta say, I'm surprised Paul is slumming it in state court," Steve said. "Much less Brooklyn."

"Only from a safe, supervisory distance."

"Ah, that sounds more like Paul," he said. "Who's the defendant?"

"Zach Grayson," I said. "It was an accident. The officer didn't even want to pursue it. Apparently somebody on the scene, an ADA possibly, pressed for the arrest. They're holding him over at Rikers without bail."

"Rikers is a tough break," Granz said casually, fingers clicking across a keyboard in the background. The fact that he didn't bat an eye at my suggesting one of his colleagues might be overreaching spoke volumes. "Ah, here it is," he said finally. "Oh, wait, is this that Park Slope thing?"

"They live in Park Slope, yes."

"The Key Party Killing." He sounded genuinely entertained. And, unfortunately, I had no idea why. "Or the Park Slope Perverts. You know, instead of Park Slope Parents? I came up with that one." He was quiet for a moment. "Sorry, they were joking in the office this morning about the headlines that'll be in the *Post* when they finally dig into the details of this thing."

Zach had mentioned a party, but a key party? It wasn't that Zach was asexual—no, actually, Zach *was* kind of asexual. It was one of the reasons I'd never considered him anything other than a friend. Then again, years had passed. Maybe a wife as beautiful as Amanda had changed him into a sex addict.

It was a risk to admit my ignorance and inquire, but I had no choice.

"Key party?" I asked, trying to sound unfazed.

"Or whatever they call it," Steve said. "Maybe it's organic, free-range fucking? I'm sure there's some four-million-dollar-brownstone way to refer to it. All I know is that my wife would cut my dick off if I ever suggested that kind of thing."

"But Amanda Grayson was found dead in her own home," I said. "Not at a party."

"Yeah, yeah," he said. "It was after the party, though. They were both there earlier, that's what I heard. There's been trouble at that party before, too. Usually it's only noise complaints, public intoxication, and whatnot. But last summer two guys got into a fight. This is all second-hand. I never heard of any of it before this morning. I'm in the organized crime section. But even I know there hasn't been a murder in Park Slope, not one like this, in—I don't know. Maybe ever. Seriously, a party like that is a bad fucking idea."

"Yeah, well, to each his own," I said casually, like I knew all about such things. "Is somebody from your office somehow getting the papers to hold off on sharing all that?"

"Come on, you know as well as I do we can't keep the papers from doing what they want." His tone was thick with sarcasm. "It is pretty ironic, though, you've got to admit. All those Park Slope Parents with their homemade organic kale baby food catching STDs from each other—" He exhaled, the sound like helium being let out of a balloon. "Ah, sorry. I'm not usually this much of an asshole. It's been a long day, and it's not even half over."

And I didn't have time for any more small talk. "Ideally, I'd like to get ahold of the ADA assigned, so I can touch base about reasonable bail. Even unreasonable bail would be fine. Anything so my client can avoid getting assaulted again at Rikers."

"I'll ask around, see if I can get you a name," he said, notably also unfazed by the mention of Zach's assault.

"That would be helpful, thanks."

"Anything for Paul," he said. "He's been trying to get me over to that firm of his for years. I think he wants to build some mini criminal defense empire. You like it there?"

"It's great," I said, because that was the only right answer under the circumstances. My tone, though, was appropriately flat.

"Right," Steve said skeptically. "I love Paul. But I'm not sure I'd want to work for his ass."

"Why?" I couldn't help asking.

"Because that fucker is a maniac. He'll always be five steps ahead," he said. "And I'm not a big fan of choking on dust."

By the time I finally opened our apartment door, I'd completely lost my momentum. There was no longer time for some big showdown with Sam; I really did need to be getting to Zach's to call Case's camp. Besides, I'd already waited, what, *years* to draw my line in the sand. What was a few more hours?

I expected to be greeted by the usual smell of strong coffee and the quiet lilt of the Gaelic music that Sam had taken to listening to lately. Inspiration to get him in the "writing mood," he said. Since he'd gotten fired from *Men's Health*, every few weeks it was a new genre, always instrumental, usually somewhat obscure. The Gaelic had been on tap for the past month or so, though it didn't seem to be doing much good. Sam wasn't banging out the pages of his book the way I'd have hoped for someone with so much free time.

"Sam!" I called out. "Hello?"

He wasn't asleep at nearly two in the afternoon, was he?

"Sam!" I called again, even louder, as I headed for the bedroom.

When I finally pushed open the door, the bed was empty and neatly made. The sharply flattened sheets, the crisp edge of the comforter folded back, it was an obvious act of contrition: perfectly executed guilt origami.

"Sam!" I called one last time before I turned out of the bedroom and headed down the short hall. Where was he? And what exactly had he been feeling so regretful about when he woke up and made the bed?

When I reached the living room, there was still no Sam. But his laptop was there, open on our small, round dining table, the screen dark in slumber. I closed the top and smoothed my fingers over the round sticker at the center, a recent purchase recalling a years-ago marathon it was difficult to believe Sam had ever run. But *he* believed he would run another someday soon. And so in his mind at least he remained a marathoner. Such was the nature of Sam's faith—unreasonable and intoxicating. There were some notebooks stacked to the left side of his computer and a small pack of matches to the right, with "Enid's" printed on them. Sam hadn't also started smoking, had he? He hated smoking. Maybe he'd just kept them as a keepsake. But a keepsake of what? Luckily, there was no name or number jotted down on the inside cover.

I took a deep breath and reopened his laptop, then typed in his password—LizzieLOVE. Sam had gotten his new computer the day after he'd thrown up in Mary Jo's living room during her annual Kentucky Derby party. The password had been a small part of a much longer apology. It had worked, too. I was always so willing to accept anything that might get us back to that perfect place where we'd begun.

The party where Sam and I met wasn't even a law school party. I'd gone along with a friend who had a friend who knew someone who claimed there would be lots of attractive eligible medical students in attendance, which had sounded like both a totally stupid reason to go to a party and a wildly appealing one. Also, the party was in The Rittenhouse, a fancy building right off the Philadelphia square, a nice change of pace from the dingy apartments the law school parties were always in.

I'd been at the party an hour, nursing a beer, when I first spotted Sam's shaggy hair, two-day growth of beard, and iridescent blue eyes across the room. He was extremely good-looking, but it was the way his whole face lit up when he smiled that made my heart leap. It was electric. When he finally looked my way, and kept on looking, it was like my scalp had been set on fire.

I felt the color in my cheeks rise as he finally made his way over to introduce himself.

"You don't look like a doctor," he said.

"What does that mean?" I asked, afraid that he was about to say something dumb like I was too pretty for that, which would ruin everything.

He pointed around the room. "The doctors all have this way of standing," he said. "They, like, lean back a little. It's because they spend so much time on their feet."

I looked around the room, ready to argue. But a fair number of people did seem to be standing that way.

"Will you all be stuck like that forever?" I asked.

"Me? Oh, I'm not in med school." He laughed. "Too cutthroat for me. I'm here visiting a friend from college. He's in med school, and he told me the thing about the standing. However, there is a decent chance that he was only fucking with me." He smiled, and on cue, my heart jumped again. "If you're not a doctor either, what do you do?"

"I'm in law school."

"That's funny. I was supposed to be a lawyer."

"What happened?"

He smiled crookedly. "I'm a lover, not a fighter."

"Seriously?" I rolled my eyes, though I was already charmed.

Sam shrugged. "Trying to best an opponent all day is not my thing," he said, then hurried to clarify. "Not that being a lawyer couldn't be noble, I mean, theoretically."

"Ah yes, theoretically." I smiled back. Maybe I should have been offended, but I was too distracted by how wobbly my legs felt.

"I just insulted your chosen profession, didn't I?"

I laughed. "A little."

"Am I fucking this up?" Sam asked.

"A little," I said, though it was hardly the truth.

"Regardless of what I think about lawyers generally, you'll do great things," he said. "That I'm sure of."

"How do you know?" I asked. "We just met."

"Oh, I can tell," he said, glancing my way. "It's a feeling. A good one."

"You have a lot of these good feelings?"

When he smiled this time, my heart nearly stopped. His eyes were so impossibly blue and bright. "Not like this."

I soon learned that though not a lawyer or a doctor, Sam was plenty accomplished. He'd recently finished up graduate school at the Columbia School of Journalism and had a job on the metro desk at the *New York Times*. He was focusing on exposing the secondary impacts of US poverty, especially on children. He even had a feature—"The Orphans of Opioids"—about to run. Sam wanted to change the status quo, just like me. He believed it was possible, too, and as we talked, his optimism swept me away. Within minutes, I suspected I'd met my destiny. Someone who would fix the world with me. Someone who might even fix me. Because I might have looked okay on the outside, but I wasn't. Ever since I'd lost my parents, I'd been like a burned-out bulb.

It wasn't until I met Sam that unseasonably warm April night that I believed I might brighten again one day. By the time we were kissing on the edge of Rittenhouse Square, I'd already started to glow.

Up on Sam's computer screen was a website for Enid's, Brooklyn, which, it turned out, was a bar in Greenpoint. I looked around the empty room again. Was that where he'd gone? To a bar in Greenpoint in the middle of the day? It had only been a matter of days since he'd bashed his head.

For fuck's sake, Sam.

My face felt hot as I dialed his number. When the call went straight to voice mail, I had a long moment where I thought I might leave a message telling him not to bother coming home. A moment when I felt like even rehab wouldn't be enough. But instead of saying that, instead of saying anything, I closed my eyes, swallowed down my sorrow and anger, and hung up the phone.

———

Fifteen minutes later I stood on the short, tree-lined stretch of Montgomery Place between Eighth Avenue and the park, staring up at Zach's impressive brownstone. In the golden late-afternoon sun, it was breathtaking. Five floors of flawless reddish-brown sandstone, with an extravagant stoop that seemed twice the width of the ones on either side. Through the huge windows in front, I could see a massive Art Deco chandelier floating under fifteen-foot ceilings.

Of course, given Zach's success, I did wonder why he and Amanda had chosen Brooklyn over Manhattan. I imagined Zach could have easily afforded a similar home in Tribeca or the West Village. Brooklyn did have a unique charm, but so did those neighborhoods. If Amanda was from a small town, though, maybe she'd been the one who preferred something quieter and more down-to-earth for Case.

I held my breath as I finally made my way up the front steps, relieved that there was no crime tape or any other indication that Zach's home was still being held by police. Not that I was looking forward to actually going inside. From Zach's own description, it had been a particularly gruesome scene, and it wouldn't have been cleaned up. The police and EMTs didn't mop up the blood and sanitize after your wife's bludgeoned body was taken away. It was left to you to put your house back in order, even when they didn't think you were the one responsible for breaking it to pieces.

At the top of the steps, I crouched down next to a large planter filled with chic fernlike greenery. It lifted easily, and there was the key on the ground underneath.

Shit. I had been hoping the key might be gone, proof that somebody other than Zach had indeed used it to gain entry the night Amanda died. Somebody who'd also used Zach's golf club to beat her to death.

But the notion that somebody had swiped the key, used it to get in, killed Amanda, and then put it back? Some things strained credulity. Like the idea that Zach had simply forgotten to tell me about the part of his hearing where an outstanding warrant was discussed.

It was bothering me. That was the honest truth. The Zach I knew from law school was meticulous about details. There was no way he had simply forgotten about the warrant. He hadn't mentioned it because he didn't want me to know. As I turned the key, I realized I still wasn't sure if it was the fact of the warrant or that Zach had tried to hide it from me that bothered me more.

Even the way Zach's front door popped open with a gentle whoosh was fancy. I kept my eyes down as I stepped inside the dim, no doubt lovely foyer, careful to avoid having to face the stairs. The typical layout of Park Slope brownstones would put them straight ahead—the stairs and the blood and the brain matter. My mouth already felt tacky. I needed to stay focused on the here and now, the task at hand.

Zach had said that the papers about Case's camp would be in Amanda's small desk in the front room. I didn't look up until I'd stepped safely into the vast, thoroughly updated open living room. It was sparkling white with fashionable midcentury modern furniture. The air was a little stale, but that was the only sign anything was amiss.

The desk—slim and graceful like Amanda—was near the windows. I headed over, stopping first for a closer look at the photos in a sleek built-in along the wall. They were in coordinating frames and so carefully curated that even the poses in the photos—taken over years— seemed somehow to have been planned to one day work together. The idyllic images made it hard to imagine that Zach and Amanda ever had an unhappy moment, much less a violent altercation that had ended in Amanda's death.

The pictures also confirmed what I'd noticed at Rikers: Zach was much more attractive than he'd been in law school. More definition in his face, brought on by age, or the twenty pounds of muscle he looked to have put on. Or maybe it was the confidence that came with success. The old twitchiness I'd noticed at Rikers had likely been an aberration brought on by the stress of the situation, or maybe by seeing an old friend. Regardless, there was no doubt that Zach had come into his own. And, appallingly, I had a momentary flicker of regret.

I tried to shake it off, to pretend I hadn't felt it—desire for a man whose dead wife's blood was all over the stairs only feet behind me. Whatever I was feeling obviously wasn't about Zach anyway.

I picked up one of the framed pictures of Amanda and Zach on their wedding day, on a beach somewhere tropical. Amanda looked stunning in a simple lace wedding dress, holding casually arranged exotic flowers; Zach was smiling in a light linen suit. They looked effortlessly happy in the way of people who have everything.

I wondered what the pictures of Sam and me from our wedding day would say. All I remembered was feeling grateful and, God, so impossibly in love. Sam had arranged our entire wedding himself. Wedding planning without my mother would have been too hard, and Sam had known that intuitively. From the moment we met, we'd been like that—connected in one continuous loop.

We were married in the beautiful backyard of a West Village town house owned by a wealthy boarding-school friend of Sam's. Sam had personally strung every inch of the backyard with the twinkling white lights I'd talked about loving on our first date, and the flowers were the blue hyacinths Sam had brought me on our second. Neither Sam nor I had family there, but we'd been surrounded by friends. A guitar played by Sam's college roommate serenaded me down the aisle, Heather from law school baked the cake, and Mary Jo performed the ceremony. We wrote our own vows. Sam's, of course, were much more beautiful than mine.

"I promise to be your light home" was his last vow. And in so many ways, meeting Sam had been like a flare shot off, startling me awake and blazing a trail through my darkness. And yet, we'd ended up so hopelessly lost. I was *still* choosing him, wasn't I? Every single day.

My phone rang, startling my eyes off the photos. I dug in my bag for it.

Sam, apparently back from Enid's. And, just like that, our wedding memory dissolved and I was angry at him all over again.

"What?" I answered.

"Well, hello to you, too," Sam replied jovially. Drunkenly? It was possible, but if so, not very. His speech always became rapidly, notably slurred, and it wasn't. "I saw you called. I was just calling you back. But you sound . . . busy."

"I am busy," I said, determined not to interrogate him about Enid's or Greenpoint. It was only the rehab that mattered now, and I couldn't exactly get into that in Zach's house. Or that seemed as good an excuse as any not to say a word. "Because I'm *working.*"

"Okay then." Sam sounded wounded. "I can let you—"

"What have *you* been up to?" I challenged.

"Oh, I've just been writing," Sam said. "Wasn't a bad day on the book. Five pages. Then again, my butt never left my chair, so maybe five pages isn't actually that impressive."

"Never left your chair, huh?" A completely voluntary, gratuitous lie.

"Well, I did go to the post office," Sam said, carving himself an out. "For stamps. What's with the third degree?"

It hasn't even been a week, Sam.

"I'm tired, that's all," I said. "It's been a long day."

I could feel Sam's guilt rise in the silence. And I was glad. A little guilt was better than nothing.

"Okay," he said finally, but tightly. Like he wished he'd said something completely different.

"I've got to go," I said. "I'll see you later tonight."

I hung up without waiting for him to say goodbye. I gripped my phone and pressed it against my lips.

Suddenly there was a loud crash, followed by a bang. It had come from the back of the house. On the other side of a door at the far end of the living room. I stared toward the closed door.

"Hello?" I called out, heart thumping. *Please don't answer. Please don't answer.* I glanced behind me toward the front door, trying to calculate how fast I could sprint out that way if necessary.

"Hello? Who's there?" I shouted in as deep and imposing a voice as I could muster. "I'm Zach Grayson's attorney!"

Only silence in return.

"Hello?"

More silence.

I threw my phone back in my bag and gripped Amanda and Zach's wedding picture in two hands as I inched toward the door, my back to the bloody stairs.

I took one last deep breath before pushing open the swinging door with my hip, picture frame held high. On the floor of the kitchen was a shattered ceramic bowl, dimes and quarters strewn about nearby. My eyes darted around. But there was no one in sight and, luckily, no closet or other obvious place to hide. The dish could have fallen on its own, I tried to tell myself. Set too close to the edge, maybe on the verge of toppling for days.

But then I spotted the back door. I walked closer, careful not to touch anything, hoping my eyes were playing tricks. The door was definitely ajar, though. Someone had been there just now. Someone who'd knocked the dish over, probably in a rush to get out the back door at the sound of my ringing phone. What would have happened if Sam hadn't called and I'd surprised them in the kitchen?

My hands trembled as I dialed 911.

"Nine-one-one. What's your emergency?"

"I'd like to report a break-in."

I waited on the front steps for the police to arrive. An endless fifteen minutes later, a patrol car finally pulled up and parked in front of a nearby hydrant. A middle-aged female officer and a younger man got out. He was short and solidly built. She was tough-looking and a head taller, with slicked-back blond hair and imposing shoulders. She walked ahead a few steps, very obviously in charge.

"This your house?" she called up.

"I called to report the break-in," I said. "But it's my client's house. I'm his attorney."

"Your client, huh?" Her eyebrows bunched. "He inside?"

"No, no," I said, making the calculated decision not to mention Zach's current residence in Rikers. "I was here to pick something up for him. I was inside when I heard a noise at the back of the house, in the kitchen." I motioned over my shoulder to the house. "When I went to check, there was a smashed dish on the floor and the back door was hanging open. Like somebody had just run out. I can show you. I didn't touch anything."

"There anything missing?" the female officer asked, peering up at the house without taking a step closer. "Signs of an actual burglary?"

"Nothing obvious—the drawers weren't opened or anything. Only the broken dish. But like I said, it's not my house."

"I thought you said there was an open door." The female officer leveled a pair of skeptical eyes at me as she made her way up the steps. "Right?"

Sarcasm. Okay, so that answered that question: she knew exactly who my client was and all about Amanda's murder. Did she think I'd staged this?

"Yeah," I said, sharply, but just short of rude. OFFICER GILL, her name-plate read, and unfortunately, I did need her help. Staying polite seemed wise. "*And* the open door."

"Well, let's get this show on the road," the male officer said, clearly oblivious to the tension as he started up the steps. Officer Kemper was his name.

"The blood hasn't been cleaned up," I said, glancing at Officer Gill. She avoided eye contact.

"Blood?" Kemper asked. "Somebody want to clue me in?"

"The Key Party Killing." I glared at Gill. "I believe that's what you all are calling it."

His eyes widened. "Oh, that's *this*?"

"Same house," Gill said, then turned back to me. "Unlock the door, then wait out here. Till we make sure it's clear."

I hovered outside the mostly closed front door, listening for a commotion—a shot fired in the dark, officers shouting, a suspect discovered, a struggle. But there was only more silence. Ten minutes later, the door swung open.

"You're good," Officer Kemper said, breathing hard from his pass through the house.

"You know, whoever was here probably had something to do with Amanda Grayson's murder," I said as I moved toward the door. It wouldn't change how the officers handled this, but it would be good to have it on the record. "It's a reasonable assumption."

"Okay," he said, but with a tone that said *That's not my department*.

We stepped back inside. And there it finally was: the staircase. Clearly a recent addition, it was pale wood with modern steel detailing in the railing and treads. Blood was splattered all over the walls near the bottom—small drops and big drops and a fine spray. Long splashed lines on top of that like a gruesome Jackson Pollock painting. There was an entryway table under a mirror knocked out of place, beneath that a small, stained towel. In the center of the polished blond wood beneath the stairs was a huge circle of smeared blood. As though somebody had made an effort to clean up, only to make matters worse. But it was one nearly black spot to the side of the last step that was most disturbing. I could picture Amanda's head lying there, the insides pouring out like a cracked egg.

"You okay?" Officer Kemper eyeballed me.

"Yeah, I just . . ." I motioned toward the stairs by way of explanation. "I'll be okay."

"I thought you'd been inside already?"

"I was. I didn't look." It did sound odd now that I'd said it out loud.

"I thought you were his lawyer?"

"I am."

"Then you'd probably better buckle the fuck up," he said before starting off toward the kitchen.

Officer Gill was crouched down, inspecting the broken dish with gloved hands. "Interrupted burglary, I'm guessing."

"But they didn't take anything?" I asked. "That doesn't make any sense."

"They tried to, though." Officer Gill motioned to the quarters. "An addict, I'd guess. Desperation break-ins usually are. They probably heard you, got startled, took off."

Officer Kemper drifted over to the back door, opened it with an elbow, then stepped through, studying the backyard for a moment. I considered objecting to this patently absurd burglary theory. Someone totally unrelated to Amanda's murder just happening to break in days later to steal a bunch of quarters? But Officer Gill would argue it wasn't a coincidence: the house had been empty since—what, Saturday or Sunday morning—anybody keeping an eye out would be able to see that.

"You can run the fingerprints, right?" I asked as Officer Kemper stepped back inside. "On the door. They probably touched it on the way out."

"Yeah," Officer Gill said, sarcastic again. "Sure we can."

"Are you saying you won't?" I demanded.

"Nothing's been taken and nobody's been hurt," Kemper offered diplomatically. "This isn't going to be a top priority."

My face flushed—part frustration, part embarrassment. "For all we know, the person who broke in here could be responsible for Amanda Grayson's death. You're telling me the police won't try to figure out who it was?"

"Wasn't your client arrested for that?" Officer Gill asked.

"He was arrested for assaulting an officer," I shot back. "Anything to keep him where the DA can watch him."

Officer Gill huffed quietly, but there was something resigned about it. Like she didn't actually disagree. She held up her hands.

"Listen, we'll put a request in to get the crime scene unit detectives back out here. We'll also call the borough evidence collection team that handles property crimes." She lowered her hands, placed them on her hips. "You'll get one or the other. All I'm saying is that you're gonna need to be patient."

———

A few minutes later the officers were gone and I was alone in the house again. I made my way back out to the living room and then finally closer to the stairs. I looked up again the length of the metal banister, back down to that large circle of smeared blood on the floor.

And then I saw something on the second to the last stair. It was to the side, hardly visible against the blackened steel of the tread. I stepped closer. It was a pattern in the blood that could have been a print—fingers, a palm. Definitely it could be. What if the police had missed it? It was very hard to see. What if they hadn't tested other prints on the wall? That also didn't seem impossible under the circumstances. The crime scene was a mess and there'd been an excellent suspect already in hand.

As soon as the police stepped through the door, they'd have seen their prime suspect standing there, his own golf club at his feet, dead wife at the bottom of his stairs. Once they heard about the sex party, they'd have been even less worried about casting a wider net. And fair enough. The vast majority of female murder victims were killed by a loved one. Having settled on Zach as suspect number one, everything from that point forward would have been about the prosecution building a case.

From a former prosecutor, that wasn't a judgment, it was a fact. It was also a fact that it was now my job to stop that particular freight train from barreling any farther down the track. And it felt more important now than ever. The outstanding warrant may have left me briefly questioning his trustworthiness, but the intruder in his house had left me more convinced than ever: Zach was an innocent man.

KRELL INDUSTRIES

CONFIDENTIAL MEMORANDUM
NOT FOR DISTRIBUTION

June 26

To: Brooklyn Country Day Board of Directors
From: Krell Industries
Subject: Data Breach & Cyber Incident Investigation—Progress Report

The following is a summary of key data collected and interviews conducted. Preliminary conclusions will be made next week.

Data Collection

A review of Brooklyn Country Day information systems has revealed a series of malicious hacks beginning on April 15 of this year. On April 30 a more significant intrusion was made into Brooklyn Country Day data systems. At that time, it appears extensive family data—including emails, home addresses, birthdates, and private phone numbers—was obtained.

Interview Summaries

SUBJECT FAMILY 0005: Female Primary Parent (FPP) received an email from an anonymous source stating that if she did not comply with $20,000 demand, details of her husband, Male Primary Parent (MPP)'s, involvement with Terry's Bench (a dating site for married individuals) would be posted on Park Slope Parents (PSP), a local parenting site.

SUBJECT FAMILY 0006: Female Primary Parent (FPP) stated voluminous and disturbing pornography, including so-called peeper porn, was emailed to her along with a demand for $20,000 cash transfer and the claim that said offensive material had been found on subject family computer. Failure to comply with the cash transfer demand would result in the offensive material being posted to PSP along with information that it belonged to Subject Family 0006.

LIZZIE

The sun set as I sat on Zach's front steps, waiting for Millie to arrive. Reaching out to her had been a reflex, though as I waited I couldn't shake a sinking sense of unease. On the one hand, as a former police sergeant turned respected private investigator and old family friend, Millie was an obvious choice. On the other hand, calling Millie came with obvious complications, especially given all her recent emails I'd ignored.

I didn't usually avoid Millie's emails, but they also didn't usually have "please call me" in the subject line. And I'd only just heard from her a few weeks ago. Something was up, clearly. And, yes, I was deliberately delaying finding out what it was. Poor Millie. All these years, all she'd been trying to do was help. And she had. Proof that no good deed goes unpunished.

Of course, Millie being Millie, when I called and asked her to come she hadn't mentioned my ignoring her. She'd asked only for Zach's address and assured me she was on her way.

At least the calls about Case were now behind me. They'd been much worse than I was prepared for. The young residential adviser who'd answered the phone at Case's camp had burst into tears when I told her about Amanda and then was in such a rush to put Case on the phone that I'd barely managed to stop her.

Luckily, I'd then spoken to the significantly calmer camp director, who'd agreed to keep Case away from the news and then had given me the number for the parents of Case's friend—Ashe, it turned out, not Billy. That call had been even more upsetting. Ashe's parents had known Amanda well, had been friends with her. The wife was so distraught she'd dropped the phone and screamed.

"This is so awful," Ashe's father said over and over when he was finally on the line. "God, Case—he's like a member of our family."

It was difficult to hear him over his wife's guttural sobbing in the background. But eventually he had pulled it together enough to come up with a plan. By the end of the call, I was certain he would pick up Case and Ashe that weekend and deliver the news in a responsible, caring fashion.

I felt so relieved when I finally spotted Millie's compact, athletic frame headed my way. Her once-forceful stride was noticeably slower, but it had been a long time. And even from that distance, Millie still exuded that air of comforting forthrightness that had always been her best quality.

I was in the eighth grade the first time I ever really talked to Millie. Lots of cops came into my parents' diner because it was right around the corner from the Tenth Precinct in Chelsea. Millie wasn't just another cop, though. She'd been a good friend of my mom's for years.

Millie was never as charmed by my dad, though. She always seemed to be peering into him, trying to figure out what made him tick. For my part, I was mostly trying to steer clear of him in those days. My father was obsessed with my studying for New York City's hypercompetitive public-high-school entrance exam. It was all he talked about. Do well on that test, and my dad was sure it would be my ticket to a whole new economic class. His ticket, too, I could tell.

Luckily, my mom could not have cared less about that stupid test. To her, I was perfection the moment I was placed in her arms. She loved me with such raw ferocity and blind faith that I was all but convinced I could fly.

My mother's love was outmatched only by her protectiveness. By eighth grade, she had finally started to let me walk alone to the Apollo in the afternoons. My school was only a few blocks from the diner, and all my friends had been taking the subway alone, much longer distances, *for years*. Still, for her it was a huge concession to permit me that small measure of independence. She worked twelve hours a day at the Apollo my entire childhood, but only when I was in school or asleep so that I would have sworn that I had the world's best stay-at-home mom— homemade costumes for the Greek Independence Day Parade and lovingly baked *koulourakia* and hours of attentive listening; my terrible piano playing, my reading aloud of the trashy romance novels she hated, and my overly detailed tales of childhood triumph and occasional tragedy.

I'd arrived late at the Apollo that day. It was pouring rain, and I'd left a book at school. But my mom didn't even seem to notice the time. She was sitting in a booth with Millie, who was dressed in plainclothes. Millie looked more human that way, but she had the usual fierce look in her eye—a woman accustomed to forcibly moving men. She always had a warm smile, too, and a big laugh that my mom seemed to find contagious. It was only with Millie that she laughed with her head tipped back. But not on that day. On that day neither of them looked happy. And they were holding hands.

"Sit, sit." My mother waved me over the second I was in the door.

When Millie looked up, I could see that her eyes were teary. Later, I would learn that her wife, Nancy, had just been moved into hospice. Breast cancer. But I was thirteen at the time, and all I cared about was not being around an adult who was about to cry. I was desperate to slip away, but no one disobeyed my mother.

"Show Millie that puzzle," my mother said, pointing until I'd sat dutifully. "The one from school you did for me yesterday. She could use some distraction."

Be kind, I could hear my mother silently commanding. *Do a good thing for this sad woman who is my friend.* And so, even though I wanted to dive under the table, I did as I was told.

"I hear your dad has killed the summer trip to Greece again this year," Millie said once my mother was gone.

I shrugged, trying to hide my surprise that my mother had shared that with her. "I guess."

"Don't worry. I'm not going to ask you lots of questions," Millie went on. "I actually don't want to be sitting with you either." My eyes shot up. But Millie's expression was straightforward, not like she meant it meanly, but like it was the truth. She leaned in closer to whisper. "I mean, we'll just pretend for a few to make your mom happy. We'd both do anything for her, right?"

Once Millie drew closer on the street, I noticed how thin her face was, her skin papery. How long had it been since we'd actually seen each other in the flesh? More than a decade maybe. Longer than I'd let myself think about. Millie and her emails were in a secret box, one that I peeked into as required, but which I otherwise stored far away.

"Look at you," Millie said quietly, staring up at me from the bottom of Zach's stairs.

I stood. "I'm sorry, Millie . . . Your emails—I've been really underwater at work, a—"

Millie held up her hand and shook her head as she made her way up the steps. "No, no," she said. "I'm glad that you called."

"It's good to see you," I said, trying to ignore the burning in my throat as Millie and I exchanged a quick, firm hug. She felt noticeably frail in my arms.

"You know I'm always here to help," she said. "In any way I can."

That was certainly true and it was because of her friendship with my mom. Guilt, too. Millie had always felt more responsible than she should have for the way things turned out. Like if she'd been able to find the guy who swindled my dad, my family would have survived.

"Thank you," I said. "For everything."

Millie looked for a moment like she might say something more, but instead she nodded and turned to eye Zach's brownstone. "Now, what the hell happened here?"

Inside, we stood at the edge of the living room side by side, staring at all that blood at the bottom of the steps. I'd given Millie the background on Zach and Amanda, such as it was. I'd explained that Zach and I had been pretty good friends in law school, but that I hadn't seen him in years.

"Well," she began, eyeing the staircase, "at least this isn't your mess to clean up."

"Look at this," I said, stepping over to that swirled pattern in the blood on the metal tread of the second to last step. I pointed. "Isn't that part of a handprint? And maybe one fingerprint?"

Millie moved closer and tilted her head. "Could be," she said, not sounding especially impressed. "Sure."

"The police tonight were pretty blasé about taking prints in the kitchen, and that was after I told them I thought whoever was here probably had something to do with what happened to Amanda. I mean, they said they'd put in the request to get a team out here, but who knows? What if whoever was here the first time missed that print? It is hard to make out. I don't see any fingerprint dust anywhere, either. Maybe they didn't print anything."

"Oh, I doubt that," Millie said. "They'd have run prints. And there's lots of ways to lift a print, tape and whatnot. Dust is only for latent prints, not visible ones. It is possible they missed this one, with what a disaster this place is. But my guess is they probably did take it. Real issue is what happens when that print doesn't belong to your guy and isn't in the system. NYPD will eventually get elimination prints from friends, housekeepers, that kind of thing. But that'll take time. They get them as they interview people. And what's the rush when they think they've got their man?" Millie frowned equivocally. "There isn't a police department in the country that's got the resources to prioritize looking for alternate suspects to undermine a good case. But you know all that. You were a prosecutor. By the way—not that it matters, I'm here to help you, not him—but do you think your client did it?"

"No," I said without hesitating. But also without elaborating. Because that remained the whole of my opinion on the matter of Zach's innocence. I didn't think he had killed Amanda.

"Of course, given the right circumstances, anyone is capable of anything." Millie turned to look at me. "We both know that."

"Yeah," I said, looking away. "We do."

We stayed quiet then for an awkward moment. I kept my eyes on the stairs. Looking at all the blood was better than facing Millie. Was she going to insist that we talk about everything, right now?

"Can whatever it is wait just a couple more days?" I asked, heading her question off at the pass. I motioned to the stairs. "I need to deal with this first, okay?"

"Okay. A couple more days." She took a deep breath. "Let me make some calls and see how fast I can get someone of our own down here to lift prints, including that one on the stairs. I'm sure the NYPD will send a team for the kitchen, and I can wait until they get here. Once we've got our own prints to work with, we can make whatever comparisons we want. We'll get a blood spatter person, too. In the meantime, why don't you try to find the golf bag—the club came from somewhere—and whatever else upstairs might be interesting. Investigators might have 'overlooked' something that wasn't useful to them. Try not to touch anything with your bare hands, though, and take off your shoes. Let's not corrupt the scene any more than necessary."

While Millie got on the phone, I made my way up the steps, trying not to look too closely as I stepped around the blood in my stocking feet. At the top, well past all the blood, there was what looked to be fingerprint dust, so the NYPD had indeed done something. Upstairs, I passed Case's spotless but cheerfully childlike bedroom and headed onward to Zach and Amanda's master suite at the front of the house. I used the edge of my shirt to open their door.

The master bedroom was massive, spa-like and serene. Every sur-face was bright white—from the linens to the curtains to the walls—and yet somehow the exact right shade so as not to be sterile or cold. I tried to imagine Zach and Amanda snuggling in that huge fluffy bed late on Saturday, Case in between them, but I just could not pic-ture it.

I turned away from the bed and headed toward the closet in search of the golf clubs or, as Millie had said, anything else that might be use-ful. A vast walk-in, with warm lighting and a small bench in the cen-ter, the closet had artfully arranged floor-to-ceiling racks and cubbies and endless amounts of extremely expensive clothing on hangers. I knew such closets existed in mansions somewhere, but in Brooklyn—even in a house as nice as Zach's—it was hard to process. It also wasn't a closet for golf clubs. Downstairs, maybe, or wherever they kept the rest of their sporting equipment. They had a child. They probably had a designated area for such things.

But first I needed to take a closer look in the bedroom closet. As Millie had pointed out, there could be something helpful tucked some-where, though it already felt uncomfortably intimate, standing there in the doorway in my nearly bare feet. Lingerie, sex toys, there was no telling what I might find. After all, Zach and Amanda had been at a sex party that night. And now, here I was mixed up in whatever they had done. As if I didn't have enough of my own problems. It had been so reckless to ask Paul about Zach's case. Stupid, actually. I braced my-self as I finally stepped inside the massive closet.

I opened one drawer after another. Clothes and more clothes, that was all. There was actually nothing very personal anywhere, much less anything scandalous. I lifted the lid on a jewelry box to an eye-popping collection—necklaces, bracelets, and earrings with colored stones and, yes, plenty of actual diamonds. It seemed to rule out a rob-bery, unless Amanda had interrupted the burglar before he'd found the stash he was looking for. Maybe I'd cut short his return trip to fin-ish the job.

I headed back out into the bedroom, where I looked over the built-in bookshelves. There were dozens of classic novels, Shakespeare plays, and Nietzsche, separated every dozen books or so by a short cluster of coffee-table and art books stacked on their sides. Amanda's, surely. Back when I'd known him, Zach hadn't been much of a reader, a fact he'd seemed to offer as a challenge to anyone willing to judge him. Amanda—poor background, uneducated, but a big reader and a great mother, not to mention gorgeous. A jury was going to make somebody pay for what had been done to her.

As I turned back from the shelves, a nearby nightstand caught my eye. The top drawer was open slightly. I made a note for myself in my phone: *Fingerprint nightstand drawer.* Then I used the edge of my shirt to open it.

The orderly, impersonal contents of the top drawer bore no resemblance to my own overstuffed night table, with its tangled headphones and receipts for store credit that had long since expired. There was a small tube of very pricey, very female hand cream next to a thin box of tissues—it was Amanda's nightstand, presumably. The only genuinely personal item was a card from Case that—judging from the childish handwriting—had likely been written years earlier: *I luv u momy. You ar the best and only momy.*

My throat tightened. That poor little boy off enjoying camp somewhere, having no idea the loss that had already befallen him. It was a loss I felt daily, even all these years later.

The bottom drawer of Amanda's nightstand was empty, apart from a single Moleskine journal. Using tissues, I lifted it out. As I flipped through the lined pages—empty, it turned out—a small card with a modern drawing of two roses at the top fell to the carpet: *Thinking of you xoxo.* No signature. Maybe Zach wasn't such a lousy husband after all. I picked up the card from the carpet, careful to hold it only by the edges. On the back was the name of a florist in stylish typeface: "Blooms on the Slope, Seventh Avenue and St. John's Place."

I set the florist's card down on the nightstand for safekeeping, only to have it fall promptly back to the floor. When I bent to retrieve it a second time, I caught sight of something under the bed. Something large and dark shoved up near the headboard.

I got down and pressed my face to the carpet, using my iPhone flashlight for illumination. More journals under the bed. Dozens of them. Stacked neatly and carefully and pushed deep against the baseboard, in a place where officers might easily have missed them.

Using the tissues, I grabbed a few of the journals from different stacks. Unlike the pricey Moleskine in the drawer, these journals were mismatched, very worn, and much cheaper looking. I flipped quickly through the first few pages of each. One seemed to be from Case's first year, two from Amanda's late childhood and early teen years. I felt guilty invading Amanda's privacy, but the journals could provide a gold mine of alternate suspects. Hopefully, I wouldn't need to read much to find one good one for a jury to latch onto. But reading through Amanda's journals in any kind of detail wasn't a project for right now. A trial and the actual need for exculpatory evidence like alternate suspects was months away. Instead, I needed to finish up at Zach's house and get back to the office to write the habeas writ. That was Zach's only way out of Rikers.

The three journals still safely under the tissues, I headed quickly back toward the steps to the floor above. Straight ahead at the top was a small guest room; the bed was adorned with more bright decorative pillows than a bed in a boutique hotel. It was a chic museum of a room that looked like it had never been used. I checked the closet for the golf clubs, but it was empty except for more pillows and a couple of extra blankets.

At the other end of the hall was what looked to be Zach's office. There was a lot of dark wood and leather and more books lining the shelves—*Sailing Alone Around the World, The Oxford Companion to Wine, A History of the Modern Middle East.* There were testosterone-fueled biographies, too: Steve Jobs, John F. Kennedy, J. P. Morgan.

Maybe the books were a front—who Zach wanted to be—or maybe Zach was a wine-drinking sailor now? Eleven years was eleven years.

I remembered then how that conversation in Mahoney's about our ambitions had ended back in law school.

"Well, I admit it: money drives me," Zach had said after my impassioned defense of my future in public interest. "And not because I care about buying things. I care about what the money says about me."

"Okay, that's gross," had been my honest response. "And what do you think money says exactly?"

"That I'm better than them."

"Them who?"

Zach had been quiet then for a moment, considering. "Them everyone." He'd looked up at me. "Everyone except you."

And then he'd started to laugh. At himself, I'd thought at the time. Standing there now in his swanky, contrived home office, I wondered if he'd simply been telling the truth.

I headed over to Zach's desk, but paused momentarily before opening the first drawer. What if I stumbled on something I'd rather not know? Something Zach hadn't been worried about, because I was going there only to look in Amanda's desk. Well, that was what attorney-client privilege was for. And while there were questions you didn't ask a maybe-guilty client, it was better to be prepared for every last bad fact the prosecution might already know about.

I needn't have worried: the contents of Zach's desk were neat, orderly, and totally unexceptional. Some desk supplies and some personal files related to Case, which seemed to undermine the whole I-knew-nothing-about-my-kid speech Zach had given me. The other drawers were much the same. There was nothing about Zach's new company either. A home office for somebody who apparently never worked from home.

Zach's computer was on, but password-protected, the lock screen a lovely photo of Zach, Amanda, and Case as a baby. The truth was more imperfect, sure. Zach had already admitted as much. But idyllic images like that wouldn't hurt with a jury.

As I moved away from the desk, my stocking feet caught on something sharp.

"Ouch!" I hissed, bending down to fish it out of the thick carpet.

It was a small white strip with some diagonal blue lines and arrows on one side above a thicker black line. It looked vaguely similar to the ovulation strips I'd used in those brief, foolish weeks I'd thought Sam was doing well enough that we could start trying to conceive.

An ovulation strip was potentially damaging evidence. Being pregnant, trying to have a baby, trying to end a pregnancy—these things could bring out the worst in a marriage. I could already imagine the scene a prosecutor might sketch: Amanda arrives home from the party later than Zach, angry that he left without her, and announces that she wants to get pregnant. Zach doesn't want another kid. They argue. Things get out of hand.

I looked down again at the little test strip. The bright side of being on the defense? It wasn't my obligation anymore to disclose facts helpful to the other side. I stuck the strip in a tissue and shoved it in my pocket. I'd use it if—and only if—it somehow became helpful to us.

I paused on my way out of the office at the closet door. It wouldn't open. I tugged harder, but it wouldn't give. For a moment, I wondered if it might be locked, but then, finally, after one last pull, it gave way. There at the back of the dark closet was the bag of Zach's silver golf clubs, gleaming in the half-dark.

I left Millie waiting for her crime scene experts as well as, hopefully, a tech from the actual NYPD, and headed back to Young & Crane to draft a very persuasive bail appeal. I also needed to get someone from the managing clerk's office down to Philadelphia first thing in the morning to resolve Zach's warrant. I wasn't showing up at a hearing with that outstanding. If staying on Paul's good side meant I had to stay on as Zach's attorney, I was at least going to do a respectable job.

On the subway from Brooklyn to Manhattan, I started paging through Amanda's journals, still under the tissues, though more half-heartedly now that Millie had pointed out we'd be unlikely to be fingerprinting them. I read first from the more recent one, from when Case was a young baby.

October 2010

He sat up today! And, oh my goodness, was he proud of himself. Huge grin! I got some video of it. Fingers crossed that it came out. I'll ask Zach tonight if he wants to see. Or maybe I'll just save it for the weekend. By then who knows what else Case will have done!

I can't believe I thought that I couldn't do this. That, after everything, I might be too clumsy or even cruel. As it turned out, loving Case has made all the difference.

Most notable was what I didn't find in any of Amanda's "new parent" entries. There was not a single complaint—not about the sleeplessness or the crying or the being overwhelmed. Everyone I knew who'd had a baby—which was most people by now—complained about such things. It was human nature. But Amanda seemed inhumanly grateful. She didn't gripe about Zach either. He worked a lot, that was obvious from her entries, but she was so genuinely understanding. In keeping with Zach's description, their marriage seemed distant, but not actually unhappy.

I flipped to the middle of the second journal, with more girlish script.

May 2005

I got a job at the Bishop's Motel! Where Momma worked, cleaning rooms just like her. The manager, Al, said absolutely no way at first. I guess it's illegal to let somebody work at thirteen (stupid). He caved when I started to cry (wasn't even on purpose). It's only part-time, so it's not going to take care of the back rent right away. But it's a start. I'll hide the money better this time, too. Daddy's gotten good at finding things. The pills—they give him a lot more energy.

So far, I'd managed to keep Amanda, the person, a hazy image at arm's length. But now I felt swamped by sadness, guilt, too, for all that I'd taken for granted. Amanda had been only thirteen when she'd started working at a motel to support her possibly drug-abusing father. And she'd been *excited* about it.

I'd been thirteen when I'd sat down in that booth with Millie, excited about my new freedom to walk those few blocks alone. Because my mother had loved me too much to let me go. How much better I'd had it. And look what a mess my life had still become.

GRAND JURY TESTIMONY

MAX CALDWELL,

called as a witness the 6th of July and was examined
and testified as follows:

EXAMINATION

BY MS. WALLACE:

Q: Mr. Caldwell, thank you for coming in to testify
today.

A: You're welcome.

Q: How did you come to be at the party at 724 First
Street on July 2nd of this year?

A: My wife knows Maude from Brooklyn Country Day. Our
kids go to school there.

Q: Before her death, did you know Amanda Grayson?

A: No. I'd never met her.

Q: Did you know of her?

A: No, I did not. My wife might have.

Q: Do you know Zach Grayson?

A: No. I think I might have heard of his company
before. And now because of this . . . But not before.

Q: I'd like to show you a picture.

(Counsel approaches witness with photograph, which is marked as People's Exhibit 5.)

Q: Is this a picture of the man you saw at the party that night?

A: Yes.

Q: Let the record reflect that People's Exhibit 5 is a photograph of Zach Grayson. Where did you see him?

A: I saw him talking to some woman about Terry's Bench. You know, the Tinder for married people? The woman was drunk and seriously pissed. She kept telling everybody at the party that her husband was on there.

Q: What did Mr. Grayson say to her?

A: That he had to go home to get some sleep. That he had something he had to do early in the morning. I remember because I thought it was bullshit.

Q: What do you mean?

A: The way he said it. It sounded like an excuse. I thought: That guy wants to get away from that woman. Like I said, she was pissed and drunk. Maybe he also wanted to leave the party. But it is like the only good thing that ever happens in Park Slope. I did sort of wonder if he was having an affair. Why otherwise would you leave a sex party unless it was for sex somewhere else?

Q: Did you see him actually leave?

A: He headed toward the front door.

Q: What time was that?

A: 9:35.

Q: Are you sure?

A: Yes. I checked my watch when he said he had to go to bed. I thought maybe I'd lost track of time and it was later than I thought. That's the kind of party it is. It makes you lose track of everything.

LIZZIE

I'd just arrived back at my office when the phone rang. It was precisely 7:00 p.m., Zach's appointed time. I looked down at my notes: "Warrant? Time line of night? Witnesses to Zach's walk? Amanda's friends, enemies? Flowers? Pregnant? Sex party?"

So many questions, but not all for right now. That last one, though, I had underlined. The sex party was an even worse fact than the pregnancy. Jurors would easily be able to imagine one spouse killing another after they'd agreed to something like that. Something that might seem like harmless good fun beforehand. Something that could not be undone after the fact. They might even want to punish Zach for breaking the rules of fidelity they were forced to live by. That was the way juries worked, judges sometimes, too. Because they were human beings. And human beings couldn't help but take things personally.

"Hello?" I answered.

"You have a collect call from a New York State correctional facility—"

I hit the number **1** on my phone.

"Hi, Zach."

"Hey, Lizzie. Thanks for taking the call." His voice was low and a little distorted, like Sam's when he'd been drinking.

"What's wrong?" I asked. "You sound . . . strange."

"I, um." He took a breath. "Had another run-in with some bars of a cell. But I—really I'm fine. My lip is swollen. That's what you're hearing."

"Jesus, Zach, again?" My stomach tightened. I really, really hated this. Thanks to Paul, everything that happened to Zach while he was stuck in Rikers now felt like my fault. "What happened this time?"

"I'd really rather not get into it," he said. "The details don't make it better. Trust me."

"These assaults—should I put a call in to the warden or something? Try to get you some protection?"

"I'm pretty sure that tattling on people in Rikers is hazardous to your health. I just need out of here. Quickly."

I regretted wasting so much time at Zach's house. The break-in had slowed me significantly. A writ of habeas corpus had nothing to do with any fingerprints or Amanda's old journals.

"Young & Crane has agreed to let me represent you," I said, trying to lead with something Zach would be happy about.

"Wow. That's great news." Zach exhaled so hard it made a rumbling sound into the phone. "I can't even tell you, Lizzie . . . Thank you."

"We'll eventually need to back up and have a longer, much more detailed background discussion where you walk me through everything you can remember about that night. But first we need to focus on getting you out of Rikers. I'm drafting the habeas writ right now. We'll get it filed first thing in the morning," I said, signing in to my computer. I felt on more solid ground than I had in days. I'd get Zach's situation sorted out, and then I'd sort out my own life, too. A drunk husband and some financial problems—even when they came with a side helping of secret baggage—were nothing compared to a murdered wife and a potential life sentence. "I'll also have someone from the managing clerk's office get down to Philadelphia to clear your outstanding warrant."

I waited a beat, hoping that Zach would jump in with an explanation for the warrant.

"Right, the warrant," he said finally, but he sounded more irritated than apologetic.

"You need to tell me about things like that," I said. "I can't represent you properly if I don't know everything. It puts me in a really bad position."

Zach was silent.

"Hello?"

"Yeah, I get that," Zach said finally, his tone icy. "But then, discovering your wife's bloody, beaten body and then getting sent to Rikers, where you are getting beaten up repeatedly yourself, can make a person loose with details."

Fuck you, Zach, that was all I could think. I got that his situation was a nightmare, but I definitely didn't ask for any of this.

"Hey, I'm trying to help you, remember?" I sounded even angrier than I'd intended. "Because *you* asked me to."

He exhaled loudly. "Uh, I'm sorry, Lizzie." He seemed genuinely chastened. "That's not— I am so lucky to have your help. I know that. I'm just starting to lose it in here a bit."

"That's understandable," I said. And Zach was being attacked, literally. Surely it was taking its toll.

"I should have told you about the warrant. Actually, I should have paid the damn ticket in the first place. The whole issue could have been avoided."

"Adam said you didn't remember what the warrant was for?"

"I do now," he said. "I've had plenty of time to think in here. It was for loitering, I'm pretty sure."

"Loitering?"

"Ridiculous, right? Do you remember that new mayor in Philly when we were there?"

"Um, maybe, I don't know." I did not.

"Well, he was going after everybody for everything. Like every jaywalker. I remember the one officer making a point that they were doing me a favor by not charging me with a misdemeanor, which supposedly they could have. So, I got the ticket for standing too long on a corner. I objected to it on the moral principle that the mayor was trying to create a police state. Hubris of law school youth, I guess. That's why I didn't pay it. Obviously, I should have."

I would have preferred an explanation that was slightly less belligerent, but at least it sounded truthful.

"Yeah, that might have been better, but it's okay. We'll get it resolved."

"Were you able to reach Case's camp?" Zach asked.

"Yes, it's all set. Ashe's parents will head to the camp this weekend, then bring both of the boys to their house and tell Case there. The camp will make sure Case doesn't hear anything before then. And Ashe's parents will let me know if Case wants to talk to you, and we'll arrange it."

"Oh, good." Zach sounded relieved. "I was so afraid that he'd accidentally—"

"That's not going to happen," I said. "His camp seems really on top of things. And his friend's parents were very upset about Amanda, obviously, but they were focused completely on Case by the time I hung up."

"Thank you, Lizzie, really," Zach said. "Ashe, huh . . ."

"We should get some other facts straight, in case they somehow come up at the writ hearing. Also, there's a good chance I'll be arguing it without you there. They're scheduled on short notice. You do have a right to be there, but having you brought up could slow things down. Are you okay waiving your appearance?"

"Sure, yeah, of course. Whatever you think is best," Zach said, the edge completely gone from his voice.

I glanced down at my list, hoping to start with the easiest things first.

"Did you send flowers to Amanda from Blooms on the Slope?"

"Flowers?" Zach asked. "Sorry, no. Why?"

"I'm sure it's nothing. She just had a card from some flowers," I said, hoping now to breeze past the question of who sent them. "What are the names of some of Amanda's friends? I should go talk to them."

"Maude was the woman who had the party that night. I know they were friends," he said. "And her other close friend in the neighborhood is a woman named Sarah. She worked with Amanda at the foundation."

"Foundation?" I asked.

"Oh, yeah, we just started a scholarship foundation," he said. "Or *I* started a scholarship foundation. Amanda ran it, because that's what the wives of successful entrepreneurs do," he said flatly. He was mocking himself, at least I hoped. "Amanda didn't complain because she never complained. But I don't think she enjoyed running the foundation. With her upbringing, she was glad to help needy kids. But she was overwhelmed by the responsibility. She was always worried she was going to mess something up and somebody was going to come after her."

"Come after her?"

"Not literally," he said. "If there was something like that, I would tell you, believe me."

"I found her journals at your—"

"Journals?"

"She kept a bunch under your bed. They go back years."

"Oh yeah, right," he said. "I knew that."

But did he? I wasn't so sure. If he was learning about the journals for the first time, though, he wasn't nervous about them. *At all.* And wasn't *that* a little weird? Who wanted a running account of their petty marital discords, especially through the eyes of their partner? I wouldn't want Sam keeping journals, and I hadn't been accused of murdering him.

"I took a quick look at a couple of them," I said. "I think maybe Amanda's childhood was worse than just being poor."

"I'm not surprised," Zach said. He also did not sound particularly intrigued. "When I met Amanda, she was a seventeen-year-old high-school dropout working and living at a motel, so—" He was silent then, abruptly. As though he'd wished he hadn't admitted quite that much. "Anyway, she didn't talk about her past except to say that 'money was tight.' She didn't seem to want to get into it, and I never pushed. We all have family crap, right? I know her mom died when she was young. Whatever else happened, she came through it all right, because she was a great mom and a good wife. A really positive person. We liked to be forward-looking, you know? Our life started when we met."

"Were you guys trying to have another baby?"

"Another baby?" Zach scoffed. "Are you asking if we were having sex?"

"No, no, I—"

"Because the answer is not very often. I worked long hours," Zach said. "Not that sex with Amanda was bad. It was great, actually, when we had it."

My cheeks flushed, but I was annoyed, too. Why was Zach talking to me about his sex life? It was weird and awkward, verging on inappropriate. But then, I reminded myself, who was "appropriate" in Rikers? "I found an ovulation test strip in your home office. That's why I asked."

"An ovulation test strip in my *office*? What were you doing in my office?"

"Um, the job *you* asked me to do?"

"Right, right, sorry," he said. "Well, after Case, Amanda couldn't have any more children. That's what she told me. So I don't know anything about an ovulation test."

"Are you sure?"

"Why would she lie?" he asked.

We were both quiet for a moment, the implication not lost on either of us. Had Amanda lied about her infertility? Had she been trying to get pregnant without Zach knowing? Or secretly trying to avoid it?

"I think maybe there was someone in your house when I was there," I went on, hoping to change the subject from sex.

"What do you mean?"

"Someone ran out the back door. I didn't see who."

"Do you think—what if they had something to do with what happened to Amanda?"

"I called the police for that reason. But it's unclear how exhaustive their investigation will be, so I also called in an independent investigator. She wants to run the house for prints and get a blood spatter expert. It won't be cheap, but it seems like there are definitely some prints in Amanda's blood on the stairs. If they're not yours—"

"They're not," Zach said. "I didn't kill her, Lizzie."

"But you did try to help her, right? So your prints should be there somewhere."

"This is it, isn't it?" Zach asked, sounding defeated.

"This is what?"

"This is how innocent people get railroaded. What if we get an expert to test the prints and they *don't* find anyone else's? Couldn't that be used against me?"

He wasn't entirely wrong. "I think it's worth that risk," I said, and now there was no putting it off anymore, though the last thing I wanted was to talk about sex again. "Also, was there a partner exchange going on at the party you were at the night Amanda died?"

"Partner exchange?" Zach asked like he had absolutely no idea what I was talking about.

"Yes, people having sex with other people's spouses?"

"Are you saying you think Amanda had sex with somebody else that night?" Zach sounded angry, very angry. "That she cheated on me?"

"No, no, no." I was taken aback by the force of his reaction. "I don't have any reason to think that Amanda did anything with anyone that night. I'm asking what you know, that's all."

There was another long, uncomfortable silence.

"I'd be surprised if Amanda had sex with somebody other than me. But then you keep telling me stuff about my wife I didn't know." He sounded more hurt now than angry, maybe a little embarrassed, too.

"Look, we didn't really talk, Amanda and I. We weren't close in *that* way." He hesitated. "You know, it wasn't like with you and me."

"Me?" I immediately regretted inquiring. The last thing I wanted was for Zach to elaborate. But the comment had just caught me so off-guard.

"Yeah, you and I had actual things in common. Our backgrounds, our work ethic. We wanted the same things out of life, not to mention that we're both lawyers and intellectual equals," he said quietly. I felt my cheeks flush again. But was I *really* that surprised? Deep down, hadn't I known back then that Zach had feelings for me? "It would have been different with you. That's all I mean. With Amanda I wasn't even looking for some kind of partnership. And neither was she. We had a pleasant arrangement that worked for both of us. That's it."

Awkward silence. What could I possibly say next? All I could think was no, we did not want the same things. Because we didn't. Did we? Returning to the facts seemed best.

"Okay, so Sarah and Maude. Anyone else I should talk to?" I asked. "The DA doesn't go around interviewing every possible person. They get the information they need for their case and that's it."

"Those are the only people she mentioned," Zach went on. "Listen, I know what this looks like. A distant marriage, a sex party, a dead wife. You don't have to be a genius to put the pieces together. Except I didn't do it, Lizzie. I did not kill Amanda. I swear. You know that, right?"

"I do," I said.

But how could I possibly? Millie was right: given the right circumstances, anyone was capable of anything.

At the office, I spent three hours drafting a damn good habeas corpus writ for Zach's bail appeal. I left it with the managing clerk's office for filing first thing in the morning, along with instructions to request an expedited hearing and for them to send someone to Philadelphia to clear Zach's old warrant.

I brought Amanda's journals home with me, and started reading the third one as my black car home sped south down the FDR toward the Brooklyn Bridge.

January 5, 2006

Christopher and I went to see Marley & Me *at the theater on Route 1. But I had a hard time even concentrating on the movie. I've thought about seeing a doctor. The pain won't go away. And it was a lot worse this time. Because I wouldn't hold still, he said. But doctors have to report things to the police. . . . I went down to the St. Colomb Falls Methodist Church instead. To see Pastor David. I'm pretty sure a minister needs to keep anything you tell them a secret. But when I saw his stooped shoulders and his kind eyes and wrinkled face, I knew there was no way I was saying a word to him either.*

I tried asking Carolyn about the pain—without telling her why I was asking. But she was way too interested. And once Carolyn gets herself in the middle of something, there's no getting her out. I love Carolyn for that. But I'm afraid she'll make a bigger mess of things.

It was past 11:00 p.m. when I finally got home, haunted by Amanda's cornered teenage voice in my head. I was glad the apartment was dark and quiet. After reading about what I could only guess was maybe Amanda's rape by a boy named Christopher, the last thing I felt like doing was talking to Sam about rehab or anything else. I would. I would. Just not right now.

I could hear Sam lightly snoring back in the bedroom as I tiptoed out to our small living room to keep reading. How much more was there about this Christopher? When had Amanda stopped seeing him? It was a long shot that he had anything to do with Amanda's death all these years later, of course. A very long shot. But also not impossible.

Everything in the living room was exactly as it had been when I'd stopped by earlier that afternoon. Sam's computer was there, open as I'd left it, his notebooks stacked up. *Enid's*. I felt a wave of fresh irritation as the bar flashed back to me.

I lifted Sam's worn messenger bag to take a seat at his computer, hoping to see on the screen some evidence of work that afternoon. As I put the bag down on the floor, something sparkling in the gaping outside pocket caught my eye. A gift? I felt a little girlish flutter—had that been what Sam was out doing? Shopping for me?

I reached in the pocket to fish it out.

For a very long time, I just stared down at it in the palm of my hand. There was only the one. Not a gift for me, that's for sure.

I blinked hard when my eyes began to burn. But when I opened them, it was still there. Long and thin and shimmering silver. A woman's earring. Coiled like a snake in the palm of my hand.

AMANDA

It was barely dawn, the light dim and gray, when Amanda came downstairs and flipped on the light over the huge island in their enormous kitchen. And to think that when they'd first arrived in Park Slope, Zach had considered purchasing two such brownstones and connecting them. Even the real estate agent, who'd stood to profit significantly from such an endeavor, had discouraged him.

"This isn't Manhattan," she'd said simply, as though that settled the matter.

Zach had been genuinely disappointed that the neighborhood culture meant not being able to go quite as far over the top as he was inclined, but he was unwilling to consider living elsewhere. "It's the ideal community," he'd kept saying.

Like every place they'd ever lived, their now very modern brownstone felt to Amanda like it belonged to someone else. As grateful as she was to live someplace so nice—and she *was* grateful to Zach for that—their homes always left her feeling like an impostor.

Oh, this drifting of Amanda's mind was not good. Things worked so much better for her when her mind was contained to the page. That's what her journals were for.

Amanda moved to make herself a cup of coffee—activities were also good. She'd just filled the carafe with water when the home phone rang. She turned to look at the cordless sitting over there in the center of the island. Her work phone, her cell phone, and now her home phone?

She stepped closer: "Unknown Caller." No, she thought. Please don't. Not so early.

"Hello?" Amanda answered, her voice quiet and trembling. Silence. And then that rough, rattling breath. "Hello?" Sharper now, more forceful. But she didn't want to make him angry. That wouldn't help anything. When she spoke again it was a whisper. "Please stop calling me."

But there was only more silence on the other end. And more of his awful breathing.

And then a click.

"Hello?" Amanda asked again, louder this time.

But the line was dead. She pressed the phone to her chest and closed her eyes. They never should have come to New York City. It was too close to St. Colomb Falls. Not that Amanda had been given a choice in the matter. Where Zach needed to go, they went. It had always been that way. And aside from the effect on Case—which she continued to worry about—Amanda hadn't considered this move any differently. Until she'd stepped off the plane at Kennedy Airport and saw that sign: "Welcome to New York."

The wind had been pounded right out of her. It wasn't until an hour later, when she'd glimpsed the Empire State Building from the back of the chauffeur-driven SUV—sparkling red, white, and blue against the glittering Manhattan skyline—that she'd finally been able to get her hands to stop shaking. This was New York City, she'd been reminding herself ever since. It was a world away from St. Colomb Falls.

Amanda caught sight of something then, someone, out of the corner of her eye. She startled back, bumping her hip into the counter and letting out a little yelp.

"It's just me!" Carolyn called, waving her hands around. "Sorry, I let myself in."

"Don't do that!" Amanda shouted, then tried to steady her breath.

"Jeez, you are jacked up," Carolyn gasped. "What did His Highness do now?"

It was a joke, of sorts. Carolyn didn't like Zach any more than Sarah did. Actually, she liked him much less.

"I'm jacked up because you just scared the hell out of me. What are you even doing in Brooklyn?" Amanda asked. "It's not Monday, is it?"

Since they'd moved to Park Slope, she and Carolyn had been running together every Monday morning in Prospect Park. Had Amanda lost track of the days? With Case gone, and the bad dreams and lack of decent sleep, time did feel especially slippery.

"Nope, it's Sunday. But let me guess, Zach is at work?" Carolyn asked. Amanda rolled her eyes in response, though that was exactly where Zach was. "Anyway, can't I come see my best friend? You sounded weird the last time we talked. I thought I should check in." Carolyn tapped at her temple and then pointed at Amanda. "Then again you are also weird on the phone. Only way to be sure was to see you with my own eyes."

Carolyn worked in advertising, as a creative executive at McCann Erickson. Zach had once said it was the most prestigious advertising agency in the whole world. And he wasn't one for false praise. Carolyn had done well for herself, which wasn't a surprise.

"I am not weird on the phone," Amanda said mildly. "And I'm fine. It's just an adjustment not having Case here."

Carolyn stopped at the kitchen island and tossed her headphones down, then put her hands on her hips. "I knew that camp was a bad idea."

Carolyn had been strongly (and loudly) against Case going to that particular sleepaway camp. She wasn't opposed to the idea of camp in general, but she thought sending a kid to camp on the opposite coast at the age of ten was ridiculous. She also didn't buy it as compensation to Case for the cross-country move. She thought that was something Zach should have made up for, as if that was how anything worked. Really, she couldn't understand why Amanda hadn't stayed behind in California with Case until he had finished the school year. But Zach needed his family at his side. With new businesses, new cities, people cared about a person's context. It was Amanda's job to give Zach that context, to complete his picture as a family man. And Amanda didn't mind. In fact, she liked it. She was good at it.

In their early days, when they didn't have two quarters to rub together, people had assumed countless things about Zach because Amanda was his wife. After all, if a guy who looked like him and who wasn't wealthy could keep a woman like her, he must be truly special. Now that Zach was rich and successful, the explanations for their uneven union were more often at Amanda's expense—what a gold digger she must be. But that was okay. People could think what they wanted. Amanda knew the truth.

For her part, Carolyn would have been happy for Amanda to leave Zach altogether. She'd long complained, among other things, that Amanda and Case were nothing more than props for Zach. But if you thought about it, props *were* useful things, and there were worse things than being useful. Besides, everything was always so mercilessly black-and-white to Carolyn—she could afford that luxury. She'd been able to live her life without worrying about how to survive.

"Case is fine. Better than fine," Amanda said, getting Carolyn a cup of coffee—light and sweet, the way she always had it. It was comforting, knowing by heart those little details about her friend. "He couldn't miss me less, in fact, which smarts a little. But I know it's a good thing." Amanda set the coffee down.

Carolyn lifted it and took a big sip, eyeing Amanda over the top of her mug. "So what is it, then?"

"I guess I miss him and I haven't been sleeping well, that's all."

"Don't tell me—your wacko dreams again?" Carolyn rolled her eyes this time. "Let me guess, a monster squid."

Once Amanda had dreamed she was trapped in a giant lobster's claw while sleeping over at Carolyn's house. Thrashing about, she'd whacked Carolyn so hard in the mouth, her lip had bled.

"No squids. But I do keep having this dream I'm running barefoot through the woods in the dark. I'm looking for Case. Frantic, really. It's ridiculous," Amanda said. She hoped confessing the details might make them stop running over and over in her head: the cold wetness of the dress against her skin, standing in Norma's diner and looking down at her bloodstained hands. A scream. "There are sirens, and I have blood on me. It's horrific."

"Yeah, horrifically literal." Carolyn laughed, then focused on Amanda, her eyes softening.

"What do you mean?" Amanda asked. She already felt better that Carolyn had laughed.

"Come on, you're running after Case in the woods, covered in blood?" Carolyn shook her head and held her arms out wide for dramatic effect. "Your subconscious has *obviously* come to the same conclusion I have: that camp on the other side of the country was a dumb idea."

"Well, you're in the dream, too," Amanda jabbed back lamely.

"Me?" Carolyn batted her eyes innocently.

"At the beginning. You're in this puffy seafoam dress, like for a bridesmaid. And I'm in a peach one. We're eating pizza on a bed."

Carolyn smirked. "Ah, see where ignoring my advice and sending Case to that camp has gotten you? It's spawned revenge of the junior prom."

"Junior prom?"

"Those definitely sound like our junior prom dresses. But you swapped them in your dream. Yours was the seafoam one, remember? I lent it to you."

Amanda shook her head a little, as though hoping to shake the memory back into place. Yes, that was right. That was where that piece of the dream had come from. Carolyn had lent her a seafoam dress. Amanda had dropped out of school by the time the junior prom came around, but she'd gone with a boy who was friends with Carolyn's boyfriend. She couldn't remember much more than that.

But the dance itself had been magical, hadn't it? She'd felt like a regular teenager for once. Even without the details there was a feeling. It was sad that she couldn't remember more. That was the problem with closing off so much of her past—sometimes the good memories went with the bad. This wasn't the first time Carolyn had reminded her of some detail from their shared history that Amanda couldn't quite drag all the way to the surface.

"Junior prom, I know," Amanda lied. "That's why the whole thing is so weird."

"Let's at least agree that *Zach* is to blame?" Carolyn smirked. "For everything?"

Amanda ignored Carolyn's baiting. She knew it came from a place of love; besides, there were times when Amanda felt a little bit of that resentment herself. It was kind of comforting to have Carolyn actually say it.

"The dream isn't the real problem anyway," Amanda said.

"Then what is?"

That stupid burn had returned to the back of her throat. "He's calling again."

"No." Carolyn dropped hard onto a kitchen barstool. She knew instantly what Amanda meant, even after all this time. "That fucker." She sounded angry, but not worried, which was a comfort. Carolyn took a deep breath and then another big swallow of coffee. Then another. She stared down at the counter, considering. "I guess he was bound to slither back out of his hole eventually. Did he say anything this time?"

"Not a word," Amanda said. "Like last time. Just that breathing."

Carolyn knew about the last time, too, back when they'd been in California. Carolyn knew everything. All the ugliness. All the shame. She was the only person in the world who did.

"He's such a disgusting pig." Carolyn's face hardened. "Someone should deal with him permanently. Erase him from the surface of the earth." Her voice was vicious, as she reached across the island to give Amanda's hand a quick squeeze. "I'm sorry. You shouldn't have to deal with this."

What a relief not to be alone with it anymore. But now she needed to tell Carolyn the rest, to confess the most frightening part.

"I think, um, I think he might be following me, too."

"I'm sorry, what?" Carolyn's eyes were like saucers as she turned toward the windows. "He's in Park Slope?"

"I don't know for sure. I haven't actually seen him," Amanda said. "But I'm pretty sure he was behind me on my way to the Gate last night. I heard footsteps following me—who else could it be?"

Carolyn's eyes were on the front window. Amanda braced for her friend to argue, to say something like *Come on, he wouldn't do that. He wouldn't go that far.* But Carolyn knew better.

"Fuck no," Carolyn said with a new can-do tone and a clap of her hands. "We are not going to stand for him following you. Nope. No way."

"No?"

"Enough of his fucking bullshit," Carolyn said firmly. "Maybe we can't have him exterminated. Or we won't, at least not yet. But he can't harass you forever. You don't have to put up with it. You can have him arrested."

"Arrested?" Amanda looked toward the windows, filled with a mix of dread and delight. "For what?"

"For following you! Get a restraining order." Carolyn took another large swallow of coffee. She'd finished more than half the mug already. She'd always been that way, a fast drinker—coffee, soda, water. "Then when he violates it—which you and I both know he definitely will—you throw his ass in jail."

"A restraining order," Amanda said, trying the words on for size.

She'd heard of it, of course. It was a thing people did. It was theoretically a thing *she* could do. She'd gone so far as to file a complaint back in Sacramento when the calls had started the first time. The nice female officer there had heard Amanda out so patiently. She'd been pretty and young with fiery red hair, pale blue eyes, and a noticeably large chest. The kind of woman who might have experienced a fair amount of harassment herself.

"His breathing," Amanda had said at the time. "I'd know his breathing anywhere."

And the female officer had seemed to know exactly what that meant. She'd suggested to Amanda that a complaint would be a good first step. It was something they could do right then at the police station—no judge or other official process required. And while it might have no real legal implications, it would at least create a record.

Carolyn was staring at Amanda intently, waiting for a response. "So?" Carolyn asked. "Will you do it?"

Amanda nodded, though she did not feel convinced. "A restraining order is a good idea."

"That doesn't sound like a yes." Carolyn knew her so well.

Amanda smiled weakly. "I'll think about it."

"There's nothing to think about, Amanda."

"There shouldn't be." Amanda's face felt hot as tears pushed into her eyes. She felt so terribly weak. "I know that."

"I believe in you," Carolyn said firmly and with such love. "And I know you'll do the right thing."

And now Amanda needed to change the subject. Because it was getting hard to breathe. She forced a bright smile. "I almost forgot, I have gossip for you." Carolyn loved gossip. "I just heard it last night."

"What's that?" Carolyn asked with narrowed eyes. She was onto this changing-of-the-subject nonsense, but she also seemed intrigued.

"It sounds like, well, like they have some kind of sex parties here, in Park Slope."

Carolyn choked on her coffee. "What?"

"Yes, apparently."

Carolyn's face was positively aglow. "The patron saints of sanctimony? That is the best thing I've ever heard."

It wasn't that Carolyn disliked Park Slope, but she was suspicious of perfect things. And Park Slope, with its picturesque tree-lined streets, gorgeous brownstones, and giggling children, had been ripped from a storybook, then had all the artificial flavoring and high-fructose corn syrup rinsed clean.

Amanda smiled. "I thought you'd enjoy it."

"Oh, yes," Carolyn breathed. "But now I need *details. All* of them."

"I'm not saying they do it every weekend, but it sounds like there's at least this one party every summer."

Carolyn's mouth was agape. "Wait, do your friends Maude and Sarah have sex with each other's husbands?"

"No, no," Amanda said, like that was so absurd. "At least I don't think so. Sarah doesn't participate—or hasn't. It sounds like that's maybe only because her husband won't. For Maude and her husband, apparently, it's a regular thing. They go with other people, not only at their parties but all the time."

"How can you sound so calm about this!" Carolyn cried.

"I don't know," Amanda said, but for some reason, none of it bothered her in the least. It seemed ordinary almost. "Maybe it was the way Maude described it. And it was her decision, not her husband's. She's so comfortable with who she is and what she wants. I don't know. It made it sound like . . . freedom."

"Well, well, well, Amanda. After all these years, you finally have surprised me." Carolyn was grinning now. "And I have to meet this Maude person. Anybody who can make *you* loosen up like *that* is definitely somebody I want to know." Carolyn set her coffee mug back down on the marble counter. She checked the time on the stove. "Oh, shit. Now I'm going to be late. I've got a meeting. Work on a Sunday. Like your husband. I've got to go."

"Go, go," Amanda said, even though what she really wanted to say was *Please stay forever*. But how needy was she going to be? Carolyn already did so much for her.

Carolyn got off her stool and walked over to Amanda. She put a hand on each of her arms. "Go to the police. Today. Enough of this shit."

"Okay," Amanda said, but too quickly.

Carolyn eyed her doubtfully. "I mean it, Amanda. I'm not trying to freak you out, but I have a bad feeling this time."

"I'll go talk to them," Amanda said. "I will."

"Today?"

Amanda nodded. "Today."

After the two hugged goodbye, Amanda watched Carolyn disappear from the kitchen, then turned to dump Carolyn's coffee in the sink. As she watched the coffee swirl down the drain, she felt her conviction sliding away with it. If Carolyn could be there at her side all the time, that would be one thing. Though it was hardly strength if you had to rely on someone else for it. Carolyn was right; *she* needed to do something. Besides, it was one thing to ignore the calls and even the following while Case was away, but what about when he got back? Amanda wouldn't allow this to continue. For the sake of her son, she could not.

Upstairs, Amanda passed by the front bedroom windows on her way to take a shower. She spotted something on the sidewalk down below, in front of their gate. Something purple and low to the ground.

Amanda squinted, but was unable to make it out. She headed back downstairs, chest growing tight. These days, there were no good surprises. She checked out the window before she opened the upstairs door to be sure there wasn't somebody out there waiting for her. With no one in sight, she stepped out on the stoop. It was chilly, especially for June, and Amanda shivered as she made her way down the front steps to the gate, barefoot. There on the ground was a huge bouquet of lilacs, wrapped in violet tissue and tied elegantly with natural twine.

Lilacs were Amanda's favorite flower. She'd planted them in large pots at every house she and Zach had ever lived in, including in the small backyard of the brownstone, where they had promptly died.

Without touching the flowers, Amanda stood up and looked around again. Maybe someone had left them there for safekeeping while they ran back to retrieve something? But they were not lilacs by coincidence. And the sidewalk was empty in either direction.

Oh, God, why had she let Carolyn leave?

There was a card. Amanda held her breath as she bent down, hands trembling, to pick it up, hoping it would be made out to someone other than her. She squinted as she tugged the card out of the envelope.

Amanda, thinking of you. xoxo

LIZZIE

The office of the Hope First Initiative was in a gritty converted factory. It was hard to imagine elegant Amanda there, and so I pictured her wearing white gloves, her hands hovering over the handrail as she glided up the cracked stairs. Amanda probably glided everywhere. I believed this even though Zach had already told me that Amanda came from a poor background, and I'd already read myself about her addicted father and her being raped by some boy who'd then made her go watch *Marley & Me* with him. It was amazing how I could conveniently disregard all these tragic details so I could return to my initial impression of rich, beautiful Amanda: that she was a woman to be envied, even when she was dead.

What an awful person I was.

At least self-loathing was *a* feeling, though. I'd been disturbingly numb since I'd found the earring. There were many ugly explanations for my husband having some other woman's earring in his bag: an affair, a prostitute, a stripper. Out of these, an affair seemed the only real possibility. Sam had a genuine aversion to anything that even hinted at exploitation.

At least, as far as I knew.

There were innocent explanations, too. Sam could have found the earring on the street or in a café; he was holding it so that he could launch a search for the rightful owner . . . But Sam had always been a big believer in the "Leave it, they'll come back for it" school of thought. I couldn't see him picking up a stranger's earring. Was I too quickly jumping to the worst-case scenario this time? Maybe. After all, I'd had a lot of experience being blindsided.

Ironically, I might have had some actual answers, had I not deliberately avoided confronting Sam. After spending the rest of the night upright and awake on the couch, I'd left while he was still sound asleep. I'd parked myself at Café du Jour near Hope First to check in on my other cases. Everything had taken a back seat to Zach these last few days, and I needed to catch up. It turned out the DOJ was filing charges against three members of the battery manufacturer's board. Paul wanted me to have a joint motion to dismiss ready to go. I'd never been so grateful for such tedious work.

When I was finished, I saved the motion document and pulled one of Amanda's journals from my bag. What I really needed was her most recent one—but I'd have to go back to Zach's to look for that. In the meantime, I couldn't stop reading the older ones. It was a compulsion now, like gawking at somebody else's car accident to distract from your own wreckage.

Finally I got to an entry that made clear what had happened to Amanda all those years ago was even worse—so much fucking worse— than I'd ever imagined.

March 2004

I watch the cross on the living room wall and pray that little Jesus will tug himself down and help me. So far he hasn't. But maybe it has to be your cross. This one was on the trailer wall when we moved in.

He always does it there in the living room. Right under the

cross. On the rough yellow couch. Maybe out there it's easier for
Daddy to pretend he's not really doing it.
   But he is. Little Jesus knows.

As I climbed the steps to the Hope First building a half hour later I still felt sick. Amanda's father had raped her, repeatedly. When she was twelve. Raped as a child and now she was dead. It was horrifying. All of it. My phone buzzed with a text, when I was almost at the door, snapping me out of my numb haze. It was Paul's friend from the DA's office, Steve Granz: Wendy Wallace. Sorry.

That was it. The whole text. While the name didn't mean anything to me, evidently having Wendy Wallace assigned to prosecute Zach's case was not good news, at least as far as Steve was concerned.

I quickly googled Wendy Wallace as I pressed the buzzer for the Hope First Initiative. "Three Heirs to the Throne" was the first article that popped up. I tapped on it and skimmed. As Zach's public defender had mentioned, there was indeed a high-profile contest brewing for a handpicked successor to the Brooklyn DA. In Brooklyn, the real race was always the primary, since no Republican stood a chance, and Wendy Wallace, the Homicide Bureau's chief prosecutor, was one of three leading contenders. The knock against her was that she lacked name recognition, but a case like Zach's would solve that problem. Her name would be all over the papers, even better if that coverage were strategically timed to maximize her involvement. This was surely the reason the most salacious details hadn't yet been in the papers.

"Hello?" A crackly voice through the intercom. I'd forgotten that I'd even rung the buzzer. "Can I help you?"

"Lizzie Kitsakis," I said. "Zach Grayson's attorney."

Such a long silence followed, I started to wonder if she'd heard me.

Finally, there was a buzz. I pushed through the two sets of locked doors and into the polished lobby.

———

The elevator opened directly into the Hope First Initiative offices, a bright open space with wood floors the color of wheat, vibrant yellow walls, and endless windows. There was a reception desk with a sign overhead—HOPE FIRST INITIATIVE—in playful blue type. And not a soul in sight.

"What do you want?" came a voice from behind me.

When I turned, there was a petite woman with short, dark brown hair standing near an office door, a sweater wrapped tight around her shoulders. Her pretty face was ashen and drawn.

She was Amanda's friend, I reminded myself. She's grieving. It's not personal.

"I have a few questions," I began. "Like I said in my voice mail."

"Why would I answer any of your questions when you're defending that monster?"

"Monster?" I asked stupidly.

Sarah advanced toward me so quickly that I reflexively took a couple steps back. "Yeah, monster. He bashed her fucking head in with a golf club, and—" Her voice caught.

Shit. Sarah knew about the golf club? Cops and investigators often shared details with witnesses when it served their interests—to get them angrier at a defendant, to make them more sympathetic to the victim. To motivate them to help. These disclosures skirted right up to the line of unethical, but didn't technically cross it. I'd done it myself. But, wow, did it seem unsavory now. Unsavory and effective.

"Nothing about the manner of Amanda's death has been confirmed," I said, careful to stay polite. "And I don't think Zach killed her."

It was a deliberate choice of words.

"You don't *think* so?" Sarah huffed. The anger had brought some color back to her face. "Well, that's not exactly a ringing endorsement. Aren't you *his* attorney? If you aren't even sure he's innocent, then he must be guilty as hell."

"To be clear, Zach hasn't even been charged with murder. There was some sort of scuffle after he found his wife, during the course of which he accidentally struck an officer with his elbow. That's what he was arrested for."

"Whatever." She rolled her eyes. "It's only a matter of time."

"And to clarify, I said I 'think' he's innocent because I do strongly believe that's the case. I could even offer you substantial evidence in support of my position. But it's circumstantial. I imagine you'll say it doesn't prove what I say it does, and it seems you've already made up your mind. So instead of trying to convince you, I'd like to hear what you know."

Sarah cocked her head, considering. Finally, her face softened the slightest bit.

"If Zach didn't kill Amanda," she asked, "who did?"

Fear, a flicker underneath. *A homicidal stranger?* I imagined Sarah thinking. No one would want to think there was a madman on the loose in Park Slope.

"I don't know yet who killed Amanda. That's what I'm trying to figure out. Though to be clear, it isn't Zach's responsibility to find the guilty party. The finger shouldn't be pointed at him just because there aren't better alternatives. Also, once the police decide on a suspect, they don't keep looking. They work to build a case against that person. I used to be a prosecutor—federal white-collar crimes—there's literally no other way to do the job. But Zach shouldn't be penalized for that." I let it hang there for a moment, hoping some part might sink in. "I also think it's important to move the focus from Zach, so we can find whoever really did kill Amanda. We need to get them off the street."

Playing on Sarah's fear of some random killer didn't make me feel particularly great. But I needed her to reconsider her assumptions. She'd worked with Amanda. She was one of her closest friends. There was no telling what she might know, even if she wasn't aware that she knew it.

"I don't mean to be such a bitch. But I'm— Amanda was the sweetest person. Not an aggressive bone in her body. I don't understand how anybody could do that to her. It's like beating a . . ." She winced. "Here, let me show you something."

Sarah waved me to an office on the opposite side of the room with a bright orange couch and a dramatic gray-striped rug. She pointed to some frames on the wall.

"They're essays from scholarship students," she said, approaching one and looking closer. "We'd barely started accepting applications. But Amanda was so touched by the essays we'd received, she framed them. Every single one. I teased her that she wouldn't be able to keep it up, and she said she'd cover all the walls if she had to. She was a really special person."

Sarah dropped down onto Amanda's couch. She was rigid for a moment, then her body sank. She stayed quiet for a long time.

I took a seat in one of the guest chairs. "Was Amanda having problems with anybody that you knew of?"

Sarah shook her head. "If you ask me, Zach was a shitty husband, though. On a good day, he treated Amanda like she was a couch he'd bought to complete his living-room set. On a bad day, she was only an accent piece. And no—to answer your next question—she never said anything about Zach being aggressive or even yelling or anything like that. And I saw no evidence that he was physically abusive." Sarah's eyes got glassy. "But deception can be its own kind of violence."

"Zach deceived her?" I asked.

Sarah's eyes darted away. "She didn't say that, specifically. But he was *always* 'working.' It didn't seem to bother Amanda." She was quiet again for a moment. "Maybe that's what bothered me. Also, personally, I do think Zach is arrogant. He can't even be bothered to show up for a birthday dinner for one of Amanda's closest friends? And I know he's a big, huge success or whatever, but that doesn't mean he can't be polite. Honestly, Zach cared more about his business than he cared about anything, including Amanda."

"Was there anything else going on in Amanda's life that she talked about?" I asked Sarah. "With Case maybe?"

"Are you kidding?" she huffed. "Case was a delight and Amanda was a devoted mother. And I mean that, like exceptionally good."

"What about issues with other friends or family?"

I didn't plan to reveal that Amanda's father had raped her as a child. If she'd kept that to herself, it should stay that way. People had a right to their secrets.

"I know that Amanda's mother died when she was young, which was probably why she was such an attentive mother herself. She grew up poor, too. She tried to make her childhood sound idyllic or charming or something, but I got the sense it was really hard."

"What do you mean?"

"Amanda was wonderful, but she was also a closed-off person. Guarded. Like she'd been damaged."

"Had she been?"

Sarah looked overwhelmed with regret. "I was her best friend in Park Slope, and honestly, I have no idea. Amanda was good at making you feel like you knew her really well, even when she was keeping you at arm's length. What did, um, what's her name . . . Carolyn. What did Carolyn say?"

"Carolyn?" I asked. Amanda had mentioned a Carolyn in her journals, but that had been years ago.

"Yes, Amanda's *best* best friend," Sarah said, with clear disdain for my investigative skills. "From what's-it-called, St. Whatever. Practically like a sister. You should definitely talk to her. She lives in Manhattan."

"Do you know how I can reach her?" I asked.

"Nope. Ask Zach. He must know, right?" She eyed me then. She knew as well as I did that he easily might not. "He *is* her husband."

"Any conflicts here at work?"

"Amanda ran from conflict of any kind. She almost had a breakdown when the foundation accountant was trying to track her down."

"About what?"

"Nothing, I'm sure." Sarah waved a hand. "What I mean is that Amanda hated dealing with anybody in a position of authority."

Except an accountant meant money, and money was another reason people were killed.

"Do you have that accountant's name?" I asked.

"I might." Sarah pushed to her feet. "I'd have to check my office. I'll be right back."

I stood once Sarah had gone, taking the opportunity alone for a quick look around Amanda's office. Like at the house, there were shelves filled with pictures, but these were fantastic candids, almost all of Case. There was one posed shot of Amanda, Case, and Zach, but it was up on a high shelf and off to the side, as though kept deliberately out of sight. As I turned to check out the shelves over Amanda's desk, I spotted a black Moleskine journal on top of a stack of papers in the corner. It looked like the fancy blank one I'd found at the house. Maybe Amanda's most recent one. I could already hear Sarah's heels clicking back down the polished concrete hallway. I lunged over the desk, grabbed the journal, and shoved it in my bag. My chair squeaked as I banged back down. Luckily, Sarah didn't seem to notice when she reentered the office. She was too flustered herself.

"I'm sorry," she said. "I have no idea where I put the accountant's name."

"That's okay. I can get it from Zach," I said, willing myself to look calm as I pressed on with my questions. "How did Amanda seem at Maude's party the night she died?"

Died, not *killed*. I'd been practicing swapping out the terms. Admit nothing, not even the most basic facts. It was the first rule of criminal procedure.

"Oh, um, she seemed fine," Sarah said. "She looked beautiful as always. I'm sure you've seen pictures. She was a woman that people gawked at. If you're looking for alternative theories, I would look into that. There are a lot of perverts in the world." She looked disgusted. "There are whole porn subgenres devoted to it."

I nodded. But somebody with a crush was not the kind of alternate theory that would be useful. Juries wanted specifics. Something, someone, they could sink their teeth into. Anything else was too much like saying the bogeyman did it; you couldn't put him behind bars.

"The two of you spoke at the party?"

"Only for a minute, and mostly about Maude—she was really worried about her daughter. So Amanda and I were worried about her."

"What's wrong with her daughter?"

"She's a teenager at camp. What isn't wrong with her?" Sarah said dismissively. "Maude's not used to it, that's all. She got some dramatic letters and panicked. I'm sure it's fine now. Then again, we've all had more important things to think about."

"Did you see Amanda talking to anyone else?"

"No, but I got all wrapped up talking to this Brooklyn Country Day mom who I barely even know—who I definitely don't even like—about the Great Email Debacle."

"Email debacle?" I asked.

"Somebody's been hacking into the computers of the Brooklyn Country Day parents, using their dirty laundry against them." She hesitated again and pressed her lips together. "Like Terry's Bench, for instance. You know, the Tinder for married people? A bunch of husbands had their account info emailed to their wives, which makes that hacker Robin Hood as far as I'm concerned. There's that and all the naked selfies that have been stolen. Oh, yes, and porn. Buckets of porn people are getting blackmailed for." She laughed in a sharp burst. "Anyway, this was all supposed to be secret because the school's investigating. But that night at the party, everyone got drunk and started spilling. Maybe if I'd been with Amanda instead of listening to all that stupid gossip, she'd be alive."

"Do you remember what time it was when you last saw Amanda at the party?"

Sarah wiped at her eyes and sniffed. "Let's see, I got there around eight thirty, and I was home by nine thirty. So sometime in there."

Suspiciously short was the first thing that jumped to mind. "That's not very long."

"I know." Sarah sounded annoyed. "My oldest was supposed to be in the Hamptons for six weeks. That turned into six days after some fight with his girlfriend. Anyway, he didn't have house keys, and Thursday nights my husband is out angling to break a hip. Believe me, I never would have left the party if my son hadn't called. Nothing is better than watching to see who uses the 'upstairs' at Maude's parties. Everyone's so hush-hush after. If you want to know, you have to be there yourself. I'm in awe of couples whose marriages are that adventurous. Like Maude and Sebe. They could walk through fire naked together and not get burned."

"Did you see Zach at the party?" I asked.

"I chatted with him for a second," Sarah said. "He was skulking at the edges of the party and then he left."

"Did you actually see him leave?"

"No, but I'm assuming . . . I didn't see him again."

"And you didn't see either Zach or Amanda go upstairs?"

"Please." Sarah laughed. "You should have seen Amanda's face when she heard about it. She actually looked like she was going to faint."

"And Zach?"

Sarah's eyes went hard. "He's your client."

"I'm asking what *you* saw."

She snorted lightly, looked away. *Lawyers*, the look seemed to say. "Aside from our two-second exchange, I only saw Zach circling like some kind of shark," she said. "Then I went home. I have no idea what he did after that."

She stood then, heading to the open door. "And now I really do have to get back to work."

I rose and followed her. "If you think of anything else, you have my cell number," I said. "It's the one I called you from."

"Yeah, I have it," Sarah said, then paused. She squinted at me, focused anew. "You look familiar. Do I know you?"

"I don't think so." I certainly hoped not.

"Do you have kids in the neighborhood?" she asked. "I'm really good with faces."

"I live all the way in Sunset Park."

"Where do your kids go to school, though?" she asked. "I feel like we all cross paths eventually in Brooklyn."

"I don't have kids."

"Smart," she said, and now she looked intrigued. She glanced at my wedding band.

"Is your better half also a lawyer?"

"No," I said, with a too hard, bitter laugh.

Sarah leaned in. "What does he or she do?"

"He's a writer."

"Oh, that sounds exciting," she said. "My husband is a lawyer. No offense, but you are all boring as hell. Or maybe that's just my husband. He's not a criminal lawyer."

"No, all lawyers are boring. Boring, but reliable," I said. "Writers, not so much."

"Ah, yes, reliable." She let out a knowing sigh. "It's not sexy, but it is useful."

"Can I ask you one last question?"

"I guess."

"Can you think of anyone other than Zach who might have sent Amanda flowers?" I asked. "Amanda saved an unsigned card."

"A secret admirer?" Sarah offered. "Like I said, Amanda inspired adoration. That's what Sebe said once."

"Sebe?"

"Maude's husband. But don't get any ideas. Sebe and Maude have an unorthodox arrangement with the whole 'upstairs' thing, but they don't sleep with each other's friends. Sebe is *devoted* to Maude. It's sickening really. The note didn't have a name?"

"No. 'Thinking of you,' that was all it said."

"Oh, men. They are *so* original," she said coldly. "Well, definitely not Sebe. He's so French. He's awkward with American colloquial-isms. You think this person who sent the flowers had something to do with what happened to Amanda?"

"I'd like to know who sent them."

"Right, an alternative theory of the case." Her tone had hardened again. "Sorry, can't help you there. Because the only theory that makes sense to me is that your client is an arrogant fuck who killed my beau-tiful friend."

AMANDA

FOUR DAYS BEFORE THE PARTY

As Amanda sat in the Seventy-Eighth Precinct waiting for her turn to speak with a detective, she was overwhelmed by second, third, and fourth thoughts about going there in the first place. It didn't help that the precinct was even rougher than she'd anticipated—louder and dirtier and far angrier. A place you'd be only if bad things had already happened to you. A place that reminded Amanda too much of St. Colomb Falls.

If it hadn't been for her promise to Carolyn, she would have gotten up to leave. Not to mention that she'd started thinking about how Zach would react to a restraining order. Were these things a matter of public record? Zach didn't like anything that violated their privacy, and now she'd be making a public spectacle? She hadn't even told him about the calls.

"Amanda Grayson?" The officer was on the short side, with dark hair and warm olive skin. His height made him seem boyish and unthreatening, like Zach when Amanda had first met him. He looked around when Amanda didn't answer, consulted his clipboard again. "Grayson, Amanda!" He was quite annoyed now. That was like Zach, too, abruptly turning on a dime.

"Yes, that's me," Amanda said, rising to her feet.

"I'm Officer Carbone." He motioned her back. "Right this way."

They headed down a short hall from the waiting area to an open room with a dozen desks occupied by other detectives interviewing witnesses, victims, maybe even suspects. It was impossible to tell the difference. Everybody seemed upset. Amanda sat in a chair alongside Officer Carbone's desk as he took his place behind an old computer monitor.

Already Amanda felt like a victim. Wasn't that the opposite of how this was supposed to make her feel?

"So, again, I'm Officer Carbone," he said, reaching out to shake her hand. His grip was moist and his manner was stiff, as though he was following a script.

"Hi," Amanda said, resisting the urge to yank her hand back.

"What is it I can do for you?"

Amanda smiled awkwardly. "Someone is, um, harassing me. They've been calling and hanging up." This was a weak start. Carolyn would not be impressed.

"Okay." Carbone leaned back in his chair. He seemed skeptical, of course he did. Why wasn't she just being direct? "Any idea who?"

"Yes, um, it's my dad. I know that it is."

"Has your father made any threats?" At least he hadn't batted an eye at the idea of a father stalking his daughter.

"No— I mean, yes, in the past. On the phone he hasn't said anything. He just breathes."

"Breathes?" The officer frowned.

"Yeah, it's like this panting. I, um, know it really well. It's definitely him."

"Okay," the officer said, like he was trying to decide exactly how hard to press her for more details. "And the calls are from his number?"

"It just says 'unknown,'" Amanda said. "But I'm sure it's him. We moved back to New York recently from the West Coast. He lives upstate," she said, hearing how thin her evidence sounded. "And he's done this before," she added. "I filed a complaint back in California, Sacramento. Back then, he only called a few times. This time it's been . . . dozens, and dozens."

"Okay," the officer said, seeming encouraged. "A complaint. That's good."

"He also has a history of . . . He has a drug problem." Even those simple words—ones that didn't even get to the half of it—were so hard to get out. "I think he probably wants money. Actually, I'm sure that's what he wants."

Carbone turned toward his computer and began to type. "Sacramento, you said? And this was how many years ago?"

Amanda considered. She couldn't remember exactly anymore. But it had been spring because the flowers were newly blooming and she'd had Case with her at the time, which meant he wasn't yet in nursery school. She never would have brought him to a police station if she'd had a choice. Wait, it was right after Case had gotten that terrible food poisoning. Four whole days in the hospital because of tainted lettuce, of all things. Or so the doctors suspected. There was no way to be sure. Whatever had caused it, though, it had been absolutely terrifying to see how quickly Case had deteriorated, and how lifeless he'd become. He'd been nearly three at the time.

"Six or seven years ago."

A minute more of typing and then Officer Carbone's fingers suddenly stopped. "Ah, here it is."

Thank goodness. It was almost like having that stern, big-breasted female officer who'd taken the report standing at Amanda's side barking at him: *She's telling the truth, asshole, and she shouldn't have to prove it to you.*

"Seven years ago," he said. "Nothing since then?"

"No."

"How did it end last time?"

"I shouted that I'd been to the police," Amanda said.

"Did he respond to that?"

"No, but after that he didn't call again, until now."

Amanda had forgotten that part. That she'd threatened him. And it had worked. That was something.

"Has he ever done anything other than call?"

"I think he's been following me. And today he left flowers right at my house."

Lilacs. Amanda and her mother used to collect them from an abandoned field where they'd grown wild. Amanda had always been so comforted by that dreamy lilac smell filling the trailer afterward, while her daddy ranted about the sweetness making him feel sick.

"Flowers?" He looked confused. "Any chance he's trying to apologize?"

Amanda glared at the officer. She couldn't help it. Hadn't they just covered this? But from the plain look on his face, it did seem to be an actual question.

"You can't apologize for some things," Amanda said, an unexpected heat in her chest. Her jaw was clenched, too. She forced herself to smile. Getting angry wouldn't help. "Anyway, he would never apologize. And he hates lilacs. They were meant to be threatening. He wants me to know that *he* knows where I live. Even if he wants money, I'm afraid he'll do something horrible to get it. I threw the flowers out, but this is the card."

Officer Carbone studied the card for a long moment, but made no move to take it. "How does he know?"

"Know what?"

"You said you just moved to New York, right?"

"Yes," Amanda said, relieved that Officer Carbone had at least been listening that much. "Four months ago."

"And the calls started up right after you got here?"

"Yes."

"And you haven't been in contact with your dad since this complaint seven years ago?" He nodded toward his computer. Was his tone slightly accusatory now?

"Yes," Amanda said. "I mean no. I haven't had contact with him since then."

"Then how did he find you?"

"I don't know. Not easily." Amanda could not imagine her dad googling or something like that. Even if he did there would be nothing to find. "My husband is—he's very careful about privacy. He always makes sure our addresses can't be found online and that kind of thing. He has a service that does these checks and removes anything personal from the internet."

The officer raised an eyebrow. "Seems like maybe you should focus then on how your dad found you. Don't you think?"

"What do you mean?"

"There's the issue of how to make this stop. But there's also the issue of how it started. Sometimes the two are related," Officer Carbone said. "Are you sure you're not connected on social media somehow? Or maybe there's family or old friends who might tell him where you are? Sometimes people think they're helping when really they're doing just the opposite."

Amanda laughed then, in a way that probably made her seem crazy. But Officer Carbone's suggestion *was* crazy. Amanda had no connections to her old life. And she wasn't on any kind of social media. Zach thought it left people too exposed.

"No, no one told him," Amanda said quietly. "And our lives have nothing—no one in common."

The only friend she had from St. Colomb Falls was Carolyn, and she would have no way of—well, not no way. Carolyn's mom had passed, but she probably had family left upstate. Amanda hadn't asked about them in a long time. Carolyn, of all people, would never have anything to do with Amanda's dad, though. Carolyn hated him. And she loved Amanda.

"Well, he found you," Officer Carbone said. "Might be worth trying to figure out how."

"I just want an order of protection, something to make him stay away."

"To get an order of protection, you're going to have to actually prove he threatened you in some way or another."

"But *he* is threatening me," Amanda said quietly. "His being here is a threat. Because of the person he is, our history."

"I'm sure it's difficult, but maybe you could be more specific about what he's done exactly?" Officer Carbone asked. "If there was a previous act of violence, there's a better chance you could make the case."

But the ugly details were sunk beneath miles of ocean, buried deep in the sediment. And Amanda lacked the will to dive after them. An actual tear slipped out of her eye, though she hadn't realized she'd been about to cry. When Amanda brushed it away, the detective shifted uncomfortably in his chair.

"Listen, I am sorry," he said more gently. "Really, I am. And you could go down to the courthouse anyway and try for that restraining order. But I do think it would be a waste of time. My advice? Try to get something on the record, some evidence of your father's bad intent—video, audio. These days with everyone having an iPhone, judges end up almost expecting that kind of smoking gun." Carbone fished a card from his drawer and held it out to her. "In the meantime, if something else happens, property damage or some more specific threat, you call and ask for me personally. I'll do whatever I can to help. Keep asking yourself how he found you, too. There might be something or someone you're not considering."

Amanda headed away from the police station feeling confused, and even more hopeless. It wasn't that she'd expected one visit to the authorities to resolve the entire situation with her dad. But maybe she had let herself get her hopes up a little. Halfway home, she tossed Carbone's card.

What if her dad continued to call after Case came back? What if things continued to escalate then? No. She would not allow it. She would protect her son no matter what. A restraining order might not be the answer, but she had to do something, and she had to do it now. No matter what Carolyn thought, it wasn't as simple as talking to Zach, either. She'd tried to talk to him about her dad before and it had not gone well. She remembered one specific time their first year together.

They'd been driving to a party at the house of Zach's first boss, Geoffrey. Zach actually liked Geoffrey, and so Amanda hadn't told Zach that Geoffrey put his hands on her ass whenever he hugged her goodbye. Geoffrey and his wife belonged to one of those modern ministries, the kind in a strip mall, with a hard rock band. He was always trying to get Amanda and Zach to come to services. As Zach pulled into Geoffrey's driveway, he was talking about how they probably should go soon or they'd risk offending these "good people."

"Having a cross on your wall doesn't necessarily mean you're a good person, you know," she'd said.

"Oh yeah?" Zach had asked as he turned the car off. And Amanda felt this hopeful little rush in her chest. Zach was actually curious what she was getting at? He wasn't usually. For a second, she even considered telling him about Geoffrey's roaming hands.

"My dad had a cross on his wall," she went on. "And he did terrible, terrible things."

Zach had nodded and stayed quiet, smiling thoughtfully. But then Amanda watched his face slowly drain of all expression until it was cold and empty. "Is this the part where I'm supposed to ask, 'What terrible things, honey?' Because I'm not going to. We've all got baggage. If I'd wanted to take on someone else's, I would have married a different kind of woman."

"Amanda!" a voice called out.

When Amanda looked up, Maude was sitting there at the top of their stoop. Amanda had been so lost in thought, she hadn't even realized she'd walked all the way home from the Seventy-Eighth Precinct.

But what was Maude doing there? Sarah, Maude, and Amanda usually met at restaurants or bars like the Gate, or for coffee or a movie. Occasionally they'd walk the loop in Prospect Park. In the past months, Amanda had been to Sarah's house a few times, and to Maude's once or twice. But she'd never had anyone over, no one except Carolyn. And she didn't count.

Zach didn't want strangers in the house—that was the bottom line. There were times when Amanda thought about trying to explain to him the difference between "friends" and "strangers." But for him, there *was* no difference.

And now here was Maude at the top of their steps. Amanda couldn't let her in. Zach's schedule was too unpredictable. He could be home anytime. Yet how could she not invite Maude in without seeming impossibly rude? Amanda inhaled deeply before waving brightly from the bottom of the steps, hoping a solution would come to her before she reached the top.

"Hi there!" she called up.

"I should have texted first," Maude began, her voice unsteady. "It's obnoxious to loom on somebody's stoop uninvited."

"Don't be silly. Besides, you're sitting, not looming."

Amanda sat down on the top step next to Maude. As they hugged briefly, Amanda noticed Case's emergency house key poking out from underneath the planter. She felt a sharp pang of missing her son as she reached behind Maude to tuck it back under. At least at sleepaway camp, Case was safe from her dad.

Amanda turned her face toward the sun. *Let's stay out here and enjoy the glorious weather.* Amanda would not say that in particular. (*Glorious* was not a good word unless you lived in the eighteenth century.) But she could say some version of it. Anything to keep them on that stoop.

"It's strange that I'm here," Maude said. "I know. I just really needed to talk to a friend. And I love Sarah, but she can be . . . flip sometimes."

Amanda felt a flush of pride that Maude had chosen her. "I'm glad you're here."

Maude was gripping several brightly colored envelopes in her hand.

"I got more letters from Sophia. And they're worse." She grimaced and shook her head, then waved the envelopes in Amanda's direction as if encouraging her to take them. "I thought sending her to that camp, being in a new country, a whole new setting, was the right thing to do under the circumstances."

"Under what circumstances?" Amanda asked, finally reaching for the envelopes. Maude had made it sound before like she didn't know what was wrong with Sophia, but it was obvious now that she did. "Maude, did something happen?"

"A boy." Maude's eyes filled with tears. "I knew Sophia was upset, but I honestly thought getting away would be best."

"That makes total sense."

"But then these letters." Maude motioned to the envelopes. "I tried calling the camp a couple times this morning to check on her, but no one is answering in the office. Such a great camp until you call them, I guess."

"What does Sebe say?"

"That I'm overreacting. That she's not a child anymore, and I need to stop smothering her." Maude sounded hurt and angry. "I know that Sebe loves Sophia. But he's not a mother. Or a woman."

Amanda nodded.

"Listen," Maude said, "I know none of this makes much sense because I'm obviously not telling you all the details. But Sophia—she made me promise I wouldn't."

"That's okay. You don't need to tell me."

Maude motioned to the letters again. "Will you read one? Tell me if you think I'm overreacting."

"Oh, I . . ." Amanda hesitated. What if she didn't react the right way?

"Please."

"Sure, okay." Amanda pulled a letter from one of the envelopes and unfolded it. The writing was so neat and pretty, the paper a cheerful sky blue.

Dear M,

I want you to know that none of this is your fault. I know you'll blame yourself. You'll think that if I had better self-esteem that I wouldn't have gotten myself into this mess. Or maybe you're going to think that you didn't tell me all the things I needed to know. That if you'd given me some different kind of advice or the right facts, I could have protected myself.

But it's not your fault. It's my fault. I'm the only one to blame. I made so many stupid choices. And you definitely taught me better. You taught me everything I needed to know. I just messed up anyway.

I'm sorry, Mom. So, so sorry.

Xoxo
Sophia

Amanda thought about her own mother's last piece of advice right before she died, when she'd wrapped her bony arms around Amanda from her hospital bed and pulled her close. "You run if you have to," she'd whispered. "You run as fast as you can."

Run where? That was all Amanda could think at the time. She'd been so very young.

"So?" Maude asked, motioning to Sophia's letter. "Do you think Sebe's right? That I should back off and let her figure it out on her own? Pretend like the whole thing isn't happening?"

Amanda considered whether there was a "right" thing to say at that moment. Probably there was. But she opted instead for something much simpler: what she actually believed.

"I don't think you can pretend your way through anything," Amanda said, reaching out and putting a hand on Maude's arm. "Closing your eyes won't stop the bad things from finding you."

GRAND JURY TESTIMONY

OFFICER DAVID FINNEGAN

called as a witness the 6th of July and was examined
and testified as follows:

EXAMINATION

BY MS. WALLACE:

Q: Good morning, Officer Finnegan.

A: Morning.

Q: Did you report to a call at 597 Montgomery Place
on the night of July 2nd at approximately 11:45 p.m.?

A: Yes.

Q: And what was the nature of that call?

A: It was a report of a suspected homicide.

Q: What occurred when you arrived at the scene?

A: My partner, Officer Romano, and I entered the
residence to assist officers already on scene.

Q: What did you observe when you entered the home?

A: There was a lot of blood on the stairs and the
walls. There was a golf club near the body. They had
marked it off so nobody touched it. The victim's husband
was there.

Q: Anything else?

A: The EMTs had arrived just before us, and they were attempting to revive the victim with CPR and to control the bleeding.

Q: Were they able to revive her?

A: No. She was pronounced dead at the scene.

Q: What did you do then?

A: My partner and I were standing with the victim's husband when the crime scene unit detectives arrived, followed by ADA Lewis and Detective Mendez. The crime scene unit started taking photos so that the body could be removed.

Q: And what was ADA Lewis doing?

A: Just observing. The ADA on homicide duty overnight comes to the scene, but they don't talk.

Q: What was Detective Mendez doing?

A: He started talking to Mr. Grayson.

Q: At any point, did Mr. Grayson appear to be crying or similarly emotional?

A: No. He made some noises. But there were no visible tears.

Q: Did Detective Mendez eventually get Mr. Grayson to move outside?

A: I don't know.

Q: Why not?

A: Because I was injured at the scene.

Q: How were you injured?

A: Mr. Grayson hit me in the face.

Q: With his fist?

A: No. Detective Mendez put his hand on Mr. Grayson's arm, you know, to encourage him to come away from his wife's body, and Mr. Grayson jerked his arm away, and I think he might have said "Fuck you" or "Fuck off" or words to that effect.

Q: To Detective Mendez, who was asking him to step away from his dead wife's body?

A: Yes.

Q: And then what happened?

A: He swung his arm back and his elbow made contact with my face, breaking my nose.

Q: Was it intentional?

A: He knew I was standing there. You tell me?

Q: Sorry, Officer Finnegan, but it's my job to ask the questions, not answer them. I need to know whether you think it was intentional.

A: Then, yeah. In my opinion, it was intentional.

LIZZIE

I took a deep breath as I rang the doorbell to Sebe and Maude's stately brownstone. It was on First Street between Seventh and Eighth Avenues, not far from Zach's and almost as impressive. As I waited for someone to answer, I tried to keep myself from imagining the upstairs goings-on at the party. Who could possibly survive a marriage where partners strayed openly? Who could possibly survive marriage, period?

I'd stopped at Café du Jour after leaving Hope First with the journal I'd swiped from Amanda's office. It was indeed her most recent one, with detailed entries for each day since they'd arrived in Park Slope. There were also summaries of life with Case, how lonely and lost Amanda felt with him at camp, her intimidating running habits, the mundane details of her trying to handle foundation business, and chats she'd had with Carolyn. But, most importantly, there was a log of incidents—somebody calling and hanging up, following her.

In the entries I'd read so far, Amanda hadn't identified this person. But she was scared of him, that was clear. Excellent reasonable doubt for Zach's case, if I could eventually find a name. Luckily, I had time. A new suspect—no matter how compelling—wouldn't be useful until trial.

When the door finally opened, there was an alarmingly good-looking man in the doorway.

"Hi?" he said like it was a question, pushing his thick black hair back with one hand, his eyes boring into me as he waited a beat for me to explain myself. "Can I help you?"

He had an accent, too. French, as Sarah had said. Sebe.

"I'm Zach Grayson's lawyer," I began, bracing myself for another hostile reception. "I called. Your wife said I could come by and ask some questions."

"Of course, come in," he said cordially. "Tragic, what happened. Amanda was a lovely person."

"Lizzie Kitsakis," I said, extending a hand once we were in the foyer.

"Sebastian Lagueux. But everyone calls me Sebe." He shook my hand firmly before motioning me onward into the house. "Come have a seat in the living room."

The inside of the house was as grand as the outside, with lots of dark polished wood and vibrant modern rugs. It had been renovated, but in a way that retained more of its historic charm than Zach's house, which really was quite modern inside. The art was particularly eye-catching, especially a large blue and red abstract painting directly through the main entryway on the living room wall.

"That's amazing," I said.

Sebe laughed gently. "Ah, did Sarah tell you to say that?"

"He means he painted it." When I turned, there was a striking woman, with reddish-brown hair falling in long tendrils, barefoot and barefaced. She was wearing a peasant-style wrap dress with a deep V-neck, so sheer it was almost see-through. "And Sebe's not even a painter—he's a doctor. A doctor and a painter and a tech start-up entrepreneur and an amateur horticulturist. He did this painting in one day with no planning. How annoying is that?" And she did seem actually annoyed.

"This is Zach's lawyer, Maude," Sebe said.

"Oh, yes." She reached forward to shake my hand. "Is Zach okay? Sarah told me he'd been arrested."

Her tone was so different from Sarah's, reserved and concerned, but not at all hostile.

"He's very upset about Amanda, obviously," I said, because that was the right thing to lead with, even if—truthfully—it wasn't necessarily the first thing that jumped to mind. "And, to clarify, he's only been arrested for assaulting an officer at this point. It was a misunderstanding. But it does seem likely he'll be charged in Amanda's death eventually. It's horrifying to be suspected of a crime you didn't commit, even more horrifying to be wrongly accused of murdering your wife. It doesn't help that he's being held at Rikers. It isn't just any jail."

I saw Maude and Sebe exchange a nervous look. "Rikers?" Sebe asked.

"There are only a few places people are held over pending trial if they aren't granted bail, which, ridiculously, Zach wasn't. Jail is jail, but none are quite as bad as Rikers." I considered how much to tell them. But the truth could motivate them to be more helpful. "He's already been assaulted more than once."

"Assaulted?" Maude looked worried, but there was something off about her affect. As though she was also suppressing some other reaction. Like a piercing scream.

"That's awful." Sebe reached over to squeeze Maude's hand. And then they exchanged a look, having an entire wordless conversation with their eyes. No wonder they could have sex with other people. Sarah was right: they were bound by some preternatural force.

"I think I need a whiskey," Sebe said finally. "Ladies?"

"Yeah, me too." Maude turned to me. "What about you, Lizzie? I feel like we could all use a drink."

Oh, no, thank you, was my immediate reaction. These days anything involving alcohol was immediately off-putting. But then why should Sam be the only one who got to drink at work? All things considered, I felt like I deserved a whiskey. Besides, there was this unearthly quality to Maude and Sebe that made me want to say *I want to do whatever you do*.

"Sure, thank you," I said. "That would be great."

Maude nodded, pleased, it seemed, by my willingness to join in. We both watched Sebe at the built-in bar at the far end of the room. And I wondered: Was this the way it happened? These upstairs affairs? Did the husband return with the drinks, and instead of sitting next to his wife, go to sit next to the other woman? Or maybe the husband and wife sat next to each other and began kissing and waited to see if the other woman would join in. I could picture all of it suddenly. I could see how it could happen. I could even see myself in the role of the other woman.

And the real dark truth? I realized I was intrigued. Less by the sex itself than by the notion of doing something wrong. Something to hurt Sam. I already had my own secrets, sure, but mine didn't have a thing to do with our marriage. My mind flashed to the earring tucked in the pocket of my bag.

How stupid had I been, and for how long?

Three years into dating, Sam proposed while we were in New Orleans for the weekend, getting down on one knee in the middle of Bourbon Street, in front of a jazz bar. By then we'd been living together in Brooklyn for a year and both so focused on our careers. We were working hard and we were tired, but we were doing things that mattered. Sam somehow made me feel challenged and yet accepted; liberated, but also taken care of. And so very undamaged.

When I first saw Sam down on the ground that night, I thought for a second he'd fallen. But then I saw that little box in his hands. People were staring. And I was glad. It was the proof I'd been waiting for. I had survived, and I was happy. I wanted the world to see.

"Lizzie, I promise to live every day trying to be the man who deserves you. Will you marry me?"

"Yes!" I'd shouted, grabbing Sam's face in my hands and kissing him. "Yes."

After Sam had slipped the eye-popping ring—a long-ago-gifted family heirloom—onto my finger, we'd raced into the jazz bar for champagne. It was after our third drink that I started thinking we should slow down. Sam was stressed working at the *Times*, though, and it was hard to blame him. The standards there were impossible, and he'd made a couple of stupid mistakes. High-pressure jobs like that weren't easy. I knew firsthand. I was finishing up a clerkship in the Southern District, on my way to another in the Second Department and then the US attorney's office. It was all lined up—a steep, prestigious, terrifying ladder. Anyway, we were celebrating. We were getting married.

"Did you ever imagine when we met that first night that we'd be getting married?" I asked him as he ordered us another round and a new jazz band began to play. The bar was smoky and packed and perfect. And I was getting *married*. After all these years, I was getting a family back.

"God only knows." Sam laughed a little too hard and then took another sip.

"Well, that wasn't exactly the romantic response I was hoping for," I joked back, but it stung. That was the problem with a night like that— the night you were engaged—the stakes were too high. "Well, *I* knew the second I met you. Maybe I was imagining things."

"That's not what I meant," Sam said lightly, oblivious. Drunk already. "I was swept off my feet by you. About that I have no doubt. It's the specifics of the conversation that get fuzzy. We had all been drinking for hours. But who needs specifics when I have you?"

I'd laughed because that was my favorite thing about Sam and me—unlike a lot of couples, we didn't pretend to be perfect. We were honest about our flaws. And truthful was so much better than perfect.

Maude had said something.

"What?" I asked.

"Why do they think Zach killed her?" she asked, seemingly for the second time.

"They found his golf club at the scene," I said. "And he found Amanda. It was their house. He's the husband. It's a routine assumption. Also, they'd been at your party, so . . ."

"Our party?" Maude sounded nervous. "What does that have to do with anything?"

"I know there was . . ." The hesitating was death. So much for passing myself off as casual about it. "The police are calling it a key party. Apparently there have been problems in the past."

"The police," Sebe scoffed. "Thanks to this unstable neighbor of ours, they get called every year. She's a very old, very angry sort—racist, too, I'm fairly certain. If Maude and I were both white, I suspect she'd never even consider calling the police. Anyway, last year the police carted off two dads because they'd gotten into some kind of foolish argument, about American football of all things. If the police hadn't been called, it would have been nothing. It *was* nothing."

"I know what it sounds like, the 'upstairs,'" Maude said, more seriously. "But it isn't that big a deal. Only a handful of people participate, and it's all very discreet."

Sebe's cell phone rang then. "I apologize. This is the hospital," he said. "I need to speak with them."

"Of course," I said, as Sebe swiftly exited the room.

"The police have already interviewed you?" I asked Maude once he was gone.

"Not yet. They're supposed to come tomorrow morning."

"They haven't been here at all?"

"Is that a problem?" she asked, nervous again.

"This *is* the last place Amanda was seen," I said. Was the prosecution's case already locked up that tight that they didn't even *need* to talk to anyone else? "I'd think they'd want the names of the party guests and that kind of thing."

"Maybe they got those from Sarah. I know they talked to her." She was quiet for a moment. "I'm sorry about Zach being assaulted in jail.

It would be awful if something really happened to him. Especially, I mean—poor Case."

And so I decided to raise the stakes. "Yes, Rikers can turn a false accusation into a death sentence."

"Death sentence?" Maude blanched. "But what would happen to Case then?"

I felt a guilty burn at the base of my gut. Maybe I was overstating the situation a bit, but it wasn't a complete fabrication. Zach had been attacked.

"I'm not saying that will happen," I went on. "I'm just saying that it could. That's why I'm focused on getting Zach out on bail. I feel confident he'll be acquitted once there is an actual trial."

"What can we do to help?" Maude asked.

"Did you speak to either Zach or Amanda at your party?"

Maude nodded. "To Amanda only briefly."

"How did she seem that night?"

"She was sweet and lovely as always. She tried to make me feel better about my daughter—she's been having some, ah, issues. Amanda was always a very good friend, so supportive." Maude stared down in silence into her whiskey glass. "Listen, I *know* that Zach didn't kill Amanda." She hesitated. "Because, um, I was with him when she died."

"I'm sorry, what?"

She closed her eyes, and I watched her jaw tighten. "Zach and I were together at the time Amanda died."

That didn't mean what it sounded like, did it?

"But not . . . You mean, *together* together?" I asked.

When Maude finally looked up, her eyes were cold, almost angry. As though she was being forced to make this disclosure, rather than volunteering it. "Yes."

"Oh." My cheeks felt warm again.

Why the hell hadn't Zach told me? Was he worried about how it would look? Assuming the time windows matched, being with Maude would give him an alibi, which was *huge*. On the other hand, being an unfaithful husband didn't exactly go down in the innocent column. A skilled prosecutor would have a field day with it. Here was a man who wanted to sleep with other women, like this gorgeous woman Maude here, exhibit A. *That's* why he killed his wife. A jury might believe that, even though Amanda was so beautiful herself. But an alibi was still an alibi.

I swallowed hard. "What time did Zach leave, then?"

"It was late, two a.m., maybe?" Maude said stiffly. "Anyway, you can say we were together. I mean, to the police."

Of course—aside from the infidelity implications for Zach—I wouldn't know whether that alibi was truly helpful until I knew Amanda's official time of death and what time Zach had placed his 911 call. And I wouldn't know either until the DA's office turned over a copy of the medical examiner's report and the 911 records. All of that was a ways off. Zach hadn't even been indicted for Amanda's murder.

"It's probably one of those helpful, not helpful things." I didn't like how flexible Maude was making the truth sound. "Though you should be completely honest when you talk to the police, of course."

"Sure, yes." Maude seemed even more agitated now. "My alibi won't get the case dismissed? I mean, if Zach wasn't there when Amanda died, he obviously didn't kill her."

"It's not that simple," I said, and it never was. "An uncorroborated alibi from a witness who is acquainted with the defendant only means so much."

"Meaning they won't believe me?"

"They might not," I said.

The truth was, I wasn't sure *I* believed her. Maude in bed with Zach didn't fit with anything Zach or Sarah had told me. Also, why did Maude seem angry?

"Did anyone see you together?"

"No," she said. "I mean, I don't think so."

"The party was ongoing at two a.m.?"

"No, no," she said. "It had ended by then."

Already the holes in her story were growing. "But Sebe was here?"

"Yes," she said, though she did not sound sure.

"Then he can corroborate the alibi," I said. "Obviously, it would be better if the two of you weren't married . . ."

"Right," Maude said, then forced a stiff smile. "Well, I guess we can't change that."

"Did Amanda mention any problems she was having with any-body?" I asked. "Before the night of the party?"

"No, she didn't."

"Anything in Amanda's past stand out for you?" I asked. "About her family, maybe?"

I needed to be careful with what I revealed about Amanda's jour-nals. It wasn't just a matter of protecting Amanda's privacy; I didn't want word of this stalker getting back to the prosecution. It would give them more time to figure out how to prove why he—whoever he was—couldn't possibly be a viable suspect. And to subpoena every last one of Amanda's journals, yanking them, and whatever other secrets they contained, right out of my hands.

"I do think she had a hard childhood," Maude said. "She was vague about it, but she mentioned something at Kerry's—Sarah's husband's—birthday dinner. I got the sense there was a story there."

"Did you know her friend Carolyn? I'm trying to track her down, too."

"Amanda mentioned her," Maude said. "But we never met."

"Any chance you know her last name or where she works?"

"No," Maude said. "I'm sorry."

"Did Amanda tell you about some anonymous flowers that had been sent to her? Or any unwanted calls or anything like that?"

Maude looked concerned. "No," she said. "Was that happening?"

"I have reason to think it was."

"Why wouldn't she have told us?"

I shrugged. "Sometimes it can be easier to pretend something isn't happening if you keep it to yourself."

Wow. That explanation had popped out of my mouth with disconcerting ease.

"We were her friends, though," she said, tears filling her eyes. "We would have helped. Whatever it was." She wiped her cheeks with the back of her hand. "I don't mean to be getting so upset. I know it's not helpful. Like I said, my daughter has been . . . Between her and Amanda, it hasn't been an easy time."

"I should be going anyway." I stood. "Thank you for your time. Can I be back in touch if I have other questions?"

"Yes. Of course," Maude said. "What'll be next exactly?"

"My first priority is getting Zach out of Rikers on bail. And that's really about some legal technicalities at the moment. After that, assuming Zach is charged with murder, we'll start factfinding, talking to witnesses. We might need your help with that."

"Yes, definitely. Would it be okay if I also checked back in to get an update? Under the circumstances, the party—I guess we feel responsible, in a way. Especially, with Case . . . Do you have a card?"

"Of course," I said, digging for one. But there weren't any in my bag. I'd been so distracted after finding the earring that I'd left them—and God knows what else important—at home. "I don't have one on me. You can reach me on my cell, the number I called you from." But from the way Maude was looking at me, she wanted something more than just that. Maybe she didn't believe I was who I claimed to be. "I can text you my other contact information if you want?"

"That would be great," Maude said.

I scrolled through my contacts to the appropriately vague "New Office" one I'd created right before I started at Young & Crane, and sent the firm address and my direct line.

"You can check in with me anytime," I said, though Maude seemed so relieved to have my contact information, I wished I hadn't given it to her. I moved toward the door. "Thank you for your time."

It was nearly four o'clock when I stopped in front of a deli at the corner of Seventh Avenue and Flatbush near the entrance to the Q train. I quickly scanned the newspaper racks for the *New York Post* or the *Daily News,* the perennial bellwethers for the city's most tawdry news. A group of rich Park Slope parents, a sex party, and one gorgeous dead mother was a tabloid trifecta. Sooner or later "Key Party Killing" or "Park Slope Perverts" would surely be emblazoned across their covers. But today they were dedicated to a corruption scandal at the MTA, something about hundreds of thousands of dollars in overtime paid to a single driver.

I felt light-headed suddenly. The heat, the sleep deprivation, the emotional drain of the night before. I also hadn't eaten all day. I rested a hand on the doorway as I made my way into the deli.

After a minute of aimless browsing, I approached the counter with a Diet Coke, a pack of M&M's, Mike and Ikes, and Twizzlers.

"I hope you won't eat this all today," the friendly man behind the counter said, shaking his head gravely. "So much sugar is no good."

"Of course not," I said, though I planned on doing just that the second I hit the sidewalk.

He was getting my change when I noticed a box of matchbooks next to the register. *Enid's.* I pulled one out, my heart picking up speed.

"Where did you get these?" I asked.

Here was an alternate theory for the case against Sam. Maybe he hadn't been off drinking during the day yesterday, after all. This particular deli was more than twenty blocks from our fourth-floor walk-up, and Sam wasn't much for Center Slope—too many bankers and five-dollar lattes—so I didn't think he'd gotten the matches there specifically. But if that deli had them, maybe others did, too. And if I was wrong about him drinking at Enid's, maybe I was jumping to the wrong conclusion about the earring, too. Maybe he was being a Good

Samaritan after all? Maybe it had even gotten accidentally dropped into his bag. Why hadn't this totally plausible explanation occurred to me before? After all, New York City was a crowded place. Who knew how many other possibilities I was not considering?

"Get what?" The man eyed me over the top of his reading glasses.

"These matches," I said, gripping a pack. "This place is in Greenpoint, isn't it?"

"Closed down. Twenty years it was in business." He shook his head in disgust. "Now the cigarette distributor gives them out for free."

GRAND JURY TESTIMONY

DETECTIVE ROBERT MENDEZ,

called as a witness the 7th of July and was examined and testified as follows:

EXAMINATION

BY MS. WALLACE:

Q: Good morning, Detective Mendez.

A: Morning.

Q: Were you at 597 Montgomery Place on the night of July 2nd?

A: Yes.

Q: What did you do after you arrived at the scene?

A: I approached Mr. Grayson and asked him to step outside with me in order to give the crime scene unit detectives room to work. I also thought Mr. Grayson would be more comfortable that way. Generally, it's best to have family members away from a scene like that.

Q: And by a "scene like that," what do you mean?

A: The condition of the body—of Mr. Grayson's wife. She had very traumatic injuries. There was a great deal of blood.

Q: Did Mr. Grayson accompany you outside?

A: Not at that time.

Q: Why?

A: He refused.

Q: Why?

A: It wasn't clear.

Q: Did he say he didn't want to leave his wife?

A: No. He didn't say anything specifically about her.

Q: Do you recall anything he did say?

A: He was more generally defensive and argumentative. He kept asking why he needed to go anywhere. I think he said it was his f-ing house, which seemed strange under the circumstances.

Q: Under what circumstances?

A: I mean, his wife was dead. The tone seemed off.

Q: Can you explain what you mean by "off"?

A: I mean he seemed more angry than upset.

Q: Did he seem angry the whole time you were there?

A: Yes.

Q: At any point did he seem sad or tearful?

A: No. I didn't see anything like that.

Q: Did you see any blood on Mr. Grayson's person? On his clothing, his hands? Anywhere?

A: Only on the soles of his shoes.

Q: Would it have been possible for him to have touched his wife to attempt CPR and not get blood on himself?

A: I don't see how.

Q: Was there any other indication that he had attempted to revive his wife?

A: Not that I am aware of.

Q: But if he'd murdered his wife, wouldn't he also have blood on him?

A: Yes. We believe he changed his clothes and disposed of them prior to our arrival on the scene.

Q: Have you located those clothes?

A: Not yet. But Park Slope is full of garbage cans.

Q: Did you ask Mr. Grayson about his whereabouts at the time of his wife's murder?

A: He said he found his wife when he got home from taking a walk on the Brooklyn Heights Promenade.

Q: Did you find that response credible?

A: No.

Q: Why not?

A: I didn't believe he would go out walking all the way over there at that time of night. And Mr. Grayson claimed he'd walked home from Brooklyn Heights. That's a couple miles from Park Slope.

Q: Were there other things that made you suspect Mr. Grayson had murdered his wife?

A: Sure, there were no signs of a break-in, it was his golf club near her body. He wasn't emotional either. His wife was dead.

Q: Did you eventually get Mr. Grayson to move outside?

A: Only after he struck one of the uniformed officers in the face and was placed under arrest.

AMANDA

THREE DAYS BEFORE THE PARTY

"Oh, here she is now. Hold on!" Sarah barked into the phone as Amanda stepped off the elevator. She was standing at the reception desk, gripping the handset with dramatic irritation. Sarah leaned over and punched a button on the console. "Thank God you're here. This *man* apparently must speak with you."

Amanda's chest seized.

"Um, who is it?" She tried to sound casual, but sweat had sprung up at the back of her neck.

"The jerk wouldn't even tell me his name. Sounds like he's afraid I'm screening your calls." Sarah's face brightened mischievously. "I could hang up if you want me to. I would very much like to."

"No, no, don't hang up," Amanda said. What if her dad was finally going to demand the money he was after? It could be her chance to be done with him. Amanda paid the household bills. She could write a check without Zach ever needing to know. "I'll take it. In my office."

"Ugh." Sarah frowned at her. "I love you, Mandy, but sometimes you really are too accommodating."

Mandy. Sarah had never called Amanda that before, and it meant far more to Amanda than it should have. She knew that. But it was yet more proof they were real friends. She couldn't let this ugliness with her dad turn everything good in her life inside out.

It needed to stop now.

"Thank you, Sarah!" Amanda called, smiling back one last time before disappearing into her office and closing the door. She took a deep breath, bracing herself against her desk as she picked up the phone. "This is Amanda Grayson."

"Hello, Mrs. Grayson. This is Teddy Buckley."

The voice on the other end sounded young, far too young to be Daddy, even trying to disguise himself.

"Mrs. Grayson?" The man sounded concerned. "Are you there?"

"Yes, yes, I'm here," Amanda said. And that was all she was going to say. She didn't know any Teddy Buckley.

"I've been reviewing Hope First Initiative's ledger in advance of the board meeting, and there are some important matters I need to discuss with you."

"What matters? Who are you?"

"Your accountant?" Teddy Buckley's voice lifted at the end, like it was a question. "With PricewaterhouseCoopers?"

"Oh," Amanda said. "Sarah, the woman you were just speaking to, she's the assistant director. She handles the budget."

"Mrs. Grayson, I need to speak with you personally," Teddy Buckley said, more insistent now. "And this really is rather urgent. I've tried speaking with your husband, but . . ."

"Sarah," Amanda repeated. "She's in charge of the finances."

"As principal, I'll need to speak with *you*," he pressed. "How about your office, tomorrow morning at eight a.m.?"

If she didn't want to meet with this accountant, she didn't have to. No matter what they scheduled.

"Sure, yes, of course," Amanda said, her voice regaining the refinement she'd spent years cultivating. "Tomorrow at eight a.m. would be lovely." *Lovely* was a good word, though probably too much under the circumstances.

"Uh, okay, great," Teddy said skeptically. "See you then. Okay, bye."

As if on cue, Sarah appeared in Amanda's office door as soon as she hung up.

"Everything okay?"

"I'm not sure. That was the accountant. He was very insistent," Amanda said. "But he wouldn't even tell me why. We have to meet in person, apparently."

Sarah narrowed her eyes. "That's weird, isn't it?"

"I suppose," Amanda said. "Maybe I should send you to the meeting in my place."

"I do love being your bad cop," Sarah said, her eyes shining with delight. "*Provided* you and Zach *both* come to Kerry's birthday dinner tonight."

Amanda smiled. "We wouldn't miss it. It sounds lovely."

Lovely was a better word now. Still a bit much, maybe, but Sarah looked pleased.

Sarah checked her watch. "And now I've got to scoot, if that's okay with you, boss? I've got a cake to bake and a house to scrub. My place, eight p.m.?" She motioned toward her own eyes, then back at Amanda. "And I'll be looking for the *both* of you."

Amanda spent more than forty minutes trying to find the perfect gift for Kerry at the Park Slope Spirit Shoppe. At least Kerry was a collector of whiskey and wine, which made him easier to shop for than Zach. Even after all these years, Amanda couldn't say with any genuine certainty what her husband would actually enjoy as a gift. The only thing he seemed to truly derive pleasure from was his work.

Amanda caught sight of one particularly pricey bottle of whiskey from Cork on a high shelf. Wasn't that the area of Ireland that Kerry's family was from? He'd mentioned it once; Amanda was almost certain he had. She looked closer. It was a very expensive bottle, though, and sometimes expensive gifts made people uncomfortable. Amanda had once given a bracelet as a birthday gift to a woman in her Palo Alto tennis group. She'd selected it because it was the woman's—Pam was her name—favorite color: blue. Amanda hadn't thought of the cost until Pam, quite forcefully, said that she couldn't possibly accept "that kind of gift." After that, Pam avoided Amanda.

KRELL INDUSTRIES

CONFIDENTIAL MEMORANDUM
NOT FOR DISTRIBUTION

June 29

To: Brooklyn Country Day Board of Directors
From: Krell Industries
Subject: Data Breach & Cyber Incident Investigation—Critical Event Report

FPP from Subject Family 0006 contacted the office today. The Junior Assigned Investigator (JAI) who spoke with FPP reported her as "extremely agitated." She wanted someone to give her additional information about the pornographic material emailed to her with the usual request for cash transfer. FPP requested that all such offensive material be removed from her computer and placed on a zip drive. JAI offered to refer her to companies that do such assessments, but indicated that Krell was not available to assist with her personal situation beyond evaluating the consequences of the hacking.

FPP of Subject Family 0006 was adamant that Brooklyn Country Day and Krell should be responsible for a forensic analysis to determine whether the pornographic material had, in fact, been installed on the family computer by Subject Perpetrator (SP) rather than found there. There is no reason to believe that SP has ever downloaded files onto a Subject Family computer. SP exploits preexisting downloads or other data. The pornographic material belongs to someone in Subject Family 0006. FPP was informed of these facts.

FPP then threatened legal action against Brooklyn Country Day, which, sustainable or not, could cause reputational damage. In order to avoid legal action, it is our recommendation that Krell conduct the requested forensic analysis of Subject Family 0006 computer.

But the whiskey was meant as a real thank-you for all of Kerry's help, which ran the gamut from the small but inconvenient—getting Case's cards down late on a Sunday—to the downright selfless—chasing off that huge, sick-looking raccoon Case had been so scared might die right there in their backyard between the already-dead lilac bushes. The gift would be a thank-you to Kerry, and an apology for Zach's absence, though it would surely be only Sarah who was offended by that. Kerry had never said anything pointed about Amanda's marriage or asked accusingly where Zach was. For his part, Sebe had probably never even noticed Zach's absence. That's how men were about such personal details: vaguely disinterested. Especially if those details hinted at any sort of problem. Honestly, sometimes it did make life much easier.

Amanda was still contemplating whether to buy the whiskey when she got a text from Sarah: Can't wait to see Zach, finally! Amanda's eyes snapped up from the text to the absurdly expensive whiskey.

"I'll take it, please," she said to the store clerk, who'd been ogling her since she'd walked in. "Could you wrap it up?"

LIZZIE

The room assigned for Zach's writ hearing at the Brooklyn Criminal Courthouse lacked the historic grandeur of the Manhattan state or federal courthouses. But it was at least on a much higher floor than arraignments had been, and was significantly larger, which made it seem more dignified.

Wendy Wallace hadn't arrived, as far as I could tell. The empty prosecution table sat there expectantly, and there were only a handful of people in the gallery. But then, I didn't know what Wendy Wallace looked like. I'd started to do more research on her, but stopped once I'd found the article that described her as bloodthirsty. Not all preparation was good preparation.

Paul wasn't there yet either. Despite the short notice—the emergency writ hearing had been scheduled through the managing attorney's office late the evening before—Paul had assured me with this annoying munificence that he would be in attendance. Like I needed his help. I did not. To the extent my hesitancy about taking Zach's case had been about my skills, I'd only been worried about the intricacies of a fast-moving, full-blown murder trial. This writ hearing was a straightforward legal argument, an area in which I had always excelled. The carefully reasoned written positions, the intellectual clarity, the comforting presence of a well-informed judge—I could win a legal argument, *any* legal argument.

Maybe even this one, though on its face it was a loser. I wasn't giving up, though. Our brief was as good as it possibly could be, our positions reasonably strong. Plus, justice was on our side: Zach didn't belong in Rikers for accidentally elbowing an officer. And while I still would have preferred not to be representing him in the first place, after reading Amanda's most recent journal with all those details about someone following her, I was at least more convinced than ever of his innocence.

I was even feeling better about Sam and that stupid earring. I had jumped too fast to the most damning possible conclusion; that was obvious to me now. And yes, years of dealing with Sam's bad behavior was largely to blame for all my worst-case scenarios. But not entirely. The weight of my own baggage had also been taking its toll. Finding that cache of matches at the deli really had put things in perspective. And then there was Sam, up already before me this morning, proving once again—all hope was not lost.

"What time is it?" I'd asked, worrying I'd somehow overslept for court. Sam was never up before me.

"Almost six," he'd said. "I'm headed out for a run."

"A run?"

Sam had been on the cross-country team in college and had finished two marathons before the age of twenty-one, or so I had been told. Sam the runner had predated me, the only remaining relics the marathon laptop stickers he replaced on each new computer.

He'd started running to please his father—a fool's errand. The only sports that counted as far as Sam's father was concerned were football, basketball, rugby, lacrosse, and maybe soccer. The colliding of male bodies was a prerequisite. I suspected that it was his father's disapproving voice in Sam's head that had sent him out in recent months to his Thursday-night rec basketball game. Despite all the other players supposedly being "old dads," there was certainly a fair amount of colliding bodies. Sam had the bruises to prove it.

"Yeah, a run," Sam had said that morning, his eyes bright as he turned back from the bureau to face me. "I'm getting myself sorted out for real this time, Lizzie. And I know I've said that like a thousand times before. But I'm going to make sure it sticks. I—" He knew better than to actually promise. "I will."

All I could do was stare back at him and his luminous face. How I wanted to believe. Like my life depended on it.

"Okay?" he'd asked finally.

I thought then about the earring. But I'd already been wrong about those matches. And so, in that moment, I chose hope once more. I chose love. And silence.

"Okay," I'd said, and left it at that.

"Good morning." Paul had appeared at my side in the courtroom. He looked even more distinguished than usual in an exquisitely tailored navy-blue-checked suit. Had he gotten his hair cut, too? I was actually glad he was there. Paul did emanate a certain air of victory.

"Morning," I said, pulling out my copy of the brief, painfully aware now that my "designer" suit from Century 21 probably wasn't fooling anybody.

There was a bustle of activity behind us as the courtroom doors opened. A silver-haired woman in an edgy camel-colored pantsuit and toothpick-thin lizard pumps strode in, two younger, dark-suited male lawyers close at her heels. A couple of reporters rushed up to her as she headed down the center aisle, but she waved them away with a demure smile. Her face was unreasonably unlined for a woman her age, features regal, with flawless makeup and a perfectly understated manicure. Her eyes glinted across the room like those of a wartime queen prone to edicts and unexpected attacks.

I tucked my own bitten nails beneath my copy of our brief.

Avoiding pictures of Wendy Wallace had been a good call. Still, there was something else about her imposingly fashionable appearance: she was awfully familiar.

"It's deliberate," Paul said flatly.

"What is?"

"All of it. The pointy shoes, the way she walks—clicking them. She likes to intimidate." He said this with an air of contempt, but also admiration. He and Wendy Wallace had obviously crossed paths. "Act oblivious. It drives her crazy."

I turned to look at him. Paul sat at the defense table to my right, elbows resting on the arms of his chair, fingertips touching so that they formed a church's steeple. He was staring straight ahead, his expression expertly neutral.

And then there it was. All at once. The photograph on Paul's credenza. Wendy Wallace was his fucking first ex-wife. The one he was supposedly pining for all these years later. I closed my eyes and pressed my hands against the table. He must have made an educated guess that Wendy would be the DA assigned. It wasn't such a leap. The case was in Brooklyn, and it was a homicide. He must also know about her ambitions.

"You could have told me you had a preexisting relationship with the prosecutor," I hissed.

"I didn't know for sure she'd be assigned." He hesitated, and I thought for a moment he might actually apologize. "Besides, you were the one who came to me, remember? You know, she took almost everything I had in the divorce, and yet she's the one who won't talk to *me*." He looked up at me like I might offer some explanation for this cruelty. His face changed then, grew sullen. "Besides, I have insight into the prosecutor's character. It could be useful."

"If she hates you, you'll do more harm than good."

"Define *hate*," he said, raising a playful eyebrow.

I lowered my head. "Zach's been attacked at Rikers more than once," I snapped, unable to conceal my fury. "This isn't a game, you know? He could end up dead."

"Well then, let's hope this hearing goes well," Paul said, matter-of-factly. He put on his black reading glasses and paged through the brief, which he quite obviously had not looked at before. "We have proof of the warrant discharge, correct?" His voice had regained its military crispness.

I nodded absently. "Exhibit C."

"It was for loitering?" Paul asked, after looking at it more closely.

"Yes," I said, already feeling defensive.

"What kind of Penn Law student doesn't just walk away when the police tell him to?" he asked. "It would be one thing if he'd been taking a political stand against racial profiling or something, but this is a white guy, right? So he was, what? Being a dick?"

"I don't know," I said, annoyed by Paul's eleventh-hour insights, accurate or not.

"Reminds me of that partner I had to get rid of," Paul said grimly, flipping through the brief. "He showed up on not one but two different legal assistants' doorsteps, offering to help carry their groceries at just the right time. When confronted about this implausible coincidence, you know what he said?"

"No, I don't know," I said, not bothering to hide my impatience.

"'Sometimes, you have to show people what they need.'" Paul shook his head. "Defiant narcissism: some assholes think the rules don't apply to them."

"That's helpful, thanks. Anyone is capable of anything. I am aware. Are you aware you're at defense counsel's table?" I asked. "Because Wendy Wallace is over there, if you'd like to go help her."

Paul's eyes shot up, but luckily the judge's chambers swung open before he had the chance to cut me back down to size.

"All rise!" a stout, angry-looking court clerk bellowed as the judge entered the courtroom. "The Honorable Reggie Yu presiding!"

It wasn't until I heard the very loud collective rustling of everyone behind me rising to their feet that I became aware of just how many people had filed into the courtroom. Glancing over my shoulder, I recognized several local crime reporters from my own high-profile cases at the US attorney's office. The press out in force, surely as Wendy Wallace had intended.

Judge Yu was a petite woman with a blunt black bob and a commanding air. Older than me but younger than Paul and Wendy.

Fifty-two, to be precise. I knew because I'd looked her up when I'd found out she was assigned. Slightly defense-leaning. I could only hope that was an understatement.

"Docket number 45362, the People versus Zach Grayson," the court officer called.

"I've read your papers," Judge Yu started in, all business. "I'll hear from defense counsel first."

"Your Honor, the defendant in this case is a successful businessman, father, and well-regarded member of his Brooklyn community," I began. Calm, assured. "He has absolutely no criminal record and has been charged only with assaulting a police officer, an accident that occurred within minutes of his discovering his wife was dead, when he was quite understandably distraught. And yet he is now being held without bail at Rikers Island, where he's been repeatedly assaulted."

Judge Yu gave me a cold stare through her funky, oversize red glasses. "Uh-huh," she said. "So you want me to substitute my judgment for that of the judge who presided over the arraignment?"

An unsurprising response. That was the standard—whether the arraignment judge had abused his discretion. I was ready for it.

"We're merely asking that the appropriate standard be applied in assessing my client's eligibility for bail. The only question before the court should have been whether or not my client was a flight risk for the crime with which he had been charged: resisting arrest. Leaving aside the glaring insufficiency of the evidence in support of that charge, the arraignment judge was shown highly prejudicial photographs of a violent homicide scene. His decision was improperly influenced, Your Honor."

"Wait, what homicide?" Judge Yu asked, growing impatient.

"Amanda Grayson, my client's wife, died in her home of an apparent head trauma which—"

"*Apparent* head trauma?" Wendy Wallace guffawed, like she just couldn't help herself. "Her skull was crushed, Your Honor. She was savagely beaten to death with a golf club belonging to the defendant, in the defendant's home, and, oh, the defendant was the one who found the body after the two of them returned home from a night of heavy drinking at a sex party."

"Objection!" I barked.

Though there really was no point. There was no jury in place, and this was not a trial. But it was enraging. Wendy Wallace had gotten in almost every single piece of damaging evidence I'd been there to object to, short of the crime scene photos themselves.

"What about this old warrant?" Judge Yu asked, brow furrowed as she motioned to her clerk, who handed up some papers. "April 2007, for loitering, apparently? The court looked into it, but there were no additional details online."

Her caution was understandable. No judge wanted to be responsible for turning a blind eye to something as glaring as an outstanding warrant in a case where someone was dead. Even if the charge before the court at the moment wasn't murder, it was the unspoken pall hanging over Zach's head.

"Yes, an unpaid ticket for loitering my client received as a law student. It was an innocent oversight, not to mention ancient history," I said. "Regardless, it's been resolved. The warrant has been discharged."

"Loitering?" Judge Yu asked, brow furrowed skeptically. "What exactly does that mean?"

Outside of a political protest, a law student acting in such a way *was* odd—Judge Yu was right. Paul was right. Why hadn't Zach just moved along when the police officer told him to? I wished now that I had more details about the warrant, but they had yet to arrive from the managing clerk. As it was, I had no choice but to rely on what Zach had told me, which wasn't all that helpful.

"There was an extremely aggressive new mayoral initiative at the time, broken windows and such," I said to Judge Yu as forcefully as I could, hoping that would make the excuse more credible than it sounded, even to me.

"'Broken windows,'" the judge said derisively. "Lucky for your client that he's white. Otherwise, he'd probably be dead."

There was that lean to the defense. I had Judge Yu on our side for a second. I needed to seize the opportunity.

"Your Honor, on the night in question, my client had just found his wife dead in his home. He was in a state of extreme emotional distress when he accidentally struck an officer standing behind him with his elbow. Under the circumstances, I submit that the prosecution will never find a jury willing to convict for the assault, and yet he's being held at Rikers, where *he's* been assaulted three times already. This is an outrageous miscarriage of justice, Your Honor. One that could cost my client his life."

"This all does sound excessive under the circumstances, Counselor," Judge Yu said to Wendy Wallace. "And while I appreciate the ingenuity of getting those pictures in front of the arraignment judge, a homicide—with which the defendant has yet to be charged—is, as the defense points out, irrelevant."

Paul wrote a note on his pad. "Ask about ADA Lewis, who was at the scene. I bet he wasn't even on duty."

Who cares? I wanted to write back, but there wasn't time, and Zach's public defender and Zach had both flagged the ADA, too.

"Further, Your Honor, this alleged assault only occurred once ADA Lewis appeared on the scene," I began, rolling the dice. "It's my understanding that he wasn't even assigned to homicides that night."

"Then what was he doing there?" Judge Yu asked. And, unfortunately, she was looking at me.

"I don't know, Your Honor. That's my question as well," I said. "Perhaps Ms. Wallace or someone else at the DA's office instructed him to find cause to make an arrest because the family involved is high-profile." I braced for Wendy to shout an objection. Instead, she glared coolly my way. It was far worse. "Once ADA Lewis arrived on the scene with Detective Mendez, my client was deliberately manhandled, escalating the situation, which directly led to his inadvertently injuring the officer. The DA's office effectively created cause for my client's arrest, which they are now using as an excuse to hold him at Rikers while they conduct a murder investigation. It's impermissible boot-strapping."

Finally Judge Yu turned to Wendy Wallace. "So what's the story with this ADA . . ." She consulted her notes. "Lewis."

"There's no story, Your Honor. It's procedure to have an ADA at the scene of all homicides. Lewis *was* that ADA. Perhaps somebody went home that night with a stomachache or had a hot date, and Lewis filled in. Last I checked, the DA's office is not obligated to provide evidence of its staffing schedule to the defense." Wendy Wallace leveled her eyes at Paul this time, and with a look that should have, by all accounts, sent him up in flames. "This entire discussion is moot anyway," she drawled, approaching the bench with a document out-stretched. "The grand jury has just returned an indictment against Zach Grayson for first-degree murder in the death of his wife, Amanda Grayson."

I had suspected this might be coming. And I was prepared.

"Your Honor, the defense objects to the amending of the indict-ment," I began. "The defendant wasn't offered the opportunity to testify. It's a clear violation of CPL 190.50. It calls for vacating the indictment."

This was all true. It was a violation of the criminal procedure rules not to give a defendant a chance to testify before the grand jury charged with indicting him. It was such a serious violation, in fact, that it could result in an indictment being thrown out after the fact. I might not have been experienced in state court, but I did excel at doing my home-work. Unfortunately, I was also prepared for how Wendy Wallace would respond, which was why I already knew I was unlikely to pre-vail.

"Oh, wait, does your client *want* to testify?" Wendy Wallace turned to me, head tilted slightly. "Because we will happily vacate the indict-ment to make that happen."

And there it was. Of course I didn't want Zach to testify. A defendant testifying before the grand jury was suicide, no matter how innocent they were. Grand jury proceedings subjected defendants to broad questioning with no judge present, resulting in reams of testimony that could easily be used to impeach them at trial. Nope. No way. But it had been worth a try raising the objection. Attorneys made mistakes, even accomplished ones like Wendy Wallace.

"What about it, Counselor, is your client going to testify?" Judge Yu asked. She knew how this was going to end, too. We all did. It was only a *meaningful* violation if Zach actually wanted to testify.

"No, Your Honor."

"Then the indictment stands." Judge Yu cast a sharp eye on Wendy Wallace. "Counselor, your tactics go that close to the line one more time, and I'll hold you in contempt."

"And, Your Honor, first degree?" I asked. "On what possible grounds?"

The premeditation involved in first-degree murder conflicted directly with the crime of passion theory Wendy Wallace had just laid out. Obviously, they could pursue any theory they liked, but there was the chance—with Judge Yu on my side—that I could at least use my objection to do a little reconnaissance. What did Wendy Wallace know that I did not?

"As counsel well knows, we are at liberty to amend the indictment to include second-degree or other lesser offenses at a later time," Wendy Wallace replied smoothly as she sauntered back to the prosecution table. *We know this happened, unless we decide this completely different thing happened.* Such were the mental gymnastics permitted by our justice system. "We are also under no obligation to share grand jury evidence with defense counsel at this time."

"But you are obligated to share some of your evidence with me," the judge countered brusquely. She didn't like being strong-armed by Wendy Wallace any more than I did. Luckily, she had the power to do something about it. "Given the context of everything else that's gone on here, I think defense counsel can be privy to your theory in broad strokes."

Wendy Wallace didn't seem the least bit bothered, which suggested her case was even stronger than I knew. "Very well. We've received a preliminary forensics report confirming that the defendant's finger-prints and the victim's blood were found on the murder weapon. We also have evidence that Amanda Grayson was having an extramarital affair, providing ample motive for the defendant to kill his wife."

"Your Honor, the prosecution has no actual evidence of an alleged affair," I protested, hoping that Wendy Wallace might give up a name. While an affair might have been proof of Zach's motive, it would also have handed me another possible suspect: Amanda's lover. Maybe this supposed paramour was even the person stalking her?

"Witnesses saw Amanda Grayson heading 'upstairs' with a lover at the sex party she and Mr. Grayson attended right before her death. And, as counsel well knows, premeditation need not occur weeks in advance. Hours or even minutes suffice." Wendy Wallace was cer-tainly correct about that. But surely she also knew *who* it was that Amanda had been with that night, and there was a reason she wasn't mentioning it. It must have been a weakness in her case. "And the defendant refuses to account for his whereabouts at the time of the murder. So we have motive, opportunity, and physical evidence that ties the defendant to the crime—certainly adequate for a first-degree indictment. Perhaps he'd like to say where he was, and we could get this all cleared up."

Zach claimed he'd been walking on the Brooklyn Heights Prome-nade. Maude was a much better alibi, even with the complications it presented. But I hadn't even had the chance to speak with Zach about it yet. Besides, Wendy Wallace was baiting me, and I wasn't falling for it. Maybe she already knew about Maude and wanted me to say some-thing. And to what end? It wouldn't get Zach bail. Alibis went to whether a defendant was guilty, not whether he was likely to flee.

The same was true of Amanda having a stalker. I could raise it now and hope the suggestion of an alternate suspect might curry favor with Judge Yu, but it wasn't actually relevant to bail. The prosecution had gotten their murder indictment, and so that train had left the station. I needed to focus on the narrow issue at hand.

"Your Honor, can we return to the issue of bail?" I pressed. And now, a frontal assault on Wendy Wallace. It was all I had left. "The decision to remand my client was an erroneous one based on prosecutorial misconduct."

"Misconduct?" Wendy Wallace laughed icily, but didn't seem remotely rattled. "That's absurd."

"The prosecution deliberately introduced photos of a murder scene, which were not relevant to the issue of bail on an unrelated charge. That initial erroneous bail determination should not be allowed to remain in effect simply because the prosecution has now amended its charges."

Out of the corner of my eye, I saw Paul nod. I had done a solid job laying out our argument.

Judge Yu took an annoyed breath, then paged again through the brief in front of her, which she was already clearly very familiar with. "The prosecution's tactics in this case certainly leave much to be desired. It's clear to me that Mr. Grayson should not have been held initially. I also have grave concerns about the circumstances that led to his arrest." Judge Yu shot another look at Wendy Wallace. "However, I cannot prevent the State from lawfully amending the indictment now. So here's what we're going to do. Let's start again, right now, in my courtroom. I will hear arguments on bail. The charge is murder in the first degree."

This was Judge Yu being generous, giving me a chance.

"Your Honor, my client has a young son, a business, deep ties to this community," I reiterated. "He has no criminal record and there is no evidence indicating he ever contemplated flight. There is absolutely no legitimate reason Zach Grayson should not be granted reasonable bail."

That was my best argument: principled, clean, straightforward. Unfortunately, it was still a loser.

"And what's 'reasonable bail' in the case of a multimillionaire like your client?" Wendy Wallace asked. "What dollar figure would he *not* be willing to walk away from? Your Honor, Zach Grayson's son isn't even living with him at the moment. He's already off in California, shipped conveniently out of state so that Mr. Grayson can retrieve him and be easily on his way to some distant foreign locale. Two weeks ago, Mr. Grayson even asked his assistant to look into flights to Brazil."

Brazil? What the fuck, Zach?

"Your Honor," I interjected. "Obviously, Mr. Grayson would happily surrender his passport. Further, the Graysons' son, Case, was already at a long-planned summer camp well before his mother died. He wasn't 'sent' to California after the fact. And with regard to international plane tickets, Mr. Grayson often travels for work."

"Yes, about that work. Mr. Grayson probably has enough money to pay for a private jet and an excellent fake passport. He certainly has good reason to, given that he'll be facing a life sentence for murdering his wife," Wendy Wallace said. Her justifiable confidence was terrible. "He has the means to flee, and, resolved or not, that outstanding warrant tells us one thing about Zach Grayson: he believes he's above the law."

Judge Yu was quiet for a moment, considering. "Ms. Wallace, I do not approve of your end run around due process in this case." She held up a hand when Wendy Wallace leaned in to protest. "But the access to the funds and the son already out of the area are problematic."

"Your Honor, if my client's son was brought back to New York, it's not clear who he would even stay with. My client and his wife only recently moved to the area. He shouldn't be penalized for wanting what's best for his son. And right now that means staying with family friends in California."

Foster care. That would be the likely upshot if Case was brought back. It might even be the upshot if Zach was convicted—unless Ashe's parents were willing to make taking care of Case a more permanent solution.

"I understand. But it presents an issue, and not the only one," Judge Yu said. She nodded then, her mind made up. She turned to the court reporter. "Please note for the record that the defendant must be given credit for all time served before and after the amending of the indictment. The defendant, Zach Grayson, will continue to be held over without bail."

And with that, Judge Yu struck her gavel down, rose to her feet, and swept back into chambers.

"That was never going to go any other way," Paul said as we watched Judge Yu disappear. "You did well with what you had."

Wendy sauntered over, leaned her fingertips down against our table, then thrust her face into Paul's. Her eyes were ablaze. Paul did an impressive job of staying perfectly still. Didn't even blink.

"Fuck. You. Paul."

"Nice to see you, too, Wendy."

And with that, she turned on a sharp lizard heel and click-clacked down the aisle and out of the courtroom.

"She's been sleeping with that ADA Lewis for months," Paul said, his jaw muscle flexing. "Guy's a prick. He's also like twenty-five years younger, and reports to her. Anyway, I'm sure they were in bed together when she got a call letting her know they had something press-worthy. She definitely told Lewis to go down and see if it would be a good case to insert herself into. Wendy's always been that way: strategic, even in who she's screwing." He finally rose from the table. "Anyway, she knows that I told you about her boyfriend."

"So now what?" I asked as I shoved my papers back into my bag. This was a rhetorical question.

"I'll tell you this much: Wendy is one hell of a storyteller. It's her trademark. Her case will be light on facts, but it'll be flashy, and it'll flow, and the jury will be riveted. You'll need a story of your own, and it had better be a goddamn good one."

I nodded. "You get what you wanted out of being here?"

Paul frowned. "She'll probably end up calling me," he said. "The more important question is whether I'll answer."

"Will you?" I asked.

Paul smirked. "What do you think?"

I walked a few blocks out of the bustling chaos surrounding Brooklyn Criminal Court to the quiet tree-lined area surrounding the more regal Kings County Supreme Court. I sat down on a bench to the side, out of the worst of the harried lunchtime foot traffic. Despite the already hot July sun, it was surprisingly cool in the shade.

Prepare for trial. That was the obvious next step. And, aggravating or not, Paul was right: if we had a hope of prevailing, we'd need a far more compelling story. The prosecution's version—a distant marriage, a controlling husband, a sex party that ended in violence—was a narrative a jury would be able to sink its teeth into. I'd need a similarly appealing one to grab their attention back. Better yet would be an alternate suspect that the jury could punish. Amanda's stalker was my best candidate, if I could find out who he was. Somebody from Amanda's troubled past seemed like the strongest possibility—her dad, Christopher, maybe even Carolyn. To know for sure, I needed to finish the rest of Amanda's final journal, and pray that she identified him, or her, there.

My phone rang. I was expecting Sam, hoping for Millie, though it was too soon for anything definitive from the lab. "Vic," my caller ID read instead. I was about to send the call to voice mail when it struck me that maybe what I really needed at that moment was a friend.

"Hey," I said.

"Hi!" Victoria exclaimed, taking my call off speakerphone. "I can't believe I got you! How's big-firm life?"

"Strange," I said without hesitation. It was the most honest thing I'd said in weeks.

"Strange?" Vic had made partner at one of the biggest entertainment law firms in L.A. in a mere six years, slipping into that elusive groove between big-firm stability and interesting work. "I guess that's better than some other alternatives like, say, excruciating."

I'd told Vic months ago that I was leaving the US attorney's office because I needed money to pay for IVF or adoption. I couldn't bring myself to tell her the truth. As close as Vic and I were, Sam's drinking was my dirty secret.

"Hey, do you remember Zach Grayson?" I asked.

"Ah." She made a sound like she was trying to think. "No. Should I?"

"I was friends with him first year at Penn."

"Oh, wait, you mean shifty eyes?" she asked. "That guy was a weirdo."

"Yeah, that's him," I said. "His wife is dead, the police think he beat her to death with a golf club."

"Yikes," Vic said. Then she was quiet, but only for a moment. "I feel like he probably did it. Don't you?"

I laughed too hard. I couldn't help it. The way she said it was so absurdly matter-of-fact. "I'm representing him," I said when I'd pulled myself together.

"What?" Vic sounded genuinely alarmed. "Why?"

"It's a long story. I kind of got cornered into it thanks to you and your obsessive need to send updates to our alumni magazine," I said. "He knew I'd moved to Young & Crane."

"Oh, no, no," she said. "I'm not taking the fall for this. I stopped sending in those updates two years ago, after Amy had her first miscarriage. She'd told me it was okay to post about her being pregnant, thank God. But still."

"Well, somebody must have posted it, because he called me at the office." Somebody probably delighted that I'd been forced off my high-minded path. I'd been pretty sanctimonious about public interest law back in the day—even though plenty of reasonable people didn't consider prosecutors public interest lawyers. "I felt bad saying no."

"You felt *bad*?" she asked. "What if he killed her? Is this because you dumped him? Because, my God, that was so long—"

"Dumped him? What are you talking about?"

"Come on," Victoria drawled. "You know exactly what I'm talking about. You were *so* in denial about the whole situation until I asked you what it was like to have sex with Zach and you freaked out. It was a totally genuine question, by the way. I'd assumed you two *were* having sex."

And then there it was—me and Vic studying for finals one night in Philly so many years ago. Vic had so casually asked me about sex with Zach and I'd been so childishly appalled. Sex, with Zach? We were friends. *Only* friends.

But by the time I was walking to meet Zach for dinner that same night—as we did several nights a week—I'd accepted that Victoria's question was a warning, one that I would ignore at my peril. As soon as I arrived at the restaurant and saw Zach, smiling so eagerly at me from a table in the corner, there was no more denying it: Zach thought we were dating, or on the verge of it. God, how stupid I had been. I did like Zach. I enjoyed his company. But I didn't want to feel his warm breath against my bare neck, did not want to curl up naked against him. I had never once—not for even one split second—pictured our bodies entwined.

And so, that night in the restaurant, I'd chosen the path of least resistance, one suggested by Victoria: an imaginary boyfriend. Richard, I'd named him. I'd thought it would be so easy, mention the boyfriend and Zach would beat a hasty retreat. But instead, he'd dug in his heels. Zach had suggested—plainly, but very seriously—that I ditch the new guy. In the end, I had no choice but to get to the point. The real point.

"I don't have romantic feelings for you."

"What does that have to do with anything?" Zach had laughed, like it was a joke. Except his laugh had been too loud and sharp. And when

I looked up from my menu, he was smiling too hard. "Lizzie, relax, I'm joking. I'm happy for you."

He wasn't. I'd known it then. But I'd decided to believe Zach. Because I'd wanted to.

I startled when someone touched my shoulder.

"Oh, I'm so sorry," Maude Lagueux gasped when I whipped around. She was standing behind me, a hand to her mouth. "I didn't see you were on the phone."

"What's wrong?" Vic asked on the other end.

"Can I call you back? There's somebody here."

"Sure," Vic said. "But you'd better. I need to know what the fertility doctor said."

I'd forgotten that I'd actually manufactured details of a whole doctor's appointment when Vic and I last spoke. The one where they did all the tests and told you what your actual chances were of having a baby. Sam wasn't the only one who was good at lying.

"I'll call back, definitely," I said. And when we spoke again, I'd finally tell Vic the truth about everything. I would.

I turned back to Maude once I'd hung up. Her face was taut, and in her fashionable but formless black shift dress and dull, earth-toned ballet flats, she looked funeral-worthy.

"I really didn't mean to interrupt," she said.

"That's okay."

"I was in court for the hearing. Why didn't you tell them about the alibi?" Her tone wasn't quite accusatory, but almost.

"The alibi is useful, but complicated."

Maude crossed her arms. She looked almost angry now. "But I was trying to help."

Help. Such an unfortunate choice of words. Had she fabricated the alibi? Honestly, I didn't want to know. Because if I knew for a fact that the alibi was false, I wouldn't be able to use it later at trial—that would be suborning perjury. Having doubts but not knowing anything for sure? That was a different story entirely.

"I understand," I said noncommittally.

"What happens now?" Maude asked, squeezing her arms tighter.

"Zach stays in jail and there'll be a trial," I said. "Between now and then we'll investigate. The best way to get Zach acquitted will be to find out who actually killed Amanda. That's not supposed to be our responsibility, but if the defendant didn't do it, a jury will want to know who did. Have the police interviewed you yet?" I asked, wondering what she'd shared with them, and whether Wendy Wallace might even already know about the alibi.

"They rescheduled the interview for tomorrow," Maude said. "Isn't that strange? That they're not in any rush? Don't they want all the facts they can get?"

They might have been worried Maude would present something contradictory to their theory of the case, maybe about this upstairs encounter Amanda supposedly had—it was the whole basis of Zach's supposed motive, as far as I could tell.

"They don't want *all* the facts," I said. "Only the ones that help their case."

"That doesn't sound right."

"It's not." I shrugged, because Wendy Wallace was only doing her job. "But it is the way the game is played."

AMANDA

Sarah swung open her door with a delighted grin. "Hell—" Her face fell when she saw the empty steps behind Amanda. "Seriously?"

"He'll be here any minute." It was stupid to keep lying, but Amanda felt so cornered.

Sarah made a face and crossed her arms. "Any minute?"

"Okay, he's not coming." Amanda hung her head. "Zach really is overwhelmed with the new business. He's working so hard that he can't even see straight, much less make it here for a dinner party. I'm sorry, I did try."

In truth, Amanda hadn't even asked Zach. He would have said no anyway, and Amanda would have had to suffer the usual back-and-forth with Zach's assistant Taylor. A sweet, plain-faced girl with a fixation on fashion magazines and an obsession with one unhealthy diet fad after another, Taylor did her best in a tough situation. If Amanda had asked about the dinner—via email, as was the procedure—Taylor would have written right back, as she always did, that she would check ASAP! Taylor would be just as kind-hearted when she wrote back to say: "Sorry! Zach can't squeeze it in tonight!"

Amanda didn't mind if Zach couldn't be there. But those exchanges with Taylor were excruciating. Just thinking about it now, standing there at Sarah's front door, Amanda's eyes filled with unexpected tears. She blinked and forced a smile, hoping Sarah wouldn't notice.

"Oh, no, no. Come on." Sarah tugged Amanda in the front door and gave her a hug. "Ignore me. I'm being a pain in the ass."

"I'll attest to that!" Kerry called cheerfully as he made his way down the stairs to the kitchen in gray sweatpants and a dark-blue Oklahoma City Thunder T-shirt. "Anyway, we don't need more husbands. *I* am plenty."

"Happy birthday!" Amanda called.

"Thank you, thank you." Kerry gestured regally as he hit the landing.

"This is for you." Amanda went over and thrust the wrapped bottle of whiskey, probably too forcefully, in Kerry's direction.

Kerry's face lit up. "For me?"

"Look at you," Sarah chirped at Kerry, then turned to Amanda. "You'd think I'd never bought him a gift in his entire life. Or that he hadn't been told only five minutes ago that sweatpants were not dinner wear."

"Yes, my love, but I like sweatpants and it is *my* birthday. As for your gifts, they come with strings," Kerry joked. "Taking the garbage out, listening to your stories. It's all so much *work*."

Sarah turned to Amanda and winked. "*That's* the true secret to a good marriage: strategic quid pro quo."

Kerry excitedly untied the ribbon at the top of the silvery bag as though it weren't already completely obvious from the shape that it was a bottle of something.

"Wow!" he exclaimed once he'd gotten it open.

His expression turned thoughtful as he studied the bottle. Did he know how much it had cost? Amanda leaned in to point at the label. "I remembered you said that your family was from—"

"I know," Kerry said quietly, seeming genuinely touched. "It's also a damn nice bottle of whiskey."

"What about his family?" Sarah moved closer to investigate.

"It's from Cork," Kerry said. "Where my grandparents live. I mentioned it once, and Amanda, *thoughtfully*, was listening. Thank you very much. And I didn't even have to take out the garbage or kill any water bugs to get it."

"But you're so good at water bug assassination," Sarah razzed him back. "Hey, there's an idea if things get really tight for us: the coveralls, the spray can, you'd be a natural."

Kerry rolled his eyes, then leaned in to hug Amanda. She felt so safe for a moment that it tugged her tears back to the surface.

Her dad had called, again, right before she'd reached Sarah and Kerry's door. She was trying to brush it off, but that was getting harder and harder to do. How *had* he found her in Brooklyn? How did he know to even look? That police officer had been right: it didn't make sense, not with all the steps Zach had taken to protect their privacy.

"Thank you again for this," Kerry said, releasing Amanda. He held the bottle up. "I will genuinely treasure it. And now I am going to retire downstairs to my man cave to watch some birthday baseball, if that's okay with you ladies. You may send Sebe down when he arrives, even though he is French and hence useless."

"Can you clean up while you're down there? Somebody's going to call the health department soon." Sarah looked at Amanda. "I won't even go down there anymore."

"Ah, my plan is working perfectly." Kerry grinned, then leaned over to kiss Sarah on the cheek and pat her rear end. "Thank you, dear, for arranging my birthday dinner. I do appreciate it and you. I will gladly slay water bugs for you any day."

Once Kerry had gone, Sarah bent over to remove a perfectly roasted chicken from the oven, then turned to toss a quinoa salad. Amanda watched, mesmerized by Sarah's effortless command of the kitchen, which was cheerful and homey if somewhat dated, like the rest of the house.

"That looks amazing," Amanda said, eyeing the roasting pan.

Sarah nodded at her handiwork. "Not bad, right? If only Zach knew what he was missing."

Amanda closed her eyes and sighed. "I really am so sorry."

"No, *I'm* sorry. My teasing is such a bad habit. It's a compulsion. Ask Kerry. But I do worry about you. It's all none of my . . ." Sarah stopped tossing abruptly, a salad spoon gripped upright in each hand. "Oh, fuck it. You already know I think everything is my business. So here it is: Amanda, you are a surrendered wife, and it is fucking disturbing. I don't know what it's like out in Palo Alto, but here in Brooklyn husbands and wives are equal partners, no matter who brings home the bigger paycheck. Up until the foundation, I've always stayed home, but Kerry listens to me. Because he loves me, and knows that I love him. That's how marriage is supposed to work. You know that, right?"

"Yes," Amanda said, and she did. In theory. "But you and Kerry have the perfect marriage."

"No, we don't!" Sarah cried. "I made out with my kid's soccer coach!" She leaned back, double-checking that Kerry really had gone downstairs.

"But Kerry forgave you," Amanda said.

"Yes, but not because we're perfect. He forgave me because we love each other. There's a difference. Believe me, we still have *plenty* of problems." Sarah looked for a moment like she was going to elaborate, but did not. "Everybody does. But you need to at least have a voice, Mandy. Period. Otherwise, I'm sorry, but it's not really a marriage—it's, I don't know, servitude."

"I have a voice," Amanda offered lamely.

"You do not!" Sarah cried, but then she closed her eyes and took a breath. She laid her palms flat against the counter. "When you cannot make your husband come to a single dinner party—I'm sorry, but you do not have a voice. That's a fact. And, as your friend, it's my job to be honest. Frankly, I think it's a risky way to live."

"Risky? What do you mean?"

"I mean in sickness and health and loneliness and despair and all that," she said. "When you're married, you're each other's first line of defense. You're supposed to take care of each other."

Sarah was right. And how could Zach possibly protect Amanda—from her loneliness or her despair, or her bad dreams, much less from her dad—if he didn't even know about any of it? They'd been together more than a decade, and Zach didn't know anything about the awful things her dad had done.

Amanda nodded. "I know what you're saying is true. I do."

"Good," Sarah said with a satisfied nod, then turned to move the chicken from the roasting pan onto the chopping block. The doorbell rang just as Sarah stuck a fork into the chicken and set down a huge knife for carving.

"That must be Maude and Sebe. I'll be right back. Watch the chicken."

A moment later, there was the sound of the front door opening, followed by Sarah's lively, high-pitched hellos.

"Oh, good. The coast is clear," Kerry said, breezing back into the kitchen. Furtively, he grabbed a roasted potato out of the pan and popped it into his mouth. He grimaced from the heat, fanning his open lips. In his sweatpants and T-shirt, he was all belly, like an oversize little boy. He peered then at Amanda's earrings. "Wow, those are something. Don't let Sarah see them, for God's sake."

Amanda put a hand up to her ear. *Drop* diamond earrings. What was wrong with her?

"Shoot," she said. "I shouldn't have worn them—you're right. They're too much. I had a donor meeting. I forgot to take them off."

"That was a joke! Actually, if I was you, I'd make sure that Sarah *does* see the earrings." He winked. "Then the next time she tries to ride you about your marriage, you can be like: Remember the earrings?"

Amanda smiled. Kerry was more perceptive than he let on.

"It's the birthday boy!" Maude called as she entered the kitchen and kissed Kerry affectionately on both cheeks. He pulled her into a long, warm hug. When they separated, she motioned to his sweatpants. "I see you pulled out all the stops. Has Sarah seen you? I can't imagine she's going to approve of that ensemble."

"It's my birthday," he protested.

Sebe appeared in the doorway behind Maude, looking handsome as always in his crisp linen shirt. But the chill between him and Maude was obvious. She was right. The situation with Sophia was causing a strain.

Sebe leaned in to kiss Amanda on both cheeks. "Very good to see you."

"Ugh," Sarah said as she emerged back into the kitchen, motioning at Amanda, Sebe, and Maude. "Why do you all have to look so good tonight?" She gestured at her own stained button-down.

"That's because you've been cooking for us!" Maude cried. Then she shot a cool look at her husband. "Sebe, make yourself useful. Pour Sarah a glass of wine."

Sebe's face tensed. He didn't look at Maude as he made his way over, filled a glass, and handed it to Sarah. They clinked glasses.

Sarah waved a hand at Kerry. "At least we're both pathetic slobs."

"Hey!" Kerry raised his arms. "It's my fucking birthday!"

And everyone laughed.

By the time they were all seated at the dinner table, Maude had brightened considerably. The couple glasses of wine she'd quickly kicked back seemed to have done the trick. But she and Sebe were avoiding even looking at each other. Amanda didn't want to take pleasure in their tension, but it was honestly a relief to see that even they did not have a stress-free marriage. Maybe Sarah was right: no one did. Soon the conversation turned back to Sarah's favorite subject of scorn: the Brooklyn Country Day PTA.

"Remember when it was the panini press everyone was shouting about?" Sebe laughed good-naturedly.

"An unconscionable risk to their bodily integrity!" Sarah bellowed. She made her voice high-pitched. "But Sawyer loves her burrata and free-range tomato. She deserves the right for self-actualization."

"I don't know, Sarah." Kerry laughed. "I think this hacking thing might finally be your undoing. If you don't have it sorted out soon, they'll have you drawn and quartered."

"Oh, yes, the *hacking*." She narrowed her eyes at Kerry, then looked away with a sharp smile. "You know, I actually got a phishing email of my own the other day."

Kerry's brow furrowed. "You haven't given away all our money to some long-lost aunt who's down on her luck in Dubai?"

"What money, Kerry?" Sarah asked. Kerry laughed as Sarah went on. "Anyway, it looked like a membership renewal from Netflix. But no, I didn't click on it. Because *I* am not stupid. But, boy, did it make me glad that *I* don't have any deep, dark secrets for the hackers to find."

"Secrets?" Amanda asked.

"Oh, yes," Sarah said. "Apparently it's secrets these people are after. Embarrassing secrets. They find something on your computer and then they threaten to post it on Park Slope Parents if you don't pay up, though I don't actually think they've done that yet. One person, who shall not be named, had an email pop up in her in-box, forwarded from her husband's account. It was an exchange between him and an escort about the next time they were going to meet. One who special-izes in S & M. The husband is a submissive, apparently."

"Someone told you that?" Maude gasped. "Who?"

"I am sworn to secrecy. Come on, I love hearing gossip, but I do not perpetuate it," Sarah said primly. "At this point, I wish people would stop telling me all the lurid details. I already know *way* more than I ever wanted to."

"Who emails with an escort?" Kerry laughed. "Did he make her fill out a W-9, too?"

Sarah ignored Kerry and turned to Sebe and Maude. "I know you guys are all free to be you and me, but I'd be careful what you put in writing these days."

"Oh, I don't need escorts," Sebe said with perfect deadpan timing.

Maude was the only one who didn't laugh. She was staring down at her untouched food.

"Touché!" Kerry cried at Sebe, though a beat too late and a little too loud. "Sebe could probably go and stand in the middle of the sidewalk and women would show up and open their legs."

Sarah made a disgusted face and swatted at Kerry. "Ew."

"Oh, come on, that was a joke." Kerry laughed. "I thought we were all joking here."

"It was colorful, Kerry," Sebe said diplomatically. "Disgusting, but colorful."

"Thank you, Sebe."

"Why don't they steal credit card numbers or something? Like normal criminals?" Maude asked with uncharacteristic spite. "This is such a sick, twisted violation."

Amanda could think only of her dad, who'd even had a cameo in her now familiar dream the night before. He'd appeared in the middle— Amanda transported nonsensically back home in the midst of all that running in those dark, damp trees—his frame so large he almost filled the doorway of her bedroom. He was silent and stooped, the way he'd been whenever he drunkenly mistook her bedroom for the bathroom in the middle of the night. She couldn't count the times he'd peed right on her floor. Thinking about it now, Amanda was sure her dad had enjoyed embarrassing her in that way.

"Some people love to shame others. They feed off of it." Amanda's voice was so venomous it was barely recognizable. "It's worse than sick. It's evil. They shouldn't be allowed to live."

And now everyone at the table was staring at her.

"Cash for escorts, Amanda," Kerry joked. "Always cash."

They were still all looking at her, though.

"Sorry. It's just—my childhood wasn't the easiest," Amanda said, because she needed to say something. And at least that was the truth. Though her explanation seemed only to make everyone more uncomfortable. "That's all."

"Then it's all the more credit to you that you turned out to be such a nice person," Kerry said as he opened another bottle of wine and began refilling everyone's glasses. "You're not wrong, anyway," he added, sitting back down. "My stepfather broke my arm—on purpose—when I was fourteen. I think to shame me in a way. Everyone's got a history. Even here on Sesame Street."

"What are you talking about?" Sarah looked confused and annoyed. "Your stepfather is such a nice guy."

Kerry smiled, but in a strange, sad way. "You don't know *everything* about me, dear."

"That's awful," Sebe said quietly.

Maude looked sick. "Kerry, I'm so sorry."

Sarah was staring at her husband. Amanda was just glad the focus was off her.

"A toast to the future." Kerry raised his glass. "And to great friends, who make the very best family."

"To friends!" everyone called.

To the future, Amanda thought as their glasses clinked like wind chimes. *To the future.*

KRELL INDUSTRIES

CONFIDENTIAL MEMORANDUM
NOT FOR DISTRIBUTION

June 30

To: Brooklyn Country Day Board of Directors
From: Krell Industries
Subject: Data Breach & Cyber Incident Investigation—Progress Report

The following is a summary of key data collected and interviews conducted.

Data Collection

Data monitoring continues. There have been no additional intrusions into the Brooklyn Country Day information systems, though additional families continue to receive new threats.

Interview Summaries

SUBJECT FAMILY 0016: MPP received an email from an anonymous source that contained screenshots of correspondence he has received from various creditors, along with a demand for a $20,000 cash transfer. Failure to comply with the cash transfer demand would result in the photos being posted to PSP.

SUBJECT FAMILY 0031: MPP has not had any personal experience with hacking. But he knows of an individual (identified herein as Person of Interest A) whose son was expelled last year for behavioral issues who indicated a desire to retaliate by damaging the reputation of Brooklyn Country Day.

EMPLOYEE INTERVIEW 0009: Current employee reports that a former employee (identified herein as Person of Interest B) said, after being fired from soccer coaching responsibilities, that he would do anything he could to "hurt" the school.

PRELIMINARY CONCLUSIONS

At this juncture, not a single victim has complied with the cash demands, and yet no information has been posted to PSP. This raises the question of whether financial gain is the true motive. Further, information uncovered suggests that the perpetrator is a preexisting affiliate of Brooklyn Country Day—an employee, student, or parent.

LIZZIE

I slid into bed, careful not to wake Sam. I'd stayed at the office late to work on that cell-phone-battery motion to dismiss. Conveniently, it also allowed me to avoid confronting Sam about the earring. In fact, I'd pretty much decided I wanted to let it go altogether. I'd already jumped to the wrong conclusion once, about Enid's and the matches. Really, my doubt was like a muscle that spasmed with the slightest pressure. I couldn't trust my knee-jerk response to anything.

So instead I kept my mouth shut and left Sam asleep, using my little booklight in the dark to read more of Amanda's troubling journals, which continued to make my shitstorm of a life seem absolutely flawless by comparison. At the office, I'd made it through three months of her time in Park Slope, but still no mention of exactly who Amanda thought was following her, just "he" and "him." And then, as I furtively read in bed, there it was, in one of the very last entries, wedged between an account of a coffee with Sarah and Maude at Blue Bottle and a meeting at Hope First:

I'm starting to worry Daddy doesn't want money. That he came to Brooklyn because he wants to drag me back to St. Colomb Falls, to prove he owns me even now. But I won't let him. I will not.

When I sat up, the journal slipped through my fingers and bumped Sam's shoulder. Amanda's father was there in Park Slope? It was him stalking her. It had to be.

Sam startled awake as if from a bad dream.

"Oh, it's you," he exhaled, relieved, then wrapped an arm tight around my hips. I bristled. So much for letting things go. "What are you reading?"

"It's a journal."

"You're reading somebody's journal?" Sam mumbled. "That's not very nice."

"It belongs to a woman who was killed in Park Slope."

"What?" Sam asked with a half laugh. "In Park Slope? When?" He sounded much more awake now.

"Center Slope. It was over last weekend, when we were away," I said.

"That's awful." He was quiet for a moment. "Where was it?"

"Montgomery Place. She had a son. Ten years old. I'm representing her husband." It was a jab—*see all the things you don't know about me.* I couldn't help it.

"Representing her husband?" Sam asked. "I didn't think Young & Crane handled cases like that."

"They don't. *I* do. We were friends in law school. Until it got . . . complicated," I said, intentionally suggestive. "I think he's innocent."

Sam rose up on his elbows. "You *think*? Who is this guy, Lizzie? What's going on?"

He sounded wounded. And I was the tiniest bit glad.

"His name is Zach Grayson," I said. "We were friends, but then he wanted to be more than friends. I didn't want that, so we weren't friends anymore."

That dinner where I'd told Zach about my imaginary boyfriend had ended politely. But, I now remembered, it had also been our last. The next time I'd seen Zach, at the law school's library, he'd smiled and said hello, but didn't stop to chat. Two weeks later and he was no longer even saying hi. I didn't push for explanations either. I figured Zach would be back in touch with me eventually. When he was ready. Instead, he'd disappeared permanently. Not from the law school, but from my life. And I'd been relieved. It made me feel guilty at the time. Maybe that was why I'd agreed to see Zach in Rikers in the first place.

"And now you're representing him?" Sam sat up. "This guy who wanted to date you?"

"Yes. I went to see him at Rikers." Another jab.

"Rikers?" he asked. "You hate Rikers. You told me you'd never go back there. Anyway, you're supposed to be doing corporate law."

"Yes, thanks to you I am doing corporate law." I yanked the blanket back and swung my feet to the floor, trying to stay calm.

"What's that supposed to mean?" Sam asked.

Oh, no, Sam didn't get to play dumb about that. Not after everything he'd put me through. Suddenly, all the anger I'd been pushing down for so long was about to blow.

"That means just what I said: that it's *your* fault I'm working at Young & Crane. That the career I worked so hard for is ruined, thanks to your accident. Isn't that what you're always apologizing for?"

Sam's eyes widened. "So because of the accident I'm not allowed to have an opinion about anything you do ever again?" He was shouting, but he sounded more hurt, which only made me more enraged. "How is that going to work, Lizzie?"

I jumped out of bed and turned to glare at him in the shadowy halo of my booklight.

"You can have an opinion. Right after you tell me whose fucking earring I found in your bag."

Sam recoiled, then froze. Only silence followed. Too much of it. *Fuck.*

Finally, Sam sucked in some air like he was about to launch into an explanation. Instead, he flopped back down on the bed. Eyes up on the ceiling, he exhaled loudly. Then he lay so flat and motionless. In the cold, endless silence, my stomach tucked into a fist.

Fuck. Fuck. Fuck.

"I don't know whose earring it is," Sam said at last, his voice small and scared. "That's the truth."

Denial or defensiveness, clumsy lying, maybe even anger, I was prepared for all those things. But not fear.

"You don't know?" *Take it back*, I wanted to say. *Take it back*.

"I wish to God that I did know. I've searched and searched and searched my memory. I've tried to picture the earring. Tried to imagine who it might belong to or how it might have gotten into my pocket. That's where I found it, in the pocket of my sweatshirt. But there's nothing, Lizzie. Nothing."

In another marriage, this would have been a ridiculous excuse. But in ours, lost time was a shameful fact of life.

"When?" I whispered. "When did you find it?"

"The night I hit my head. I found it in my pocket before we left for the hospital."

I swallowed. "Where did you go drinking that night?" I'd specifically avoided asking this the day after. I'd avoided asking it in all the days that followed.

In my defense, there'd been an emergency to attend to. I'd found Sam bleeding, called the ambulance, then dealt with the EMTs in our apartment. Once they'd realized that all that blood had been from just the one cut—apparently heads bleed a lot—they'd recommended we go on our own by taxi to Methodist Hospital, a much cheaper option than the unnecessary ambulance. After that there was the waiting in the ER, and then the stitches and the ride home and cleaning up. When all that was done, I needed to head in to the office before we left for the weekend.

Besides, when you were married to an alcoholic, you got tired of excavating details. Don't ask, don't tell. It was easier that way to pretend you had absolutely zero role in anything that happened to you. Or not you. Me. That was what *I* had always done—wipe away the inconvenient facts to keep my eyes on the prize: forward momentum.

"We went to Freddy's for a drink."

"Freddy's?" I shot back. Sam had said "the old dads" went to the dive bar Freddy's every week after basketball, but that he never joined them. A bonus, ongoing lie tacked onto a single betrayal. Perfect. "I suppose you've been going every week?"

"I figured you knew," he said.

"You figured I *knew* you were lying to me?" I shouted. "Why the hell wouldn't I say something?"

"It does sound stupid now," he said. "But that is what I thought. That we were just agreeing to disagree."

"For the record, I have never thought you were being anything other than completely honest with me." I swallowed hard. What a lie that was. "I guess I'm the asshole then."

"You're not an asshole, Lizzie. I am, obviously," Sam said quietly. "But I don't know whose earring it is. That's the honest truth."

"Did you ask the other guys you were with about that night?"

"I only have an email for the guy from the *Journal* who got me into the league, and he's away for work. He hasn't gotten back to me. And that was the last game for the summer," he said. "I know I was at the bar when my friend left. I remember wishing him luck on his story. After that, I was with one of the other guys. But he's got a wife and kids and a big career so I don't know how late he would have been out. Then again, he was also always trying to get us to go to a strip club, so who knows."

"A strip club?" My voice was shaking. "I thought these were old dads."

"Who do you think goes to strip clubs? Anyway, I wouldn't have gone. I hate those places. You know that."

"Awesome. What a relief."

"I don't think I did anything with anyone, Lizzie. I honestly don't. I wouldn't do that. I love you."

"Oh please, Sam!" I snapped back. "In a blackout you're a completely different person. You've said that to me so many times. You can't turn around now and claim you weren't with someone while blacked out because you're not that person. I've been here the whole time, remember! I know how this works. *You don't know what happened.* So *anything* could have."

Sam took a deep breath. "I don't think there was any other woman. I don't want that to be true," he said evenly. "But you're right. If I'm one hundred percent honest, I can't be sure."

And there it was: Sam had admitted there was a possibility he'd been with another woman. And to think I'd almost let the whole thing go. I pushed myself off the wall and turned for the door.

"Lizzie, where are you going?" Sam called after me, his voice desperate.

"I don't know," I said. "I have no fucking idea."

In daylight first thing the next morning, Rikers looked even more like a refugee encampment, my view of it probably not improved by the three fitful hours of sleep I'd gotten on our lumpy couch. There were more visiting families this time, including children, lined up along the wall as I stood in the attorney security line to request that Zach be brought up. A guard in uniform walked a drug- or bomb-sniffing dog back and forth in front of them as though they were nothing more than terrified suitcases. One little girl started to cry. What kind of justice was this, and for whom? Zach was rich and white and had the resources of a huge Manhattan law firm at his disposal, and even his best-case scenario at the moment was to live long enough to make it to trial.

When Zach finally appeared in the attorney room, his eye looked a bit better, but there was a new long purple bruise across his left cheekbone and a fresh cut at the corner of his mouth.

He moved slowly as he lowered into the chair across from me. "It looks worse than it is."

But this time he sounded less sure.

"I'm sorry," I said.

"It's not your fault."

"We might be able to get you moved," I offered, though I wasn't even sure that was true.

"Moved where? To protective custody?" Zach's leg started to bounce, but weakly. "The box?"

"I guess, maybe."

"That's solitary. Literally there is no difference. They protect you by giving you the same thing they punish other people with. Ironic, huh?" He sounded so wizened, like he'd been in Rikers years and not days. He wouldn't look at me. "The box might kill me faster than the guys in here. I need out, that's all."

Time was up. Zach deserved the truth.

"We lost the bail appeal." There was no way to sugarcoat it. "And they've brought the murder indictment. As we expected."

Zach was silent for a long time. Finally he shook his head as his leg began to bounce with more vigor. "There was a part of me that was really hoping for a miracle: that the actual truth would matter."

"The truth will matter," I said. "Facts will matter. But at trial. Not so much at bail hearings." I pulled out a pad. "Which means I am going to have to ask some tough questions, and you're going to need to be completely honest with me, okay?"

"Okay," Zach said, but he seemed so utterly dejected.

I wondered if I should come back, give him a chance to process. It wasn't as if there was some big rush to get all the details now. His trial wouldn't be for months. But then, I was there already. It was probably best to get to work.

"Why were you looking into plane tickets to Brazil?" It was the one fact that Wendy Wallace had raised that did trouble me. Prosecutors loved consciousness of guilt. Wendy would probably try to use this "proof of flight" at trial to show premeditation.

"Oh, jaguars," Zach said, like this should have been obvious.

"The car?"

Zach's eyes snapped up to mine in that sudden, too forceful way of his. "No, no, the animal. There's this place in Brazil, the Pantanal, where you're supposed to be able to see them really easily," he said. "Case is obsessed with jaguars. I was thinking about taking him to see them in Brazil when he got back from camp. You know, a father-and-son adventure." He was quiet for a moment. "Let's face it, I probably never would have actually taken the time off from work. But I do think about things like that. It's the following through I'm not so good at."

It was a decent explanation, one that I was hoping would hold up once I cross-referenced it with the dates of the actual tickets and his assistant's recollection.

"Do you know why an accountant for the foundation would have been trying to meet with Amanda?"

Zach shook his head, but seemed unconcerned. "Not to sound like a jerk, but when you get to a certain point financially, money becomes more of an administrative detail. I hire accountants so I don't have to deal with that sort of thing. But if it had been something serious, Amanda would have come to me. And she didn't."

"I'll follow up myself. If that's okay with you," I said. "I'm going to need to access some funds anyway to pay our experts. Lab tests aren't cheap. I'm assuming the accountant can help me with that, too?"

"Definitely," Zach said. "You'll need an authorization, though."

"I assumed. I brought a form that should work. Before I go, I'll get the guard to have you sign it. I'll need the firm name and the name of the actual accountant, too."

"I know it's PricewaterhouseCoopers, and the guy's name is Teddy. I don't know his last name. I only remember his first name because it's ridiculous. There can't be more than one adult man named Teddy working there, right? And let me know what he says," Zach said. "It would be good to know if I'm about to be sandbagged by something else."

"Speaking of being sandbagged . . . ," I began. "I know we touched on this. But just to revisit that warrant from the loitering for a second, are you sure—"

"Jesus, let it go, Lizzie!" Zach's outburst was so loud and sudden I flinched. Immediately, he held up his hands. "I'm sorry. I didn't mean to shout. I know the warrant looks bad. Believe me, I do. But it was, what, thirteen years ago? Anyway, there's nothing I can do about it."

Zach looked beaten and defenseless on the other side of the plexiglass.

"It's okay, it's fine," I said, though it wasn't really. "I do have one potential piece of good news. I mean, good news might be a poor characterization. But it looks like Amanda's father is a legitimate alternate suspect."

"Her father?" Zach looked confused. "What do you mean?"

"He was harassing her. Calling and hanging up. Following her, too. And he . . . I think he was abusive, sexually, when she was younger. Amanda recounts a series of rapes in her older journals when she was twelve, maybe thirteen."

"What?" Zach looked disgusted, then enraged. "Why didn't she tell me?"

"I don't know," I said, though Zach had said himself that he and Amanda had a distant marriage. Why was he so surprised? "I think we should at least try to track him down. What was Amanda's maiden name?"

"Lynch," he said without hesitation. "But I don't know her dad's first name or where he lives now or anything like that. I never met the guy, and the few times Amanda mentioned him, it was only in passing: 'my dad.' Actually, I think she called him 'daddy,' which now seems even creepier." He grimaced. "*Twelve?* Case is ten. That's disgusting."

I nodded. "It is."

I wrote down "Lynch" and underlined it. Now I had a last name, and the town—St. Colomb Falls—even the name of her old church from her journals. Enough to build on.

"It shouldn't be our job to provide alternate suspects. But a jury will want somebody else to blame," I said. "It will be good to find him."

But was I seriously going to be the person defending Zach by the time a jury was empaneled? It had been one thing to handle Zach's bail appeal, but a full-blown murder trial? Because Paul had a thing for Wendy Wallace? Because I felt guilty I'd let Zach down easy a million years ago? Because I was angry at Sam? Or was it actually something else, *someone* else, I was compensating for? The thought had occurred to me. But none of those were good reasons for staying on as Zach's lawyer. Not when what I really needed to do was deal with the mess my life had become.

"I'd also like to talk to Amanda's friend Carolyn. Seems like she'd probably have some insight. Do you have her number?"

"I don't know who that is, I'm sorry."

"Amanda's best friend from growing up?" I pressed, sounding almost as judgmental as Sarah had with me. "She lives in the city. Apparently Amanda spent a fair amount of time with her."

"I don't think I've ever even heard that name," Zach said. Again his response seemed authentic.

"Amanda wrote about Carolyn in her journal. Sarah and Maude knew about her, too." I was hoping something would click for him. "But they hadn't met her."

"Maybe she's the one who killed Amanda, then," Zach said, his face brightening. "I mean, if there's somebody here from her life back then, I guarantee it wasn't for a good reason." He took a sharp breath, shook his head. "I was Amanda's knight in shining armor, you know. And I did rescue her in some ways, which felt good. I worked my ass off so she—well, we—could have all the comforts money could buy. Maybe that's not all that mattered, though." Zach looked down. "I should have taken better care of her. Isn't that what a good spouse does? Look at you."

"Me?" I asked.

Zach's eyes flicked up, then back down. "Taking care of your husband, by changing jobs and all that."

"I guess," I said, feeling the fog of shame descend. Was my story with Sam that obvious?

"You guess?" he asked. "You've made *huge* sacrifices. I mean, your job of all things. But you did that because your husband needed you. You accepted his problems as your problems. You're a much better person than me."

Except I hate him for it.

"I also spoke to Maude," I said, anything to move the conversation off Sam.

"The one who had the party?" he asked. "What about her?"

"She told me that you and she were together at the time of Amanda's death." I hesitated, but only for a second. "*Together* together." I paused again. "Upstairs."

"Upstairs?" Zach asked, curious but not remotely defensive. "I feel like you're trying to telegraph something, but I don't know what you mean. I'm sorry."

"Upstairs at the party where the partner-swapping was going on."

"What?" Zach laughed hard. "Maude said we had sex that night?"

"Yes," I said. "She said you were with her until two a.m., providing you with an alibi, assuming the time line ends up corresponding with Amanda's official time of death and your call to the police. It's complicated under the circumstances, but it could be potentially useful."

"Um, maybe. If it was true. First of all, I called the police, well, I don't remember exactly what time, but it was well before midnight." Zach looked exasperated. "And not only did Maude and I not have sex that night, we never even met. I saw her at the party because somebody pointed her out, but we didn't talk." He shook his head in disbelief. "I have no idea why she'd say that. Maybe she's had sex with so many people, she's lost track."

I approached one of the three guards near the exit after Zach and I were done. He was young and wiry, with a cynical but not unkind look in his eyes.

"Could you have Zach Grayson sign this?" I handed him the power-of-attorney letter. "I need to take it with me."

He regarded it skeptically for a moment. "Sure thing."

I leaned back against the chilled cinder block to wait. Before I left Zach, I'd had him go over the rest of the time line from the night Amanda died.

They arrived at Maude's party shortly before 9:00 p.m., at which point he and Amanda had gone their separate ways. He'd chatted with a few people at the party, but mostly he just "observed" from the edge of the living room. The most substantial conversation Zach had was with Sarah, who'd wanted to know all about how he'd become such a wildly successful self-made man, which sounded to me like she'd been mocking him. After that, Zach left. To take that walk on the Brooklyn Heights Promenade. It was around 9:30 p.m. by then, and he'd texted Amanda after he'd gone. It wasn't clear if he'd looked for her before leaving, but I got the sense that he did not. Zach was only at the party for thirty minutes. When he returned home, approximately two hours later, Amanda was dead.

Zach did provide me with a few physical descriptions of people from the party who might be able to attest to his departure time: *Guy with the jester's hat? Old woman in pigtails? Bald guy, Wellfleet T-shirt?* I asked him several times about this walk on the promenade, which was perhaps the weakest alibi in the history of all alibis. It sounded like a lie on its face. Who left a party to go out walking alone at that time of night in a place that was a cab ride away? Yet Zach insisted that was exactly what had happened. Could someone have seen him? I'd asked. "Sure, maybe," he'd said, but not in a way that made me feel like I should send Millie searching for witnesses. There was the driver of the cab Zach claimed to have taken to Brooklyn Heights, for instance. He'd hailed it from the street, though—there was no record of it. But why would Zach be lying about his alibi and yet be unwilling to take the one Maude had offered him?

Amanda's father—viable alternate suspect no. 1—remained our best defense. We—or ideally somebody other than me—needed to find him and prove he'd been in Brooklyn that night. Otherwise, I had a bad feeling that Wendy Wallace's very well-crafted story would bury Zach alive.

And I didn't want to be responsible. I needed to go back to Paul and tell him that we should hand Zach's defense off to someone now, well before trial. I could say that a murder trial would interfere with my other matters, all of which were also Paul's. He might even be happy for an excuse to drop the case; he'd been able to see Wendy, maybe he'd already gotten it out of his system.

"Here you go," the guard said when he returned, handing back Zach's signed power of attorney. "You know, you should tell your client to be careful. He's going to get hurt for real one of these times."

"I know," I said, relieved and surprised that a guard was acknowledging the assaults. "Is there something we could do, or I—I could do to help him? Maybe some advice, or someplace he could be moved?"

The guard tilted his head, like he was sure I was messing with him.

"Uh, how about you start by telling him to stop bashing his own head in."

GRAND JURY TESTIMONY

KENNETH JAMESON,

called as a witness the 7th of July and was examined and testified as follows:

EXAMINATION

BY MS. WALLACE:

Q: Thank you for being here, Mr. Jameson.

A: Yes. Okay.

Q: Can you state your job title for the record, please?

A: Senior New York City crime scene analyst, Second Department.

Q: And how long have you been a crime scene analyst?

A: Twenty-five years. I've been a senior analyst for fifteen years.

Q: Did you visit the scene at 597 Montgomery Place in the early morning hours of July 3rd?

A: Yes.

Q: And what did you observe at the scene?

A: There was a deceased female. Extensive blood spatter.

Q: Could you determine the cause of death at that time?

A: I made a preliminary determination. Cause,
homicide. Method, blunt-force trauma.

Q: Have you identified the murder weapon?

A: Not definitively. We are waiting for final test
results.

Q: Have you made a preliminary assessment?

A: Yes.

Q: And what is that assessment?

A: That Mrs. Grayson was struck with a golf club.

Q: How did you reach this conclusion?

A: First, it was found at the scene right next to the
body. Second, it was found to have blood on it matching
the victim's.

Q: Anything else?

A: She had a defensive wound to her arm. She held it
up to block the blow.

Q: Anything else?

A: The blood spatter patterns in the area of the body
are consistent with that object being used to strike the
victim repeatedly.

Q: Can you elaborate, please?

A: You can tell from the shape of the blood drops and
their pattern the manner in which they were left. Blood
spatter provides a blueprint for the way a particular
crime was committed.

Q: And what did you discern from the blood spatter
pattern in this case?

A: That Mrs. Grayson was struck multiple times about
the head.

Q: Anything else that points to the golf club as the
murder weapon?

A: Preliminary analysis suggests that the wounds are
consistent with the size and shape of the golf club.

Q: Meaning?

A: I believe she was struck with a golf club about the head when she was standing, then again several times after she had fallen. Her being at different heights as the attack continued accounts for the various locations and the variety in the type of blood spatter.

Q: So, in layman's terms and based only on your preliminary analysis, of course, what is your professional conclusion as to the manner and cause of Mrs. Grayson's death?

A: That she was beaten to death with a golf club while at the bottom of the stairs in her home.

AMANDA

Amanda awoke later than usual the day after Kerry's birthday dinner, her body beginning to acclimate to her child-free days. Almost as if Case had never even existed. It frightened her a little. But at least Amanda hadn't had the dream again, had she? That was something. Maybe getting used to Case being gone wasn't the worst thing.

It was 8:15 a.m., the bed next to her long empty. Zach was always up and out at 5:30 a.m. to the gym and then to work. He did not believe in idleness.

What was he doing, though, she wondered, at this exact moment? And why was he always at the office so late, and so early? Did he *really* need to work quite *that* much? Kerry was a lawyer and Sebe was a doctor and a tech start-up entrepreneur, and neither of them put in hours like Zach. Or was he not really working the whole time he was gone? The thought had, of course, occurred to Amanda before. She was not stupid.

But when Case was around, Amanda always had more important things to worry about. And their life moved more smoothly when she held her tongue. Amanda thought back to the last time she'd forgotten that. They'd been in their second home in Davis and Zach had been complaining again about his most recent boss—he was not as smart or talented or hardworking or insightful as Zach. And Amanda was pregnant and so nauseous at the time. It was like their entire reality slipped her mind.

"You never like anybody," she'd snapped at Zach. "Have you ever thought about whether the problem is you?"

Zach's eyes had flashed. But then Amanda watched his face shift like he'd just decided something. Calmly he set down his knife and fork and leaned back in his chair, arms crossed. Just glaring at her. In silence. Amanda had squirmed in her chair. It felt like an eternity before he finally spoke.

"What did you just say?"

Zach was looking at Amanda like he despised her. Like he wanted her dead. No, like she already was dead, and all that remained was the disposing of her body.

"Nothing," she'd said quickly, wrapping her hands around her belly. "I didn't say anything."

Even now, Amanda felt queasy remembering. But she couldn't risk staying silent. Certainly not about her dad. Case would be back in a few weeks. Amanda needed to find her voice immediately.

She could even start right then, but with something small. She could call Zach at work and tell Taylor she needed to speak with him directly. Then she could do that simple, ordinary thing other wives did every single goddamn day: ask her husband if he would be home for dinner. And she could act like she was entitled to the answer.

Full of purpose, Amanda rolled over and grabbed her phone. But there was already a new voice mail. Not from an unknown number, luckily. This was a 212 area code. She tapped to listen.

"Hello, Mrs. Grayson, this is Teddy Buckley, your accountant from PricewaterhouseCoopers?" he began. "We had an appointment this morning? I'm at your office, and no one is answering. I don't know if we got our signals crossed, but I really do need to meet with you as soon as possible. I'll come back tomorrow."

Shoot. Had she really just forgotten, though? Or had it been more deliberate than that? But leaving Teddy Buckley waiting outside the foundation's office at such an early hour was rude, not assertive. Amanda was going to need to be a lot more precise in how she stood up for herself if she was going to get Zach to listen.

The phone lit up with another call. Carolyn.

"Hello?"

"How was the dinner party?" Carolyn asked. The sound of a busy Manhattan street was in the background—horns, voices—and Carolyn was breathing hard, as though she was walking quickly. "Did Sarah give you shit about Zach not being there?"

The "shit about Zach" role belonged to Carolyn. She got territorial.

"It was a little awkward," Amanda said. "But they were all really sweet and understanding in the end."

"Hmm. Sweet," Carolyn said skeptically. "Just don't get too sucked in. You know how those women can be."

"Those women" were any of the wives and mothers Amanda had become friends with in any of the towns they'd moved to over the years. To Carolyn they were all the same. But Amanda believed that Sarah and Maude were different. They were real friends. They cared about her. She didn't want Carolyn to undermine that.

"Hey, could you meet for a run after work?" Amanda asked. "I need to talk to you about something."

"What?"

"I've been thinking about what you said—what you've been saying—about Zach." Amanda sucked in a breath. It was amazing how scary it was, admitting just that.

"And?" Carolyn sounded cautiously optimistic.

"I want to talk to you about it when I see you."

"Um, okay, sure." Carolyn sounded disappointed now. "But I can't tonight. Tomorrow?"

Amanda resisted the urge to press. "Great. See you at the usual spot, eight o'clock tomorrow night."

When Amanda got out of the shower, there was a text from Sarah: Coffee? Maude and me. In 15 at Blue Bottle. They often met at the café on the corner of Seventh Avenue and Third Street before starting their day. Amanda used to go to Blue Bottle even more often, to read in the afternoon, before things with the foundation began heating up. She'd loved sitting there, watching the neighborhood writers at work—Park Slope had so many—like the young, shaggy-haired dad with the 26.2 sticker on his computer who always seemed so focused. Amanda could feel it in the air, the magic of all those stories being built. Sometimes, she imagined asking that dad what he was writing, or how many marathons he'd run. But of course she never had.

Yes! See you there, Amanda replied.

It was amazing that Amanda and her friends all had the flexibility for late-morning coffee dates. But then both Maude and Amanda were their own bosses, and Sarah was technically an employee, but only of Amanda's. Sarah did like mentioning that at every opportunity, though. Not in a hostile or resentful way, more like she wanted to be sure that Amanda knew she hadn't forgotten. Sarah didn't need the paycheck, of course. She'd taken the job at the foundation to give something back to parents who really needed it—a break from the ungrateful contingent of the Brooklyn Country Day PTA.

Amanda dressed quickly in one of her casual, quirky summer dresses, the kind she'd finally learned were exactly right for daytime summer in Park Slope (when paired with pricey but "minimalist" sandals). She headed down the hallway feeling almost cheerful. It had been nearly twelve hours since the last call. More than two days since she'd last thought Daddy was following her. She knew better than to get her hopes up, but there was the chance that he'd slithered back into his hole.

Amanda was about to turn down the stairs when she caught sight of Zach's open office door up on the third floor. Zach didn't usually leave the door open when he wasn't home. His office was his private space. Even Amanda didn't go in unless she needed to do something specific like fix the closet (finally scheduled for next week). This had been true in every house they'd ever lived in, once their houses were big enough for luxuries like an office.

"Zach!" Amanda called up. Maybe he'd gone to work early but stopped back home on his way to the airport or something. Often Amanda had no idea he was scheduled to travel until he'd come and gone. She took a couple steps back and aimed her voice more directly. "Zach!"

The house was utterly quiet.

Amanda made her way up and toward the open door with a rising sense of dread. But what exactly was she afraid of? She'd lived for so long—always, really—by such a clear set of rules. There had been the rules for surviving back with Daddy in the trailer—hide, lie still, run. There were the rules for avoiding conflict with Zach—don't complain, don't ask questions, don't be where you're not supposed to go. Simple, really. Considering breaking any of them—intentionally—was bound to feel dangerous. Amanda was holding her breath by the time she finally reached the top of the stairs and peeked into the office.

An empty room. She exhaled.

Three massive computer screens, wrapped around like a cockpit on Zach's sleek midcentury modern desk. The shelves were lined with the books that Amanda was sure Zach had never read. She'd been there, back in Palo Alto, when the "personal library curator" had selected the books to give the precise intellectual impression Zach desired—not that he ever had anyone in his home office to appreciate it. It was too bad. The books did paint a convincing picture of someone who was adventurous and curious, a casual athlete and an open-minded traveler. A person who was interested less in the finer things in life and more in a life well lived. It was an appealing idea of a man, just not one that had anything to do with Zach.

The only thing that Zach had ever cared about, as far as Amanda could tell, was success. And not even for the money—which she might have understood better—but for the pure satisfaction of coming out on top. Winning for winning's sake. Zach didn't just want it. He needed it. As if without it, he'd have vanished into thin air.

Amanda had never cared before about Zach's obsession with success or those pretend books. But today, all of it grated. Amanda thought about those novels she'd pored over so longingly at the library, the stories that had saved her life. And yet here was Zach, thinking he could have all that just by laying down some cash. But then, why not? After all, he'd bought her.

Amanda's face felt hot suddenly. Her heart was throbbing in her ears. No. She was not a thing that belonged to Zach. Of course she wasn't, and neither was Case. This was her home, too.

Amanda felt a little rush as she stepped inside the office, arms crossed tight.

On the floating shelves on either side of Zach's desk was a scattering of the framed photographs that had been taken over the years by an assortment of paid photographers Zach had insisted Amanda hire. The pictures, displayed throughout the house, were lovely. But Amanda longed for family photos like Sarah's, with mussed hair and chocolate-covered faces and closed eyelids. Even Maude and Sebe had these kinds of pictures—of life in all its perfect imperfection. For Zach, that kind of thing simply wouldn't do. For him, their family had always been an airbrushed abstraction, something to be put on a shelf and admired from a distance.

But what did Amanda want out of her family, her marriage? She'd never seriously considered the question. To be able to tell her own husband that she was scared. She wanted at least that much. And she wanted him to care.

Amanda made her way over to Zach's desk chair and sat down. When she put her hand over the mouse, the computer screens came to life. Yet another photo of the three of them, taken by a photographer in Sunnydale, where they'd lived until Case was a year old. Outlined in light, they were standing by the window of their loft apartment— which looked far more glamorous than it had actually been. Zach had Case cradled in his forearms. Amanda stood behind them, her hands on Zach's shoulders, gazing down at Case. As if this was a thing they did: touched each other, gazed adoringly.

When Amanda swiped the mouse again, a password request popped up. She tried her birthday and Case's together, halfheartedly. As she expected, the password was rejected. It was too demoralizing to consider other possible alternatives.

Instead, Amanda pulled at the drawer to her right. To her surprise, it slid open, unlocked. Inside, were several manila folders, crisp and neatly stacked. Amanda lifted them out and set them on her lap. The top was labeled *Case Camp*. There were brochures for several of the camps they had discussed, including the one that Case had ultimately attended. Amanda maintained all the files for Case—school, camp, activities. She'd had no idea Zach ever kept anything.

Amanda flipped to the next file, *Case Activities*. There was a brochure for the Brooklyn Conservatory of Music, where Case took guitar lessons, and for the DUSC Soccer League. *Case School* had copies of Case's Brooklyn Country Day report card, the school newsletter they'd gotten at spring parent-teacher conferences (the only one Zach would probably ever attend—he knew the minimum that was required), and the student directory. Looking at all of it, Amanda felt such a strange mix of confusion, guilt, and sadness. Like she'd stumbled upon some rebellious teenager's secret collection of well-loved toys. Was this the true Zach? Was this what he really wanted? To be more involved. Maybe he didn't know how to ask for what he needed, any more than Amanda did.

At the bottom of the stack was something she'd never seen before: emails from the Brooklyn Country Day headmaster's office to Zach's personal email. Three of them, to be exact, all with the exact same text, though slightly different formatting—there'd been an unfortunate incident involving Case that Country Day needed to discuss as soon as possible—followed by details about how a meeting could be set up, with what was probably a drag-down selection of dates. Three such messages over the past three months, starting about a month after they'd arrived—April 24, May 19, June 5.

Of all the clerical mix-ups, Country Day had emailed *Zach* about something so important? They might as well have flushed the emails straight down the toilet. She couldn't even blame Zach for ignoring them. He would have assumed that Amanda had gotten them, too. That she was dealing with the "incident" as she ordinarily would have, completely and thoroughly and alone. The messages were maddeningly vague, too. Were they about something Case had done or something that had been done *to* him? Was *he* the problem, or was it a problem he was having?

Amanda closed the folder and clutched it to her chest. She couldn't even call Country Day now to find out, because they were closed for the first two weeks of summer. And how could she ask Zach about the emails without revealing that she'd discovered them by rifling through his desk?

She'd have to figure out a way. She couldn't let Zach's absurd rules, the ridiculous standards she'd come to accept, get between her and protecting Case. She'd already let Zach haul them to Brooklyn in the middle of the year, which was probably what had caused the school problems to begin with. It had been a mistake not to speak up then. It would be a mistake not to speak up now—about her dad, about these emails, about her right to a voice. She would not, could not, let her son pay the price for her weakness any longer.

LIZZIE

JULY 10, FRIDAY

I stood there, ears ringing, as the guard at Rikers walked away and left me holding Zach's signed power of attorney. The paper trembled in my hand.

Zach's been hurting himself. Zach's been hurting himself.
What. The. Fuck.

I went to sit outside the Bantum building, letting bus after bus back to the Rikers main exit come and go. I couldn't stay there much longer without somebody telling me to move. Attorney or not, you couldn't just hang out on Rikers Island. But I also couldn't leave without confronting Zach.

I let one last bus pass before going back inside, hoping the guards would be willing to let me talk to him again without requiring I go all the way to the main building to make a formal request.

"Excuse me," I asked the same guard who'd helped me with the power of attorney. I smiled helplessly. "I forgot to ask my client something."

"About the face thing, huh?" The guard looked vaguely annoyed, but also sympathetic.

I nodded. "I'd really appreciate it."

"All right," he relented. "Just this once."

Fifteen minutes later, Zach and I were seated again in the same interview room.

"Couldn't get enough, huh?" he asked, eyes darting down. Leg bouncing.

I stared at him in silence. Where to even begin.

"Why did you lie?" I asked finally.

"Sorry, you'll have to be, um, more specific," he said. "There are quite a few allegations swirling around at the moment."

I pointed at Zach's face, even though he was looking down, then clasped my hands tight so they wouldn't shake. "You did all that to yourself."

Zach's leg froze. And for the longest time, he didn't move.

His head lifted first, eyes meeting mine, then his hands came to rest on the metal shelf in front of him as he sat up straighter. He blinked, once, his gaze strong and steady. He was suddenly someone I did not recognize. Someone I had never seen before.

"Surprise," he said. And then he smiled. "It took you long enough."

I squeezed my hands tighter, my fingernails digging into my flesh.

"Why?" I asked, the word scratching the back of my dry throat.

"Why am I surprised it took you this long?"

"No, why *me*?" My voice was too loud. The guards might come. But I couldn't help it. "There are so many other lawyers. *You* have so many other lawyers."

"Well, we've already established that you're loyal to a fault." He smirked. "Determined, too. Once you started helping me, I knew you wouldn't give up." He motioned to his face. "This was added incentive."

"Is this because I didn't want to date you?"

"Please, Lizzie," Zach huffed. "That's patronizing. This isn't some *love* thing. Though what you did back then—both you and I know it was wrong. You used me."

"We were *friends*."

"It wasn't that simple," he said, casually. "Anyway, it doesn't matter now. Like I said, it's not like I've been sitting around thinking about you all these years. You've seen what Amanda looked like, right? I did okay in the wife department. This is just me wanting to get the hell out of jail."

I pushed to my feet. "I'm withdrawing from your case, effective immediately. I'll find you replacement counsel."

"You and these fucking referrals, Lizzie." He laughed and leaned back in his chair, arms crossed. "Nope. No thank you. You need to see this through."

"Zach, I am not representing you. You can't force me to," I said. "This is over."

I turned for the door. I needed to get outside, to the fresh air.

"You know, Young & Crane asked for that financial disclosure for a reason," Zach called after me. "They don't hire associates with significant credit issues."

Breathe.

"What are you talking about?" I asked without turning around.

"Come on. Your husband's lawsuit is a joint obligation. You knew that," Zach said. "Creditors can go after you just as much as they can poor wayward Sam, the drunk writer. And because that debt is a joint obligation, you were required to include it on your financial disclosure form. And yet you left it off."

I reached out to the wall to steady myself, then turned back to face him.

"How do you know about that?"

"That's a valid question," Zach said. His voice was restrained, but the look in his eyes could only be described as glee. "But the more *important* question is, if *I* found out, how can you be sure Young & Crane won't, too? Honestly, Lizzie, it's pretty brazen, lying to that kind of law firm on that type of document. And you, of all people. Has Sam destroyed your ethics, too?"

My stomach lurched.

"What do you want?"

"I didn't kill my wife, Lizzie," Zach said. "All I'm asking is that you stick around and help me prove it."

"And if I won't, you'll get me fired?"

"If you won't, I'll be sure your firm knows the truth about what *you* did," he said. "So *you'll* get *you* fired. Blame yourself. Or blame Sam. He's the drunk."

My hands trembled the whole drive back from Rikers. At one point, I had to pull over on the frenetic Brooklyn-Queens Expressway to dry heave. Was Zach always this monster, and I'd somehow missed it? Or had I known deep down? Was that why I'd been glad when he cut ties? It didn't matter now, of course. I just needed a way out. But every path I considered ended in the same brick wall: the financial disclosure form. Young & Crane would almost certainly fire me if they found out—they might even bring me up on ethics charges. And without my job, my professional reputation, what was I? An orphaned, childless, disbarred liar, married to an alcoholic and saddled with massive debts. So much like my parents in the end. Except the person who had defrauded me wasn't a stranger. It was my own husband. And now Zach.

The only way to wrest myself from this situation was to get Zach out of Rikers. That meant a trial, which could take months, if not years. I couldn't survive living under Zach's thumb for that long. Find the real killer—that was a much better alternative. If I did that, and could prove it at least to some reasonable degree, maybe even get some press, Wendy Wallace would have no choice but to dismiss the charges against Zach.

Of course, this approach depended on one critical fact: that Zach hadn't actually killed Amanda. And right now, he seemed guilty as hell.

Lynch, it turned out, was an extremely popular last name in St. Colomb Falls, shared by more than a dozen men. I studied the list of names on the computer screen once I was back in my office at Young & Crane. I was trying to focus on the task at hand—find Amanda's dad—and not on the fact that I was being blackmailed into doing it. That was the only way forward now: to pretend.

A search on Amanda Lynch had already yielded nothing; not a single Facebook account or article, not even a reference from an old school paper. But then, Amanda Lynch had become Amanda Grayson at only seventeen or eighteen. She'd barely existed before she met Zach.

I sorted the male Lynches by age—I guessed Amanda's father would now be at least fifty—and was left with a list of eight people: Joseph, Daniel, Robert, Charles, Xavier, Michael, Richard, and Anthony. I cross-referenced those with the sex offender registry. If Amanda's dad had assaulted her, maybe he'd assaulted others. But every name came back clean. Within a few minutes, I had a phone number for each of them. A direct approach wasn't exactly subtle, but it was efficient. And I was pressed for time.

I dialed the first number: Joseph Lynch. It rang and rang before I finally got a voice mail. My entire investigative approach was predicated on people answering a call from a number they didn't recognize. Who did that anymore? But I had no better options.

"Hi, this is Josephine," a gruff woman's voice intoned. "Leave a message at the—"

I hung up. "Joseph" was probably Josephine. I took a deep breath and moved on to the second number: Robert Lynch.

I was startled when somebody actually answered on the second ring.

"This is Robert." His voice was loud and excessively jovial.

"Oh, hi. My name is Lizzie. I'm trying to find Amanda Lynch. We went to high school together, and we lost touch."

The old friend: a casual, innocuous gateway to disarm Amanda's father into accidentally identifying himself.

"Amanda?" Robert Lynch repeated enthusiastically. "I'm sorry, I don't believe I know any Amanda Lynch. I'm afraid you've reached the wrong number."

"Sorry to have bothered you."

"That's okay," he said, like my call was the highlight of his day. "Anything else I can help you with?"

Zach. Help me with Zach.

"I don't think so, but thank you for your time."

"You have a blessed evening."

Charles Lynch was next. Straight to a recorded message: *"The number you are trying to reach has been disconnected."* Three down. Four to go. *Fuck.* There were other avenues to try, probably more unlisted Lynches out there, and a disconnected number alone certainly didn't rule someone out. Amanda's dad could also have moved from St. Colomb Falls. I took another deep breath as I dialed the next number: Xavier. I repeated the name in my head. Biblical. Righteous. The name of a prophet, not an abusive father.

"Hello?" The voice was low and clipped.

"Oh, yes, sorry. My name is Lizzie Kitsakis."

"Yeah?"

"I'm trying to find Amanda Lyn—"

A click. Distinct but quiet.

"Hello?" I asked. There was no answer. "Hello?"

I redialed and immediately got a recorded message: *"This number is not receiving calls at this time."* It was what happened when someone blocked your specific number. I knew this because we'd blocked the Anglers' lawyer when he'd started calling our home at all hours.

Was it *proof* that Xavier was Amanda's father? Of course not. But it was suspicious.

I ran a search on Xavier Lynch and was immediately swamped with results. There were two Xavier Lynches in the United States with a substantial digital footprint. One was a thirty-one-year-old dentist from El Paso, Texas, the other a nineteen-year-old sophomore at Florida State University who had a half-dozen vlogs of himself playing different video games. I got distracted for a second scrolling through the irrelevant links before adding St. Colomb Falls to my search. And there he was right at the top: a third Xavier Lynch. He was mentioned in the St. Colomb Falls Methodist Church newsletter from a year earlier, in an article about a church rummage sale. It was the very same church that Amanda had written about in her journal.

Xavier Lynch's name appeared only once, in the caption below one of the photographs. In the photo, he was standing next to a much older couple, who each held a birdhouse in their hands. "Susan and Charlie Davidson and Xavier Lynch about to Treat Some Birds Thanks to Our Annual RUMMAGE!" Xavier Lynch was a very large man, several inches taller than the couple and very, very broad, with short gray hair, a wide face, and heavy-framed glasses. He was standing stiffly, with not even a trace of a smile.

Now what? When I'd been a US attorney, the answer was simple: send the FBI to shake the truth out of Xavier Lynch. But I didn't have armed professionals at my disposal anymore. Managing law clerks paid fines. They didn't go interview murder suspects.

"Um, hello?"

When I looked up, my legal assistant, Thomas, was standing in my office doorway, knuckles resting against the door as though he'd already knocked once. He was dressed in slim-fit pants and an expensive-looking bright-yellow-and-orange-striped polo shirt. Thomas had lively eyes and a sly grin that always left me feeling like he'd just heard some gossip, maybe about me. He'd proved a great legal assistant, though, and a loyal ally.

"What's up?" I sounded more annoyed than I'd intended.

He raised an envelope like a shield. "The warrant documents from Philadelphia?" He stepped forward to hand them to me. "You wanted me to bring them to you as soon as they arrived?"

The warrant. What difference did it make now? The judge knew it had been cleared, and she'd refused to grant bail on the murder charge.

"Right. An unpaid loitering ticket?" I asked.

"I deliver envelopes; I don't inspect their contents unless specifically directed to," Thomas said. "Remember?"

Thomas was looking at me like I was supposed to know what he meant.

"No, I don't remember."

"Oh, right, that was before your time," he said. "I don't want to call myself a hero or anything, but the partner who got fired? *I* was the whistleblower. He sent me to pick up something at the printers and, overachieving legal assistant that I am, I decided to take it out of the envelope so said partner wouldn't cut his fat fingers. Let's just say the envelope did not contain the contracts I'd expected."

"What was it?"

"Compromising photos of a certain female legal assistant, obviously taken without her knowledge."

"Ugh," I said, disgusted. What was wrong with *everyone*.

"You know, I think the other partners would have let it go if it wasn't for Paul. He's a maniac, but at least he has a modicum of integrity."

"Yes, a modicum," I said dryly as I reached for the envelope.

I opened it and quickly skimmed the warrant until I spotted the bottom line—it was indeed for loitering.

"You all right?" Thomas's voice had lost its snarky edge.

"Not really."

"Can I help?" he asked, and quite genuinely.

"Thank you, but no," I said, avoiding his eyes. "I don't think anyone can."

The Brooklyn DA's office was in a newer, taller building than the Manhattan DA's office, yet somehow the lobby smelled the same— cardboard with a dash of urine—and the longer I sat there, the more it was getting to me.

I'd been told by reception that, despite our 11:45 a.m. appointment, Wendy Wallace had yet to arrive. It was already 12:15. Sitting there waiting, staring up at oil paintings of DAs gone by, it occurred to me that maybe Wendy had only agreed to meet because she'd never intended to show.

Finally I heard high heels down the marble hallway from the elevators, like a clacking of knives. Wendy Wallace. Surely she assumed I was there to discuss a plea deal. She was not going to be pleased by the bait and switch and the last thing I wanted was to be asking for her help. But if I could somehow manage to get the prosecution to look into Xavier Lynch themselves, it would be a far better alternative.

When Wendy Wallace emerged from the hallway, she looked even more beautiful than she had in court: pale blue eyes set off by her silver hair, sharp gray linen suit and black heels. She held her head up, peering down her nose like a sphinx. I stood, hoping it would make me feel less intimidated. It did not.

"Counselor," she said, expertly unreadable. "Come back to my office. You'll be more comfortable there."

Would I, though? Everything with Wendy Wallace felt like a puzzle encased in a lie. Surely this was why Paul remained stuck on her. She was probably one of the few people who had ever left *him* choking on dust.

Wendy Wallace's office was crisply decorated with a few designer touches—a Herman Miller chair in the corner, a signed print on the wall—that probably reflected the money she'd gotten from Paul. Certainly they were not paid for with her ADA's salary alone. But nothing too ostentatious either. Precisely enough to signal that she was worth substantially more than her yearly income might suggest.

Wendy motioned toward a guest chair. "What can I do for you?"

I sat. But too upright. And once Wendy was seated across from me, I had no choice but to maintain my overly erect, exhausting posture.

"I need your help," I began.

"My help," she repeated with an awful calibrated flatness.

"I've found Amanda Grayson's father." I pulled Amanda's most recent journal out of my bag. "He was stalking her." I held up the journal for emphasis. "I believe there's a very good chance he killed her. He needs to be interviewed, immediately."

It was a risk, pulling this ace out of my sleeve. Wendy would now be ready for this alternate theory of the crime, once we got to trial. But if this case got that far, I had to hope I'd have figured a way out of representing Zach by then.

"Her father?" Wendy's eyebrows pulled together and her nose wrinkled slightly. She eyed the journal.

"I'm not one hundred percent sure I've found him, but I think so," I said. "He raped her as a child, and he's been harassing her since they returned to New York. He's been in Park Slope, following her. It's documented in her journal."

"Your client killed his wife, Counselor. I don't need to consult her journal or talk to her father to know that."

Was her response a shade too emphatic, though? Like maybe she wasn't one hundred percent sure of anything. I understood her not being thrilled to open up some can of worms. As a prosecutor, I never would have made it my business to go around interviewing random family members in search of alternative theories that might conflict with mine. You used evidence selectively to build on your story, not because you were an evil asshole, but because you *believed* your story. But genuinely exculpatory evidence was a different matter. No prosecutor would ignore that, not even Wendy Wallace. It could be career ending.

"Amanda Grayson's father was stalking her, and she was terrified," I said more forcefully. I waited a beat for her face to register concern. It did not. "I think he killed her."

"Ha," Wendy said quietly. She looked genuinely amused. "You know, I wasn't worried about Paul, because I know how to throw him off his game. But I'd heard you were like a tenacious little dog at the US attorney's office. Thank you for making it abundantly clear that description was not intended as a compliment."

Annoyingly, my cheeks flushed. And Wendy's eyes gleamed.

"The police need to talk to the father. Someone needs to check his alibi. Have your investigators even seen these journals? They were under the bed. Amanda recorded dates and times—phone calls, occasions her father was following her. It's potentially exculpatory."

Wendy was nodding thoughtfully. It seemed I might finally be getting through to her. But then she suddenly shook her head, as though coming to.

"I'm sorry," she said. "Did you say something? I heard the word *potentially*, and then my brain exploded inside my skull."

"Look, I don't think it's so unreasonable to expect—"

"Oh, it's clear that you don't think," she snapped. "Your client is a millionaire. If you want to go on some wild-goose chase that's not going to lead anywhere but straight back to him, be my guest. *He's* going to pay for it, though, not the taxpayers of the state of New York. We're not obligated to run down every stray fact just because you think it might 'potentially' lead somewhere. They also didn't interview your client's high school friends, or his dentist. So fucking what? None of that's relevant just because you think it *could* be. But I've got an idea: I'll subpoena all those journals just in case. Take them right off your hands. That way we can be sure to take our time reading them."

"And what if this does lead somewhere? What if Amanda's dad says something incriminating to my investigator?"

"Then you call your fucking investigator to testify!" she shouted, though we both knew damn well that she would make it her mission to undermine said investigator on the stand. She sat back calmly, a hand on each arm of the chair, like it was a throne. "I only agreed to meet with you because I thought that you wanted to grovel for a plea deal, and I was looking forward to saying no. Instead, you come in here asking me to do your fucking job for you?" She shook her head and let out a small dismissive huff. "You want to waste your time interviewing this fucking guy, that's up to you. Now, if you'll excuse me, I've got actual work to do."

"Fine," I said as I stood. "I disagree, but obviously you have to do what you think is right."

"Yes, *obviously*."

"Though prosecutorial misconduct is reversible error. If this lead pans out, and you deliberately ignored it . . ." I left the rest to her imagination.

Wendy Wallace glared at me for a moment, then smiled. "I look forward to responding to *that* brief."

"Thank you for your time," I said finally before turning for the door. "This has been illuminating."

"A word of warning," she called after me. "Woman to woman."

I paused and turned back.

"Be careful with Paul. He's charming, but sooner or later he'll dig out your heart and make you swallow it whole."

I cocked my head. "Oh, don't worry," I said with a smile. "Woman to woman: I'm way too smart to fall for Paul."

GRAND JURY TESTIMONY

TAYLOR PELLSTEIN,

called as a witness the 7th of July and was examined
and testified as follows:

EXAMINATION

BY MS. WALLACE:

Q: Good morning, Ms. Pellstein. Thank you for being
here.

A: You told me I didn't have a choice.

Q: You were subpoenaed to testify, that is correct.

A: Are you saying that I do have a choice?

Q: You are legally required to appear as a witness.

A: Because I really like Mr. Grayson. He's a really
good boss, and I really don't want to lose my job.

Q: You don't have to worry about that, Ms. Pellstein.
The proceedings of the grand jury are secret.

A: So you say.

Q: No, those are the facts, Ms. Pellstein. So the
law says.

A: Whatever.

Q: Let's move on then, and get you out of here as

quickly as possible. I only have a couple questions. You work for Mr. Grayson, is that correct?

A: Yes.

Q: In what capacity?

A: I'm his assistant.

Q: And what duties does that job entail?

A: I organize Mr. Grayson's calendar, book meetings, schedule appointments, arrange travel, answer his phone.

Q: And how long have you had this job?

A: Three years.

Q: So you worked for Mr. Grayson in California?

A: Yes.

Q: Unusual to move an assistant across the country, isn't it?

A: How would I know? I don't have an assistant.

Q: Did you ever have occasion to speak with Mrs. Grayson?

A: Of course. Whenever she called.

Q: Did Mr. Grayson ever give you any special instructions where his wife was concerned?

A: I don't know what you mean.

Q: Let me remind you, you're under oath. You could be charged with perjury if you do not tell the truth. Did Mr. Grayson give you any special instructions where his wife was concerned?

A: He told me not to put her calls through.

Q: Was this on a specific occasion that Mr. Grayson told you not to put his wife's calls through?

A: No.

Q: You were never supposed to put through her calls?

A: I was always supposed to take a message. But I want to say that I felt bad about that. Mrs. Grayson—I didn't know her or whatever—but she seemed like a

nice person. I think Mr. Grayson was just busy. It was
nothing personal.

Q: You must have also felt bad that you were having
an affair with Mr. Grayson, then?

A: What? I'm not having an affair with Mr. Grayson.

Q: Have you had sexual relations with Mr. Grayson?

A: Yes. But it wasn't an affair.

Q: How many times have you had sex with Mr. Grayson?

A: I don't know.

Q: More than once?

A: Yes. More than once.

Q: More than ten times?

A: Yes. More than ten times.

Q: More than a hundred times?

A: I don't know. Maybe. It wasn't like a love thing.
Or a relationship. Or whatever.

Q: Why do you say that?

A: Because Zach told me that: "This is not a love
thing. This is not anything." He told me that all the
time.

AMANDA

TWO DAYS BEFORE THE PARTY

By the time Amanda was rushing down to Blue Bottle, she was more than ten minutes late. Sarah and Maude were already seated at an outside table in the small gravel patio area, the late June morning quite warm, but not humid. One of those perfect New York City summer days that Amanda had been repeatedly warned would soon give way to an unbearable August of stifling smells and furious people. Eventually even most of the adults would be off in the Hamptons or Cape Cod or on assorted European adventures, and by the last weeks of summer, Park Slope would be rendered nearly a ghost town.

Maude's back was to Amanda as she approached, but she could see Sarah—big sunglasses on, her mouth a flat line. Amanda waited for her to look up, to smile broadly and wave theatrically as she usually did. But Sarah stayed fixated on Maude.

"I'm so sorry I'm late," Amanda murmured when she'd finally rushed through the café and out onto the patio.

She hadn't decided yet whether she would mention the emails about Case. She was so ashamed that she'd somehow missed them. But then hadn't Sarah said something about getting similar emails and ignoring them?

"That's okay," Sarah said, her voice grave. "Maude and I were just talking."

Once Amanda sat down, she could see that Maude's eyes were puffy from crying.

"What happened?" Amanda asked. "Is Sophia okay?"

Maude shook her head. "I don't know. I got another letter. It didn't say anything different exactly—but I have such a bad feeling. I finally reached somebody at the camp, and they said she seems absolutely fine, but she's gone on some stupid backpacking excursion, so I can't actually talk to her directly until Thursday. I don't think I'm going to feel better until I hear her voice."

"Maude, honey," Sarah said more forcefully. "What happened to Sophia? There is obviously something going on. Tell us so that we can help."

"All Sebe wants me to do is stay calm," Maude said. "And I just—he's wrong. She's not okay. I can feel it."

"That's because husbands are useless," Sarah said. "Even the gorgeous ones. Maude, tell *us* what happened."

"But I promised Sophia I wouldn't." Maude looked pained.

"Please," Sarah huffed. "Parent promises are kept at the discretion of the parent. Everybody knows that."

Maude stared out into the distance for a moment, chewing on her lip.

"Sophia took some naked pictures of herself," she finally blurted out, and then her body sank. "For this boy she's seeing."

"Oh, Maude, they *all* do that!" Sarah exclaimed. "*I've* done that, which, by the way, I do not recommend—no matter how high your self-esteem, naked at forty-eight years old is much better in your head than in a selfie—but you wouldn't believe the pictures my son and his friends get *sent to them*. All the time. And I am not blaming the girls, either. No, no, no. I know the boys *ask*. Even my boys, I'm sure. Like it's nothing. And for that I blame porn. And not regular old *Playboy* either. That was healthy curiosity. This online garbage?" Sarah closed her eyes and shuddered. "Anyway, my point is, it's a bottomless cauldron of twisted depravity out there. There are apparently whole websites devoted to things like 'peeper porn.'"

"Peeper porn?" Amanda asked.

"Oh, just people videotaping up women's skirts or setting up cameras in public bathrooms, that kind of thing." Sarah blushed uncharacteristically. "No big deal, right?"

Maude's eyes filled with tears.

"Oh, Maude, I'm so sorry!" Sarah cupped a hand over her mouth. "That peeper bullshit has nothing to do with Sophia! Really, it has nothing to do with anything. So Sophia took the pictures, and I'm assuming she gave them to the boy? It's not a big deal. Seriously. We just need to make sure Sophia knows that."

"Think of how amazing it is that Sophia told you about any of it, Maude," Amanda pointed out. "It shows how much she trusts you."

"Exactly. It's a testament to what a good mother you are," Sarah added. "I like to ride you about hovering, but, you know, my boys don't tell me a damn thing."

Maude blinked, sending the tears rushing down her cheeks.

"There's more," she said.

"What?" Sarah asked.

"Our computer was one of the ones hacked into," Maude said. "And the pictures Sophia took of herself, they're provocative, really provocative. They've threatened to post them."

"Those motherfuckers," Sarah growled.

Maude's tears were coming even faster now. Her cheeks were glistening. "The worst part is, some of Sophia's letters from camp have made it seem like there's even *more* than that. Something I don't know." Maude looked from Sarah to Amanda and back again, like surely they must have some answers. "What else could there be?"

Sarah shook her head. "She's going to be fine. You just need to talk to her. All that time away from home without her phone? She's had too much time to think."

But Maude continued to look so worried. And Amanda felt worried for her.

"You can talk to her on Thursday, you said?" Amanda asked.

Maude nodded. "Yes. But they can't even tell me what time. What if it's in the middle of the stupid party? I should cancel."

"Oh, don't cancel!" Sarah cried, then recovered with a wave of her hand. "I mean, getting ready will keep you distracted. There's nothing you can do right now anyway. What's happened has happened." Then she smiled playfully, like she was trying to lighten the mood. "Besides, you cannot have this be my last sex party and then cancel. I'll have no closure."

"Maybe you should host my party then." Maude smiled tearfully. "Speaking of the party, I should be getting home. There are deliveries coming."

"Will you be okay?" Amanda asked. "Do you want one of us to come with you?"

"No, no," Maude said. "I must seem spectacularly unhinged, but I'll be fine. I think I just need some time to myself."

"You're sure?" Sarah pressed.

"Yes," Maude said, taking a deep breath as she stood. "I promise."

Amanda and Sarah watched as Maude gathered her things and left. They did not speak again until Maude was safely out of sight.

"God, what the fuck is wrong with me?" Sarah shook her head. "Peeper porn? I am such an asshole. It's because I'm exhausted. Fucking Kerry."

"Kerry?" Amanda asked.

Sarah looked startled by the question. "Oh, an argument. It was silly. Too much wine more than anything," she said. "I was just mad about that fairy tale Kerry told about his stepfather."

"Fairy tale?" Amanda asked.

"Kerry's stepfather never broke his arm, though according to Kerry he was quite the jerk once upon a time," she scoffed. "Anyway Kerry felt like everybody was gawking at you, and he didn't want you to feel bad."

"Oh," Amanda said, indeed feeling bad. "I'm so sorry."

"Don't be sorry. It's not your fault. That was only how the fight started, anyway . . . it blew up from there." Sarah waved her hand. "But that's a discussion for another time. Right now, poor Maude is what matters. I can't believe I made her feel worse."

"No, no," Amanda said, even though she was pretty sure that Sarah *had* made it worse.

"I'll call her later and check in."

"Can I ask you something totally unrelated?" Amanda began tentatively. She should have probably let the conversation go on a little longer before changing the subject. But she couldn't bear to wait anymore. "It's about that email you received from Country Day. About Will?"

"You mean the one I decided to ignore because I wanted to get on with the business of enjoying my kid-free summer? Another example of my sterling judgment. Sure, why not? Ask away."

"We got a similar one about Case," Amanda said. "A couple of them actually. But I overlooked them, so I didn't respond."

"Well, at least you *accidentally* didn't respond, instead of intentionally not responding like me."

"Will the school hold it against Case?" Amanda asked. "That I didn't answer and set up the meeting?"

"Absolutely not. Especially since the meeting was probably about nothing. All that school does is set up meetings. I get it. Bad things have happened because some other schools around here were asleep at the wheel. But how about a happy medium. Honestly, a kid stubs their toe and Brooklyn Country Day wants to have a meeting between you, the kid, and the offending piece of furniture. If Case was having an actual problem, they would have called you."

"They would?" Amanda asked.

"Definitely," Sarah went on. "When that school really wants to find you, they hunt you down. Watch what happens if you're late with a tuition bill."

Amanda smiled. She felt genuinely relieved. "Oh, good, then maybe it's not serious."

"One hundred percent it's *absolutely* not serious. I'd put it out of your mind completely. Pretend you never even got it. Like me." Sarah was quiet then, her face grave as she looked toward the exit. "Trust me, ignorance sometimes really is bliss."

KRELL INDUSTRIES

CONFIDENTIAL MEMORANDUM

NOT FOR DISTRIBUTION

Attorney-Client Work Product
Privileged & Confidential

July 1

To: Brooklyn Country Day Board of Directors
From: Krell Industries
Subject: Data Breach & Cyber Incident Investigation—Progress Report

Interview Summaries:

SUBJECT FAMILY 0005: Does not know whether they received a conference request from Brooklyn Country Day due to shared family email. Will inquire of all family members once they have returned from camp.

SUBJECT FAMILY 0006: Received Brooklyn Country Day conference scheduling request but did not reply. Did receive other suspicious emails from different household accounts. May have responded.

SUBJECT FAMILY 0016: Received Brooklyn Country Day conference scheduling request and scheduled conference. A later message indicated that conference had been canceled and would be rescheduled.

PRELIMINARY CONCLUSIONS:

Brooklyn Country Day systems were compromised on or about April 30. At that time, extensive personal information about Brooklyn Country Day families was gathered, including children's names, family emails, and other contact information. Access was obtained to the personal computers of individual families once they interacted with a counterfeit conference scheduling form. If a conference was scheduled it would subsequently be canceled with an automated follow-up email. If this access attempt failed, a second attempt was made using an alternate forged account. Based on syntactical variation and disparate IP locations, it appears likely that several individuals are responsible for the specific exchanges with subject families.

LIZZIE

The building that housed Millie's company, Evidentiary Analytics, was tall and wrapped in mirrored glass like so many others in that stretch of Midtown East, north of the UN. The vast lobby was floor-to-ceiling marble with three different reception desks, the two most imposing reserved for Sony and Credit Suisse. The third, smaller desk was the catch-all for the remaining tenants. Millie had mentioned that she'd expanded her company into a partnership with a forensic expert. But this was already more impressive than I'd expected, which was encouraging. And after that meeting with Wendy Wallace, I was badly in need of encouragement.

On the thirty-sixth floor, I made my way down a long, fancy hallway—expensive-looking textured wallpaper, exceptionally clean carpets—and rang the bell under the polished sign for Evidentiary Analytics. A second later Millie, in a sensible if not exactly fashionable navy-blue suit, opened the door. Under the glare of the office lights, her skin had a distinct grayish tinge.

"Hi, sweetheart," she said, reaching forward and pulling me into a hug.

This time, hugging Millie was like squeezing a pile of twigs. "Okay, why are you so thin?"

"Why, thank you, dear," she said cheerfully, though it was obvious I hadn't meant it as a compliment. She waved me inside. "Come on, come on. We've got some good stuff for you here. Real good."

I'd called Millie right after I'd left Wendy Wallace's office. I told her that Zach had been indicted and that I urgently needed some actual proof that someone else had been at the scene. This was all true, though I'd notably left out that the real urgency was that I was being blackmailed by my client. I was too ashamed. Also, Millie wouldn't believe in caving to Zach's demands, and I couldn't risk her refusing to help because of it. Finding a new investigator would just mean more time on Zach's case.

Inside the sleek, open-plan Evidentiary Analytics office, there was a small man with a thick, dark mustache and a mane of jet-black hair standing alongside the reception desk. Behind him a petite blond, curly-haired receptionist sat answering the phone. The man had droopy but kind eyes, which I tried to focus on instead of his hair, which was so unnatural in its blackness that it had to be a wig, a very bad one. Given how nice the office was, it seemed strange he hadn't considered an upgrade.

"This is my partner, Vinnie," Millie said. "Vinnie, this is Lizzie. She's an old friend, so be friendly. It isn't easy for Vinnie. Forensic guys aren't known for their people skills."

The droopy-eyed man scowled at Millie, then advanced toward me with an outstretched hand. His grip was surprisingly soft and puffy, like he was wearing a mitten.

"Lizzie Kitsakis," I said. "Thank you so much for your help."

"Don't worry. It'll cost you." If this was meant as a joke, it wasn't accompanied by even a hint of a smile.

Millie motioned to a low black leather and walnut seating area in the far corner. "Come, sit."

"This is so nice," I said as we made our way across the room.

There were huge windows on one side, with decent peek-a-boo views of the East River. The half-dozen desks, artfully arranged, were occupied only by men, presumably other investigators, all but one talking on the phone. At the back there were three large private offices, glass-fronted, but each with a door.

"We're making a decent go of it here," Millie said, looking around with a satisfied nod as we sat on the couches. "Don't have an actual lab of our own yet, so we have to outsource the testing—print analyses, blood typing. But someday, I'm hoping. Vinnie makes the initial strategic assessment, figures out the right tests, the approach, while I run down witnesses and other investigative leads. Vinnie also has the connections at the medical examiner's office."

"Yeah, Vinnie has the connections," he grumbled, taking a seat on the couch farthest away. "And he likes to get paid for using them."

"Vinnie," Millie snapped. "Stop with the money. She's going to pay, for Christ's sake."

"She'd better."

Millie rolled her eyes. "I explained to him that we couldn't wait for a retainer, given that time is of the essence and your client is locked up at Rikers." She shot a scathing look Vinnie's way and then turned back to me. "We got burned a couple times when we first started. In Vinnie's defense, it was on my say-so each time."

"I can get Zach's accountant to wire money today," I said, turning to Vinnie. "I need to call him, anyway."

He nodded, though he looked unconvinced. "Well, from what I hear from *my* contacts at the ME, this is a blood case, no doubt."

"That could be good news, right?" I asked tentatively. "At least they're planning to rely on actual evidence. And blood evidence has got to be more reliable than eyewitnesses, or something, right?"

I was wading into unfamiliar waters now. Fraud cases were data and document cases. They didn't involve blood, sometimes not even eyewitnesses. They were all about numbers, emails, invoices, and accounting ledgers. Over the years, I'd intentionally avoided learning much about violent crime scene forensics. But here I was. No more looking away. I'd have no choice but to suck it up and educate myself.

"Fuck, no. Blood spatter analysis is completely unreliable," Vinnie grumbled. "In New York City, at least the people doing the analysis have *some* actual training. A lot of places send some regular old cops to a six-hour seminar before they get to start pretending they got the lead on *CSI Fucking Fresno*. Regardless, blood spatter in and of itself is more art than science, always."

"That sounds bad," I said. Sweat was trickling down my lower back. This was all getting to be too much.

"Look at this case—there's so much blood spatter, in so many different variations. They can use it to prove anything they want. For sure, the DA will get some lab tech to walk the jury through every step of this crime like he watched it happen. Meanwhile, he might as well be reading his own fucking palm. In a case like this, I could find you three different blood guys who'd come to three totally different conclusions about the sequence of events on that staircase. That would say to me that they shouldn't be using blood spatter, period, in a case like this. But I'm not the prosecutor, so fuck me."

That sounded very, very bad. Hadn't Millie said there was good news?

"And you heard all this from the medical examiner's office?" I asked.

Vinnie nodded. "Apparently they've got the golf club with our guy's prints on it, and rumor is the victim's injuries are 'consistent with' a golf club, but there's too much damage to get an exact match. My guess is all of that sounded a lot more definitive in front of the grand jury. That's easy to do with no cross. For sure, they'll spend hours crowing about their bullshit 'airtight blood spatter' at trial. And we'll do the best we can to knock it down. But you ask me: we shouldn't have to."

We. Our guy. I tried to focus on the way Vinnie had said that, and not the rest of it. It was a relief to share the burden of Zach's awfulness with somebody—if only for a second and somewhat begrudgingly. Vinnie was certainly right about the way grand juries worked, though. With no defense attorney present to point out the holes, testimony ended up being entirely one-sided. Witnesses weren't encouraged to outright lie—after all, if they testified at trial, they could be confronted then by the defense—but there was an ocean of distance between a lie and a carefully asked series of questions.

"Which is why it was good that you called me over to the house," Millie said, trying to strike a more optimistic tone. "The prints are gonna help."

"You found something?"

"Yeah, a fuckload of prints," Vinnie said, holding up a folder and eyeing Millie. "That we already fronted a shitload of cash to get some rushed comparison results on."

"It's nothing conclusive." Millie tugged the folder out of Vinnie's hands and handed it to me. Inside were twenty pages of item numbers, percentage ratings, and descriptive language. It was all completely indecipherable. "But we did run comparisons between some prints in key locations."

"I'm sorry . . . ," I began. "I'm not sure I follow."

"Here." Vinnie flipped to a page toward the back of the stack. "See this? We found two sets of prints on the golf bag, Zach's and an unknown."

"Amanda's?"

Vinnie shook his head. "We had a control set from Zach and the victim. The other prints on the golf bag aren't hers."

But there had to be countless innocuous explanations for prints on the golf bag—housekeepers, movers, caddies, valets. Any number of people could have had a legitimate reason to touch it.

"Who do they belong to?"

Vinnie scowled. "How the fuck should I know?"

"He means the unidentified print on the golf bag wasn't in the system. We were able to pull some strings and get it run through at the NYPD." Millie motioned for Vinnie to continue. "Get to the good part, Vin."

"We've got a partial of that same hand from the bag, here." Vinnie indicated a place on the photograph of the staircase. "In Amanda Grayson's blood."

My heart surged. "What?"

"That palm and single fingerprint you spotted in the blood on the metal tread," Millie said, "that same print is *also* on the golf bag. Lots of people might have had a legitimate reason to have their hands on that golf bag, but they sure as hell didn't also have a legitimate reason to have their hands in Amanda's blood the night she died."

"Oh my God," I said. "Are you sure?"

Millie smiled slyly. "We're sure. And the print definitely doesn't belong to an EMT or anyone at the NYPD. We had those checked, too. But somebody was there the night Amanda Grayson died. Somebody other than Zach Grayson."

Holy shit. Zach really hadn't killed Amanda? He was just a sick fuck who was extorting me?

"Now, we can have our lab run this print against everybody who was in the victim's life, anybody you get us a sample on. It'll be a hell of a lot faster than whatever the NYPD does, sure as hell more comprehensive. But we're not doing that until we get paid," Vinnie said. "Lucky for Millie, she's got me to be sure we don't get kicked out of this fancy office here for nonpayment of rent."

Millie frowned at Vinnie, then turned to me. "I pushed him as far as I could," she said by way of explanation. "He's right that running print comparisons can get expensive fast. It's good for clients to be fully on board before we get too far ahead of ourselves."

"Zach is on board, definitely. I warned him the lab work could be expensive, too. Why don't I call his accountant right now, from here?" I offered. And I actually did feel the tiniest bit better for the first time since Zach had threatened me. If Zach hadn't done it, maybe I really could get him off with a clear conscience and save myself. Even Wendy Wallace would be hard-pressed to ignore bloody prints belonging to the real perpetrator. "I'll get you guys paid, and then we can get on with this."

Millie shook her head. "Oh, you don't have to call right now, that's—"

"Great," Vinnie said. "A great idea. Call right now."

"Can I first ask—are the same person's prints also on the golf club?"

Millie and Vinnie glanced at each other, then back at me.

"Um, the police have the golf club, hon," Millie said, her tone polite but sharp. Like she was nicely reminding me to wake the fuck up. "So we've got no idea."

"Oh, right," I said. It was the prosecutor in me, forgetting.

Of course we didn't have the golf club yet. Or Amanda's all-important phone, which could contain God only knows how much further confirmation of her father's stalking. That is, if the prosecution decided to go digging. Deleted messages, unknown numbers—those things weren't looked into unless the prosecution needed to *find* a suspect. In Zach's case, they were convinced they had their man, and they certainly didn't need phone calls to prove a connection between him and Amanda. It was only thanks to very recent changes in New York law that we would soon even be privy to something like Amanda's phone log. Up until now, all of the prosecution's evidence would have been sprung on us right before trial, a procedure that had—of course—always seemed perfectly reasonable to me when I was on the other side of the equation. It did make me think about getting Zach's phone. I was no expert on the specificity of cell phone pings in a place as densely populated as Brooklyn, but if we could locate Zach's phone on the Brooklyn Heights Promenade at the time Amanda was killed, that would be extremely helpful.

"Could be for the best we don't have the club," Vinnie offered. "You test that particular golf club, and it *doesn't* have the same prints you're hoping for? Then all the evidence you have becomes about all the evidence you don't have. Because maybe this other guy, whoever he is, was smart enough to wear a glove on the one hand he used to hold the club, but not on the other. Maybe he only touched the bag and that one step with his nondominant hand because he lost his balance? Like this—" He imitated the motion. "Those scenarios sound ridiculous, but no more ridiculous than their blood spatter story. Weird, fucked-up shit happens during the commission of a crime."

"I think I might know who the prints belong to," I said.

"Care to fucking share?" Vinnie asked.

"Amanda's father. Her estranged father. He lives upstate. He was sexually abusive when she was young, and ever since they moved back to New York, she thought he was stalking her. That he had been, for months. She kept a log in her journal about it. There were phone calls, and he was following her. He even left some flowers."

"Really?" Millie asked, intrigued. "Well, that sure as hell sounds like a solid lead."

"I think I've got him tracked down, too. But I'll need to go upstate, to a town called St. Colomb Falls, to talk to him to be—"

"No, no, no," Millie said. "Absolutely not. Rapists don't love it when you show up out of nowhere, accusing them of murder." I hadn't wanted to ask Millie to go to St. Colomb Falls, not when she was already helping me so much. But I had brought up Xavier Lynch, hoping she might offer.

"I'd go myself, but . . ." Millie looked down, uncomfortable. "I've got this thing I can't miss, starting tomorrow. It'll last a few days. And Vinnie's no good in the field. Sending him would be worse than sending no one."

"Gee, thanks," Vinnie said mildly.

"I know a couple other guys I trust, though. I use them sometimes for canvassing. They're not cheap, and they don't always have time. But I can ask."

"I think someone needs to talk to him soon," I said.

"Okay, let me reach out and see what they say. Otherwise, we'll just have to wait. It's not like there's some big rush anyway. We've got time until trial."

"If you don't mind asking, that would be great," I said, already knowing there was no way I was waiting. "Can I take that file with me? I'd like to look at the photos and the rest of it."

When Vinnie showed me the fingerprint analysis, I'd glimpsed some other documents in the file: what looked like maps of the neighborhood, printouts of internet search results, notes from interviews. I was partly hoping there might be something in there that made Zach look guilty. Maybe something I could use to reverse-extort him. It wasn't exactly ethical to threaten to rat out your own client—especially when you suspected he was innocent—but Zach and I were well past ethical now.

"Oh, sure, we'll hand over all our work product. Just as soon as your client pays us," Vinnie said, gripping the folder tighter. "Fifteen thousand for past fees and a twenty-thousand retainer for future costs should do it. I can provide an itemization, if needed."

"Jesus, Vinnie," Millie groaned, but in a resigned way.

"No, no, it's okay," I said. "Can I use an office phone for a minute? I'll call Zach's accountant right now and get it sorted out."

"Sure. Come this way." Millie guided me toward an unoccupied office at the back. "I'm sorry about Vinnie," she said as we walked. "He's spent most of his life dealing with criminals. He doesn't trust anybody. Worst part is that he's been right most of the time."

"I understand," I said as we stopped at the office door. "And it shouldn't be a problem."

I reached for the doorknob.

"I have cancer, Lizzie," Millie said quietly from behind me.

"What?" I spun around to face her.

"That's why I'm so thin," she said. "And all the emails. It could have implications, you know, for our arrangement."

My mouth felt so dry. "God, I'm sorry, Millie. And I'm so sorry that I've been—that you even have to think about this right now . . . you've done so much for me. I'm sure when you first offered—I'm sure you didn't think you'd still be on the hook, what, seventeen years later. Is there anything I can do for you?"

Anything except talking about our whole entire situation. I'm sorry you have cancer. But I just can't. Not right now.

Millie smiled, but her eyes looked so sad. "I start chemo tomorrow. Mandatory. That's why I can't do your interview."

"Will you be . . . What do the doctors say?"

"Um, well . . ." Her voice drifted. "It's breast cancer, like Nancy.

They were always 'optimistic' with her, and look how that turned out."
She smiled stiffly. "I'm gonna fight, though. Because I'm a fighter." It
was as forced as her expression.

"Please let me do something."

"Pretend like I didn't tell you. That's what you can do for me," she
said. "And promise me you won't go upstate yourself."

"Of course not," I said, even though it was definitely an extra sin to
lie to a sick person.

"And we will need to talk about the rest," she said, then cleared her
throat. "But I assume you'd like to wait on that, given this case you're
dealing with."

I nodded. "Thank you."

Millie pressed her lips tight. "Okay," she said. "A few days, though,
tops. In the meantime, start thinking about what you want to do, because this—our arrangement—I think maybe it's run its course."

It was a relief to be in the empty office with the door closed. I was even
more grateful for the excuse of having to pull myself together to dial
Zach's accountant. I would face Millie's news later. I would.

He answered almost immediately. "Teddy Buckley."

"This is Lizzie Kitsakis. I'm Zach Grayson's attorney, and he's
given me power of attorney to have financial discussions with you on
his behalf. I can email an authorization before we speak further, if you
like."

"Okay," Teddy said, drawing out the word warily. "Yes, that would
be great. I'm sure, under the circumstances, you can understand why
I have to wait until I have the authorization in hand before we proceed."

A by-the-book, nervous guy. Not surprising for an accountant. But
there was something else in his voice: relief. He'd been hoping for a
call. From somebody.

"Yeah, hold on one second. I'll send it right through."

"No problem," he said. "I can wait."

I held my phone away from my ear, snapped a photo of Zach's executed authorization, then attached the image to an email. The whole process took less than a minute.

"Okay, you should have it in a—"

"Got it. Yep, all looks in order." Teddy Buckley exhaled. "I was so sorry to hear about Mrs. Grayson."

"You knew her?"

"Not really," Teddy Buckley said. "Everything I heard about her, though. She seemed . . . human. People who are that wealthy, or who've been that wealthy, aren't always. Anyway, it's sad what happened to her."

"Before we go any further, could you get a payment over to Evidentiary Analytics? They're the expert investigation firm we're using to assist with Zach's defense, and they need a payment for services rendered, also a retainer for future services. Thirty-five thousand total. And if you could wire it ideally right now, while I wait, that would be helpful. Apologies for the fire drill, but as you can imagine in a situation like this, they've already fronted a significant amount of money for lab tests and so on."

"You want me to wire thirty-five thousand dollars?" Teddy Buckley asked. He sounded wary again. No, actually, he sounded confused. "Right now?"

"The power of attorney extends to payment requests."

"Yes, I can see that. But I'm afraid I can't wire the money."

"I don't understand."

"There are no funds available to transfer."

I pressed my eyes shut. "What do you mean?"

"That there is no money. Not in the foundation's accounts or in the Graysons' personal ones, at least none that I have access to. Frankly, I'm surprised that Mr. Grayson didn't tell you this himself when he signed the authorization. He is fully aware. I can't imagine why he'd sign an authorization for money he knows full well he does not have."

But the answer was clear to me: Zach had been hoping to get as much out of me and my experts as he could before the truth caught up. It was a decent strategy. Look how far it had already gotten him.

"What happened to the money?" I asked, trying to keep my voice steady. "Do you know?"

"No. I discovered several large transfers at Mr. Grayson's direction. When I inquired, he quite angrily told me it was none of my business. But technically, I also have a fiduciary responsibility to the foundation's board of directors."

"Why would Zach need to take the foundation's money?" I asked. "Didn't he just sell his company for millions of dollars?"

"That's not my understanding," Teddy Buckley said, but carefully.

"Then what *is* your understanding?"

"Listen, this is really all gossip and conjecture. I wasn't involved at the time. I only took over after the company was sold, once the foundation was established. I don't handle financial matters for Mr. Grayson's new company," he said. "It wouldn't be appropriate for me to—"

"Mr. Buckley!" I shouted, even though I was probably on thin ice. "I don't have time for this. I'm just trying to get an innocent man out of jail, and I have experts who need to be paid. You have an authorization allowing you to speak with me. Believe me, I am acting on Mr. Grayson's legal authority. You are obligated to answer my questions."

Teddy Buckley took a nervous breath. "My understanding is that Mr. Grayson was bought out by the board of ZAG, but that they were able to pay him a significantly reduced amount because of alleged malfeasance."

"Malfeasance?"

"I don't know the specifics and it's not been proven legally, of course. But apparently, it was discovered that Mr. Grayson had some . . . unorthodox methods. It made ZAG, Inc. vulnerable," he said. "Surely he was paid enough to cover personal expenses, to establish the foundation and start the new venture. As for the ongoing costs of that venture . . . Again, this is speculation."

"Oh," I said, feeling queasy. "I didn't realize."

But now I did. This was probably the real reason Zach had sought me out to represent him: he was broke. Any other attorney would have demanded a huge retainer up front. And they would have—smartly— waited for the check to clear before getting to work. How much better if he could get me, for free? It hadn't even occurred to me yet to ask about a retainer. Evidently, it hadn't occurred to Paul either. After all, Zach was rich. What could possibly go wrong?

"Mr. Grayson stopped taking my calls about a month ago, but Mrs. Grayson had agreed to meet before she died. I was going to explain the issue to her, and then escalate to the board of directors if need be. But when I showed up at the foundation last week, she wasn't there." He paused, then took another breath. "I returned the next afternoon and then the one after that, but Mrs. Grayson continued to be unavailable. I ended up telling the foundation's assistant director what was going on. It was against my better judgment, and I'll admit it skirted an ethical line. But I felt that somebody at the foundation needed to know before they started awarding nonexistent funds to needy students."

"Assistant director?"

"Let me look at my notes," Teddy said, reluctantly. "Her name is Sarah Novak."

"You met with Sarah Novak?"

"Yes, briefly."

Sarah had specifically mentioned this accountant trying to track Amanda down, and yet she'd left out the fact that she'd met with him herself? And that during that meeting he'd dropped a *bankruptcy* bombshell? What was she hiding? Was it possible that she'd been in- volved somehow with Zach in taking the foundation's money?

"When exactly was this?"

"Hold on," he said. There was the sound of tapping on a keyboard in the background. "It was Thursday, July second, at four p.m. I will say Mrs. Novak wasn't happy when I told her. Actually, she was very, very angry. Honestly, it took me by surprise. I had expected concern, but she seemed to be taking it all very personally."

"What do you mean?" I asked.

"Um, well, she said something like, 'Great, so now I'm out of a fucking job? What am I supposed to fucking do?'" Teddy sounded very awkward swearing, like he was speaking a foreign language. "There was more, but all along those lines. With more profanity and more shouting. She seemed very worried about the financial consequences for her personally."

"Okay, thank you," I said.

"Please let me know if there's anything else I can do."

I hung up and looked through the glass office door as Millie paced back and forth in the distance, shaking her head and waving her finger in the air, as though she was reaming out Vinnie for doubting me. Unfortunate, given that he'd been right from the start.

Zach was a failure—a loser—the very thing he swore he'd never be. Who knew how far he'd go to cover it up? Maybe he was in on some scheme with Sarah. Maybe it was the two of them who'd been together the night of the party, not Zach and Maude. Was Maude protecting Sarah? Was Sarah's disdain for Zach part of some elaborate ruse?

The possibilities multiplied before my eyes so rapidly that soon I felt sure of only one thing: I'd been flying blind.

AMANDA

Amanda entered Prospect Park near Garfield Place and headed south. She and Carolyn always met on the far side of the park, near the skating rink. Close by was the most convenient subway stop from Carolyn's work, and Amanda liked walking through the center of the park, across the long meadow where the dogs could play off-leash before 9:00 a.m. and after 5:00 p.m. The sun was low as Amanda crossed the meadow, the late summer light bathing everything in a buttery gold.

When she finally arrived at the entrance to the rink, Carolyn was nowhere in sight. But she was never late. Was Amanda early? She didn't know what time it was. She never brought her phone. She hated jogging with the huge thing strapped to her arm.

Amanda looked up and down Prospect Park's East Drive, then across to the Flatbush Avenue side. No Carolyn.

"Excuse me," Amanda asked a determined-looking woman with a stroller who was speed-walking her way. "Could you tell me what time it is?"

"Oh, sure," the woman said as she whipped past. "Eight oh five p.m."

Carolyn was only five minutes late, though the light was rapidly thinning back there in all those trees and Amanda was beginning to feel nervous standing there all alone. But she needed to be patient. Carolyn worked long hours. She was entitled to be a few minutes late. Besides, Amanda could use the time to decide exactly how she wanted Carolyn to help her.

Because aside from confronting Zach in Amanda's place, it wasn't obvious what Carolyn could do. Surely she would tell Amanda she needed to speak up with Zach. But that was easy for Carolyn to say. It came as second nature to her. Without specifics, it would be useless advice for Amanda. All she really knew how to do was run. As far and as fast as she possibly could. She'd been doing it for years. It had a way of steadying her, even when she felt most lost. That was probably why she was doing it now, even in her dreams.

It was six months after her mom died that Daddy came for Amanda in the dark for the first time. After that, she knew exactly why her mom had said "You run if you have to. You run as fast as you can." Though where Amanda was supposed to go remained a mystery. After all, she was only twelve years old. And so Amanda had started running everywhere she could: to the bus stop and back, to the library, out to Route 24, and around and around the Walmart parking lot. She ran in the flat, uncushioned Keds she wore to school and the one pair of sweatpants she owned, so bulky her knees brushed together. Soon she could run nearly ten miles without much effort, and she was fast. So fast it seemed there might actually be a chance she'd get away, just as soon as she figured out where to go.

Amanda looked around again. Still, no Carolyn. The crowds of bikers and runners were sparser now that twilight had started to sink its long fingers into the sky.

This time, Amanda asked an older man the time. He was wearing headphones, so she had to shout at him twice.

"Eight twenty-one," he finally shouted back.

Sixteen minutes gone. Had she really been standing there that long? What if something had happened to Carolyn? The subway was incredibly safe—or so Amanda had been told—but people were mugged, they got pushed. And Carolyn could be overconfident.

Or there was that other, much more obvious explanation: her dad. He could have followed Amanda to the park and somehow found a way to head Carolyn off. He was clever that way. What if he'd made it so that Carolyn could never meet Amanda again? A flash of him came at her from the dream, so large and strong, looming in the doorway. All she could think about was him cornering her best friend in some desolate section of the park. Amanda felt light-headed, and then sick. Like she might pass out. She hung her head between her knees until the feeling passed. No, no, no. Her dad had not hurt Carolyn. She was—that was a crazy, crazy thought. Amanda's nerves had her inventing things. How could her dad possibly follow her *and* get to Carolyn? Even he could not do that. It was nonsense. A subway delay was so much more likely.

Of all the times for Amanda not to have her phone. Maybe she should go home. If she ran at her usual pace, she could be there within ten minutes, hopefully to a message waiting from Carolyn.

The quickest way was down Center Drive and then up the stairs that cut through the woods. Much faster than heading back up the busier outer loop. Of course, the first rule of city living was that safety lay with the crowd. Even Amanda knew that. But the shortcut would save so much time.

Amanda eyed the quiet trees one last time before spinning toward the woods. She jogged quickly past a series of dark-green dumpsters along the desolate Center Drive, hulking like monsters in the shadows. Between them, the perfect place for someone to hide.

Soon Amanda was at the tall wooden steps, though, rising crooked and steep through the trees—so many trees—running faster than her daddy ever could. She was breathing hard, but feeling strong as she raced up the stairs, two at a time. Even if he was there, he'd never be able to catch her.

Halfway to the top there was a sound to the side, rustling in the trees. Amanda stumbled.

But she sped right back up. *Calm down. Keep going. Calm down. Keep going.* Just a squirrel, a bird, or one of those sickly raccoons. *Go,* Amanda commanded herself. *It's nothing. Get home.*

But she'd only gone a few more steps when she heard the voice. A man's voice. Deep and gruff, shredded from a lifetime of Marlboro Reds. Unforgettable. Daddy growling: *Amanda*. From the same direction as the rustling. He was right there. Close enough to grab hold.

Faster. Faster.

Amanda sprinted up the rest of the steps, away from the voice. Away from the rustling. Her father had left the flowers. He knew where she lived. He'd followed her out there tonight. When Carolyn hadn't shown up, he'd decided to seize the opportunity.

Amanda could outrun him, though. She was older now. Stronger.

She was almost at the top of the staircase. After that there was only a short stretch of trees before the path opened up to the meadow alongside the baseball fields. There were always people there. Her daddy wouldn't try to grab her in front of them. He'd always been a coward.

"Amanda!" Louder. She could feel the threat in it.

She sprang forward from the last step toward the opening in the distance. Feet pounding against the pavement. Teeth rattling.

Then out of the corner of her right eye: movement. A body hurtling toward her.

Amanda screamed. Raw and earsplitting. Not a word, just a sound. Like an animal. And then she dropped to the ground. You were harder to drag that way. She waited to feel Daddy's rough hands. Got ready to kick.

"Whoa! Hey!" A different voice. "Are you okay?"

Amanda scrambled backward and looked up. There was a very muscular, bare-chested man in running shorts, headphones dangling from his neck, headband pulling back his black curls. His hands were raised, mouth open, hazel eyes bulging. Amanda knew him, and didn't know him. She couldn't make out the details of his face. Definitely not her dad, though.

"Amanda, are you all right?" The man had an accent. French. "Did I— I'm so sorry. I called out when I saw you. I didn't mean to frighten you. Maude is always telling me that men don't think."

Maude. Sebe. Of course that was him. As she caught her breath, his face came into view.

"Oh, yes, I'm sorry," Amanda breathed. "I'm okay . . . I don't know what happened. I heard a noise. I thought somebody was following me. I guess I panicked. I shouldn't have taken that shortcut."

Sebe reached down a gallant hand. "Let's get you up at least."

"Thanks," Amanda said, letting him tug her to her feet. Her knees felt weak from the adrenaline.

"Are you sure you're okay?" Sebe asked, looking down at her leg. Amanda really wished he had a shirt on. "The way you fell was so sudden——did your ankle give way or something? Orthopedics isn't my area, but I have people I could call."

Amanda felt her cheeks flush. An ankle giving way would certainly be better than the truth: that she'd freaked out because her monster of a dad was stalking her.

"No, no. It was silly, really."

"I think there's a food vendor still up on the hill," Sebe said, calm and in charge despite being half naked. "Let's walk up and get you some water at least. Could be dehydration. You'd be shocked, the havoc it can wreak."

"You don't have to do that," Amanda said. The knee she'd fallen on had begun to throb, but she wasn't about to mention it. "Really, I'm fi—"

"Arguing is futile," Sebe said with a definitive shake of his head. "I am a doctor. I have an ethical obligation. Besides, Maude is angry enough at me already. If I leave you, she might kill me in my sleep." He smiled warmly. It made Amanda's chest burn. *Don't cry. Don't cry.*

"Okay," she said finally.

They walked on slowly up the hill, Amanda doing her best to hide the pain jabbing her knee with each step.

"There was somebody behind you?" Sebe asked, turning back toward the trees.

"I'm sure it was in my head," she said. "I have a really active imagination."

"I could walk you home? As a precaution. That will be Maude's first question: *Did you walk her home?*"

It might not be the worst idea. Sebe was so tall and athletic. His mere presence would scare her daddy away at least for the time being. But she didn't want to put him out.

"I'll be fine," Amanda said. "Really."

"This park is usually safe," Sebe said as they walked on. He was breathing quickly. "But then a city is a city. One should never get too comfortable."

He was quiet then until they'd reached the hot dog vendor. It was a merciful reprieve, though Amanda could feel him expecting some further explanation.

"Can I have two waters, please?" Sebe asked the man, pulling a twenty-dollar bill out of the phone holder strapped to his well-defined bicep.

Amanda wondered what it might be like to be married to a man like Sebe or Kerry: so kind and present and attentive. Being loved, really loved, like that. Amanda knew that Maude was frustrated with Sebe right now, and that Sarah and Kerry had had their issues. But the love between both couples was a thing you could use to steady yourself when the waters got rough. Zach and Amanda's marriage would never rescue her from anything.

"Thank you," Amanda said, taking the water from Sebe.

With each swallow, she realized how very thirsty she actually was. Within seconds, she'd finished the entire bottle.

Sebe laughed. "You do know that water is a thing you are supposed to be drinking, right?"

Amanda nodded. "I am dehydrated. You're right, so stupid," she said. "I'm sorry that I ruined your run."

"No, no. You saved me. I promised Maude I would start running. Her father died of a heart attack when he was my age. She lives in fear." He made a face. "Or maybe she wants to kill me. Either way, I would rather not run, but anything to get back on Maude's good side."

Amanda took a deep breath as they continued on toward the Ninth Street exit to the park. "Can I ask you something that's none of my business?"

"Sure," Sebe said. "Seeing as I was responsible for you falling."

"How do you and Maude do it?"

"Do what?" he asked, and it was clear from the wary look on his face that he was worried Amanda meant his and Maude's unorthodox sex life.

"How can you be angry at each other and stay so, I don't know, connected?"

Sebe considered this for a moment as they walked on. Darkness was descending quickly around them. "Forgiveness is a side effect of love," he said finally. And sadly, almost. "If you are going to be married, share the ups and downs of life. What other choice is there?"

"Right," Amanda said, like this was indeed a thing that was obvious.

They were quiet until they reached Prospect Park West, when Amanda saw two women running together and suddenly remembered: Carolyn.

"Oh, shoot," Amanda said. "Can you tell me what time it is?"

"Sure." Sebe pulled his phone out. "It's eight thirty-nine. Do you need to be somewhere?"

"I was supposed to meet my friend, and she never showed up. I was running home because I was worried about her."

"Do you want to call?" Sebe offered his phone.

"Oh, yes." Amanda reached for it. "Wait, I don't have her number memorized."

"Ah, damn technology. None of us know anything by heart anymore. Here, wait, a cab." Sebe raced forward to flag down a lime-green sedan. "You take it. I'd better finish my run. Got to pay penance to Maude." He handed Amanda the change from the water. "Take this for the cab fare. Are you sure you'll be okay?"

"I'm fine. Thank you so much. For everything."

———

Amanda had not fallen asleep when Zach finally got home at 11:45. Late, even for Zach. Not that Amanda had been waiting up for him. It was the conversation she'd had with Carolyn when she got home from the park that was gnawing at her as she lay alone in the dark.

"Are you okay?" Amanda had gasped when Carolyn finally answered the phone. "What happened?"

She'd truly panicked when there'd been no explanatory message waiting for her when she rushed in the house. Her legs had felt shaky as she'd dialed Carolyn's number. But there her friend was: alive and well. Not only that—Carolyn sounded irritated.

"What happened where?"

"You were supposed to meet me in the park. Remember? Eight p.m."

"Oh, shit. Sorry." But there was something nonchalant about it, and Amanda wondered if maybe she hadn't been planning to show up in the first place. "I forgot."

That was it. No explanation. No extenuating circumstances.

"You forgot?" Amanda had asked.

"Yes." Carolyn had snapped. "I got busy. I have a job, remember?"

"Oh, I was just so worried about you. I kind of freaked out." And, weirdly, Amanda was unable to shake the feeling that something terrible *had* happened to Carolyn. Even though Carolyn was there on the phone, proving that it hadn't. "And I just— I was going to tell you that I plan to do what you said. I'm going to stand up to Zach. You're right. I need to change things. I wasn't okay moving Case here, and I'm still not. I sent him to that stupid camp to make up for it, and now that's giving me nightmares. It's ridiculous. All this because I didn't say something earlier. With my dad around again, especially, I need to— I'm going to have to tell Zach."

She waited for Carolyn to say "Hooray!" To tell her how fantastic she was and then launch into one of those excellent Carolyn pep talks.

"Great," was all Carolyn said. Like she didn't care at all.

Anger bubbled up in Amanda's chest. "You know, I think maybe my dad was following me in the park because I was stuck there alone waiting for you."

"Really?" Carolyn asked, paying attention finally. But she did not sound nearly as remorseful as Amanda wanted her to.

"Yeah, *really.*"

"Listen, Amanda, there's something I need to tell you," Carolyn said. "I should have told you this before. But I didn't want to freak you out. It sounds like you already are, though, so . . ."

"What is it?" Amanda's palm was damp beneath the phone.

"I think I saw him." Carolyn exhaled in a gasp, like she'd been holding her breath.

"Saw who?"

"Your dad. When I was leaving your house."

"What?" Amanda's slick hand had started to tremble. She tried to take a deep breath, but her chest resisted.

"He was a few houses down, sitting on a stoop," Carolyn said. "He got up to leave when he saw me coming. It was dark, so I can't be one hundred percent sure. But I think it was him. He's so big. He's kind of hard to miss."

Amanda should have felt a fresh wave of terror then, but something about what Carolyn was saying didn't make sense.

"What do you mean, dark?" Carolyn had come by early in the morning the other day. "You were at my house at night also?"

"Whatever, morning then."

"But you just said it was dark."

"No, no. I just meant that I couldn't see his face well. That's all. Why are you interrogating *me*? I'm just trying to help."

Amanda thought back to Officer Carbone: *Keep asking yourself how he found you.* How did her dad track her down in Brooklyn, and after all this time?

"Yeah, okay," Amanda said. "Thank you."

"Listen, I have to go." Carolyn had sounded annoyed again. "I'll call you later."

But that was an hour ago, and Carolyn never had called back. Honestly, Amanda wasn't sure she wanted her to. Whatever was going on with Carolyn, it was giving Amanda the most unpleasant tightness in the pit of her stomach.

It was past midnight by the time Amanda finally heard Zach's feet on the stairs. Once in their bedroom, he would undress in their huge closet—as he always did—and then slide ever so quietly into bed so as not to wake her. As though she were a ticking bomb and not a wife. Sure enough, a moment later there he was, opening the door, changing in the shadows, then inching into bed, so careful not to make contact. *Forgiveness is a side effect of love.* What if that was her problem? What if she needed to try harder to forgive her husband his shortcomings? After all, she had them, too, didn't she?

Zach, Amanda imagined herself whispering to him. *I'm scared.*

But then Zach sighed heavily, in that way he so often did. Like he was steeling himself to weather their unbearable nighttime closeness. No, Amanda wouldn't say that. Her dad was getting closer, though. Zach needed to know. But for that, she'd need some actual time with Zach, to ease into telling him. Such a small thing to demand. A little time.

Amanda squeezed her eyes shut. "I need you to do something tomorrow night," she began, her heart already galloping away in the dark.

"Oh yeah?" Zach asked, like she always asked him to do things in the middle of the night. "What's that?"

Their marriage wasn't strong enough to keep her afloat, definitely not. And yet it was all she had. Amanda had no choice but to reach out and grab hold.

"I need you to go somewhere with me."

Another exhale. This one more annoyed. "Where?"

"A party," Amanda managed. "At my friend Maude's house. She's a friend of Sarah's, the woman who works at the foundation? It's uncomfortable that you never come to anything. They're insulted."

"That's absurd," Zach said, as though this were a scientifically verifiable fact.

"You need to be there. Because I need you to be there."

And Zach being there would be something. They could walk there together, and that would be a good opportunity to tell him about her dad. Could she just have told him right then? Yes, she could have. She did know that. But also, she couldn't.

"Who else will be there?" Zach asked.

"Mostly Country Day parents, I think."

"Ah," he said. Then he was quiet for an endless moment. "Fine, then. But I won't be able to stay long. I've got a work thing later on."

And then he turned over on his side and fell fast asleep.

LIZZIE

I got off the Q train at Seventh Avenue near Flatbush and headed toward Sarah's brownstone on First Street. I had suspicions about Sarah now, though it was hard to imagine someone as petite as her having the physical strength to kill anyone with a golf club. Still, there was a reason she'd lied about the accountant. And it didn't seem impossible that she and Zach might be in on something together—defrauding the foundation, or maybe even Amanda's death.

In the end, with no payment forthcoming, I'd left Evidentiary Analytics without Amanda's file but with a promise from Millie: "I'll work on Vinnie. I'll get it to you."

"I'm so sorry," I'd said to her, again. And there was so much to apologize for. "I obviously had no idea about Zach's finances. But I will get you paid. Zach has the brownstone. There has to be some equity there."

Millie also mentioned that a single print comparison might be an option even Zach could afford. Though it was surely the opposite of what Millie intended, that said to me one thing: *if* I got a sample from Xavier Lynch, and *if* that print matched the ones in the blood from the stairs that night, it could exonerate Zach. And I'd be free and clear.

If. If.

There were many problems with this plan. Not the least of which was how speculative it was. I'd also have to go alone to St. Colomb

Falls. There was no money to pay Millie's other investigators now, even if I'd been willing to wait until they were available. And I wasn't.

As I crossed Seventh Avenue at St. Johns Place, I spotted a standing sign on the opposite side, perfectly chalked, neon-pink rose in its center. "Blooms on the Slope" was written in an arc over the rose, an arrow pointing to the right. Once I crossed the street, I paused and searched through my bag. Sure enough, I had the card from Amanda's nightstand. I could at least check in to see if anybody at the florist recognized Xavier Lynch as the one who'd sent the flowers. It wouldn't necessarily get me out of a road trip to see a rapist, but it would be a start.

A small bell jingled when I opened the door. Blooms on the Slope was a narrow but chic shop, with an attractive older woman behind the counter, hair piled high and tied with a scarf. Her mouth was slightly upturned as she concentrated on an arrangement of all-yellow flowers. She was even humming contentedly. Watching her, I was overwhelmed by regret.

I'd imagined myself happy like her by now, with my dream job and Sam at my side, my past neatly wiped clean. And yet here I was, drafting email after email to my best friend from law school about what a disaster my life had become. Emails I was too ashamed to even send. Deep down I did know that these things—the secrets I'd kept, my marriage to Sam despite his problems, maybe even my getting sucked in by Zach—were not unrelated. Once this mess with Zach was over, I needed to reach out of my own darkness and at least tell Victoria about Sam's drinking. It was reckless to live with secrets. After all, if I hadn't kept so many, Zach wouldn't be able to use them against me now.

"Well, hello there!" the woman behind the counter called brightly when she finally noticed me, then appraised me with an air of concern. "You certainly look like someone who could use a little floral harmonizing."

I swallowed over the lump in my throat. "I'm trying to figure out who sent some flowers?" I began as I approached the counter. Though the shop did sell flowers, not guns. What type of records was I expecting them to keep? "I have a card, but it's unsigned. I know it's a long shot."

She stepped to the counter, looking concerned.

"Unsigned?" she asked, reaching out for the card. "I've got a policy against anonymous flowers. A sister of mine was stalked mercilessly in high school. Bastard left *roses* for her everywhere. Last thing I want is my flowers making somebody upset." She looked down at the card. "But it is one of ours, and this looks like Matthew's handwriting. Hold on a second. Hey, Matthew!" she called toward the back of the shop. "Can you come out here for a second?"

A moment later a gangly teenage boy with considerable acne, all black clothing, and a disaffected air emerged.

"Did you deliver flowers with this card?" she asked, holding it out to him. "This looks like your handwriting."

He hesitated for a long moment before finally reaching out and snatching the card. He looked down, shrugged. "Whatever. His wife was really mad at him. He came in and asked me to make out the card like it was from a secret admirer. He thought she would recognize his handwriting."

"Thank you, honey," the woman said, notably unfazed by his surly attitude. She turned back to me. "Sometimes we all have a hard time saying no to the people in this neighborhood. They can be, well, insistent would be a nice way of putting it. I hope the flowers didn't cause a problem."

"Could I show you a picture?" I asked Matthew. "To see if you recognize the person who bought them?"

"I guess," he offered, in that brooding yet curious teenaged way.

I pulled up a screenshot of the rummage-sale photo on my phone and handed it over to Matthew. "Do you see him in this picture?"

Matthew immediately shook his head. "Nope. Not him."

"Are you sure?" He'd answered so quickly it was like he hadn't even looked. "This picture was taken a couple years ago. He could look different now."

"That dude in the picture is a diamond," Matthew said with abso-lute surety. "The guy who came in here was a circle."

"Um . . ."

"He means the shape of the face," the woman said. "Officially there are seven. But Matthew—"

"Mom, twelve," he corrected sharply. When she raised an eyebrow at him, he shrugged again. "Whatever. But there *are* twelve."

"Mathew has identified some new subclasses, too," his mother said, smiling. "We had him tested when he was little—long story how we got there, which has everything to do with my opportunistic ex-husband—but he is officially gifted at facial recognition. If Matthew says it wasn't that man in here, it wasn't him."

Mathew finally looked directly at me. "If you have other pictures, I could definitely pick the guy out. No doubt."

I tried not to feel dejected as I approached Sarah's house. Even if they had recognized Xavier Lynch at Blooms on the Slope, that wouldn't be the same as having his fingerprint to compare. I'd probably be headed to St. Colomb Falls regardless.

Sarah's brownstone had seen better days. As I made my way up the steps, I noticed the signs of wear and tear—the cracked facade, a slope to the stairs, peeling paint on the shutters. Nonetheless it was a Park Slope brownstone, a four-million-dollar home I could never afford, but I did wonder if its relatively ailing condition was a sign of Sarah's need for money.

"Can I help you?" a man's voice called up to me as I was about to knock on the door. I turned, feeling like a trespasser.

At the bottom of the steps, in a Brooklyn Nets T-shirt and dark athletic shorts, was a burly guy with saggy eyes and a warm smile, presumably Sarah's husband. He had a pizza box in one hand and a six-pack in the other—at three in the afternoon on a weekday. Not a lawyer at a big firm, that was for sure—then again, successful people everywhere did play hooky occasionally. People other than me.

"Oh, I'm looking for Sarah?" I began, hoping I could get through this without having to identify myself as Zach's lawyer. The thought made me want to gag.

"Lunch and then a book-club outing to some author event at the 92nd Street Y," he said. "I'd say come in and wait, but it's more of a wine club than a book club. She'll probably be gone for hours. You're here about the emails, I suppose?"

"Yes," I said, grateful for the gift of an alternate explanation as I made my way down the steps.

"You and the rest of the world," he said with a rueful shake of his head. "I can take your name if you want. But I do know she's working on making the school get more information out to everyone. And I'm sure she'll have another meeting about it soon. There are *always* more meetings. And they are *always* in my home."

"I'll try her another time then," I said, smiling as I turned away and started down the sidewalk. "Thank you."

"No problem," he called after me. "Only do me a favor and don't tell her you saw me here at home at this hour. I wanted to watch a little Wimbledon, and that woman will never understand the importance of sports."

I nodded and smiled back. It was so hard to imagine this soft, affable guy with Sarah. "No problem."

By evening, Sam had sent half a dozen texts I'd ignored—all some version of: "Please, Lizzie, can we talk?" He'd called, too. In the third voice mail, he'd started to cry.

"I never deserved you," he'd said. *"You're kind and understanding and honorable. You're a much better person than me, Lizzie. You always have been."*

I felt sick to my stomach.

I parked myself at Café du Jour again. I checked in with Thomas and my secretary, answered emails, then spent a couple hours finalizing the overdue cell-phone-battery motion to dismiss. When the café closed, I moved to Purity Diner near our apartment, which somehow survived even though it was always empty. Their spanakopita was crap, but even my mother would have approved of their fries. "A front," I imagined my dad proclaiming as he so often did about such restaurants, with no evidence whatsoever. He never did like cheaters.

I stayed at Purity until there was at least a reasonable chance Sam would be asleep. If we'd had more money, I would have gone to a hotel. If we'd had more money, I probably would never have gone home. It wasn't as if there was anything Sam could say now that would make me feel better. He didn't know where the earring had come from and also couldn't say for sure that it didn't belong to some woman he'd screwed while too drunk to remember. That was really the beginning and the end of the conversation, at least the conversation I wanted to have.

And I was convinced Sam was telling the truth about not remembering. It would have been too much easier to lie. Part of me wished Sam had. That way we could have just continued on as we had been. We had deep fissures, sure, but we were still in one piece. Now we'd be trapped in a place where doubt would nibble at our edges until, at long last, it devoured us whole.

When I finally got home, Sam was asleep as I'd hoped, propped up on the living room couch, having apparently lost the battle to wait up for me. His head was tilted back, mouth slightly open. When I leaned in close, he didn't smell of alcohol. Asleep and not passed out drunk. Victory once again.

Standing there watching him sleep, I wasn't even angry anymore, only overwhelmed by grief. Alcoholic or not, Sam was *still* smart and kind and passionate. Seeing him across a room *still* made my heart pick up speed. My life had begun again when I met him. And yet none of that meant we should stay together. I'd been so foolish to think love could change the essential nature of anything.

My phone rang in my bag.

Sam bolted awake. "What's wrong?"

"Nothing, go back to sleep," I said, hurrying into the bedroom and closing the door. I dug my phone out and answered. "Hello?"

"You have a collect call from a New York State—"

I hit **1**, cutting short the recording. Zach must have bribed somebody at Rikers—with what I didn't want to know—to let him use a phone at that late hour.

"Hi," Zach said, sounding positively cheerful once he was on the line. What a relief it must have been for him not to have to pretend anymore. *Asshole.*

"I spoke with your accountant," I launched in. "As you are aware, there are no funds available to cover the experts' retainer. It's potentially soured your relationship with them, which was stupid because they're really good. You will also need to pay them for the work they've already done. They'll sue you if they have to. And then no one will work for you. You *are* going to need experts, too—a lot of them—in order to win this case."

"Meaning what?" he asked, notably not sounding surprised.

"Meaning you'll need to get the money from somewhere," I said. "The fingerprint evidence is potentially exculpatory, and they only just got started. It's the best chance you've got."

"Exculpatory?" Zach sounded delighted.

I hated making him happy. But I refused to give him the satisfaction of getting emotional in response. This was something I was being forced to do, but I could treat it like any other job. If nothing else, I had always known how to get a job done.

"There are some prints on your golf bag that match some others in Amanda's blood from your stairs," I said. "The prints aren't yours, but they do belong to someone who was there that night."

"Oh, thank God." He exhaled loudly. "I've got to be honest, I was starting to get a little worried you weren't going to pull this off."

"Fuck you, Zach." So much for staying unemotional. I was so angry now it was making my eyeballs throb.

"Fuck me?" He laughed. "Hey, you're the one who's been lying to everyone. First on that form, and then about your marriage. And who knows what else." Oh, I did not like the way he had said that. What else did he know? "I may have been a shitty husband, but at least I was honest about it. Getting back to the money, I'll be honest about that, too: there is none. But we'll need those fingerprint results, obviously. So use your creativity. I'm sure you'll figure something out."

"Zach, this is ridiculous," I said, though I knew there was no point.

"Agreed, this entire situation *is* ridiculous," he said crisply. "I'd much rather have avoided the complication of our shared history. But where else was I going to find a great lawyer, with access to the world's best experts, who was willing to work for free? And to think, you never would have even occurred to me as a possibility if I hadn't seen you at the farmer's market in Prospect Park."

"You go to the farmer's market?" I asked. I could not remotely imagine Zach buying organic produce and bringing it home in a reusable shopping bag.

"As you can imagine, not to shop," he said. "It's great for observing people, though. It's important to know people's strengths if you're going to work with them. But you know what's more important?"

"No, Zach," I said. "What's more important than knowing someone's strengths?"

"Knowing their weaknesses."

There was a click. I'd been hung up on by a man locked away in Rikers. A man who somehow still held the key.

GRAND JURY TESTIMONY

BENJI PANKIN,

called as a witness the 8th of July and was examined
and testified as follows:

EXAMINATION

BY MS. WALLACE:

Q: Good afternoon, Mr. Pankin. Thank you for coming
to testify today.

A: You're welcome.

Q: Were you at the party at 724 First Street on the
night of July 2nd?

A: Yes.

Q: How did you come to be there?

A: We were invited. I used to play basketball in a
league in the neighborhood with Sebe. Neither of us
play anymore, but I know some of the guys, Kerry and
them.

Q: Who did you attend the party with?

A: My wife, Tara Pankin.

Q: Were you aware that there were sexual activities
going on at the party that night?

A: Not that night specifically. But we've been to
that party before. I'd heard about that kind of thing
previously.

Q: Did you participate in those activities?

A: No.

Q: Why not?

A: Why not? Because my wife would fucking kill—
sorry, excuse me. Poor choice of words. I know some
marriages . . . I know that people do that kind of
thing and it works out fine. They even manage to keep it
all a secret. Who ends up with who at that party never
gets out. To each his own and all that. But it wouldn't
work for us. I'd kill my wife, too, by the way.

Q: I see.

A: Shit. I'm sorry. I don't know why I keep saying
kill. This whole thing is just . . . Anyway, no, we
didn't have sex with each other or anybody else at the
party. We did drink too much sangria. For half the night
I was wearing a jester's hat I found on the floor, if
that tells you anything.

Q: Do you have a clear memory of that night?

A: I do. I remember everything that happened. I'm not
like an alcoholic or something. I had three glasses of
sangria. That's it.

Q: Did you know Amanda Grayson?

A: No.

Q: Did you see a woman exit abruptly out the back of
the party that night?

A: I did.

Q: Can you describe what happened?

A: She came down the stairs and was trying to leave
out the front, but it was too crowded. She looked upset

and in a hurry, so I told her to go out the back. I warned her that we weren't really supposed to do that. One year, Sebe's neighbor called the cops.

Q: What time was that?

A: 9:47 p.m.

Q: How do you know so precisely?

A: Because somebody had just asked me what time it was.

Q: I would like to show you a photograph.

(Counsel approaches witness with photograph, which was previously marked as People's Exhibit 6.)

Q: Is that the woman you pointed the exit out to?

A: Yes.

Q: Let the record reflect that Exhibit 6 is a photograph of Amanda Grayson. Shortly before you pointed that woman out toward the back door, did you have an interaction with a man?

(Counsel approaches witness with photograph, which was previously marked as People's Exhibit 5.)

Q: Is this that man?

A: Yeah.

Q: Let the record reflect that the witness has been shown a photograph of Zach Grayson. What did Zach Grayson say to you?

A: He told me to get out of his fucking way.

Q: Why did he say that?

A: He was in a hurry, too, I guess. I probably was in the way. Like I said, I was drunk.

Q: What happened after that?

A: After that, he shoved me to the side and headed out the front door.

Q: Are you sure that Mr. Grayson left before Amanda left?

A: Yeah, like right before. Because after I saw her,
I got up and I went to find the bathroom. I ended up
passing out in there for a while on the floor. When
my wife found me it was after 10:00 p.m. and she was
seriously pissed.

LIZZIE

St. Colomb Falls was farm country, but not the quaint Vermont farms that I'd so loved when Sam and I had been there for his thirtieth birthday. My memories of that weekend had always been of charming red barns and white fences, and Sam and me dancing alone to distant country music in the Echo Lake Inn's moonlit backyard. But now I'd also remembered how wasted Sam had gotten on Dark and Stormies, sleeping both days until noon. It was as though Sam's admission about the earring had finally ripped my blinders off, taking the top layer of skin along with them. I could now see every memory for what it was: corrupted by the reality of Sam's alcoholism. And my pathological willingness to overlook it.

Unlike picturesque Vermont, St. Colomb Falls was filled with working farms, where hundreds of cows were raised for slaughter and chickens were crammed into feather-filled warehouses the length of football fields. It was gritty and dirty and desolate.

The farms were set off the main highway that ran through the center of town, which, it turned out, consisted only of a post office, gas station, Dollar General store, and Norma's Diner—a rusted metal box that looked like it had been there for decades. On the far side of town, there were occasional signs for hiking trailheads and campgrounds and the Adirondacks, though it was hard to imagine anything remotely recreational or scenic taking place anywhere nearby.

The homes were heavy with wear and tear, the worst downright disintegrating. And why was St. Colomb Falls so empty at ten on a Saturday morning? Like everyone was hiding from some threat about which I was stupidly unaware. I was feeling extra jittery, too, maybe because I'd gotten up so early. In an effort to continue avoiding Sam, I'd left well before dawn. He'd woken anyway, long enough to demand to know where I was going and for me to turn my destination into an attack.

When Xavier Lynch's house finally appeared ahead on the left, I felt a small wave of relief. The low ranch was the same shape and size as all the others, but it was painted a deep gray with sparkling white trim and a cheerful red door. There were large planters on either side of the small front porch, too, filled with fuchsia and purple flowers. Even the mailbox was painted to match the house with some steel detail. I double-checked the address. Definitely the right house. Of course, Xavier Lynch having a nice house did not make him a good person. But a monster with a well-tended home might be less likely to kill an uninvited lawyer from New York.

All I needed to do in this first visit was to confirm that the person who lived here was, in fact, Xavier Lynch, bonus points if he admitted he was Amanda's dad. My plan was then to occupy myself somehow until dark. Under cover of night, I'd return to Xavier's home and quietly rifle through his garbage in search of some things likely to provide fingerprints—a bottle, a can, a plastic fork.

I took a deep breath as I got out of the car and headed up the manicured front walk. I knocked hard on the screen door and waited, bracing myself for the door to snap open, for someone to lead with *What the fuck do you want?* Or worse, for pain—a hand on my throat, a fist to the jaw.

But the door opened slow and calm, the huge man looming on the other side of the screen the very same, very large Xavier Lynch from the church newsletter. He was even wearing similar khakis and a button-down with the same large, nearly fashionable glasses covering half his big face. A diamond, maybe. These shapes weren't obvious to me. He was even taller than he'd appeared in the picture, though. Maybe it had been the angle, or that the woman pictured had also been exceptionally tall. Xavier Lynch was bigger than Sam, six foot three or four, and must have been pushing 225 pounds. I suddenly felt very easy to kill.

"Can I help you?" His voice was taut. He looked past me out to the driveway, as though worried I might not be alone.

"My name is Lizzie Kitsakis, and I'm an attorney. I've been asked to locate the beneficiaries of a significant financial estate," I began, sounding—I now realized—like an email scam.

"I'd highly doubt you're looking for me," he said, skeptical but not aggressive. "I don't stand to inherit nothing from nobody."

He adjusted his glasses then, and in a way that made me wonder if they were just for show. He also opened his door some more—hopefully not to invite me inside. My entire strategy—such as it was—had been predicated on staying in the relative safety of the outdoors.

"Are you Xavier Lynch?" I asked, not moving a step closer.

"I am." He adjusted his glasses again. Then he slid his hands into the pockets of his pleated pants. There was something so deliberate about each gesture, as if he had carefully studied the steps of a normal-person routine.

"The inheritance is actually in the name of Amanda Lynch. She didn't leave a will, and under the circumstances, you are her sole heir."

That wasn't true, of course. Amanda had a son. I also had no idea if she'd left a will. If she hadn't, any money in her name would have gone to Case, then Zach. Not that there was any money anyway, apparently.

"Amanda," he said, then hung his head. It was over his bowed head that I glimpsed the large cross on the wall behind him. Little Jesus.

But when Xavier finally looked up, his expression was more resigned than guilty. "You're the person who called before?"

I nodded. "I thought it might be easier if I came in person to explain."

He looked embarrassed. "I'm sorry that I hung up on you."

I nodded. "That's okay."

"No, it's not. That's not the person I am anymore. I mean, I have been that person, God knows." He shook his head. "Once upon a time, hanging up on a nice lady would have been the least of the bad things I did in a day."

Nice lady. The way he said it gave me the chills.

"I understand," I said, though I did not.

"I've tried so hard to make it right," he went on, leaning against the doorframe and gesturing behind him, to the cross maybe, to a family inside. I had no idea, though others living in that house would complicate any fingerprint analysis. What if I didn't pull Xavier's? "I've tried so hard to make *me* right. I've had whole years I'd just as soon forget. But this house, my job—I'm a supervisor at the Perdue processing plant two towns over. I'm even thinking about marrying my girlfriend if she wears me down a little more. Anyway, I've been keeping myself on the straight and narrow. It hasn't always been easy, but these days I'm making my way."

"I understand," I said again, but dread was creeping up the back of my scalp.

Xavier Lynch looked away as he sniffled. Was he actually crying, or only pretending to? "How did Amanda die?"

I needed to be careful now. He was fishing for what I knew. And, polite or not, there was something decidedly off about Xavier Lynch. Like every moment that passed was yet another he'd survived without doing something monstrous. Xavier and I were doing okay so far, but maybe that was only because I hadn't tried to bolt.

"She was found at the bottom of the stairs in her house. She died of a head injury," I said. All true facts. "They've arrested her husband."

Xavier winced slightly. "She always was on borrowed time."

Well now, what did *that* mean?

"Had she told you about problems she was having?"

"Me?" He shook his head, frowned. "Oh, I haven't talked to Amanda for at least twelve years, longer probably, since . . . you know." He made a vague motion with his hand.

"No. I don't know. Since what?"

His eyes narrowed and turned colder. "Who did you say you were again?"

"An attorney." I tried to imagine how far the car was behind me. How quickly I could turn and race toward it. "Amanda's estate needs to be divided."

My mouth felt tacky, and my eyes had started to burn. Like I was staring into the lights of an oncoming train. *Brace yourself.*

Xavier was staring at me differently now. Not quite hostile, but nearly. "Why don't you tell me why you're really here?"

"I'm here because of the will, like I told you," I said as calmly as I could. "As Amanda's father, you're her rightful next of kin."

"What?" Xavier sounded almost offended. He shook his head vigorously. "No, no, no. Amanda is—was—my niece."

Fuck. All the time I'd already wasted.

I tried to keep myself composed. "Excuse the mistake. Do you know where I can find Amanda's father? I really do need to talk to him."

Xavier's eyebrows bunched as he tilted his head to the side. Like maybe I was messing with him. "Saint Ann's Cemetery."

"He's *dead*?" I asked, my heart picking up speed. "What do you mean? When?"

"Oh, twelve, thirteen years ago now."

"That's not possible."

"Afraid it sure is." Angry now, definitely. "What the hell is this anyway? Are you fucking with me?"

What the hell was he talking about, dead?

"No, no. I'm sorry, Mr. Lynch, I just— I don't understand. My information didn't say anything about his having passed away."

"I don't know how you can know Amanda and not know that she killed her father. Not that it was her fault. My brother William always was a fucking asshole."

My ears were ringing. *Holy. Shit.*

"I'm sorry, what?" My voice was high and shrill.

"Amanda killed her father. Twelve, thirteen years ago," he said, with less of an edge this time. "But he deserved it for sure."

"What happened?"

"Apparently Amanda came up on William in the bathroom on top of one of her girlfriends. They'd been spending the night at that dump of a trailer on prom weekend, of all damn things. William was drunk and, um, violating the friend, or trying to. Cops said the friend was already dead by then—William had hit her head on the bathtub. My guess is that part was an accident. He probably didn't even notice. William was so damn huge, bigger than me. I know that doesn't make what he was doing better, but . . ."

Xavier glanced up at me. His eyes were sad now, and ashamed.

"I'm sorry," I said reflexively.

"Yeah, well, Amanda tried to save her friend, I guess. There was a straight razor sitting right there on the sink. And that was that." Xavier shook his head, looked down, and kicked at the doorframe. "And that was that. Fucking waste. My brother never was right, though, not even as a little kid. Not crazy, just wrong. As a grown-ass man, he was one sick son of a bitch."

My mouth felt glued shut. I swallowed hard.

"What was Amanda's friend's name?" I asked, pressing my heels down. The ground felt unsteady beneath me. "Do you know?"

Xavier looked up toward the sky. "Cathy or Connie . . ."

"Carolyn?"

"That's it. Carolyn," he said with a nod. "Her and Amanda were like sisters. Or that's what people said. I got to be honest—details were lost on me back then. I had a lot of problems. That's why I've stopped drinking—that garbage will ruin your life."

KRELL INDUSTRIES

CONFIDENTIAL MEMORANDUM
NOT FOR DISTRIBUTION

July 2

To: Brooklyn Country Day Board of Directors
From: Krell Industries
Subject: Data Breach & Cyber Incident Investigation—Progress Report

Interview Summaries:

A total of 56 families have come forward to be interviewed regarding hacking of their personal information. Each occurrence involved the theft of personally compromising information. In no instance did anyone comply with the demand for money. Nonetheless, in no case was the threatened retaliatory action ever taken—no potentially defamatory information has yet been made public.

Preliminary Conclusions:

Evidence continues to suggest that the individual responsible:

- Had some change in circumstance with respect to Brooklyn Country Day in April or May of this year.

- Stands to benefit in some secondary way from the harassment, such as a reporter who would then move in to cover the alleged hacking.

- It is possible a Brooklyn Country Day student is seeking to inflict discomfort or embarrassment on fellow students. We will work with the administration to isolate any such students.

LIZZIE

I drove from St. Colomb Falls straight to Weill-Cornell Hospital on the Upper East Side. Nestled behind a gate and between dozens of trees, the hospital looked, in the setting sun, more like a leafy college campus than home to Millie's cancer ward.

When I got off the elevator on Millie's floor, patients were shuffling about, dragging IVs behind them like stubborn dogs. I hadn't been in a hospital since my mother's untimely death, and I'd forgotten how instantly claustrophobic the misery could be.

But then, my lungs had felt caged ever since I'd pulled away from Xavier Lynch's house, haunted by the thought of Amanda running for all those months from someone who wasn't even there. Or so Xavier's story would suggest. It wasn't as if I planned just to take his word for it. He'd seemed credible, sure, but also definitely threatening. For all I knew, he'd made up the entire thing and really was Amanda's dad, after all.

Xavier's story was certainly hard to process, too: Amanda had clearly thought her dad and Carolyn were very much alive. She'd written about both of them in her most recent journal. In one entry, Amanda had even described, in great detail, Carolyn visiting her house in Park Slope. Was that just how deep her commitment to her imagined world had gone? How badly she'd needed to believe? By the time I'd pulled into the St. Colomb Falls County Clerk's cracked, weed-filled parking lot, I felt nauseous thinking about it.

After some back-and-forth and lots of polite chitchat, the tiny old woman inside the small, brick clerk's office—mercifully open on a Saturday—had finally confirmed that William Lynch had indeed been killed twelve years earlier, after having murdered a teenage girl named Carolyn Thompson—his daughter's best friend. No one had gone to jail because the perpetrator—Amanda Lynch, the clerk told me in a loud stage whisper presumably meant to preserve confidentiality— was deemed to have been acting in defense of her best friend.

And so Amanda's dad really *was* dead. And so was her best friend Carolyn.

Afterward, I'd sat there in the blazing sun, trying to google my way to an understanding of how Amanda might have completely erased such a traumatic episode from her memory, and what her hallucina- tions might mean about her mental state. One of Amanda's older jour- nals had talked about Carolyn always getting herself in the middle of things. Was that what had happened that awful night all those years ago? Had Carolyn put herself in harm's way to protect Amanda and ended up dead herself?

According to the ever-unreliable internet, there were many possible causes for Amanda's hallucinations: schizophrenia, bipolar disorder, psychotic depression. Some illnesses were more serious than others. Some were episodic, others would have disrupted Amanda's thinking so completely it was hard to imagine she'd have been as high-functioning as she was. But I did come upon one that seemed to click: delusional disorder. According to the Harvard Medical School website I ended up on, a person with delusional disorder "holds a false belief firmly, de- spite clear evidence or proof to the contrary . . . Unlike people with schizophrenia, they tend not to have major problems with day-to-day functioning. Other than behaviors related to delusional content, they do not appear odd."

Fucking Zach. Could I say for sure that a better husband would have been paying close enough attention to see that Amanda needed help? That they might have even saved her from whatever terrible thing had happened to her the night she died? No. I, of all people, could not say that. I could not even say for sure that Amanda had delusional disorder, much less that it was directly tied to her death. But thinking of how tragically isolated Amanda had been was making my chest ache.

"I'm looking for Millie Faber," I said once I'd made my way to the nurse's station.

The nurse scanned a list of names. "Room six oh three. Down the hall and to the left." She pointed without looking up.

I made my way down the hushed hallway, the stillness back there even worse than the sick, shuffling crowd up front. At least those patients had been able to move. In the back, everyone seemed confined to their beds. How could Millie have seemed okay yesterday, only to be staying on the extra sick hallway today? Of course, my mother had gone from completely fine to absolutely dead in seconds. Also, Millie hadn't actually seemed fine.

I knocked gently as I pushed open the door to 603, relieved to see Millie sitting upright in a corner chair, laptop on her knees, papers spread out across the dirty linoleum floor. She was in a well-fitting navy-blue sweat suit, not a hospital gown, and she had not lost her hair overnight or shed any more pounds.

"Are you supposed to be doing that?" I asked.

"Doing what?" Millie's tone was gruff, her eyes still on her computer screen. But her face had brightened for a second when she heard my voice.

"Working," I said.

She shrugged. "It's work or worry. Better to keep busy."

The longer I stared at Millie, the worse she looked, though. "It's more serious than you said, isn't it?" I asked.

Millie frowned, eyes locked on her computer. She was quiet for a moment more. Finally, she looked up at me. "It had already metastasized by the time they found it—lung, bones, *and* liver. The trifecta. Apparently, it's very unique. Lucky me."

"Millie, holy shit." I dropped myself down hard on the nearby windowsill. "I'm so—"

Millie held up a hand. "You know I don't want pity. What I *do* want to talk about is how goddamn stupid it was for you to go up there. I thought we had an agreement?"

"Go up where?"

She scowled. "Let's not lie right to my face. Sam told me."

"Sam?" I asked. "You don't even have his number."

"I went by your house this morning, on my way here," she said flatly. "Had a feeling you'd gone AWOL. I am a detective, remember?"

Sam had known I was headed to St. Colomb Falls. I'd thrown it at him like a threat: *If something happens to me, it will be all your fault.* Everything was Sam's fault now.

"And what did Sam have to say, exactly?"

Millie put the folder down on her lap and rested her hands on top of it. They looked old, bony. "That you'd gone upstate to talk to the dead woman's father. Who, if I'm not mistaken, you suspect of killing her." She raised an eyebrow at me. "But Sam didn't seem to know that part. He seemed confused why you were helping some random guy charged with murder in the first place. There was a lot he didn't seem to know. Nice guy, though. Chatty."

"What's that supposed to mean?" Had she caught Sam buzzed at noon?

"Well, among other things, I could tell he didn't have a clue who I was." She lifted her chin and leveled her bloodshot eyes at me.

I moved my mouth to say something. But what? *Please can we not do this now? Can we not do it ever?* Millie seemed to register the panic in my eyes. Her face softened.

"Anyway," she went on, "I would have postponed this nonsense by a day if you'd told me you were going to go yourself."

"It couldn't wait," I said, then motioned to the hospital room. "And you couldn't postpone this."

"It can always wait. Trust me. This guy isn't worth risking your life for."

"It couldn't wait," I said again. "For my sake."

"What does that mean?"

I took a deep breath. I was out of places to hide. "Zach Grayson is extorting me," I said. "He's using some compromising information to make me stay on the case until he's cleared."

"Seriously?"

"Yes, seriously."

"Tell him to fuck off then!" Millie shouted.

"You do know how extortion works, right?" I asked. "You tell them to fuck off, and then they do the bad things you don't want them to do."

"Wait, this isn't about—"

"No, no," I said. "Zach doesn't know about that. At least, as far as I know."

"Then what the hell else could he possibly have on you?" She sniffed. Then she leaned in, an eyebrow raised again. "Wait, you didn't go to one of those sex parties, did you?"

I shook my head. "It's Sam. He's an . . . alcoholic." The word tore at my throat even now. "That's where the problem started. The rest spirals out from there. There's a lawsuit relating to a car accident Sam had, and now we owe a lot of money. I lied about it on a financial disclosure form when I took the job at Young & Crane, because I was worried they wouldn't hire me. And we so badly needed the money to dig us out of debt. For sure, they'll fire me if Zach tells them. I could be disbarred. It would ruin my career."

"That motherfucker." She shook her head in disgust. "How the hell did he even find that out?"

I shrugged. "Who knows. Other detectives?"

"Bet he pays them." She smiled.

A nurse came in then with a tray of needles and small bottles of medicine. She set it on the counter behind Millie and, without making eye contact with either one of us, moved about, methodically adjusting various tubes. "You ready to get started in ten, sweetheart?" she asked Millie in a voice that was two parts robot, one part genuinely kind.

"Sure thing," Millie said. "Soon as I'm done with my friend here."

"Okay, sweetheart," the nurse said distractedly as her phone buzzed. "I'll be right back."

She hustled out then, already on her phone.

"All right, we'll figure out how to deal with Zach Grayson in a second," Millie said once she was gone. "In the meantime, what did you find upstate? You have the prints? Not to reward your dumb-ass judgment, but as soon as I found out you went up there, I reached out to the lab. Got them to agree to run one more comparator sample for us on a rush basis whenever we have it. Just the one, and only to the print on the stair, and maybe the golf bag. But at least they agreed to bill us after the fact. All I need to do is call and say the word."

"What about Vinnie?"

Millie waved a hand. "It's one sample. He'll survive."

"You didn't tell him."

"Not yet."

"Thank you," I said with a dejected exhale. "But unfortunately all I discovered in St. Colomb Falls was that everything I thought I knew was wrong. Turns out Xavier Lynch is Amanda's uncle, not her father. And Amanda's father couldn't have killed her because he's dead. It happened twelve years ago. The father attacked Amanda's friend; Amanda intervened. Her father and the friend both ended up dead."

Millie let out a long whistle.

"I confirmed it with the St. Colomb Falls clerk's office. Amanda was a juvenile, so the criminal records are sealed, but they told me enough."

"I thought she had a whole journal about her dad stalking her?"

I nodded. "And she'd told her Park Slope friends that the dead friend was alive and well in Manhattan," I said. "Amanda was troubled, clearly—seems to have been delusional, which calls into question all her observations. Or so the prosecution will say."

"So no one was stalking her?"

I shrugged. "No one. Or someone other than her dad."

"Weird that your friend Zach didn't notice, huh?" And she meant *weird* as in: *There's no fucking way that's true.*

"Apparently, Amanda was high-functioning. Her friends didn't notice anything wrong either. Then again, they'd only known her for a few months. But she had a job and took great care of her son, everyone agrees about that. Her delusions must have been contained. Zach claims she hadn't said a word about her dad in years, not about any stalker either," I said. "Sounds like they didn't talk much about anything."

"You believe him?"

"About that I do. Zach's a narcissist. I don't think he had any interest in hearing about Amanda's problems. My guess is he made clear she was on her own."

"Well, that's fucking awful," Millie said. "Where does it leave you?"

"Stuck on a case, and with a client I want the hell away from. But I'm pretty sure the only way to do that is to get the charges dismissed. Some unidentified person's fingerprints are in the blood on those stairs. Which means somebody else was there that night. Somebody who didn't call the police and who hasn't come forward."

"Of course it doesn't necessarily mean your client didn't kill her. He could have been there, too. He could have hired someone."

"I know," I said. "But even if he did, I've got to get him off if I want to keep my job. Unless I can figure some other way out, like finding something I can use against Zach. Make it worth his while to let me off the hook."

Millie nodded. "I like that idea much better. Either way, just get your ass away from this whole thing. Life's way too fucking short for this bullshit. Trust me." She lifted one of the folders off the floor and held it out to me, but didn't relinquish her grip. "This is everything I've got.

And I'm giving it to you on the condition that you don't do any more of your own sleuthing out in the field. I will find you someone to help for free if need be."

I nodded too quickly. "Of course not."

She let go of the file. "Hmm. That's what you said yesterday. It's bad karma to lie to people who are dying."

"Come on, you're not—"

"I am, Lizzie," she said. Her expression was serious, but also calm. "That's the reality. And it could happen anytime. That's what the doctors have said. Point-blank. A bunch of times. They don't go around telling you to get your affairs in order just for shits and giggles. This whole chemo thing is a Hail Mary pass. It's possible it'll even make me worse, fast. That's why all the emails. I wanted to be sure I'd spoken to you . . . in case. You know I've always been more than happy to do anything that might make things a little bit easier for you. After everything your mother did for me when Nancy was sick, that's the least I could do. But me being the intermediary—it was always a Band-Aid, wasn't it?" She was quiet for a moment, then looked up at me through narrowed eyes. My heart was picking up speed. "What does Sam know, exactly?"

"He knows about the fraud, and my mom's heart attack," I offered weakly. "But Sam . . . he thinks that my dad is dead, too. That's, um, what everyone thinks."

"You've been telling everybody your dad is dead?" Millie asked, her expression a mixture of disappointed and dumbfounded. "All this time?"

"I needed distance from the whole situation," I said, and God, did I sound defensive. "You saw me. I was a mess."

And I was, for a long time. Of course I did eventually pull out of my depression. Enough so that I made my way to college and law school, made friends, got married. All of that a long time ago. And yet I'd let Millie keep on running interference for me like I was still a seventeen-year-old girl so grief-stricken I couldn't get out of bed.

But that was eighteen years ago. I hadn't spoken to my dad for eighteen years. And I could live with that, but what about my mother? How sad she would be that I'd never gone to Greece myself in all these years, that I'd never set foot again in a Greek church.

He'd sent a few letters over the years. Not the desperate pleas you might expect, though, no begging for forgiveness, no proclamations of love. Because that wasn't my dad. He didn't feel any of those things. His few letters had been matter-of-fact updates—mechanical, obligatory. Like he was trying to keep me in play in case he needed me later. Millie had also told me over the years when he'd asked about me. Was I doing well in school? What kind of money was I making? Never really about me. And he never once asked Millie why I hadn't visited myself. She'd made that very clear to me, always. She'd never wanted me to feel guilty.

"But distance is different than complete amnesia, Lizzie," Millie went on. "And you're *married* to Sam."

"I know." My heart was hammering.

Millie stared at me then, for such a terribly long time. My whole body felt hot, shame blazing through me. I was ashamed of what my father had done, yes. But even more of my inability to face it. Instead I'd shoved it deep down, where it was now buried beneath all those other things I'd tried to will out of existence—Sam's persistent drinking, our debt, my derailed career, my nonexistent baby.

"Well," Millie continued. "You can keep on pretending he's gone, I guess. That's your choice. But it might feel different without a go-between."

"Have you seen him recently?" I asked.

"Few months ago. I still try to go once a year. And he still calls occasionally, once every six months. In between, I can get enough information from my contacts at Elmira. Your dad's the same old, three-quarters asshole, one-quarter charming son of a bitch," she said. "Listen, I'm not defending him or what he did. Hell, he wasn't the best guy to begin with. But eventually he is going to get out, could be as soon as three or four years from now. Then what? It's a free country. He could come see you."

"It's been better for me this way."

"Has it, though?" Millie asked, and the concern in her eyes made my own eyes burn.

I looked away when the tears finally came, trying to will my voice strong. "You and I both know what he did that night wasn't some accident. He stabbed that guy, Millie. My dad *killed* someone, and yeah, he was upset about my mother, but you know what I think? I think my dad was more angry that guy took his money. He wanted revenge."

Millie held up her hands as if in surrender. "Maybe so. Listen, I don't have a horse in this race. I'm not trying to talk you into forgiveness. I'm here because I loved your mother and she loved you. All she ever cared about was you feeling safe and happy. I want you to be happy." She handed me a pack of tissues from her bag; I was crying hard now. "And for what it's worth, you don't seem so great. I do not think pretending your dad is dead has been helping you. Not one fucking bit."

LIZZIE

I stopped back at work on my way home, intent on starting to set things right. One by one, that's how I'd deal with all the problems I'd been trying to ignore. First up: my financial disclosure form. Without that, Zach had nothing on me and I could be done with him and his case. Two birds, one stone. I was hoping to find Paul at the office on a Saturday. He often was, along with many other, more junior Young & Crane lawyers. Confessing to Paul my misrepresentations on the financial disclosure was a risk. I'd need to test the waters first, talk vaguely and in hypotheticals and bring up the financial disclosure tangentially somehow. Maybe I could be allowed the one misstep, especially after Paul had exposed to me his Wendy Wallace Achilles' heel.

Young & Crane was quieter than I'd expected. Paul's office was dark, but Gloria was there outside his office, typing away, looking disgruntled about something—though surely not the overtime. Gloria loved overtime. I checked my watch: 7:27 p.m.

"Is Paul coming back?" I asked.

She shook her head and pursed her lips judgmentally, but kept typing. "Unlikely, don't you think?" She shot me a loaded look.

Why couldn't Paul's secretary just come back? Everything with Gloria was so exhausting.

"What do you mean?" I asked, trying to keep the impatience from my voice.

Gloria stopped typing. This time when she looked up, a sly smile spread across her face.

"He didn't even tell *you*? Interesting." Her voice was smug. "Wendy Wallace. They're having *drinks*. Or something," she said coyly. "Isn't she on that case of yours? Pretty ironic—Paul, of all people, thinking he's got the right to run around being the morality police."

I hoped the sense of betrayal didn't register on my face. But Paul having drinks with Wendy Wallace? *After* I'd told him how nasty she'd been when I went to see her? Of course it was a betrayal, even if it was probably one I should have seen coming.

"Oh right, I forgot," I said to Gloria. "If you could just let him know I stopped by."

I wandered back to my office to collect some files to work on at home, feeling wounded. Not that I was one to judge Paul. All I did was curate the truth—about my marriage, my family, myself. But what I'd said to Millie was the actual truth: it wasn't like I'd set out to lie.

I'd arrived by bus at Cornell's manicured campus for the start of freshman year upright, but barely. By then, I'd had precisely enough therapy to keep moving, but not really to heal, not in any meaningful sense. Standing in my empty dorm room, with no parents to deliver me or to help set up my room or to cry at the door when they said good-bye, I felt myself backsliding with alarming speed. Like there was a giant black hole of desperation about to suck me away. And then my roommate appeared, so blond and sunny with these big innocent eyes and two warm parents. And just like that a new version of my story— two dead parents, no one in jail—popped out fully formed to rescue me. From that moment on, *that* became my truth.

And it had been so much more palatable than the actual facts: that my dad had finally found that regular who'd stolen from him and destroyed his business and—in my dad's view—killed my mother by bringing on her heart attack. They'd argued in the man's apartment, which the prosecution proved my dad had broken into, though he insisted he'd done so only to find evidence of the fraud. There was a struggle, and the man ended up with a kitchen knife in his stomach. All of it an accident, my dad claimed. But the jury hadn't believed it—he was convicted of felony murder, sentenced to twenty-five years to life. That was what happened when you killed someone while committing a burglary. And how upset had my dad really been in the aftermath? I was the only one who knew he'd come home that night and eaten dinner like nothing had happened, wolfing down his food with remarkable zeal. I was also the only one who knew he'd asked me to lie and give him an alibi. A request I'd politely declined.

And so my mom *was* dead and my dad *was* gone—like I'd told my Cornell roommate and then Victoria and Heather at Penn, and then Zach and, finally, Sam. He was just "gone" upstate at the Elmira Correctional Facility. Right before law school, I'd even legally taken my mother's maiden name—I figured law firms might be judgmental. They were; I was right about that. So was the US attorney's office, but I had made it through the background check anyway, after a few scary follow-up questions. What I had been wrong about was my ability to will the truth away.

It had been right there with me the entire time.

Waiting for the elevator, I bristled when I spotted Gloria again, this time at the far end of the reception area, talking with a woman standing at the polished lobby desk. Talking *at* the woman, more likely. I jabbed the elevator button repeatedly.

"Oh, there she is now," Gloria called out in my direction, just as I was about to step onto the elevator. *Shit.* "Um, hello, Lizzie, Maude is here!"

When I turned, there was Amanda's friend Maude headed my way. She looked distressed, and I absolutely did not want to be dealing with her. From the instantly apologetic expression on her face, my aversion must have been readily apparent.

"I'm sorry to just show up like this, especially on a Saturday. But I did leave a couple messages for you. The prosecutor came by my house . . . And there's something I need to tell you. I don't think it can wait."

Awesome.

"Sure, no problem," I lied. "Why don't you come back for a minute, and we can talk?"

We started toward my office.

"You know, I didn't even look at your contact information until today. I didn't realize you worked here, too, of all places . . ." Maude motioned over her shoulder, gesturing to Gloria. I couldn't imagine how the two knew each other, and honestly I didn't want to know. I just wanted to get Maude in and out as fast as possible. "I wasn't even sure the office would be open. But I thought it couldn't hurt to try."

"Yes, with the endless hours we all work here," I said, aiming for lighthearted but landing closer to caustic, "we are easy to find."

I flipped on the lights in my office and put down my bag. Maude swayed slightly as she sat.

"Whoa, are you okay?" I asked.

"Oh, um, yes. It's probably just low blood sugar," she offered weakly. "I'm diabetic. I'll be fine, but do you have some juice maybe?"

"Yes, sure. Of course," I said, hustling out to the nearby snack station.

When I returned, I handed Maude a small bottle of orange juice. Luckily, she had already regained some of her color. The last thing I wanted was her passing out in my office.

"Thank you," she said, taking a large swallow.

"Do you want me to call somebody?" *Ideally, somebody to take you home so we don't have to talk anymore.* I'd already decided not to mention Amanda's delusions until I figured out what I was going to do about them. But I was tempted to ask Maude, now that she was here. Maybe she'd noticed something.

"No, no, I'm fine," she said.

"So you said the prosecutor came by?" I prompted. "Did you get a name?"

"It was that same Wendy Wallace," Maude said. "She is . . . very intimidating."

This wasn't the worst news for Zach. A personal visit from Wendy meant that she was at least a little worried about her case.

"What exactly did she say?"

"Well, I told her that Zach was with me . . . ," Maude said, and now she definitely didn't sound like she was telling the truth. "Anyway, she said that if I testified to that at trial, she would personally see to it that I spent a year in jail."

"She means if you're lying," I said, trying to be diplomatic.

"I guess, yes," Maude said, though this didn't seem like much comfort to her. "But she also said something about our party, that it could make Sebe and me accessories to murder. She mentioned us getting sued civilly, too, by Amanda's family for wrongful death."

"First of all, you can't be accessories to murder because you threw a party that the victim attended *before* she died. And Amanda doesn't really have any family, so a civil lawsuit would not only be unsustainable but highly unlikely. Wendy Wallace is bluffing. As to the perjury, you haven't even testified yet," I said. Though I'd sure as hell still use Maude's alibi if I couldn't extract myself from the case—provided I could get away with it—even if I had some unconfirmed doubts about its veracity. Because that's who I was now, thanks to Zach: someone willing to maybe suborn perjury as long as I didn't know *for sure* that's what I was doing. "You have nothing to worry about at the moment."

"Right," she said, though she didn't look very relieved. When Maude pressed her lips together, her mouth quivered. "I'm here, really, because of Sebe."

Sebe? If Amanda had indeed been upstairs with somebody, as Wendy Wallace had suggested at the hearing, could it have been Sebe? He was certainly attractive, and he and Maude presumably participated in this swapping. It was their party. I reached forward and squeezed the edge of my desk.

"What do you mean?"

Maude looked for a moment like she might cry, then grimaced and closed her eyes. *Holy shit.* Had Sebe killed Amanda? Was that possible?

"Sebe convinced me that I needed to come down here and tell you the truth," she began finally. I gripped my desk tighter. "I wasn't with Zach the night of the party."

"Oh." It was all I could muster. Maude was snatching back one of the only things I had stashed in my paltry defensive arsenal: Zach's alibi.

"I'm sorry," she said, sounding genuinely distressed. "I was— I was trying to help. . . . I realize that sounds ridiculous. But I just felt so responsible, with the party and everything. To be honest, I've been having some serious problems with my daughter, too, so I haven't exactly been thinking clearly. Zach didn't kill Amanda, though. I'm sure of it. And when you came to me, all I could think about was poor Case. Amanda loved him so much. What will happen to him if Zach is in jail? Especially if there is no extended family?"

"I don't know," I said.

"Oh, that sweet child." Maude pressed her trembling fingers to her lips, then shook her head as her eyes filled with tears. Finally she swallowed and tried to compose herself. "I'm sorry if I've made your job harder. And I'll never forgive myself if I've made things worse for Case."

"Listen," I said, taking pity on her. I had no doubt that she was genuinely worried about Case, and it made me feel like a bad person that I hadn't been thinking more about him. My anger at Zach had all but erased Case's existence. "Don't worry. Your alibi isn't even part of any official record. Withdrawing it now will have no impact on the outcome. But I am glad you told me. It could have complicated things later."

She nodded, looking down. Finally, she stood. "And please, with Case . . . if Zach—if he needs someone to help with him. We will. We will do anything for Case that we can."

"I'll let you know," I said.

"Thank you," she said. She looked for a moment like she might say something more, before smiling unsteadily and turning for the door.

I took home everything I had on Zach's case—his public defender files, the defense package, the preliminary filings, the research I had on Xavier Lynch, Amanda's diary, the documents related to Zach's loitering warrant, the file Millie had given me. I was determined to find a needle in that haystack. One I could stab Zach with, or one I could use to poke a hole in Wendy Wallace's case against him. I was fine with either. This just needed to end.

It was past nine when I got home. The apartment was empty; I tried not to consider where Sam might be and simply be glad that he was gone. I was digging myself out, yes, but I could only deal with one problem at a time, and getting away from Zach was still the most pressing.

I spread everything I had on Zach's case across our living room floor, hoping some new story might effortlessly emerge. But the disjointed pieces just lay there. There would be additional evidence to work with eventually, once the prosecution turned over its own material. But I could not do Zach's bidding for one moment more.

I picked up Amanda's journal and flipped through it again, trying to see what to make of it now that I knew that Amanda's dad and Carolyn were both dead. The descriptions of the calls and hang-ups, of the moments she believed she was being followed, were extremely detailed. They also seemed to fit a pattern. The calls were almost always during the day; the times that Amanda believed she was being followed, at night. Week after week. Often on a Wednesday or Thursday night. Detailed or not, they could have been a part of Amanda's delusion, but it did seem odd that something completely imagined would fit such a realistic pattern.

Then I spotted the card from Blooms on the Slope. Also, there were the anonymous flowers. Those had not been a figment of Amanda's troubled imagination. *Somebody* had sent them. Not her stalker, necessarily—she was a beautiful woman, she could have had any number of "secret admirers"—but it could have been.

Could Zach have been pretending to stalk Amanda as a cover? Had it all been a setup so that he could kill her and get away with it? I'd invented an insurance policy when I went to talk to Xavier, but Amanda's death triggering some huge financial payout was something to consider, especially given that Zach needed money to save his company. I regretted not showing Matthew at the flower shop a photo of Zach. He'd said that the man was a "circle." Zach had sort of a round face, I supposed. Doughy, actually.

Like Millie had suggested, maybe Zach had even paid someone to kill Amanda for him, and the fingerprint on the stairs belonged to that person. The thought of Zach hiring someone so incompetent sparked the tiniest bit of satisfaction.

I picked up the envelope containing Zach's warrant records from the loitering incident. I slid the papers out, reading through them more closely this time. It was very easy now to picture Zach being so belligerent with the cops that spring night all those years ago. "April 16, 2007," it said on the papers. *Wait,* that date rang a bell. Then it came to me: April 16, 2007, was the night Sam and I met.

Come on, Zach, seriously?

I typed the name of the street corner where Zach had been loitering into Google Maps. Sure enough, there was the blue dot on the corner of an alley tucked behind The Rittenhouse, the fancy building where that med school party was held. Zach had been arrested because he refused to leave a spot where he'd been waiting, watching for me? I wondered for a moment if Zach had been there, in the shadows, watching as Sam and I kissed for the first time. What would have happened if the police hadn't made Zach move along?

I shuddered as I put down the warrant papers and picked up Millie's investigation file. I turned to the fingerprint results and the close-up images of that bloody print Millie had taken the night I first called her. It looked so innocuous in these photos—a swirled pattern in a brownish red barely visible on the dark metal. But there were other, more vivid photographs taken from a few paces back, ones of the blood-soaked stairs and the walls that told a much more terrifying story.

Such violence in an otherwise empty room. So much blood in so many places. The force it would have taken. The rage.

Zach. It wasn't impossible.

Behind the crime scene photos and the fingerprint analysis, there were internet searches, old printouts about Zach from ZAG, Inc.'s website, information on the Hope First Initiative, and maps of the neighborhood, but nothing about Zach's new company, as far as I could tell. There were also notes in Millie's handwriting. It seemed she'd gotten at least one of the patrol officers to talk to her. "Off the record" she'd scrawled at the top in big letters, probably to humor him. It was a list of who they had spoken to and when. "7/2 Party Guests," followed by a list of names.

I flipped through more of the pages in the file, my eyes catching on a preliminary medical examiner's report (blunt force trauma) that Millie and Vinnie definitely had no legitimate business possessing. There was a time of death estimate, between 10:00 p.m. and 11:00 p.m. on Thursday, July 2. July 2 was a Thursday? I'd assumed the party had been Friday or Saturday night. But Friday, July 3, was a legal holiday because the Fourth of July fell on a Saturday, making a wild Thursday-night party possible. With the holiday, Zach's arraignment could easily have been delayed until Monday.

The party had been on a Thursday. Last Thursday.

The same awful night Sam had his blackout.

I forced myself to focus as I flipped more quickly through the rest of the pages, pausing on a personal items inventory, also from the medical examiner's office. It was a list of the clothing and personal belongings Amanda had on her the night she died, alongside a photograph of each item. "Two black YSL sandals, one pair white jeans, one white top, silver Cartier watch, one silver earring." I turned to the next document—the fingerprint analysis. The blood whooshing in my ears was deafening. But wait, no—

I flipped back a page. *One silver earring.* My hands were shaking so hard, it was difficult to make out the image in the photograph.

But there it was: long and thin and shimmering silver. I'd seen the earring before. Of course I had. Or its twin, coiled like a snake in the palm of my hand.

I flashed back to Sam as I'd found him that Friday morning in our living room: he'd been covered in blood; his hands, his shirt. So frightening—my husband hurt. My husband covered in blood.

I jumped up. I only made it a single step before I threw up all over our hardwood floor.

GRAND JURY TESTIMONY

JESSICA KIM,

called as a witness the 8th of July and was examined
and testified as follows:

EXAMINATION

BY MS. WALLACE:

Q: Ms. Kim, thank you for testifying.

A: Yeah, um, sure.

Q: You seem nervous.

A: I am. This whole thing is making me nervous.

Q: You don't need to worry. You're not the subject of
any criminal investigation.

A: I'm not nervous about that. I didn't do anything
illegal. But I've heard what you're doing in here. I
have friends who have testified. We all know each other.
You're trying to embarrass us.

Q: Perhaps we should move on.

A: Yes. Let's do that.

Q: Were you at the party at 724 First Street on July
2nd of this year?

A: Yes. I was.

Q: And how did you come to be invited?

A: Like everyone else, I received an invitation. That is generally how it works.

Q: How do you know Maude and Sebe Lagueux?

A: My children go to Country Day. But we got to know Maude when we bought some pieces of art from her.

Q: Who is we?

A: My husband David and I.

Q: Was David at the party that night as well?

A: He was. Should I save you the trouble of drawing out what you're definitely after? Yes, I fucked somebody that night who was not my husband. And, yes, my husband knew about it. And, no, I don't think he fucked somebody. Though he may have if he found that dad he has a crush on. Honestly, we've gone to this party six years running, and we don't ask each other afterward for details. And we like it that way. However, we don't pee in front of each other. So there you go. I guess every couple sets their own limits.

Q: Did you see Amanda Grayson as you were headed upstairs the night of the party?

A: (Inaudible.)

Q: I'm sorry, I couldn't hear what you said.

A: I saw a woman going up the stairs.

Q: Is this the woman you saw on the stairs?

(Counsel approaches witness with photograph, which was previously marked as People's Exhibit 6.)

A: Yes.

Q: Let the record reflect that the witness has identified Amanda Grayson as the woman she saw on the stairs. What time was that?

A: I don't know exactly.

Q: Could you estimate?

A: Um, let's see. I guess around 9:30 p.m. probably.

Q: Did anyone go upstairs at this Sleepaway Soiree for any purpose other than sex?

A: I doubt it.

Q: Why not?

A: Because it would have been confusing. People who weren't interested tended to stay far away from the stairs. That way it was clear.

Q: So Amanda Grayson headed to the upstairs of the party?

A: Yes. But I don't know if she went all the way up. I don't have the faintest idea what happened to her after I saw her on the stairs.

Q: Yes, you do, Ms. Kim. You know exactly what happened to her. She ended up dead.

AMANDA

THE PARTY

Amanda was actually feeling pretty good as she dressed for Maude and Sebe's party, better than she had in days. There had been two hang-ups only hours earlier, and the following in the park, not to mention everything with Carolyn, but right now she was preparing to tell Zach about all of it. Or at least some of it. Also, she might not start with her dad. But that was okay. Speaking up with Zach, changing things, was going to be a process.

Besides, she'd said *something* already. Hadn't she? She'd demanded that Zach go to the party with her. And he was going. Amanda was pleased about that as she pulled on her white capri jeans and off-the-shoulder ruffled top, slipped her feet into black wedge sandals, and pulled her hair into a high ponytail. The long silver earrings, too, nice but not overdone. It was the right outfit for that party, finally.

Of course, when they were still not speaking as they descended their brownstone steps, the satisfaction of asking Zach to come had been replaced by the reality of getting what she'd wanted. She and her husband were awkward strangers. *That* was their reality. This was not news, but it chafed now more than it ever had.

As Amanda and Zach walked up tree-lined Montgomery Place, past all the meticulous brownstones, Amanda kept thinking they should at least be chitchatting. But everything she thought to say felt wrong. When you've been married for eleven years, resorting to a conversation about the rising humidity was humiliating. And so they were left with silence.

And right now, all that quiet was making Amanda want to scream.

She glanced over at Zach, who was smiling slightly as they turned right onto the busier, two-lane Prospect Park West. He almost looked handsome in his white linen shirt and perfectly worn designer jeans. Strangely pleased, too, for someone who hated parties, and people. Amanda looked away, across the street to where a man was jogging alone in the bike lane and a small older woman was walking an enormous white dog. Up ahead on their side of the street, it was empty and dark except for the squares of light cast by the entrances of the larger buildings that overlooked the park.

And then Zach started to whistle. Why was he whistling? Nothing her husband did made any sense to her. It was much worse than his silence, though. Depressing, actually. This conversation would not have a happy ending, would it? Zach wasn't going to suddenly be the husband she wanted—attentive and loving. People didn't just change because you wanted them to. But Amanda had to at least tell Zach about her dad. If not to protect herself, then to protect her son. If Zach got angry, so be it. Amanda wasn't sure she cared anymore what he did.

"Yes, I had a great day today. Thank you so much for asking," Zach said sarcastically as they passed the intersection of Prospect Park West and Garfield. "Things at work are finally looking up. Way up."

"That's good . . . What does your new company even do?" Amanda asked. This hadn't been where she'd planned to start—but maybe it was as good a place as any. "I don't even know, and I think I should. I'm your wife."

"You want to know about my business, huh?" Zach asked, seeming amused. "You want me to break down its capital formation plan or its strategic plan?"

"I just want to know what you do all day."

"The details would bore you to death, trust me, but it'll make us a lot richer once I get it right. As usual with these things, it was the engineering that almost did us in. People, boards especially, don't realize how important those technical details are. But thanks to my own creative thinking, it's finally sorted out. Beta testing. That's the key."

"It doesn't sound boring. I wish you'd told me about the problems," Amanda said. "Maybe I could have, I don't know, helped."

"I didn't realize you were a software engineer." Zach laughed. "Next time I will come right to you."

Amanda balled her hands into fists. "I'm your wife."

"What does that have to do with anything?"

She stopped walking. "It's supposed to have something to do with everything."

"You know your problem, Amanda?" Zach stopped a few paces ahead. "You've always overestimated the value of human connection. I'm not saying connections don't matter. That's all ZAG was about: connecting people with the things they've bought, the life they want. It's a billion-dollar concept. But connections between people? You ask me, they just create more problems. *That's* what my new company is about."

He seemed so pleased with himself as he turned his back on her and began to walk again.

Amanda didn't move. Her eyes burned as she stared after her husband. *Forgiveness is a side effect of love.* Sebe was right about that. The truth was, she didn't forgive her husband his limitations. Because whatever was between Zach and Amanda had nothing to do with love. But it had produced one thing that Amanda did love, more than anything: Case. Amanda had failed him by letting Zach move them to Park Slope for some business she didn't even know about. But she would do now what she had to, to protect her son.

"Wait!" Amanda called after Zach, jogging to catch up. "I've been meaning to—we have to talk about Case. The move was too hard on him. I think he really struggled at Country Day at the end of the year. That's not like him."

"Struggled? Since when?" Zach scoffed. "For the amount of money we're paying that school, I sure as hell hope they'd notify us if they thought he was struggling."

"Didn't they notify you?"

"Me?" Zach asked. "Why would they notify me?"

"The school has your email, too."

"They sure as hell do not," he said. "You know how I feel about that. Might as well give everyone the keys to your front door. Speaking of which, I thought you were going to get our alarm fixed, and that damn closet door in my office is still sticking."

There it was. That was all Amanda was to Zach. Another employee.

"They're coming next week to fix the door and the alarm," she said numbly.

And there she was: doing her job, the one that Zach could fire her from at any time. He could probably even take Case if he decided to leave her—or if she had the guts to leave him. After all, she was an unemployed high-school dropout. How stupid she had been. She couldn't possibly tell Zach about her dad. What if he later tried to use it against her? Like in some kind of custody battle. Such a thing would already be a nightmare—Amanda had signed a draconian (the lawyer had quietly told her) prenuptial agreement. And Zach believed, maybe above all else, in vengeance. No, there was no way she could tell him about her dad.

"Whose house is this we're going to again?" Zach asked as they approached the intersection of First Street and passed a group of cackling teens.

Zach liked to be prepared. That way he could pretend to be charming. He was good at it, provided there was something in it for him and it was for a limited period of time. Because Zach was only *acting* like a normal person, and that took effort. In the end, maybe it was only this that he and Amanda had in common: the pretending.

"It's Maude's party. She owns a gallery. Her husband, Sebe, is a doctor," Amanda said, trying to ignore the singed feeling in her chest. "Their daughter goes to Country Day, but she's older than Case. She's been having a hard time lately."

Amanda wasn't even sure why she'd added that, but to her surprise Zach slowed and looked at her, intrigued.

"What hard time?" he asked. Amanda didn't like the idea of violating Maude's confidence by telling Zach about Sophia. But on the rare occasion Zach did get interested in something, he'd sink his teeth in until he'd drawn blood. She'd be better off telling him something. At least the gossip would stop with him. He had no friends to share it with.

"Her daughter did something she regrets."

"What's that?" Zach asked, with a weird, laserlike focus.

"Some compromising photos, I guess," Amanda said. "A teenage thing."

"Oh." Zach pulled his chin back and let out an exasperated huff as he finally walked on toward First Street. "There's no accounting for stupidity."

From the corner of Prospect Park West and First Street, Amanda could already hear giddy laughter and music floating up from Maude and Sebe's backyard and filling the warm summer night. She closed her eyes for a moment and breathed in the distant sounds of joy.

"People are always worried about the wrong things—their bank accounts or their credit cards," Zach went on, as if Amanda had asked. "No one thinks about the things that really make them vulnerable. That's why I'm so careful about our information. That's also why I've succeeded in business. I've always known what people need before they do."

What an asshole her husband was. There really wasn't anything more to it than that.

Just then a couple stumbled out Maude's front door, laughing hysterically. They were a bit older than Zach and a lot older than Amanda, early fifties maybe. But they were attractive and fit and also very visibly tipsy. The woman had a hand over her mouth, and the man was flushed, and they were both laughing so hard they were gasping for breath. They each wore several leis, and the man had a huge beach ball squeezed under his arm.

"Stop, stop, stop," the woman giggled to her husband.

"Come on," her husband hissed. "Pull it together. Or we'll never get out of here with this ball."

They glanced in Amanda and Zach's direction before feigning sobriety and making their way unevenly down the steps and onward toward Seventh Avenue. It wasn't until seeing the couple that Amanda even remembered the "upstairs." What if some unwitting party guest ended up explaining that to Zach? Talk about "risky connections." Zach might tell everyone how dumb he thought they were right to their faces. Because Zach believed his opinions were facts, he never hesitated to deliver them directly. The truth, he believed, could never be insulting.

"There's something you need to know before we go in," Amanda said when Zach started toward the stairs with that noticeable gleam in his eye. "They, um, have an upstairs."

Zach looked up at the four-floor brownstone. "I can see that."

"No, I mean, they . . . swap partners. Upstairs," she blurted out. "Not everybody. Not even most people, I don't think. Only if you want. I mean, if *somebody* wants. Not you. I didn't mean that." She was blushing now. "I'm only telling you so you're aware. It's not a big deal."

"Not a big deal?" Zach laughed. Hard and for about a minute. His face was flushed and he was pitched forward. "That's truly hilarious," he said, sighing to a stop. He looked up at the house for a moment more. "These people are full of . . . stupidity. Speaking of which, make sure you don't tell anyone anything about the new company. I don't want word of it getting out early and ruining the announcement." He pointed a finger in Amanda's face. "You wanted me to trust you, and I have. Don't fuck it up."

With that, Zach continued on up the steps. And Amanda was left standing there alone on the sidewalk, thinking about all the things a husband might have said at that moment to a wife when faced with the prospect of entering a sex party together. Things like: *We should talk about this. What are our rules? We're not doing that, right? Huh, what do we think?*

They could have giggled together. They could have wondered. They could have been two people who shared in everything, even the unknown. But not Amanda and Zach.

Because there was no *they*. There never had been. And there never would be.

GRAND JURY TESTIMONY

STEVE ABRUZZI,

called as a witness the 8th of July and was examined and testified as follows:

EXAMINATION

BY MS. WALLACE:

Q: Mr. Abruzzi, thank you for being here.

A: Of course, anything I can do to help. Everything here is confidential, right?

Q: Yes, the grand jury proceedings are confidential.

A: Okay, okay. Good.

Q: Mr. Abruzzi, were you at the party at 724 First Street on July 2nd of this year?

A: Yes.

Q: Did you spend time at the party with Jessica Kim?

A: Yes.

Q: Are you married, Mr. Abruzzi?

A: Yes.

Q: To Ms. Kim?

A: No.

Q: Did your wife know that you and Ms. Kim were together that night?

A: Yes.

Q: What did you and Ms. Kim do together?

A: You mean, like, specifically?

Q: Did you engage in sexual activities together?

A: Yes.

Q: Sexual intercourse?

A: Yes.

Q: You'll need to speak up. We can't hear you, Mr. Abruzzi.

A: Yes.

Q: Do you have children, Mr. Abruzzi?

A: What does that have to do with anything? Are you trying to make me feel like a bad person?

Q: Can you answer the question, please?

A: Yes. They weren't at the party, obviously. And they don't know anything about it. Trust me. People are discreet. Except for this, here, now. No one ever talks about it afterward.

Q: Do these children go to Brooklyn Country Day?

A: Yes.

Q: Is that how you know Maude Lagueux?

A: We know Sarah and Kerry. My wife met Sarah at the PTA. Kerry and I are friends, too. Sebe, Kerry, and I go out sometimes to concerts. I'm big into indie bands. But Kerry wasn't there that night. He texted me, looking for Sebe.

Q: What time was it that you went upstairs to have sexual intercourse with Jessica Kim?

A: Do you have to keep saying it like that?

Q: Like what?

A: Never mind. I think it was like 9:30 or 10:00 p.m. Sometime in there.

Q: Did you see anyone on your way upstairs? Somebody on the stairs?

A: Oh, um, yeah, there was a woman behind us. But I didn't know her.

Q: I'm going to show you a photograph, Mr. Abruzzi.

(Counsel approaches witness with a photograph, previously marked as People's Exhibit 6.)

Q: Is this the woman you saw on the steps?

A: Yes.

Q: Let the record reflect that Mr. Abruzzi has identified Mrs. Grayson as the woman he saw going up the stairs on the night in question.

A: If this is all secret, why is there a transcript?

Q: For the record, Mr. Abruzzi. That's all. One last question. You said someone was looking for Sebe Lagueux. Did you happen to notice where Mr. Lagueux was while you were upstairs?

A: Yes.

Q: Where was that?

A: In a room with Mrs. Grayson.

LIZZIE

I didn't hear Sam come in, but there he was in the bedroom doorway. He looked around at his scattered clothes, his bright eyes dimmed by sadness. But he also did not seem especially surprised. I'd torn our apartment apart, looking for more evidence. I'd opened every cabinet and every drawer, felt for something suspicious between Sam's T-shirts, and thrown his socks all over the floor. I was shaking the whole time, a wordless howl roaring inside my head.

I lifted the earring off the bed next to me, my eyes so raw from crying they felt about to bleed. "This belongs to Amanda Grayson." I shook the dangling earring. "She was wearing it the night she died."

Sam crossed his arms over his chest, then leaned back against the wall opposite me. I braced myself for his threadbare excuses, his well-worn defense. I wondered whether I could listen to any of it without launching at him. I could already feel my fingernails digging into his pretty face.

He looked down.

Say something, Sam. Fucking say something.

"You knew her." It was a statement, not a question. I couldn't bear to ask any more questions.

Sam looked up, eyes wide. "No. I didn't know her." He sounded panicky as his eyes darted back down. "I mean, not that I know of."

"Why do you not seem surprised that you had her earring, then?" My heart was beating so hard, it was making my head ache.

"I *am* surprised that's her earring," he stammered back. "But I— Once you told me that a woman from the neighborhood was dead, I went and read about it. I have a memory of being on a bench along Prospect Park West that night. Just like a flash. I think it might have been in front of that little playground that's near Montgomery Place. Isn't that where her house was?"

"What the hell are you saying?" I asked.

"I'm saying: I don't know."

"I don't understand." My voice was high now, even more panicked than Sam's. It felt like the room was running out of air. "If you didn't know her, how could you have possibly ended up at her house? How could you have gotten her earring?"

He didn't answer. He just stood there, frozen, eyes locked on the pile of clothes on the floor. Then, suddenly, he started to pace, back and forth, like some kind of frightened animal. *Stop, Sam,* I pleaded in my head. *Please stop.* But I was too afraid to say a word.

"I don't think I knew her," he said finally, continuing to stalk back and forth. "But I do think maybe I'd seen her before, at Blue Bottle."

"Blue Bottle? What's that?"

"It's a café."

"Not around here, it's not." The bile was creeping back up my throat.

"It's in Center Slope," he said. "Also not that far from where she lives. I saw a picture of her—I think maybe I did see her a couple times at Blue Bottle, reading there, while I was working."

"Since when do you work at some café in Center Slope?" I snapped. "You hate Center Slope!"

"I needed a change of scenery," he said, defensive. "I didn't tell you because I felt guilty spending extra money on fancy coffee. Anyway, I don't know for sure that it was her, but she was, um, striking. Similar to the woman who was killed."

"Striking? Are you fucking kidding me!" I shouted. "So what? You're saying you guys hooked up that night or something?"

"I can't see how," Sam said. "I'm just trying to tell you absolutely everything I know. I'm trying to come clean."

"Great," I whispered. "That's so fucking great."

Suddenly Sam stopped pacing and headed over to the clothes pile and started digging through like he was searching for something in particular. *No,* was all I could think. *I don't want to know anything more.*

When he stood, he was holding out one of his white basketball sneakers. He pointed to a long brown streak across the side, about an inch wide and three inches long.

"Also, I found this earlier today."

"What is that?"

Sam set the shoe down on our bureau, where we both stared at it. "It could be blood, right?"

"Sam, what the hell are you—" My voice cracked so hard I winced.

"I don't know, Lizzie."

"You hit your head that same night. That's got to be your blood," I said, even though all that blood was already nagging at me.

Sam shook his head. "I'd left my basketball sneakers out in the hall. Probably so I could sneak in quietly. I saw them out there when we got home from Methodist. I wore my Vans to the hospital."

I stood. And the room began to spin.

"Well, then somebody must have seen you that night. At the time she was killed, I mean." I moved away, backed up against the windows to steady myself. "What about the bartender after basketball—"

"I already asked," Sam said. His face was all angles in the shadows, beautiful, but menacing now. "He doesn't remember me."

"Or bar receipts," I pressed, frantic for anything to hold on to, for something to save us. "They put Amanda's time of death between ten p.m. and eleven p.m. Basketball isn't over until ten p.m., right? Even staying past eleven, that would hardly give you enough time for one or two drinks. Obviously, to be that drunk, you had way more than that."

Sam shook his head again. "We didn't end up playing basketball that night. There weren't enough guys, beginning of summer and all that. We were at Freddy's by seven. Somebody suggested doing shots. Wasn't me, I swear. But I had a bunch in a row. I do remember that."

"For Christ's sake, Sam!" I screamed so loud this time it hurt my throat. "How many more fucking things are you leaving out!"

Sam wouldn't even look at me now. We both knew what this meant. At that pace, he'd have been plenty drunk by the critical window.

"There's nothing else, Lizzie. That's—it's everything."

"Think, Sam!" I shouted, terrified and fucking furious.

"All I've done is think!" he shouted right back. "I'm sorry, Lizzie. All I want to do is tell you there's no way I could have been with her that night, much less hurt her. That I could never hurt anybody. And like that?" Sam's voice caught now. He closed his eyes and pressed his lips together. When he finally spoke again, it was with this determined sadness. "But I can't lie anymore, Lizzie. I've blacked out so many times I've lost count. I've driven a car wasted, told my boss—a guy I liked—to fuck off. And I don't remember any of it. Everybody has that dark part of themselves they keep safely locked away. When you're drunk like that, your grip slips and out the dark part comes. Is that dark part of me someone who could kill? I sure as hell fucking hope not. But how can I say for sure, when he and I have never met?"

Anyone is capable of anything. I knew that, didn't I? How many times had I pictured my own father plunging a knife into another man's gut, then coming home to eat spaghetti? My skin was on fire. I wanted Sam's denials back. I wanted our slow unraveling, not this free fall.

The fingerprints in Amanda's blood. What if they were Sam's?

I thought of the stairs in her home, of all that blood. Of the force it would have taken to bash Amanda's head in with that golf club. I pressed my body harder against the windows, felt the cool glass behind my fingers. Wondered how hard I'd have to push to send myself sailing through.

My phone rang. I lunged for the nightstand, praying that whoever was calling might have something to say that would make it impossible that this man I loved, the man I'd forgiven so often, was a murderer. The call was from a random New York cell phone. It could have been anybody. But anybody was better than this conversation.

"Hello?" I gasped.

"It's Sarah Novak." She sounded tipsy. Drunk, actually. But the boozy book club was yesterday. Why was everyone always so fucking drunk? "It's late, isn't it? Sorry, I wasn't even— I lost track. My husband said you came by yesterday? I got curious."

"Oh, yeah," I said, momentarily confused. I didn't remember telling him my name. But then Sarah had probably told him to be on the lookout for me.

"And *why*, pray tell, did you come by?"

"I spoke with the accountant for the foundation," I began, slipping numbly into professional mode.

There was a long silence. "Uh-huh." And that was all. Even drunk, Sarah was too sharp to start accidentally confessing.

"I think maybe I misunderstood when we spoke the other day," I went on, carving her the out of a "misunderstanding." "I didn't realize that you ended up meeting with Teddy Buckley, the accountant for the foundation, yourself."

"Ugh, yes, I did meet with him in the end." She was drawing out her words like a disgusted child. "And yeah, I didn't tell you because I was worried he might— I was *sure* he wouldn't have very nice things to say about me." The more she spoke, the drunker she sounded. "Anyway, being bankrupt only makes your client look *more* guilty."

"He mentioned that you were very upset that you might lose your job if the foundation had no money."

She took another breath. "That's true. And if that's all he said about me, then he's a very nice person, because I totally lost it on him. Look, my husband was laid off recently. I was worried you'd start asking questions about why I was so upset about losing my pathetic salary. Eventually, it might have come out that my husband is unemployed. I couldn't bear the thought. It's absurd, I know, but *that's* how ashamed

I am, and I'm not even the one who lost their job. Fucking marriage." She was whispering now, which made her seem even more wasted. "We both thought my husband would be right back to work. Or at least *I* did. But he hasn't exactly been pounding the pavement." *That's because he watches Wimbledon*, I wanted to say. *And eats pizza*. She sighed dramatically. "So now I'm the breadwinner. Or the *crumb*winner. It's not exactly what I signed up for, if you know what I mean."

I did know exactly what she meant.

"Did you tell Amanda?"

"Are you kidding?" she exclaimed. "I haven't told anyone. What part of I'm-mortified-my-husband-got-laid-off didn't you understand? I know it's appalling that I lied to my friends. I love my friends. But sometimes it's easier to stay married if you pretend. Willful blindness, isn't that what you lawyers call it?"

It was easier to pretend. Sarah was right about that, too. "I didn't mean about your husband's job. I meant did you tell Amanda what the accountant told you, about the foundation not having any money?"

"Oh, that," Sarah said dismissively. "I was going to tell her, but not at Maude's party. It *was* a party, and I didn't want to stress her out. Besides, Zach was there. It would have been really awkward. Maude thought I should tell Amanda anyway. But Maude wasn't exactly thinking clearly because of everything with Sophia."

"You told Maude about the foundation's financial problems?"

"Of course! The second I saw her at the party. I mean, the foundation bust, and all of Zach's millionaire bullshit a lie? It was too great. I know that's petty, but I never claimed to be perfect," she said, her words slurring even more. "Anyway, Maude cared more about the email investigation."

"Email investigation?" I asked, though Sarah had mentioned it before.

"Yup. Some of the Country Day families' computers have been hacked into." Sarah sighed. "And all their dirty laundry is now out in the open. I told Maude it was an inside job, a parent, they think—one of the investigators slipped and told me. Maude and I spend half our time saying: 'Don't tell anyone I told you this, but . . .' Maude did the same thing when she told me about the golf club. Right away she was like, 'Oh, wait, don't tell anyone about that.'"

"The golf club?" I asked, remembering how Sarah had thrown that in my face during our first conversation, proof of exactly what a monster Zach was. "I thought the police told you about that."

"The police? Please. They pumped *me* for information about who was at the party, but they wouldn't tell me shit," Sarah said. "Maude told me about the golf club. She said they found it at the bottom of the stairs in Amanda's house. Right next to her body. Zach might as well have signed his name to the scene of the crime."

"When did Maude tell you about the golf club?"

"The morning after Amanda died," she said. "The police must have told her."

But Maude hadn't spoken to anyone until today, when Wendy Wallace showed up at her house. Certainly she shouldn't have known about the golf club only hours after Amanda was killed with it. It was hard to think with that whooshing sound back in my ears. I looked over at Sam, staring at me from his spot on the wall.

I gripped the phone tighter. *Maude and not Sam.* A flicker of hope.

AMANDA

THE PARTY

A crowd of people holding large red plastic cups filled with pink punch were pressed up against each other in the entryway to Maude and Sebe's brownstone. It reminded Amanda of the college party she'd attended at the University of Albany with a girl who'd worked one summer at the motel. It was packed and noisy like this, but everyone here looked so strangely young and so old at the same time.

Amanda had to shout "Excuse me" more than once for anyone to hear her over the blasting Nirvana. She was relieved to finally wriggle her way through the bodies and escape into the more spacious living room, filled with exquisite art and colorful keepsakes from Maude and Sebe's extensive travels and lots and lots of family photos—more refined than Sarah's but no less genuine. Covering a nearby table were small bags of trail mix and scavenger-hunt maps and a big pile of leis and other party favors.

Amanda looked around for Zach, but he'd already slipped out of sight into the throng of couples—tall and short, fat and thin, fashionable, unfashionable, beautiful, ordinary. One nearby twosome exchanged some sharp barbs, but then in an instant seemed to smile and forgive. Soon they were laughing, faces close, a hand on a waist, fingers linked, hips touching. Messy and imperfect, yes, but connected.

Zach was wrong. Human connections were a good thing. They were the only thing that mattered.

Amanda deserved that, didn't she? A real connection. Love. Zach had rescued her, yes. But she'd made for him a life the past eleven years; she'd given him a son. Her debt had been repaid.

There was really only one solution now—Amanda needed to leave Zach. She'd known that for some time, if she was being honest. She couldn't even tell him about her dad. How could she protect herself? How could she protect her son? Not only wouldn't their marriage keep her afloat, she was pretty sure it was the thing that would eventually drag her under.

"Excuse me," somebody behind Amanda said.

She shifted out of the living room entryway so more newcomers could tumble in and spotted Maude making sangria at the marble island in their glamourous open kitchen. She was smiling, enjoying the party. Or so it seemed. Once Amanda was closer, though, she saw Maude's lips tremble.

Maude's face brightened a little when she saw Amanda. But her skin was noticeably clammy when she kissed Amanda on the cheek. "So glad you're here," she said mechanically.

"Zach is, too," Amanda quipped, ashamed that, despite everything, she felt the need to point out this small, sad victory. "I don't know where he went, but we came in together."

"Oh." Maude smiled distractedly. "Great."

"Yes, it's a big night," Amanda said, surprised by the depth of her own hostility. She could hardly contain it anymore. "Zach even deigned to tell me what he does all day."

"What's that?" Maude asked. She was focused on cutting up huge hunks of fruit, but with the wrong type of knife so that it was ending up unappetizingly mashed. Amanda wondered if she should offer to take over before Maude cut her own fingers off.

"Something about people and their connections and him being ahead of everyone. Related to logistics, I'm assuming. It doesn't matter," Amanda said, realizing now that Zach really hadn't told her much of anything. "Is Sarah here?"

"Yes, she was just updating me on the school email investigation." Maude pressed her lips tight as her eyes flooded with tears. She squeezed them shut. "I'm sorry," she said, wiping at her face. "I, um, I just spoke with Sophia a few minutes ago. I'm trying to hold it together here, but it's not exactly easy."

"You spoke with her tonight?" Amanda asked, looking around at the chaos. "In the middle of all this?"

"I know, right?" Maude nodded with grim exasperation. "But they only just got back from their camping trip and into cell phone range thirty minutes ago."

"Are you— Is she okay?"

"No. She's not." Maude's face was stiff as she sawed at another orange. "It was worse than she . . . Whoever was threatening to post those pictures if we didn't pay them also blackmailed Sophia directly. They said they'd post them if she didn't do more sexual things, live on camera for them. And once she did one thing . . ." Maude shuddered in disgust.

"Oh, poor Sophia," Amanda said.

Maude glared off into the distance, the knife gripped in her hand. "She told me she snuck away from the group while they were off on this camping trip and walked out into the ocean. Wanted to keep on walking forever, that's what she said. She woke up on the beach a couple hours later, by some grace of—" Maude's voice choked out.

Amanda reached out for Maude, pulling her tight. Amanda didn't even have time to consider what a person should do in that situation. She was already doing it. Because she was a person and a mother and a friend.

"She'll be okay," Amanda said into Maude's thick curls. Her friend felt so fragile in her arms. "She has parents who love her, no matter what."

Maude shook her head as the two separated. "The camp has a staff member flying home with her. It was faster than us going down there.

And so, right now, my daughter is out there, broken apart. And here I am, at a party in my home with a bunch of drunk people having sex upstairs. Fantastic."

"Do you want me to help get rid of everyone?" Amanda asked, guiding Maude's hand down until the knife was safely resting on the counter. "We could tell them you're sick or something."

"It's okay," she said. "There's nothing I can do right now anyway. Not until I find the person who is behind this. Sarah told me they think it's a parent. Whoever it is could be here, right now." Her eyes scanned the room. "Brooklyn Country Day isn't that big. Anyway, I'll let everyone stay for a bit. Then I'll have Sebe make himself useful and throw them out."

Amanda stepped closer and put a hand on Maude's back. "She's going to be okay. When I was younger I had all sorts of— Well, it doesn't matter," Amanda said. "Teenagers are very resilient. You'll see."

"But why didn't she tell me . . ." Maude's voice drifted off. "I should have known from the start that there was something more."

"We all miss things. I just found emails in Zach's desk drawer from Country Day from weeks ago about some problems with Case. I had no idea he was having trouble at school. We never even responded to schedule the meeting they requested."

"You found scheduling emails?" Maude asked, eyebrows pinched. "From Brooklyn Country Day?"

"Yeah," Amanda went on, wishing she could take it back. "They went to Zach, for some reason, though he claims they don't even have his email."

"Then how did he get them?" Maude asked.

"I don't know. But I found the printouts in his office drawer."

"Printouts." Maude's jaw clenched. Amanda knew she shouldn't have brought it up. It was so silly compared to Sophia's situation.

"Maude!" Sebe called from the steps out to the backyard. The back door was wide open. "Can you come out here? We need your expert opinion."

Maude glared in Sebe's direction. "If Sebe and I survive this mess, it will be a miracle," she said. "He's always so calm and rational. It's the doctor in him. He doesn't care who's responsible. He just wants Sophia to be okay. I want that, too. But I also need him to be out for blood, like me."

"Maude!" Sebe called again with a hangdog look on his face. "Come on. For a second, please!"

Maude looked aggravated. "Sorry, I'll be right back." She headed out of the open kitchen toward Sebe and the backyard with the pitcher of sangria, then paused and turned back. "Oh, and I want to meet Zach. I'd like to talk to him."

Amanda looked around until she spotted Zach circling the edge of the crowded living room. Watching everyone. "He's over there." Amanda pointed. "I'll introduce you guys later." Though Amanda hoped that would never happen. She didn't love the idea of Zach talking to Maude, not with Maude already so upset.

"Great." Maude smiled, though it was strained. "Be right back."

As Maude disappeared into the crowd, Amanda's phone rang in her clutch. She froze. *Come on. Not now.* It rang again. She braced herself as she dug it out. A blocked number. She could let the call go straight to voice mail. But he'd just call back, wouldn't he?

Amanda needed to stop running, once and for all. From everything. And everyone. She clenched her teeth as she answered the phone.

"Hello?" Silence.

"Hello?" Still, nothing.

And then there it was: her spine. So much stronger than she had ever supposed. When she spoke again, her voice was a menacing growl.

"Leave me the fuck alone, you bastard."

LIZZIE

JULY 12, SUNDAY

I went to Maude and Sebe's house first thing in the morning, hoping to finally get the whole story. A story I was praying would put Sam fully in the clear. Maude wasn't under any obligation to tell me anything, of course, but she'd already come close. I felt sure that was why she kept showing up. She wanted to come clean. And now I had actual evidence to help convince her that was the right thing to do.

It was only by the grace of God that the juice bottle Maude had drunk from in my office was still there, sitting on the corner of my desk, when I'd raced back to Young & Crane the night before. At my request, Millie had called Halo Diagnostics to ask for that one last comparative test. Rushed, in the middle of the night. On a weekend.

When a disgruntled Halo technician finally emerged, it had been close to 3:00 a.m. He'd been very short and walked with the arm-swinging stride of someone in a military parade. He'd slapped a nine-by-twelve envelope into my hand. "Your sample was a match to the print in the blood on the stair. And the golf bag."

"Are you sure?"

He pulled his chin back. "Of course. This isn't DNA. Fingerprints match or they don't. Period."

"Okay. Thank you."

"By the way, tell Millie this one is on the house. We've all got a soft spot for her, which is why she needs to get better and get her ass back to work, soon."

Sebe answered the door. He didn't look happy to see me, but he also did not seem especially surprised. "She's in the living room," he said without asking why I'd come.

Maude was sitting on the couch, arms wrapped tight around her. She looked up at me, then down at the folder in my hands with "Halo Diagnostics" written in big bold letters across it.

I held it out toward her. "Your fingerprints were found in Amanda's blood on one of the stairs in her home and on Zach's golf club bag. My guess is they're on the club, too."

Maude made no move to take the folder.

"I'm sorry," she said finally, and then the tears came, rolling silently down her cheeks at an alarming rate. "I almost told you so many times."

"I'm not your lawyer," I said as I sat on the edge of the chair across from her. "I want to make that clear. Nothing you tell me will be privileged. In fact, I could even be obligated to let the police know I found your fingerprints at the scene, to help Zach. He's my client. But I'm— I read parts of Amanda's journal. I know the two of you were really good friends. If there's something I can tell the police that will help explain what happened when I talk to them, I want to do that, too."

This was true. But it was also true I was there for the much more selfish purpose of categorically ruling out Sam. And to do that, I needed Maude to tell me what had actually happened. I needed to hear her say it—that she was responsible. She and not Sam.

"Maude," Sebe said sharply. "That's the second time she's told you to retain your own lawyer. You should. *We* should. Before you speak more."

Maude closed her eyes and shook her head. She patted the couch next to her, encouraging Sebe to come sit. Once he had, she reached over for his hand and linked their fingers tight.

"He's always trying to protect me from myself," she said to me. "You know, he went back to Amanda's house to see if he could find something I was afraid I'd dropped there. Almost got himself arrested, or worse, all for me."

The test strip. The one I had in a pocket somewhere. Of course, it could have been for glucose monitoring, not ovulation. Maude had said she was diabetic. It was Sebe who had been in the house when I was there; his prints were surely on the back door.

"I *am* trying to protect you," Sebe said. "That's why I'm telling you to stop talking."

"Come on, Sebe." Maude put a hand on his back when he looked away. "How can we tell Sophia to live her truth, not to be ashamed, if we're not brave enough to face the mistakes we've made? And I made a mistake that night, there's no doubt. I never should have gone to Zach and Amanda's house."

AMANDA

THE PARTY

When Amanda hung up, she felt like she could fly. She'd never told anyone to fuck off before, not in her entire life. And her dad, of all people? She'd stood her ground. She'd used her voice. And she was not struck dead. The world did not disappear. Amanda was smiling as she looked down at her phone.

Maybe Zach could not be changed, but perhaps the world could be. Not with a single conversation or one long scream. But little by little. Like the small clicks of a combination lock, each notch bringing her one step closer to freedom.

But when Amanda looked up, her heart immediately sank. Sarah and Zach were talking on the far side of the room. Zach was moving his hands around in that way he did when he was explaining something to someone he thought was especially stupid; Sarah's eyebrows were pinched, in that way they always were whenever she talked to someone she hated. There Zach went, ruining everything again.

Amanda's phone vibrated with a text.

NO FUCK YOU FUCKING BITCH

Rage pulsed through the screen. Amanda's hand felt scalded. She almost dropped the phone.

She looked around for Maude. She couldn't tell Zach about her dad, but she could tell her friends. They would try to help her. But before she could find Maude, her phone vibrated again.

Keep looking. I'm here.

Amanda jerked back, knocking right into a busty woman with short curly hair and a full glass of red wine who was standing behind her. The wine tipped all over the woman's white blouse.

"Oh, God, I'm so sorry," Amanda gasped.

But the woman only laughed, looking down at the damp stain covering her huge breasts. She was rocking visibly. "Who cares! My kids are at camp. I have *all day* tomorrow to wash my own fucking shirt."

Another pulse in Amanda's hand.

Come find me! And try not to spill any more wine.

Amanda felt light-headed as she scanned the faces in the crowd. He was there, watching her. He was inside that house. But surely he'd stand right out. Was he watching her through a window? Like the peepers Sarah had talked about? If he was outside, that meant it wasn't safe to leave. Amanda was trapped.

She needed someplace safe to think.

There was a couple on the staircase already, drifting up awkwardly. They were talking and laughing. The woman had a spiky pixie cut, the man a shaved head. They made an attractive couple. Not married, though, definitely not. There was a flirtatious bashfulness to the whole thing, and a politeness, as if giving each other space to change their minds.

Amanda paused, giving them another second to get all the way up, before darting upstairs herself. She peeked carefully down the hall, walking quickly past two closed doors until she found a small open room at the back. On the opposite side of the hall was a big sign taped to one door that read "Off Limits." Sophia's room, probably.

Amanda turned into the open guest room and pulled the door shut behind her. She barely had the door locked when someone knocked. He'd followed her up the stairs. She looked around frantically for a way out—the window, but it was too high; she'd have no way to get down. Amanda tried to take a deep breath. She was starting to feel dizzy. Was everyone there so drunk they'd honestly let her deadbeat dad waltz on in *and* up the stairs?

Amanda backed up, away from the door. Almost to the other side of the room.

"Amanda, it's me, Sebe." She recognized his accent. "Are you okay? I saw you race up here. You looked upset."

Amanda rushed back to the door, unlocking it. Sebe looked startled when she jerked it open.

"What's wrong?" he asked. "Are you okay? You look— You're pale."

When she went to speak, Amanda started to cry. "I'm sorry," she gasped.

"Don't apologize," Sebe said. He put a hand on her shoulder and guided her over to the bed, glancing back at the door. He moved to secure it open with a doorstop in the shape of Peter Rabbit. "Sit, sit. What happened?" Sebe stayed standing, though, even took a step back.

Amanda thought about showing him the texts on her phone. But from her own father? She was too ashamed to admit it. Any of it.

"It's nothing," she began. "It's just— I'm not great at parties. I get overwhelmed."

Sebe frowned. "But it's something more than that, isn't it?" he asked, more concerned now, and in a clinical, doctorly way. "Because you really don't seem yourself."

Amanda jumped when her phone vibrated once more. But it was only Zach this time: Left party. Have to stop at office. See you later at home.

"Who's that?" Sebe asked, even more alarmed.

"Zach," Amanda said, her voice hoarse. "He left. Without even finding me to say goodbye or offering to walk me home. What kind of husband does that?"

"A not very good one," Sebe said, but delicately. He finally came over to sit down on the bed next to her.

"Zach is an awful husband actually," Amanda said. It was the first time she'd ever said anything like that out loud about her marriage: the sad, ugly truth. "He always has been. He doesn't love me. I don't think he loves anybody."

Sebe was quiet for a moment. "I'm sorry," he said finally. "Do you want *me* to walk you home?"

Amanda did her best not to burst into tears again. "Maybe, but I'm not—"

Her phone had vibrated again.

Get the fuck away from Sebe.

Amanda jumped to her feet and bolted. She flew down the stairs as Sebe shouted after her.

When Amanda hit the living room, there were even more people near the front door. Way too many to push through. She tried anyway. She was scared enough to shove. But everyone was so drunk they didn't even notice.

"Go out the back." A drunken man in a jester's hat pointed a wavering finger on his way to the bathroom. "There's an alley with a gate to the street. All the *lazy* assholes are going out that way. The racist neighbor lady calls the police. But fuck her, anyway."

Amanda ran out the back door and raced down the alley, waiting for somebody to yell at her, for hands to grab hold as she sprinted all the way down Prospect Park West in her platform heels. But she heard nothing except the ragged sound of her own breathing, and the desperate pounding of her frantic heart.

LIZZIE

"At the party, I finally started putting the pieces together," Maude went on. "Everyone was so drunk, and all the confidentiality with the email investigation went right out the window. Before long, I'd learned that the person behind the hacking was possibly a parent, and that it had all started in April. Then Amanda tells me about some printouts of scheduling emails from Brooklyn Country Day she found in Zach's desk drawer. Even though he claimed the school didn't have his email. That was how they'd hacked in, the scheduling emails. And why would he have printouts? Then Sarah adds that Zach is bankrupt. All of it together . . ." She shook her head. "I didn't know for sure, obviously. That's why I wanted to confront Zach. I thought I'd be able to tell from his reaction. But when I tried to find him at the party, he was already gone."

"Maude, please," Sebe whispered, then closed his eyes. "Stop."

She squeezed his hand again, until he opened his eyes. "I love you, Sebe. But there isn't going to be any way through this except with the truth." Maude turned back to look at me. "I'm not saying it was Zach himself who contacted Sophia. According to that security company, there were probably a bunch of different people doing the actual hacking. And Sophia said she got the feeling it was somebody younger who was messaging her. But it doesn't really matter: Zach, given who he was, must have been in charge—it's all his responsibility. Everything that happened is. Sophia is fifteen years old, and that man had her performing live sex acts on camera." She blanched, then closed her eyes. "He probably recorded them."

Zach had been hacking into the neighborhood parents' computers? It was possible. He'd have the technological know-how. From what that *New York Times* profile had described, logistics involved a lot of personal information, didn't it? And at this point Zach certainly seemed capable of anything. The financial disclosure, Sam's drinking— had he hacked into our computer, too?

"What happened after you couldn't find Zach at the party?" I asked, trying to stay focused. I still needed hard evidence to clear Sam.

"I'll admit it: I was out of my mind. In a complete rage. I was going to make Zach admit what I was sure he'd done to Sophia. Somebody said he'd gone home, so I went to his house to find him. But when I got to Zach and Amanda's, no one was there. I wasn't about to give up, though. I decided to go in and get those emails that Amanda had talked about. I was going to go to the police with them. I figured it would be enough—at least for them to look into Zach and the hacking. And I'd seen once where Amanda kept her spare key."

"I wish you'd told me you were going, Maude," Sebe said quietly.

"You were upstairs talking to Amanda. Somebody said she ran up-stairs, and you followed," Maude said, so certain, it seemed, that they were only talking—she and Sebe did have their limits, after all. "And I wanted to go while Amanda was here and not at home. I didn't want to lose it on Zach in front of her. I knew she'd feel responsible. Besides, you would have stopped me."

"But Amanda came home while you were in the house?" I asked.

An accident. That had to be where all of this was going. Maude hit Amanda by accident somehow.

"I wasn't sure at first. I'd stupidly left the door unlocked behind me, and I was upstairs in Zach's office when I heard somebody come in. I'd only been in there a second; it took me a while to find the of-fice," she said. "Anyway, as soon as I heard someone I ducked into the closet. It wasn't until I was in there that I saw the golf bag."

"Maude," Sebe whispered, wincing.

"Sophia almost killed herself, Sebe," Maude pleaded. She looked from Sebe to me. "We have her at an inpatient facility right now. Hopefully, she'll be okay. Teenagers are resilient. But who knows. And for what? You know, that guy is *still* contacting her, which I guess proves it wasn't Zach himself, given that he's in Rikers. I also heard another parent just got one of those blackmailing emails yesterday for the first time. Zach may be in jail, but his soldiers are keeping on with their work. What if they're doing the same thing to other girls?"

I refuse to lose. I could hear Zach's voice in my head from all those years ago. But to what end had Zach done all of it? Surely not for cash. He wasn't going to get enough that way. And Zach didn't do anything for pure entertainment value. Whatever Zach was doing, I had no doubt his intent was to put himself back on top. And I knew Zach well enough to know: he could care less who had to lose, as long as he was the one to win.

"What happened after you saw the golf clubs?" I asked.

Maude had mistaken Amanda for Zach. It had to be.

"I pulled one out and held it. I imagined swinging it at Zach's head." Maude looked squarely at me then, her eyes defiant, fists clenched. "And I know, I didn't even have actual hard evidence. But in that moment, I felt so, so sure. And all I could think about was how much I wanted Zach dead."

KRELL INDUSTRIES

CONFIDENTIAL MEMORANDUM
NOT FOR DISTRIBUTION

Attorney-Client Work Product
Privileged & Confidential

July 9

To: Brooklyn Country Day Board of Directors
From: Krell Industries
Subject: Data Breach & Cyber Incident Investigation—Critical Event Report

The memorandum should serve to notify the board that the recommended forensic examination of Subject Family 0006 computer is now complete. Numerous pornographic images were located on the computer in question. These images were removed, and placed on a jump drive at FPP request for further investigation within Subject Family.

Despite Krell having conducted the desired forensic analysis, it remains the FPP position that the pornography must have been placed onto the family computer by the hackers in question.

JIA explained that there is clear evidence this is not the case. That the pornographic material was downloaded to the computer over many months preceding the alleged hacking.

However, FPP has continued to threaten legal action, or, alternatively, public disclosure of the security breach, specifically that she will contact local media.

We believe it imperative, under the circumstances, that the board be made aware of the identity of Family 0006, as the situation continues to evolve. They are Sarah Novak and Kerry Tanner.

AMANDA

THE PARTY

Amanda didn't look back over her shoulder or down at her phone again until she'd gotten to her front steps. Luckily, there was no one behind her, and there were no new texts. Amanda dared to hope for a moment that she'd imagined the others. But when she finally got to the top of her stoop and checked, all the disgusting, frightening messages she'd gotten earlier from her dad were still there. She deleted every last one of them.

When Amanda turned her key, the lock didn't make its usual pop. Zach was home? It wouldn't be the first time he'd used work as an excuse to leave someplace.

But as soon as Amanda opened the door, she noticed the foyer chair pushed slightly to the side. Like someone drunk had stumbled into it. Zach didn't drink, and he wasn't clumsy. There were a couple of lights on—at the top of the steps, and the front of the living room—but it was pretty dark. Amanda's heart again took flight.

"Zach!" Amanda called out as she headed for the stairs. Not a sound as she made her way halfway up. "Zach!"

Her daddy had been good at picking locks once upon a time, hadn't he? And he was determined. If he wanted in her house, he could easily have found a way.

"Zach!" she called out again, about to turn back down the steps. She should leave. Go somepla—

A hand slammed over Amanda's mouth, a leather glove on her lips.

She could smell it. She could taste it. Her head was jerked back so hard, she thought her neck might snap. Her dad smelled musky. Like an animal.

"Calm down!" A hoarse whisper—her dad disguising his voice. "Calm down. I'm not going to hurt you."

She tried to pull her head to the side, to get out from under his huge hand, but he yanked her head back even harder this time. She yelped in pain.

This was it. Where all this had been headed. Her dad wasn't going to let her go this time. This wasn't just some random burglar who would take off if she only did as she was told. Her dad had come to finish what he'd started—to kill her. She could feel the rage in his grip, too. Amanda needed to make noise. She needed to scream. And so she did. She screamed as loud as she could. She tried to kick and fight. But the sound was muffled under his hand, and he was so strong. She could barely move.

"Hey! Calm down. I'm not going to hurt you. I'm going to let you go."

But that was a lie. Amanda knew it was. She knew her dad. He had hurt her before, over and over again. He had hurt the only person on earth who had loved her besides her mother: Carolyn. He had done that. He had. It was starting to come back to her.

Amanda tried to bite his fingers. But his hand was clamped over her mouth so hard, she couldn't even open her lips. There was a taste, too. Blood. Her teeth were tearing at the insides of her cheeks. And she could feel her earring being ripped out as she struggled.

He'd never let her go. She'd have to kill him. She could, too. She'd done it once before, hadn't she? Yes—she remembered it all now— Carolyn motionless under him in the bathroom. The razor, the blood all over Amanda's seafoam taffeta dress. How cold and wet it had been when she raced through the woods to Norma's for help. How the soles of her feet had burned, the branches and rocks slicing into them.

Case. The name hit her like a bolt of electricity. She loved her son more than her own life. She'd survive for him. She'd kill her dad again now to protect him. She'd kill him as many times as she had to. Anything for Case. Amanda flung an elbow back, whacking into his stomach, soft after all these years.

"Fuck." He coughed, releasing his grip a little. She kicked him as hard as she could in the knee. "Fuck!"

He released again for a second, and Amanda lunged forward up a few more steps. Her only path was up. He was blocking the way down.

"What the fuck are you doing?" he roared. "All you had to do was listen."

Heavy feet right behind her. And the sour heat of him. Amanda was almost at the top of the stairs now, almost where she could turn and run down the hall. Lock the bedroom door. Call the police. Scamper out a window. They had that big tree out front. Maybe she could reach it.

But then a thousand needles being driven into her scalp. He'd grabbed her ponytail. She tried once more to get free. He was above her on the stairs now. She jerked to the side and screamed, "Let go of me, you disgusting pig!"

Then, a shove. Hands on her back. Just a little. But enough. And there at the top of the steps, she was suddenly and so unexpectedly free.

In free fall. Picking up speed. Amanda reached out to stop herself, even as she thought, *No, don't.* Her arm cracked against the metal handrail, but she did not slow down. And then the wind was knocked hard out of her. Amanda was on the ground. Stars exploding overhead, then blackness.

Light. Amanda was on the ground at the bottom of the stairs. Pain everywhere. But alive. A chance. Her eyes were blurry and wet. Something—or someone—was there near the top of the stairs. All in black, and with the ski mask. So big and tall. Blocking the light the way he always had. Amanda needed to get up. She needed to run. And she could. She had survived all this time. She could survive again. She would. For Case.

Amanda pushed herself to her feet but slipped. What was that all over the floor? She cracked her head against the railing as she went down again. The floor was wet and warm and so slippery. Her vision was clouded. But she saw red. All over the floor. And him, standing there above.

Amanda pushed herself up a second time. She could see him still at the top of the stairs, through the water in her eyes. It tasted of iron.

Then again she was down. Her head smacking hard against the metal edge of the stairs this time. She needed to stop hitting her head. Or something—more stars. Case. He loved stars. So many, too. Like that night she raced away from St. Colomb Falls, top down, wind in her hair. Alive. Free. The stars. And then the dark.

And then—

LIZZIE

"Was it Amanda," I asked, "that you heard downstairs while you were in the office closet?"

"No, it was definitely somebody else at first," Maude said. "Because then I heard a second person come in. That was Amanda. She called out right away for Zach. I thought there was a chance it was Zach who'd come in first, that maybe I'd have to wait there in the closet until they'd gone to bed, and then slip out. To be honest, I was thinking I'd keep looking for the emails maybe, or some other proof of what I was sure Zach had done. I was utterly consumed." Maude's voice caught, and then she fell silent.

I tried to be patient, to let her take her time in getting the rest of the story out. But I couldn't wait any longer. All I could think about was Sam's face. I needed her to say the words: I did it.

"And then what?" I asked.

Amanda had panicked in the midst of one of her delusions and had fallen down the steps? An awful, tragic accident that—as far as I was concerned—remained Zach's fault.

"Amanda screamed. And it was such a horrible, frantic sound— like nothing I'd ever heard. There were other noises, too, grunting and this awful scrambling. Like an animal. Then there was a really loud crash. I wanted to help. I had the golf club already, but when I tried the closet door, it was stuck—I couldn't get out. I thought maybe somebody had locked me in there." Her voice broke again. "I heard crashing, another scream—maybe more than one. By the time I finally got the door open and was down the first set of steps, I saw—I saw Amanda at the bottom of the lower staircase. I only caught a glimpse of a man running out."

"Wait, there *was* a man?"

Fuck.

"Yes, definitely. Like I said, I only saw him for a split second. And he had on dark clothes and a horribly creepy ski mask, so I couldn't see his face. But I'm convinced it wasn't Zach. As much as I hate him, I'm sure it wasn't. I saw Zach across the room at my party. He's noticeably short. Shorter than me. This man was much taller."

Sam was tall. But this guy had come with a ski mask? Could the monster in Sam's cage be that bad?

"Not just tall." Maude held her arms out, demonstrating. "Big, too. At least I think. I'm less sure about that. I only saw him for a second, and he was already turning around."

Sam wasn't big like that, was he? No, but Xavier Lynch was. *Shit.* I'd been so quick to write him off entirely because his story was true. But that didn't mean he wasn't involved somehow. At least, theoretically.

"Nothing else identifying?" I pressed, trying to sound calm.

"Amanda was all I could see." Maude was ashen now. "There was so much blood, too. Everywhere at the bottom of the steps. I raced down, and she didn't have a pulse. I started CPR, right away. I know how to do it. And I called Sebe. I was going to call nine-one-one, too, but then I looked down, and there was blood all over me. My hands, my arms, my shirt. I think it was on my face. And the golf club that I'd been holding with my fingerprints all over it? It was on the ground *in* Amanda's blood. How was I going to explain any of that to the police? How could I explain why I was in the house in the first place, and hiding in a closet? My prints would have been in there, too. I'm sorry, I know I should have called them anyway. But all I could think about was Sophia needing me and I panicked."

"I was there faster than an ambulance would have been anyway," Sebe said. "And I can assure you that Amanda was dead when I arrived. Her head wounds were very traumatic. I think the result of multiple impacts. Maybe that man hit her with something, or maybe she hit her head by falling more than once. Even postmortem it would be difficult to tell the difference between the long side of a golf club and the rounded metal edge of those stairs. You could see in the blood where somebody had slipped. It could have been Amanda."

"There was so much blood," Maude said again. "Sebe had to physically lift me out so I didn't track it everywhere. I didn't leave the golf club there on purpose to confuse things either. I want to make that clear. I dropped it when I tried to help Amanda. And I was so sure they'd come for me anyway, once they found it. My prints must have been all over it. But then they didn't come, even after I stupidly slipped and mentioned the golf club to Sarah. To be honest, for a little while I thought it was justice if Zach went to jail for Amanda's murder after what he did to Sophia." She shook her head. "But once he was getting beaten up, I knew I couldn't be that person, couldn't let him get killed, not with Case. And then I thought about whoever it was who had really hurt Amanda. The fact that he was still out there because they'd arrested Zach. . . . So I gave Zach the alibi." She looked up at me, her eyes aglow once more. "I didn't actually mean to imply that we'd had sex. In the context of the party, you assumed, which was understandable . . ." Maude grimaced. "After everything with Sophia, that made me absolutely sick. Not that the alibi mattered in the end."

"And you have no idea who the man in Amanda's house was?" I asked.

"All I know is that he was big and wearing all black. I was at the top of the steps, and he took off right away. I didn't see much. Oh, and he also had on these red sneakers."

My breath caught. *Sam's basketball sneakers are white. Sam's basketball sneakers are white.*

"Red sneakers?" I asked. "You're sure?"

"Yes, they were very noticeable," Maude said. "Red high-tops."

I held my breath, legs trembling, impatiently counting the floors as the Young & Crane elevator glided up. It was obvious now that I'd had too much riding on Maude's fingerprints. I'd been so sure they'd do all the work: prove that Maude had killed Amanda—accidentally—thereby exonerating Zach. *And* clearing Sam. As it turned out, Maude's fingerprints had given me only a witness to the crime and a vague partial description of the actual killer: male and large, with red sneakers.

Xavier Lynch. He was still a totally reasonable possibility, at least I was determined for him to be. Maybe he'd been after Amanda's money or had some other twisted reason for killing her. He'd hinted at a criminal past. I'd call the St. Colomb Falls police department. Someone there could easily know more about him. It was a small town.

I considered texting Sam, too, but to say what? *Good news! I've almost proved you're not a murderer!* In my defense, Sam had seemed pretty worried he was a murderer, too.

The receptionist desk was empty as I swiped my key card and headed fast for my office. There were several doors open, lights on, at my end of the hall. I could hear voices and spotted a couple of weekend secretaries scattered at the outer desks.

In the far corner, Paul's door was also open. He'd sent me an email late the night before, asking for three different things on three matters having nothing to do with Zach. Apparently he'd moved on. I turned toward my office, hoping not to see him.

"Oh!" a woman exclaimed. I'd slammed right into Gloria as I turned the corner, sending everything in her hands raining down to the floor.

"I'm so sorry," I said, bending to help her retrieve the papers.

"Darn it," she grumbled sourly. "Now everything is out of order."

"I'm really sorry," I said, hating that we were crouched there making a commotion in clear view of Paul's door. "I wasn't paying attention."

"Well, that's obvious."

I clenched my jaw to keep myself from taking her head off. I gathered the papers as best I could and handed them back to her in what was, admittedly, a messy stack.

"Do you want me to help you?"

"No, I'm fine," she snapped.

I heard Paul's voice. I needed to get out of the hallway and behind my closed office door.

"Sorry, again," I said as I began to edge past Gloria.

"Hey, how do you know Maude anyway?" she asked. It sounded like something of an accusation. "I couldn't believe when she called up from the lobby—once she realized you worked here, too. She told me she wasn't a client. But I didn't want to pry."

"Oh, do you know her? She's involved in a case I'm handling. But she's not a client, no." And that was all I was saying.

"Hmm." Gloria narrowed her eyes. She could tell I was being evasive. "Maude's so beautiful and so nice, isn't she? I only met her once, at a party—I knew all of one person there, and she was kind enough to spend half the night talking to me."

A party? Presumably not the ones Maude threw. "That's nice," I said. "Okay, well, sorry again. I really have to be—"

"It was my old boss's holiday party," she went on. "He was a *very* senior partner. I don't know if you know that. I was his secretary, for *years*. What a party that was, too. They threw one every year in Park Slope, but I was only able to go the one time, two years ago. *Very* glamorous. But no more, thanks to him." She ticked her head toward Paul's office. "Your hypocritical friend over there had my boss fired. You know, those legal assistants who cried wolf were just looking to make money. Hashtag MeToo my ass. Everyone is looking for a handout these days."

I didn't know you worked here, too. Maude had said that to me, hadn't she? I felt light-headed, my hands ice cold as I stepped toward Gloria.

"Who was your old boss?"

"Kerry Tanner," Gloria said with a nostalgic smile, shellacked with pride. Then her face darkened. "He was railroaded, pure and simple. I worked for him for eighteen years, and he never once did anything inappropriate. Ask Maude. She was absolutely flabbergasted when I told her he'd been fired. I thought she was going to pass out. And I didn't even get the chance to tell her *why* he was let go."

In my office, it only took a second to pull up an image of Kerry Tanner: a lawyer headshot, the kind of photo that had probably been on Young & Crane's own website before Kerry was fired.

Sure enough, I'd seen him before, at the bottom of Sarah's steps, pizza box in hand, six-pack tucked under his arm. Kerry Tanner was married to Sarah Novak and friends with Maude. Surely he'd also known Amanda. And Kerry Tanner had somehow known exactly who I was—probably because he stood to gain the most from Zach staying in jail.

I headed back toward Paul's office, the image of Kerry Tanner on my phone. When I looked in the open door, Paul was muttering angrily as he squinted through his reading glasses at his computer screen. I inhaled sharply.

"Sorry to interrupt," I began, "but I need to ask you something."

"If you can sort out why the hell I can't get back to the other case I was just reading in this damn Westlaw program, then I might answer you," Paul said without taking his eyes off his computer. "It was here a second ago, and now I'm in this other case I have no goddamn interest in."

Paul didn't even like communicating via email. If he was surfing cases online, it was because some associate had screwed something up. I came up behind him, and within a few, very obvious keystrokes had him back on the original case he'd been reading.

"Be careful not to click on any of the cited cases," I said. "Or it will bring you to them."

"I did not click on anything," Paul said, quietly defensive as he glared at his computer. "If this asshole's summary judgment brief wasn't all fucked up, I wouldn't even have to be on this damn system in the first place."

"Can you tell me if you recognize this man?" I asked as neutrally as possible—I didn't want to prime the pump. I held out my phone to him.

Paul furrowed his brow and leaned over to look. "Of course," he said, disgusted. "That's Kerry Tanner. The partner I told you about. Defiant narcissistic asshole." He looked up at me with an annoyed expression. "Is this the best use of your time? If I recall, you owe me several—"

"He knew Zach Grayson's wife," I said. "They were friends in Park Slope."

Paul looked up at me. He pulled his chin back. "Really?"

"Yes."

"He did live in Brooklyn," Paul said, considering. Then he was quiet for a moment. "You think he . . ."

"I don't know," I said. "But Amanda was being stalked by someone, and Kerry Tanner had stalked people in the past, right? Seems like one hell of a coincidence. There's a couple things I still need to check out, to be sure."

Paul nodded. "Well, with that guy . . . nothing would surprise me. I've got a whole investigatory file on him. He did follow those women around, showed up places. Sent harassing texts. 'All you had to do was listen.' Sick shit. Not to mention all the pictures he took, and the porn we found on his work computer." He grimaced. "From what we could tell he'd been doing it for years. Five, maybe ten, who knows? I bet some of the other partners would still have let it go if it hadn't been for the pictures. There was no ignoring those."

I took another deep breath. There was more I needed to say, too. No more running. No more pretending. Millie was right. None of it was working for me.

"There is something else I need to tell you," I said. "My financial disclosure form. There were some inaccuracies in it. Intentional ones." Paul's jaw tightened, and his eyes narrowed a tiny bit, almost imperceptibly. But otherwise, his face was completely still. "My husband is an alcoholic. He got into a car accident, and we were sued. We settled the case and are in full compliance with our obligation. We will pay off the debt, but it's a big one. I should have included it on the form."

Paul frowned more deeply, his brow scrunched. Then he took off his reading glasses and stared at me in silence for what felt like an eternity. I stared right back. It was all I could do. Maude was right: there was no way through but with the truth.

"You should have included it," Paul said finally. Then he put his reading glasses back on and turned to face his computer once more. "Call Human Resources and get it amended first thing Monday."

The woman at Blooms on the Slope was locking up for the night when I knocked on the door. Her hair was piled high as before, and she had on a bright yellow blouse and the same sunny expression. She shook her head, smiled sympathetically, and pointed to the store hours written on the door. It didn't seem like she recognized me.

I held up my phone with Kerry Tanner's picture on it. "For Matthew," I said, hoping she'd take pity on me. "I think he's the circle."

She peered through the glass at the photo, and then I saw it click. She reached forward to unlock the door. "Come in, come in," she said, waving me inside and locking the door behind me. "Let me see if I can grab Matthew. I think he's in back."

A moment later Matthew emerged, a skateboard under his arm, headphones already on.

"Is this the man you made the card out for?" I asked, holding out my phone.

Matthew smiled. "Nailed it." He held up a hand until I gave him a high five. "See, this guy's a perfect circle. And lilacs. I remember now. That's what he bought. He said all the ones his wife planted in her backyard had died."

I walked away from the florist up St. Johns, then turned right on Plaza Street, headed past the gracious doorman buildings and, finally, onto Prospect Park West. I walked to the top of Montgomery Place and stopped at a bench along the stone wall surrounding the park. Maybe even the bench that Sam had passed out on. The early evening summer sun was thin and gold as I sat down.

I was not looking forward to the last call I had to make. I found Sarah's number in my phone log and dialed her back. She answered after a few rings.

"Hi, Sarah," I began, my voice sounding strangled and foreign. "This is Lizzie Kitsakis, Zach Grayson's lawyer."

"Yes?" she asked. "What can I do for you?"

Was there a tone to her voice now? Trepidation? Maude might have already asked Sarah about what Gloria had told her: that Kerry had been fired months ago. But Maude didn't know *why* he'd been fired. Honestly, I didn't think Sarah did either. She didn't strike me as the kind of woman to keep on sleeping with her husband knowing all that. And I did not believe for one second that she had connected Kerry to Amanda's death. If she had, I couldn't imagine she would have been able to pick up the phone.

"I think maybe you were right," I said.

"Yeah," she said. "Right about what?"

"About us being connected from the neighborhood," I said. "I think our husbands might play basketball together. In that rec league. Thursday nights?"

I'd remembered Sam had said he'd been at Freddy's with a guy with a big job and a wife and kids. Maybe a lawyer who decided not to mention he'd been fired. And Sarah had said her husband had regular plans on Thursday nights, "trying to break a hip." Just like Sam.

"Oh," she said, with the quietest little gasp of relief. Only this I was calling about? Who cared about this? "Sure, he plays basketball. Hard to believe he's found the time, given what I recently discovered is his voracious appetite for pornography," she spat out. She was pissed, no doubt. Not shattered, though, not in the way she would be if she knew the rest. "But yes, he does also play basketball. I even went to watch once. Maybe I saw your husband. Let me guess: he's one of the young, hot ones, right?"

She was angry, but there was a grim humor underneath—like she might forgive her husband even a porn addiction. Like she loved him still. I felt gutted, thinking of how destroyed Sarah would feel once she learned the whole ugly truth about the man she'd built a life with. After all, the mere possibility had all but consumed what was left of my shredded heart.

"I don't know," I said. "I guess maybe my husband—"

"You should go watch sometime yourself. It's fun." Sarah's voice was brittle now, broken. "If you do, be sure to be on the lookout for my husband. He's the asshole in the dumb red shoes."

LIZZIE

When Zach came into the small attorney interview room, he looked so goddamn pleased with himself. I clenched my fists and tried to stay calm.

"I told you. I didn't do it," he singsonged. No twitchy eye contact. No bouncing leg. He was only the new and improved Zach from those staged photos now.

"You already heard?"

"A guy here was at a court date, and there was talk about somebody else being arrested for Amanda's murder. A 'fancy corporate lawyer,'" he went on, with a smile. "I may not have paid attention after that first year of law school, but even I know they can't charge two people with the same murder. So I'm out, right?"

Maude had gone to the prosecutor's office herself soon after I left her house, which I agreed would be much better than me delivering the news. Being associated with me would not curry her any favor with Wendy Wallace. I did ask Maude to emphasize that she was sure the figure she'd seen hadn't been Zach.

I waited until the next day to call Wendy Wallace myself. She'd been far from happy to hear about Kerry Tanner when we finally spoke, but to her credit—and likely at Paul's cajoling—she did hear me out, and she did seem to be listening. After all, at least she now had a new suspect in hand, and a case still high-profile enough to land her in the Brooklyn District Attorney's Office.

As of that morning, as I headed to Rikers, Kerry was in custody.

"They're processing your release as we speak," I said to Zach. "You should be out soon."

Zach closed his eyes and exhaled sharply. He'd been more worried than his cocky grin let on.

"That's great news. Great news," he said. "Thank you."

"Can I ask you something?"

"Sure, why not?"

"You were the one who compromised Brooklyn Country Day's email list, right?" This was the part of this conversation that mattered to me. The *real* reason I was there. "Clever, the way you used it to hack into the parents' computers."

There was nothing to stop Zach from lying to me now. Nothing but his own arrogance. And Zach's arrogance was one thing you could always count on. That, and the fact that he would want to be sure I knew: he'd beaten everyone.

"What do you mean?" he asked. But I could see him trying not to smile; a trace of it was there in his eyes.

"The phishing emails," I said. "You compromised the computers of the Brooklyn Country Day parents, exposed all their dirty laundry. Impressive stuff. But what I don't get is how that's going to save your failing company."

Zach rolled his eyes. "First of all, *failing* is a huge overstatement. The world of start-ups is always high risk, high reward." He was quiet then, and with a determined look on his face, like he was trying to stay quiet. But I already knew, if I waited, he wouldn't be able to contain himself. "Anyway, this new enterprise is going to take off like a shot. People have absolutely no idea how exposed they are, or why. You want to know how I learned? Working in logistics. An industry the average person has probably never even heard of. If they have, they think it's just about shipping. But we knew *everything* about hundreds of thousands of people—we knew when they had a baby because they started ordering diapers, when they were going on a long trip because they ordered power converters, when not to buy their home because they'd bought a whole bunch of mold removal products. And here people think they're just ordering stuff. It's not just stuff, it's who they are. As soon as people realize how dangerous this could be, they'll be falling all over themselves to pay the hundred-dollar yearly subscription for my family cybersecurity app."

I nodded, to look interested. But not too interested. Anything to keep Zach talking.

He leaned in a little closer to the plexiglass. "I was specifically attracted to Brooklyn Country Day because they are actually somewhat on top of things. You learn from hard targets, not easy ones. Also, I did figure the whole hacking thing might get some press because of the school's stellar reputation, and maybe that would flow over to my app if I stepped in to help at the right time. But in the end, the Brooklyn Country Day parents helped us solve more of a technical problem. We needed to reverse-engineer some of the software by seeing how actual victims might respond to that kind of intrusion."

"So you hired people to do the hacking for you?"

"You want to find out how to protect people from hackers, you hire some hackers to show you what they really do."

"One of those hackers of yours blackmailed a fifteen-year-old girl for live video of her performing sex acts," I said. "He's continuing to contact her. Did you know that?"

"It's hard to find good people." Zach shrugged. "But I am impressed that you put as much together as you did. I always knew you were special, Lizzie, which is why when I saw you near the farmer's market, I was curious about what you'd been up to. Obviously, I had no idea I'd soon need a lawyer I didn't have to pay. Amanda was alive and well then, and I hadn't thought about you in *years*—a decade at least. But then there you were, and I could see it right away." He paused, smiled a little. "Can you see it now?"

"See what?"

"That you made the wrong choice."

"What the hell are you talking about?"

"Sam instead of me," he said. "Oh, I know you hadn't even met him yet, not when you ended things with me. The 'other guy' story was a lie. I knew that the whole time. I'll admit I was angry for a while. More disappointed, though. We were the same you and I—eyes always focused on the prize. Maybe not quite as similar as some of my stories about my 'blue-collar' family might have suggested." Zach's fingers hooked the word in the air. "But I thought that would resonate more with you than two Poughkeepsie crack addicts. But then, you left things out, too. Like the Elmira Correctional Facility." He smirked. "I did actually think we might make a real go of it, though. That was true. Instead, you chose a husband with zero drive. Everything for you could have ended up differently."

"Yeah," I said, glaring at him. "I could have ended up dead at the bottom of your stairs. You know, Amanda might be alive right now if you'd paid more attention to her."

"Please, Amanda had plenty of problems long before I met her." Zach sniffed, but his face quickly brightened. "I was surprised when you clicked on that Netflix membership renewal link without even a second's hesitation, though. I mean, you should be smarter than that. One click, and boom, I was in." He smiled slightly. "I did that myself, of course. I wasn't going to outsource you. Within minutes I knew everything about you and Sam. As a friend, I have to say: researching dozens of alcohol rehab facilities on a daily basis for weeks on end isn't nearly as effective as Sam actually going to a single one. Also, you should buy some shades if you're going to walk around undressed." He shook his head. Then he smiled, and raised his eyebrows. "At least I can say exactly where you were the night Amanda died. And now you know why *I* wasn't anxious to tell you where I was."

This was what Zach wanted, maybe even what he'd planned from the start: this moment. The one when he got to really embarrass me, the way I had embarrassed him all those years ago. When he finally got to win.

Unbeknownst to him, I already knew much of what he was telling me—though not the bit about him spying on me through my windows. I'd brought in my personal laptop to the investigators I knew in the Manhattan US attorney's cybercrime unit. Within seconds they'd found the spyware Zach had installed. I'd felt humiliated that I'd fallen for it so easily, but the kind twentysomething tech investigator kept saying: "Yeah, seriously, it could happen to anyone. It does all the time."

Then I'd contacted the New York City Bar Association's Ethics Hotline for anonymous advice about how I could proceed under the circumstances without being disbarred. From now on, everything I did would at least be clear-eyed and aboveboard.

"You know, I've been thinking about that thing you said," I went on.

"What's that?" Zach asked, delighted that I was willing to play.

"About how it's more important to know somebody's weaknesses than their strengths."

"Ah, yes," Zach said. "I do think that's true."

I pressed both of my hands on the table for a moment, looking down, nodding. Finally, I stood. "You know what your weakness is, Zach?"

He smiled. So fucking satisfied. "No, Lizzie. By all means, tell me: What's my weakness?"

"You think people are things you can win."

He frowned. "I don't know. I'd say things have turned out okay for me in the end."

"Your wife is dead," I said, but Zach didn't even flinch. "Also, cyber fraud is a federal crime."

"Come on, Lizzie." He laughed. "Even if you wanted to tell them what I just told you, you can't. You're my *lawyer*, remember. Attorney-client privilege? You'd be disbarred. And I *know* you care way more about your job than you do about going after me."

"See, that's where you're wrong, Zach." I shook my head and frowned. "Maybe you should have paid more attention in law school. Because that malware you had the Brooklyn Country Day parents download is still on some of their computers. Your team is still using it to blackmail new families and the person who exploited that fifteen-year-old is still contacting her. That means this crime of yours is *ongoing,* so what you just admitted falls within the crime-fraud exception to attorney-client privilege. As your lawyer, I'm not obligated to keep quiet about crimes you are still in the process of committing." I leaned in close to the plexiglass. "So enjoy your time on the outside, Zach. It won't last for long."

Name: Kerry W. Tanner
Address: 571 2nd St. Brooklyn 11215
Date of Birth: 6/28/71
Age: 48
Telephone: 718.555.2615

New York City Police Dept.
Borough of Brooklyn
Date: July 15th
Time: 3:00 pm
Case Number: 62984415

I, Kerry W. Tanner, willingly and voluntarily give this statement to
Detective Robert Mendez, who I know to be a member of the New York
City Police Department. I know that I do not need to give a statement and
that any statement can be used against me in a court of law. Prior to giving
this statement, I was read my Miranda rights. I understand those rights and
I signed a separate written waiver of my Miranda rights before making this
statement.

Signed: _____*Kerry W. Tanner*_____

STATEMENT

I am making a statement here today about this situation because I love my
wife, Sarah, and she asked me to. So maybe this whole thing can be resolved
without a trial. We've been together for more than thirty years and Sarah
is everything to me. We have a good marriage. I love my sons, too. What
happened was a terrible, terrible accident. But it was an accident. Obviously,
I didn't <u>kill</u> anyone.

Amanda and I were friends. Close friends. She got to know my wife, Sarah,
first. Over time we developed feelings for each other. I didn't mean for that
to happen and it doesn't change how much I love Sarah. Some things you
just can't control. Over months, Amanda and I started doing little things for
each other to express our affection. Amanda would buy me thoughtful gifts
and I did things to help her because her husband was never around. He's
an asshole, that guy. Anyway, for months our relationship got closer in this
secret special way. It made me feel good about myself. Amanda made me
feel good.

But then Sebe, this other friend of ours—I think maybe he was trying to get in between us. He has an open marriage. And I couldn't let that happen.

I didn't even plan on seeing Amanda that night or going to the party. But then my basketball game got canceled and I went for a few drinks and one thing led to another. I ended up leaving with one of the other guys who I think has some kind of drinking problem. He wanted to rest on a bench on the way to Sebe and Maude's because he was so wasted and ended up passing out. So I left him there and went myself. I was just going to stop by the party. I didn't want Sarah to see me because she'd spend the whole night dragging me around to talk to people. I love my wife, but so does <u>everyone</u> else. I just wanted to see Amanda and I did, but then somebody told me later she'd disappeared upstairs with Sebe. I'll admit I kind of snapped.

I knew if I sent her a couple texts she'd go home. I just wanted her to see that she needed me. I thought if I created a little situation where Amanda got scared, I could take off and then come right back to her rescue. Luckily, I happened to have a few things with me in my gym bag that I could use so she wouldn't know it was me. That's what I mean—obviously I thought she'd be fine after. Otherwise why would I care if she knew it was me?

None of it happened the way it was supposed to, though. Amanda completely freaked out. Started hitting me. We were on the stairs at the time. I had to defend myself. And then she just fell. It was an accident. She hit her head on the railing. And then she came to and stood up and slipped. She hit her head again on the stairs. That kept happening. A bunch of times. Until finally she stopped moving. There was so much blood everywhere.

I panicked and ran. I was going to call an ambulance but all I could think about was my family. I really do love Sarah more than anything. I have <u>never</u> been unfaithful to her. Unlike Sebe and all the other guys who go to that swapping party, I would never have sex with another woman.

After I left Amanda's house, I ran toward the park to pull myself together. That was when I saw Amanda's earring hooked on my sleeve and some blood on the back of my hand. I was careful to walk around everything, but I must have brushed the wall trying to get down the stairs. My friend was still passed out. I could see him up ahead, his leg hanging over the end of the bench. So I stuck Amanda's earring in his pocket, and put a little blood on his shoe. I was panicked like I said, not thinking clearly. And he didn't do it anyway. I knew the police would figure that out eventually. All I could think about was my family. And doing what I had to, to protect them.

The above statement was given freely and voluntarily by me. I have read the above statement and it is true and correct to the best of my knowledge.

Signed: _____ *Kerry Tanner* _____

Date: _____ *July 15, 2019* _____

Witness: _____ *Robert Mendez* _____

Date: _____ *July 15, 2019* _____

LIZZIE

JULY 15, WEDNESDAY

Sam was waiting outside Young & Crane's office building when I finally got back from Rikers. He had a small duffel bag on the bench next to him. Sunglasses on, his face turned toward the setting sun. He's leaving me, I thought.

Sad. That was how I felt. Sad that Sam wanted to leave. Sad that I knew it might not be the worst thing for either one of us. Where could we possibly go from here? So much damage done. Sam had admitted he could have been unfaithful. I had believed him capable of murder. I'd been desperate to prove it wasn't true, sure. But I had entertained the possibility. And what of the things I had done? All the times I had turned a blind eye to Sam's drinking under the guise of loving him. Not to mention all my own lies.

I sat down next to Sam. I closed my eyes, too, and turned my own face toward the sun. We sat there like that, side by side in the glow. Silent, for a long time. Finally Sam reached over and took my hand.

"Going somewhere?" I asked.

"Yeah," he said. "It's ninety days to start. That's the minimum."

I opened my eyes and turned to look at him. "Really?"

"It's all arranged. I called my mom. She's paying. And, you know, she was surprisingly kind about it. In that noncommittal way of hers. Not sure she'll actually tell my father. But maybe that's for the best," Sam said. He sighed. "I'm sorry it took me so long. I'm sorry . . . about everything."

I squeezed Sam's hand. "Me too."

"I'm going to fix this," Sam went on. "Or at least, I'm going to fix me. I promise." Sam hesitated, looked down. "I promise to try."

My throat felt tight. "You know, you're not the only one who's made mistakes."

Sam turned to look at me. "What do you mean?"

The full story about my dad was too much to explain in that moment, and there was so much I hadn't decided—how much I owed my dad, how much I owed myself. But I had no doubt anymore that a lie of omission was a lie all the same. And I wasn't lying anymore, not to anyone.

I shook my head. "It's not something about us. It's about my family, but it's something you have a right to know. That you *had* a right to know, from the start. Especially because it's been with us this whole time. It'll keep, though, I promise. What matters now is that you get better. You need to focus on that," I said. "Just know that I'm not perfect either. I never have been."

We were quiet once more.

"Do you think if I do this, if I *can* do this, it'll be enough?" Sam asked.

For us to make it, he meant. And so I searched his eyes for a future neither of us could possibly see. Then I did the only thing that felt right: I leaned forward and kissed him. And I told him the truth.

"I hope so."

ACKNOWLEDGMENTS

My deepest gratitude to my extremely wise and insightful editor, Jennifer Barth. Thank you for understanding immediately what this book was supposed to be. I will be forever grateful for your keen editorial perspective, remarkable tenacity, and tireless commitment that got it all the way there. I'm lucky to have had the privilege to work with you.

Thank you to the brilliant Jonathan Burnham and the generous Doug Jones for your continued support and dedication—I'm thrilled to call Harper my home. Thank you to everyone in the marketing, publicity, sales, and library departments for all your unsung efforts on my behalf. A special shout-out to my publicity and marketing dynamic duo: Leslie Cohen and Katie O'Callaghan. Ladies, you are rock stars. Thanks also to Sarah Ried for your assistance, and to production editor Lydia Weaver, copy editor Miranda Ottewell, and the rest of the Harper managing editorial team for working so hard to turn this idea of mine into a real live book. A special thank-you to Robin Bilardello for such a gorgeous cover.

To my genius agent, Dorian Karchmar—thank you, for so many things. Most especially, for understanding me and my work intuitively, then constantly striving to make every sentence—which you could surely now recite from memory—as good as it could possibly be. I am extremely fortunate to have such a superbly gifted creative partner. Thank you to my marvelous film agent, Anna DeRoy, for your astute observations and unflagging commitment. Thanks also to Matilda

Forbes Watson and James Munro. And to Alex Kane and everyone else at WME: I'm grateful for your hard work.

To my kick-ass lawyer and dear friend, Victoria Cook, thank you for your shrewd advice and the years of love. Thanks also to the wonderful Mark Merriman. Thank you, Hannah Wood, for your sage comments and for always being there to lend a hand. And to Katherine Faw for saving the day—and me—repeatedly.

Sincerest thanks to tenacious and kind criminal defense attorney Eric Franz, who patiently gave so much of himself throughout the writing of this book, answering endless questions, letting me attend hearings, and never making me feel like a bother—even when I couldn't find my car registration at Rikers. Eric, your dedication and skills are truly remarkable, which is why I will definitely be calling you should I ever get arrested. Thanks also to Aviva Franz, who made me feel like family, and Gulnora Tali, who made me feel like part of the team.

Thank you to Allyson Meierhans, former Bronx County Assistant District Attorney, for going through the manuscript with a fine-tooth comb, then gently pointing out my many missteps. Your advice was invaluable. To William "Billy" McNeely, who was also kind enough to read large parts of this manuscript and answer emails and have long phone calls—thank you for helping me get the details right. There would have been no substitute for your wisdom.

To these other outstanding experts and incredibly generous humans who so patiently answered my occasionally stupid, often randomly specific questions, or who found me someone who could: I am indebted to all of you—David Fischer, Andrew Gallo, Dr. Tara Galovski, Hallie Levin, Teresa Maloney, Dr. Theo Manschreck, Brendan McGuire, Daniel Rodriguez, Professor Linda C. Rourke, David Schumacher, and Ron Stanilus.

Thank you to Marco Ricci, Jim Hoppin, and Beowulf Sheehan for sharing your creative gifts.

Boundless love to Megan Crane, Heather Frattone, Nicole Kear,

Tara Pometti, and Motoko Rich—your excellence as early readers is surpassed only by your fabulous friendship. I'd like to say I won't be asking any of you lovelies to read another early draft, but that would be a lie. A most special thank-you to the wonderful, warm, and always generous Elena Evangelo for your kind help. Thank you to Nike Arrowolo—there would be no words here at all were it not for your warmth and hard work.

Thank you to my family and many dear friends who are always so supportive: it means more to me than you will ever know. A special thank-you to Martin and Clare Prentice for all you have done.

Thank you, Emerson, for your patience, and for being such a wonderful example of what it means to be fierce. And thank you, Harper, for amazing me daily with your brilliance and your beauty. I live in awe of both of you.

And to Tony: thank you for absolutely everything else.

ABOUT THE AUTHOR

KIMBERLY MCCREIGHT is the *New York Times* bestselling author of *Reconstructing Amelia*, which was nominated for the Edgar, Anthony, and Alex awards; *Where They Found Her*; and *The Outliers*, a young adult trilogy. She attended Vassar College and graduated cum laude from the University of Pennsylvania Law School. She lives in Brooklyn with her husband and two daughters.